WEAR IT LIKE A CROWN

ZARAH DETAND

DISCLAIMER

Fictional Work

The characters and events portrayed in this book are fictitious.

1

This early in the morning, Clarence House was disconcertingly quiet.

Joshua was used to the hustle and bustle of his mother's royal household. He'd grown up expecting conversations in the corridors, people greeting him as he walked by, the murmur of voices drifting out of George Atkin's meeting room whenever George fed calculated bites of information to select journalists. Right now, even servants were few and far between. Daylight was only just beginning to creep up over London, and when Joshua had parked his car a few minutes ago, night shadows had still been wrapped around the trees of Green Park.

In the eerie absence of other human beings, the Horse Corridor was creepier than usual, which Joshua considered a feat. Heavy, red drapes mourned the passage of time, horse statues tracked his every step from porcelain eyes, and the oil paintings on the wall loomed like relics from another century. They were, in a way. Since the death of Joshua's grandfather, Mum had been talking about a thorough renovation. As it wasn't a priority concern, it had yet to move beyond the planning stage when there were always so many other issues clamouring for attention. Ruling a country was no part-time job.

Joshua caught snatches of a conversation from the sitting room and stood quietly for a moment, straining his ears so as to gain an idea of why he'd been roused at an ungodly hour to put in an appearance. Nothing translated through the thick wood of the door.

Joshua knocked and entered without waiting for a response. And halted his steps.

George was there. That was not a good sign. It was *never* a good sign if the Head of Royal Communications was present outside of normal office hours.

"Good morning." Clearing his throat, Joshua glanced from his mother to George, to the full English breakfast laid out on the table, and then over at a man he'd never seen before—slightly stocky, with a pleasant smile and intelligent eyes. He struck Joshua as someone who was easily underestimated. "Where's the fire?"

Mum set her cup down with a dainty clink of porcelain and gave him a kind look. Her voice was even. "Darling. Do sit down, please. This is James Boyle. He'll be joining us for breakfast."

Okay. This was *definitely* not good.

Seeing as Joshua had returned from two weeks in Spain just last night, there was absolutely nothing reassuring about being called in for an early breakfast with a man whose name was practically an institution: *James Boyle, professional fixer.* He worked in the background, word-of-mouth the only promotion he needed now that he'd managed to establish himself as the person you called on the eve of a serious crisis. He and his team had handled the fallout when the Duke of Kent's pregnant mistress had gone to the press, they'd been involved in negotiations with a kidnapper threatening to harm the only child of the Leader of the Opposition, and when Tristan had fallen for a Victoria's Secret model, the Marquess of Waterford had called Boyle in so he would spin the public narrative in a way that would protect the reputation of the old Irish family.

"Pleasure to meet you," Joshua lied, shaking the man's hand and taking note of a strong, confident grasp. He greeted George with a clap on the shoulder and his mother with a kiss on the cheek, then sank into the fourth chair and smoothed his expression into one of pleasant expectations.

Shit. He was in serious trouble. What had he *done*?

Nothing came to mind. Female underwear models and their curves held little appeal for him, and it wasn't as though he was likely to father a child, illicit or not, that could then be kidnapped.

Glancing around the table, he took in Boyle's easy smile and the perpetual glint of amusement in George's eyes. Mum looked regal in her simple dress, her hair tied back and her expression grave. It wasn't often that Joshua found his mother intimidating, but right now was one of those moments. To cover up his nerves, he helped himself to a bread roll and reached for the butter. "Thank you for the invitation to breakfast," he said out loud. "It's bound to be a lovely day, so I guess it's good I was prompted to rise early. Gives me a chance to make the most of it."

"Oh, a *very* lovely day," his mother told him. To anyone else, the hint of irony would be undetectable.

Joshua swallowed and shot George a quick, pleading look. They were friends, after all, and as such, it was George's duty to rescue him from Awkward Central.

After a moment of consideration, George did. "There's a problem." He retrieved his iPad and unlocked it, slid it across the table for Joshua to see.

Joshua felt the bread roll slip from his grasp. His muscles locked up.

Oh. Oh no. Oh no, no, no. Holy bloody... *fuck*.

How had—no. *No*. They'd been in a hotel room, he and Mo. They'd been *inside*, curtains drawn, no open doors or anything. No one should have been able to catch them in the act, and all right, the picture filling the screen was fairly tame and *could* pass for two lads horsing around on the floor, Mo straddling Joshua's hips with a wide grin. But. Shit. If this picture existed, there were bound to be others that would be far more... revealing.

Had there been a camera in the room? Oh God. *Oh God.*

Joshua swallowed and pushed the iPad back towards George,

didn't dare glance at his mum. There were some things a mother did *not* need to know.

"This was sent to my email late last night," George said. "By an anonymous beneficiary, as they call themselves. A friendly warning. It's the only picture that was sent, but they say there is more. To paraphrase: they threaten to flood the internet with shocking insights into the private conduct of His Royal Highness Prince Joshua—which would obviously mean exposing your sexuality." A frown ghosted over his high forehead. "As you well know. It's either that, or we pay a million to an untraceable account, followed by instructions and conditions, yadda, yadda."

Joshua gripped the edge of his seat and forced himself to keep breathing.

And out.

And in.

"Sweetheart." His mother's voice originated from somewhere far away. A different universe, possibly. "We need to discuss what to do about this. The damage to the Crown could be considerable, which is why I took the liberty of calling in James Boyle."

Over the rush in his ears, Joshua had trouble processing so much as a single word. "Excuse me," he muttered.

With that, he pushed to his feet and left the room as quickly as he could without breaking into an actual run. He bumped into a servant outside the room, ducked around the startled woman with a quick apology and took refuge in the nearest toilet. His stomach was trying to claw a way up his throat, to turn itself inside out the way he'd seen from a frog in some video, stomach all out, Joshua's sexuality all out, right there for the world to see, and what, *what*, what even *was* this mess in his head?

Breathing hurt.

～

MORNING LIGHT SPILLED into the meeting room and revealed the tiredness in everyone's eyes. Nate was clutching a cup of coffee Carole had set down in front of him, jealously guarding it against anyone who might want to rob him of it. As Leo was clinging to his own mug of tea in a similar fashion, he was in no position to judge.

"Why us?" he asked.

Nate's response consisted of a sidelong look that conveyed flat disbelief.

"I'm serious," Leo insisted. "So some noble brat is being blackmailed over a bunch of gay pictures, and I just bet the preferred option is shutting the whole thing down instead of coming clean. Fucking hooray. I don't see why *we* have to be a part of this."

"I know you don't like nobles," Nate began, and Leo interrupted.

"Damn right, I don't. Privileged twats, the whole lot of them." Or at least nine out of ten were, and Leo's opinion was perfectly sound and thoroughly unbiased. He would know; he'd been one of them. Still was, technically, unless his parents had found a way to erase him from the family tree.

Nate sighed. "Look, I know you don't like it. But please try to keep your mouth shut? James knows what he's doing."

James did, was the thing. He had a knack for reading people and cutting through the bullshit. Leo trusted him without question, and owed him a whole damn lot on top of that. And while Leo did not appreciate the idea that they might be expected to cover up some spoilt noble's gay exploits—well. He'd do it. For James, and because Leo was a professional and took pride in his job.

"I'll try," he agreed quietly, cupping Nate's elbow for a moment before he leaned back in his chair and ducked his head over his tea, waiting for the bitter scent to revive his will to live. Or James and their client to arrive, whichever happened first.

The tight worry lines around Nate's eyes faded. "Good," he said quietly.

At the end of the long conference table, Carole was setting up James' laptop, connecting it to the big screen. Usually, anything related to computers would be Nate's job, but Nate wasn't a morning person and Carole was. Things like that reminded Leo just how well they worked as a team. James' little band of strays.

Dropping his forehead onto the tabletop, Leo attempted to squeeze in another few minutes of sleep.

He startled upright when Ben strolled into the room and set a heavy folder on the table. As Leo doubted Ben had been told more than the rest of them—noble client of high standing, blackmailed with evidence of a gay sex scandal, all options on the table for now—Leo suspected that all that paper served merely decorative purposes. Maybe it was the kind of thing lawyers were taught in the course of their education: never be caught without a heavy load of documents. If arguments failed, they could always resort to knocking an opponent out with the folder.

"James just called," Ben announced. "Said they're downstairs, about to come up, and to put on our best game faces."

Leo took a calm sip of tea and shrugged. "He always says that."

"Sounded like he really meant it this time," Ben said.

The room fell back into an expectant silence while they all straightened up and spread strategically around the table. Leo glanced down at himself. His outfit of skinny jeans and a wrinkled shirt were no match for Ben's suit, Nate's tie, or Carole's pencil skirt. But then, Leo did the fieldwork and needed to blend into various settings, so he was allowed a hint more leeway. He'd explained that precise point to Nate. Several times.

A ping from outside the room announced the arrival of the lift. Leo set down his tea, laced his hands on the table and turned to peer into the corridor.

That was... Holy *fuck*.

Holy *fucking* fuck.

Because right there—behind some bulky type of bodyguard and a lanky, quiffed bloke Leo knew from the news, walking next to James with his hands in his pockets... well. That was Prince Joshua.

Prince Joshua. His Royal Highness Prince Joshua Edward of Wales, second in line to the throne and unknown star of Leo's teenage fantasies.

Leo's plans for the day had not included this. Jesus fucking Christ. Prince Joshua. *Prince Joshua* was at the centre of a potential gay scandal. Prince Joshua was gay, or at the very least bi-curious. Prince Joshua was the kind of person who was open to paying off a blackmailer so as to protect his effortlessly privileged life from getting complicated.

Prince Joshua was a royally spoilt brat. Pun intended.

Schooling his features into an approximation of polite interest, Leo watched James lead the Prince and the quiffed bloke into the meeting room while the bodyguard positioned himself outside the door. "Prince Joshua of Wales," James announced, after a glance around. "And Sir George Atkin, Head of Royal Communications. Allow me to introduce my team. Carole Edwards," he waved his hand, and Carole jumped to her feet for a wobbly curtsy, "along with Ben Collins, Nate Biggs and Leo Graham."

Ben and Nate gave bows that went far too deep, bending at the waist. For a beat, Leo considered boycotting the whole ordeal, then he caught Nate's pointed look and got up as well, catching the Prince's eyes before he inclined his head just enough to satisfy protocol. The Prince held Leo's gaze for an instant before his attention slid back to James.

When Leo sat back down before anyone else, he felt oddly breathless, as though he'd been briefly submerged in his past. He didn't appreciate it one bit. Neither did he appreciate Atkin asking, "No offence, James, but can we cut your team down to the essential people? This is a delicate matter."

"Everyone is essential," James replied, his tone both pleasant and confident. "Everyone in this room can also be trusted without question."

And this was why Leo loved his boss.

It looked as though Atkin might argue, but he settled down when the Prince muttered a soft, "George, please. Let's just get this over with."

Wow, thanks. So kind of Prince Joshua to convey his desire to be anywhere but here.

Picking up his tea, Leo kept quiet throughout the explanation delivered by Atkin; some basics about Joshua—*Prince* Joshua—

returning from a holiday in Spain with friends, and how it coincided with an email sent to Atkin's account, an email containing a sample of what promised to be fairly incriminating material. At James' reminder that full disclosure was part of his terms, Atkin grimaced, cast the Prince a sideways glance and then retrieved an iPad. Next to Leo, Nate tensed up, and Leo could tell that he was forcibly holding back a rant about the risks of cloud storage and Apple's thirst for data.

When Carole looked at the screen, the Prince, who'd been sitting primly so far, seemed to curl slightly into himself as he stared resolutely at the tabletop. Ashamed, was he? No pity from Leo, that was for certain. If you made your bed, you'd better be prepared to lie in it.

Accepting the tablet from Ben, Leo studied the picture for longer than necessary. *Sweet Jesus*, fuck everything. Ten years ago, a visual of Prince Joshua stretched out on the floor, partly undressed and straddled by a hot man, would have fuelled Leo's imagination for months. He was no longer seventeen and horny, though. Also, Prince Joshua was no longer the cherubic, curly-haired boy Leo had glimpsed around the hallways of Eton; at twenty-five, the Prince was very much a man, tall and slender, with a wide mouth, clear green eyes and a loose tumble of chocolate curls. Still irritatingly attractive.

Not that it mattered in any way.

Leo passed the iPad on to Nate, took another sip of tea and avoided staring at the Prince's hands, long fingers twisted together on the table, the same fingers which had been clutching the other man's biceps in the picture, and—and Leo was *not* staring at the Prince's hands. Definitely not.

Once Atkin had pocketed the iPad again, there was a moment of silence before Carole spoke up, sounding highly uncomfortable. "Um, Your Grace?"

"Your Royal Highness," Leo corrected without thinking. A moment later, he wished he hadn't, especially because Carole looked even more uncertain than before. "Sorry," he told her quietly. "If you want to follow conventions, it's Your Royal Highness for the first address, and then Sir afterwards. Just, you know. If you want to be precise."

"Just Joshua is fine," the Prince said into this awkwardness, followed by a curious look at Leo. Leo arched a brow and turned away.

So much for his ability to keep his stupid fucking mouth shut.

"Carole, you were saying?" James asked, and Carole cleared her throat.

"I was just wondering, Sir—excuse me, *Joshua*." She tried for a smile that still looked a little overwhelmed by the situation. Oh, for fuck's sake, prince or not, the bloke was still bloody *human*, wasn't he? "I was wondering about the guy in the picture. Is there a chance he set you up?"

"Absolutely not," Joshua replied immediately. For the first time, there was a hint of authority to his tone. "Mo is one of my best mates. Also, if he'd have wanted, he could have done this years ago. There is zero chance it was him. Just *no*."

"Interesting concept of friendship," Leo said. Since he clearly had no brain-to-mouth filter whatsoever.

Under the table, Nate kicked him in the shin, and Leo suppressed a flinch. He'd probably deserved that, what with how he'd promised to at least *try* to keep his comments to himself. Then again, Nate knew Leo and should thus be aware of just how impossible a request it had been in the first place.

Joshua must have caught the mocking edge to Leo's voice, a frown wrinkling his forehead. The gentle morning light washing over his features brought out the colour of his eyes. "Do you have a problem with," a short pause, "homosexual actions?"

"A problem with dicks touching?" Leo laughed, unable to help it. Out of the corner of his eye, he noticed James giving him a warning glare, and oh. Um, right. *Client*. Leo tamped down on his amusement and met Joshua's gaze evenly. "Beg your pardon, *Sir*. I'm gay, so no, I certainly don't have a problem with homosexual actions. What I do have a problem with is dishonesty. Why not do your *friend* the courtesy of calling him your boyfriend? Or fuck buddy, whichever."

"*Leo*," James said with a sharpness Leo rarely heard directed at himself. In parallel, Nate delivered another kick to Leo's shin, more forceful than the first. Still Leo refused to break eye contact with Joshua, refused to apologise just because Joshua happened to possess several titles and a shitload of money. Little twat.

"Not that it's any of your business..." Joshua's voice was deep and precise, each syllable shaped carefully. "But Mo is indeed my *friend*, first and foremost. We also happen to get each other off sometimes. Mostly because I can't very well pick up random guys at a club, now can I?"

Leo lifted both shoulders and smiled. His fingertips throbbed, keeping pace with his rapid pulse. He felt oddly dizzy. "You could if you came clean. Being gay is no cause for shame, little prince."

The informal address made Joshua sit up a little straighter, eyes narrowing, chin tipping up in challenge. Hell yeah, bring it *on*.

Only then Leo glanced over, and the open disappointment in James' eyes had him swallow and shrink back into his chair. Fuck. *Fuck*. "I apologise," he said, rushed. Meeting Joshua's gaze, he tried to ignore the unsteady thump of his own heart, beating high up in his throat. He also tried to ignore the way Atkin was glaring at him. "That was out of line, and it won't happen again. I'm in no position to judge, obviously."

After a second that stretched like a brittle rubber band, ready to tear with the strain, Joshua nodded once, barely perceptible, and looked away. Leo found that he could breathe again. Focusing on his tea, he resolved to keep his mouth shut for the rest of the meeting.

It was going to be a long day, and it had barely even started.

THERE WERE FOUR VIABLE OPTIONS: one, the Royal Family could pay the money and hope to never hear from the blackmailer again; two, Joshua could come out and render the blackmailer's material much less valuable; three, they could stall for time and try to catch the culprit before anything went public; four, they could do nothing and wait it out. Of course there were further details, such as the question of whether they were looking at one blackmailer or several, or whether the ramifications of a potential coming-out would be cushioned if Joshua's friend were to pose as his boyfriend, at least for a short while. The basic options remained the same, though.

Throughout the discussion Prince Joshua had been remarkably quiet, listening with his hands clasped in his lap and his gaze lowered, lashes hiding his eyes. Atkin had been much more vocal, although he hadn't displayed a clear preference. For all that Leo considered himself quite skilled at reading people, he honestly couldn't predict the outcome when Joshua and Atkin—*George*—asked for a few minutes of privacy.

While James and Ben went to check their emails in their respective offices and Carole popped down to the deli to grab something for lunch, Nate grabbed Leo's arm and pulled him into their tea kitchen.

"What the *fuck* was that?" he hissed.

Leo twisted his arm free. "Don't, okay?" He shook his head. "I know. I *know*. But I'm tired and hungry and cranky, and—it doesn't matter. I'm sure James will have plenty to say to me later, so just... bloody save it, yeah?"

Nate was quiet for the time it took Leo to fill the kettle, but his frown hadn't softened. His thick brows were drawn together, arms crossed where he was leaning back against the work surface, staring at Leo. It was highly irritating. Leo refused to rise to the bait. *Refused*.

"Stop staring," he told Nate a moment later. "It's creepy."

"Why were you like that in there?" Nate shot back. He didn't budge an inch, and Leo moved around him to retrieve their selection of tea.

"You know I don't like nobles."

If Leo had hoped that the finality in his tone would put Nate off, he'd been mistaken; Nate wasn't easily riled up, but once his mind was made up, he turned into a dog with a bone. One of those tiny, vicious ones that would growl and shake their victim until it squeaked. "You don't like nobles, sure," he said. "But I've never seen you like that. Like... He's a client, Leo. James' client. *Our* client. We have a responsibility here, and you can't just go and—he's the bloody *Prince of Wales.*"

"Actually, he's Prince Joshua of Wales," Leo corrected. "Since he's not the heir-apparent."

Nate gave him a hard look and went on as though there had been no interruption. "This must be tough for him, you know, and you can't expect him to just say 'whatever, fuck it' and come out. I think he'd be the first royal to do that, and being the first is hard."

"Fuck the monarchy," Leo stated, clear and decisive. He chose his tea, then raised his head and met Nate's gaze just in time to see Nate's eyes widen, colour draining from his cheeks as he focused on something behind Leo.

Slowly, Leo turned around.

Oh.

Just his fucking luck.

~

"FUCK THE MONARCHY," was the first thing Joshua heard when he rounded the corner.

He stopped dead in his tracks, his quest to find the toilets all but forgotten. There was no mistaking that voice, the slight rasp and strange mixture of soft vowels and sharp contours to the words. Leo Graham it was.

Joshua should have been used to it. There were more than enough people who sneered at his status, minds made up before they'd exchanged so much as a single word with him. But usually, these people weren't part of a team hired to help Joshua; they weren't privy to a secret he'd been forced to hide for years, and they weren't unfairly attractive even when they regarded him with poorly concealed contempt. While Joshua had avoided all eye contact with Leo throughout the meeting, he'd been all too aware of him, the derision radiating from Leo like an itch under Joshua's skin, a low hum in his bones. Strangely, it had been coupled with a vague sense of recognition, like a memory that was just beyond Joshua's grasp.

Either way, Leo had apologised, and Joshua had accepted it. But Leo's words just now made it blatantly clear he hadn't meant it at all.

Screw this. Joshua found it hard enough to submit to the demands of a stranger who'd robbed him of an intimate moment, had violated both his and Mo's privacy; he wasn't going to be a doormat to Leo Graham as well.

He squared his shoulders and moved forward.

It was Nate who caught sight of him first, and the obvious shock on his face felt gratifying, proof that Joshua was still able to collect a few crumbs of respect, even if it was all down to his status. His bloody *status*, the reason he was here in the first place. If it wasn't for that, no one would have thought to set up a camera in his hotel room and blackmail him with something that was supposed to be private. Of course, he knew what the likes of Leo would say if he dared utter so much as a word about how it wasn't all fun and games, how the golden cage could make it difficult to breathe at times.

Poor little rich boy, yes; Joshua had heard it all before. Knowing he was privileged didn't mean he couldn't hurt. He wasn't a bloody *robot*.

When Leo turned around, his expression was largely neutral, the light that spilled through a small window emphasising one half of his face and bringing out the cut of his cheekbones, the clear blue of his eyes. Light brown hair was swept off his forehead, tousled in a way that might be careless or deliberate, and upon catching sight of Joshua, his lips pressed into a thin line. He tilted his head up, and Joshua drew bitter satisfaction from being taller. Leo was slight, with strong thighs and strong arms, and if Joshua wanted, he could easily crowd Leo back against a wall, loom over him and—and *nothing*.

"You're a judgmental prick," Joshua said. His voice wasn't made for carrying emotion, so it came out calmer than he felt. "I have a name to uphold, you know? That's not just—it's not that simple for me. I can't just strut down the street shouting, 'Hello, I'm gay.' There are *consequences*."

Behind Leo, Nate made an unsuccessful attempt to blend in with the wallpaper. Leo, on the other hand, smiled to expose a row of sharp teeth. "All I see is a lie that makes your life easier."

"You think this is easier? I have no chance at an actual relationship, and you think that's me taking the easy way out?"

Leo didn't bat an eye. "Ever thought about how much it would mean if someone like you did come out? The significance of it?"

Oh, fuck him. As if Joshua hadn't considered the idea so often he'd lost count, as if he hadn't examined it from all angles and arrived at a different conclusion every single time. No matter what Leo thought, it *wasn't* that simple. Not all Commonwealth Realms were as accepting as the UK, and an openly gay representative of the British Crown could affect foreign relations even beyond that. Even progressive countries might hesitate to welcome a guy they'd seen choking on another man's dick. The Crown's reputation was built on soft power, and the unfortunate fact of Joshua's sexuality could undermine its basis. He wasn't that selfish. He *wasn't*.

"You have no idea of the potential costs," Joshua managed, a weak repartee. Why did he even bother? It was his decision, his very own, very personal decision, and he shouldn't have to justify himself to Leo, or anyone.

"Don't talk to me about costs, *Sir*. Just don't." Leo made the title sound like an insult, but there was something else swinging in his voice, a darkness that might not be directed at Joshua alone. For a moment, Joshua stared at him and then shook his head, suddenly tired.

"For someone who's so disdainful of the monarchy, you certainly know a lot about its conventions."

Leo pursed his lips, everything about him spelling a challenge. "The more I know, the less of a fuck I give."

"Leo," Nate mumbled, the warning clear in his tone.

"Paying them off is the best option," Joshua told both of them. It was. It *was*. And if he repeated it often enough, it would eventually start to feel like it. "It's the best way to limit the damage to the Crown, and it's not like I made the decision alone. George agrees, and he has plenty of experience with crisis communication."

"Being gay isn't a crisis." Leo snorted with disdain, eyes sharp. "Also, you do realise that this is the digital age, correct? It's not just a couple of negatives. Each copy of a file is as good as the original, so how will you know that the material really is gone? And won't pop up anyway?"

That...

Well. *Shit.*

It was both obvious and so very, very *true* that Joshua's stomach sagged to his knees. Before he could think of an adequate response, Nate spoke up for the first time since Joshua had barged in on them. "Leo is right, you know? You don't know how many copies there are, how many pictures and videos, and where they're stored. What if you pay, and then those people get greedy and want another million? Or something else?"

Joshua had no answer.

～

LEO COULDN'T BELIEVE IT. How had the thought of a blackmailer disregarding an agreement not occurred to Joshua? If it had been about buying time to put a plan into action, about controlling what would be released when—fine. But for fuck's sake, did Joshua expect that it really would be that straight-forward? *Freedom—buy today!*

It was never that easy.

Taking in the way Joshua bit down on his bottom lip, eyes a little distant with thought, Leo counted to five before he asked, "Did that honestly not cross your mind?"

Joshua's gaze snagged to settle on Leo. His voice held a defensive note. "I was raised to believe that a person's word actually means something."

Well. Now that was just naive. It was also strangely sweet, and a little sad. Leo wondered whether he might have said the same at age seventeen, before he'd crash-landed in reality.

"Look," he said slowly. "Where I come from, the only currencies are money, sex, and power. More often than not, they're one and the same." He raised his brows. "You can't expect a blackmailer to operate by the ethical code preached in College Chapel, you know?"

At Joshua's surprised glance, Leo realised that he might have betrayed a familiarity with Eton's traditions that not everyone possessed. Fuck, he was usually better at guarding himself, but Joshua's presence was disorienting, cut through walls Leo had diligently erected and exposed the shoddy foundation underneath. Joshua was a fragment of Leo's past. He didn't belong into this present.

"How," Joshua began, and Leo cut him off.

"A gentleman's agreement only works if both sides are behaving like gentlemen. Not applicable in this case."

It was highly, *highly* impolite to interrupt a member of the Royal Family. There was a distinct possibility that in dark and long-gone times, people had been hanged for this kind of thing. Joshua merely blinked at him, though, and yes, his eyes were still so very green, and his mouth was still a tad too wide for his face—the same mouth Leo had fantasised about with a hand stuffed down his pants, face turned into a pillow to muffle all sounds. Back then, sex had been a sticky-sweet promise.

"Because blackmailers aren't gentlemen? Or because you consider me a coward?" Joshua was looking directly at Leo as though challenging him to say... *something*, Leo didn't know. It was strange and unwelcome to have that kind of focus turned to him, like a spotlight that would catch each twitch of a muscle, each blemish on his facade. He opened his mouth without any clear idea of what he was going to say.

He was saved by Nate inserting himself into the conversation once more. Bless him.

"What about your friend?" Nate asked carefully, and he didn't twist the word 'friend' into a mockery of itself, the way Leo would have done. "What'd he say?"

When Joshua glanced away, the claustrophobic pressure around Leo's chest eased just slightly. He watched Joshua direct a tiny smile at Nate before answering.

"Mo told me he's fine with whatever. And he's mostly already out as bi, so there's that, and since he doesn't come from a noble family, it's not like... They're not..." Joshua paused. For someone who had likely been trained in eloquence from an early age, he had a surprising tendency to ramble and trip over his own words. "He's a model. So he's not too keen on having his private bits on the news, but it wouldn't be quite as bad for him. His words, not mine."

A model, huh? Now that it had been brought up, Leo supposed that the man straddling Joshua had seemed vaguely familiar, someone Leo might know from the pages of glossy fashion magazines. Not that Leo was into that kind of reading material, really. He only flicked through *GQ* when he was high-strung and overtired, and because James insisted on a subscription for their waiting room even though they only consulted by appointment and dealt in clients thoroughly unused to waiting.

Also, trust bloody Prince Joshua of Wales to hang out in the closet and still get to shag models. Just went to prove that clichés existed for a reason.

Leo was about to make a comment along those lines—screw appropriateness—when Joshua took a step back, shaking his head. "Anyway," he said. "Could you point me to the gents?"

"You mean you need to *piss*?" Leo asked pointedly. "Or is that too plebeian for you?" It was barely out when Nate pinched him in the hip, hard. He may have deserved that.

Joshua drew himself up, clearly aware of his height advantage. "Yes. I need to piss. Because I'm *human*, surprisingly."

Nate interfered before Leo got a chance to dig himself into an even deeper hole. "Loos are down the corridor, last door on the left."

"Thank you," Joshua said, all dignity. With a blank look directed at Leo, he headed off in the indicated direction.

"What the actual fuck?" Nate hissed as soon as Joshua was out of earshot.

"Don't." Abruptly, Leo felt tired. Like water rushing down his body, the energy that had been sizzling in his blood drained away and left him mildly nauseous. This wasn't *him*. "Just don't, please."

"Leo," Nate began, not as harsh anymore.

"Please," Leo repeated, and the wrinkles in Nate's forehead smoothed out.

"Okay. Just remember that he's a client, yeah? Remember that we're on his side."

"I know." Leo inhaled, held the air in his lungs while he counted to five, and exhaled. "I *know*. I just think he's making a mistake."

"Wouldn't be the first time we've had a client make the wrong call. What's your personal stake in this?"

Leo swallowed around the lump in his throat. "None. Absolutely none. I should probably apologise, or something."

It was clear Nate didn't quite believe Leo's claim, but he also didn't stop Leo from dumping his untouched tea into the sink before setting off for the toilets. He'd apologise, yes. That was what he'd do. He'd apologise, and he'd be professional and calm about it, and he would give it a rest.

Really. It was *exactly* what he'd do.

Just as soon as he'd had a chance to explain his reasoning.

Joshua's lumberjack of a bodyguard assessed Leo with a rather distrusting expression when Leo stepped around him to enter the toilets, but made no move to stop Leo. So far, so good. Letting the door fall shut, Leo found Joshua at the sink, washing his hands. Joshua stiffened when he caught sight of Leo, then made a point of acting as though he hadn't even noticed Leo's presence.

On second thought, there might have been places better suited to this conversation than the loo. Too late, though. Leo had made his move.

"Hey. Princeling?" In the mirror, he caught Joshua's eyes and held them.

Joshua cocked his head and levelled Leo with an unreadable look. He remained silent as he shut the tap off, shaking water off his hands.

"Allow me to ask a question," Leo said. "Just one."

Joshua didn't break their eye contact in the mirror, and Leo supposed that was enough of an invitation. As a teenager, Leo had dreamed of something a little like this: happening upon Joshua in the toilets, Joshua alone for once, less intimidating without his usual entourage and hangers-on. They'd bump into each other somehow, Leo would make a clever comment and Joshua would laugh, the one where he threw his head back to expose the bare column of his throat. Then they'd become friends and fall in love and into bed. In that order.

Teenage Leo had been mildly ridiculous. Teenage Leo had also been funnier, brighter, more optimistic and social, high on life and unfamiliar with worrying about his next warm meal and a roof for the night. He might have been Joshua's type.

Not the point.

"How closely have you examined the idea that someone might have tipped them off?" Leo asked slowly. "Because that camera in your hotel room was no lucky coincidence."

"I told you that Mo wouldn't do that." Joshua's tone was sharp, and Leo raised both hands, palms up.

"I'm not saying it was your Mo. Just someone. Someone who would know what to look for, and who knew you'd be staying in that hotel. That couldn't be more than a handful of people, correct?" When it looked as though Joshua was about to interrupt, Leo continued quickly, leaning forward as he turned his head to study Joshua's profile rather than a reflection of his face. "And yes, it *might* have been a stranger who stalked you long enough to know things. But maybe it wasn't. You should at least consider the possibility."

After a frozen moment, the stillness all-encompassing, Joshua ducked his head. He ran damp fingers through his hair, making it stick up in odd strands, the corkscrew curls at his temples reminiscent of the teenager Leo had once been infatuated with. Joshua's nostrils flared, but he didn't reply.

Something about that ached in Leo's chest, made his next breath feel as cold and smooth as liquid nitrogen. "I know it sucks, having to doubt everyone around you," he murmured, softer than he'd intended. "But you shouldn't trust blindly."

"I don't." Joshua glanced over, a flicker of darkness in his expression. "I've learned as much."

"Okay." Leo inhaled and kept the air in his lungs for a beat. "But how about you give us a chance to find out more? Nate is one of the best hackers in this country, so really... One day, all right? Give us *one day* to find out something, see whether his computer wizardry reveals anything."

The stark overhead light made Joshua's lashes cast shadows on his cheeks. When he abruptly raised his head and turned to look at Leo, it was too quickly for Leo to pretend that he hadn't been staring. Joshua exhaled in a rush. "What if you stir them up? Like, what if they notice you're on to them, and they release the stuff before we have any kind of plan?"

Who's rushing you? Leo didn't ask. Instead, he settled for, "I wasn't kidding about Nate being one of the best. If you keep your mouth shut, don't tell *anyone* about it—not even your Mo—"

"Not *my* Mo," Joshua cut in, followed by a tiny twitch of his shoulders. "I mean. Not that it matters, I guess, but I'd prefer if you stopped it with the mocking undertone. He's one of my best friends, and I'd rather you didn't... belittle that."

Leo squashed the impulse to argue just for the sake of it. "Fair enough," he allowed.

The ghost of a smile skimmed across Joshua's face, and he nodded, about to say something when the door opened and Ben joined them in the small space. While Leo saw no need to hide anything from the team, Joshua closed off and moved past Leo to dry his hands. He acted as though their conversation hadn't happened at all.

Leo wanted to push, argue his point. Instead, he held the door for Joshua and then followed him into the corridor, Joshua's bodyguard falling into step. They didn't speak as they returned to the conference room, Joshua's stance inviting no further input. His face was set into a frown.

Five minutes later, Joshua declared that he hadn't made up his mind about which option to pursue, that he needed a night to sleep on it. He didn't back down when George warned him that they couldn't afford the luxury of time, George's body coiled tight with suppressed energy. "One night," Joshua insisted. "Surely that's not too much to ask for, right? We're talking about a million pounds, which —that's a *lot*, so just... tell them we'll let them know by tomorrow morning at ten?"

For a few seconds, George stared at Joshua. Then he deflated, nodding sharply. "All right. I'll respond to their email, tell them we need some time to sort out the payment process from our side. And James and I will work on the details of the follow-up plan, see how we can avoid running into something like this in the future."

Ah, so developing a follow-up plan had occurred to them, after all. Good to know—even if Joshua hadn't realised that the future might hold a simple rehash of this very situation. Had George considered it, and simply neglected to tell Joshua so as not to trouble him? Or to steer him in a certain direction? Inquiring minds wanted to know. Inquiring minds *craved* to know.

"That would be great, George," Joshua said softly. "Please do. And thank you."

While he didn't look at Leo, it felt as though Joshua was addressing him as much as he was addressing George and James. Leo kept his face blank, biting down on the smile that wanted to creep up on him.

TRISTAN PICKED up on the second ring. It had to be some kind of record, and Joshua took it as a sign that Mo had already filled Tristan in on this morning's unpleasant news. Joshua's suspicions proved true when Tristan opened with, "Porn star! How's it hanging?"

"Funny," Joshua said. "True comedian, you are. And *you* are the one dating a Victoria's Secret model, so I think I'm in good company."

The thought flared that Leo had told him not to trust anyone. It was *Tristan*, though.

Tristan had been the first and best friend Joshua had made at Eton, and when Joshua had broken down over how he might fancy boys, Tristan had hugged him for about a century, then proceeded to get him drunk and tuck him into bed. "You like who you like," he'd said. That statement had plunged into the abyss of sleep with Joshua, winding through his dreams. His head had housed a marching band in the morning, but his chest had felt just slightly lighter.

There had been countless chances for Tristan to expose Joshua much, much earlier than this, and he hadn't used a single one.

The same was true for Mo, who'd been a part of Joshua's life ever since Joshua's first week at university, Joshua drenched with rain and stumbling—literally—into the café where Mo had worked. Mo had known Joshua's secret ever since they'd ended up snogging one night in Mo's room, *just to see what it was like to kiss a boy, right, just between friends.* Not much use in pretending to be as straight as a ruler after that. Also, it had given Joshua the chance to pick up a shred of experience, just enough that he wouldn't embarrass himself completely if he ever got a shot at something real.

Anyway. Mo and Tristan were above suspicion. Joshua acquiesced to treat everyone else with the kind of caution that Leo guy had recommended, yes, *fine*, but Tristan and Mo were as dependable as Joshua's mother and sister. Joshua wouldn't let some worthless criminal drive a wedge between them.

It was out of the question.

He made a vague noise of agreement at whatever Tristan had said, then pressed the button to slide up the partition between the front and the backseat. When he tuned back in, Tristan was ranting about "the fucking *nerve* of some people, seriously, fucking cunts who wouldn't know how to spell privacy if it bit them in the arse, and also, mate, *also,* this is the 21st century and you shouldn't have to hide anymore, that's so beyond unfair I want to hit something." The cascade of Tristan's words, the genuine outrage on Joshua's behalf, went a long way in calming the rush of blood in Joshua's ears that had been present since he'd rolled out of bed and straight into a nightmare.

"Hey, Tristan?" Joshua said eventually, tipping his head back against the seat. "When you were working with James Boyle, what was your impression of him and his team?"

Tristan made a disgruntled noise. "Wasn't me working with them, was my parents. I don't think there's anything wrong with Kels that needs to be fucking *handled*, just so we're clear."

"I know." In spite of the general gloom clinging to his nerve endings, Joshua smiled, just slightly. Tristan was amazing like that. "But you met the team a couple of times, didn't you? What did you think?"

"They're good," Tristan said. "Might not look it, what with how most of them are pretty young. Like, Carole and Nate and Leo, I think they're in their mid-twenties? But they're really good, know what they're doing. Good people. I actually went to have a pint with Leo and Nate, meant to stay in touch and forgot." He paused, as though considering a sudden thought. When he spoke again, there was delight in his voice. "Leo giving you trouble? He's not a fan of nobility, made that plenty clear, what with my parents' antiquated ideas of honour and all. You being a swaggering prince—"

"I don't *swagger*," Joshua injected.

Tristan continued as though he hadn't heard it. "—would probably raise his hackles."

Joshua huffed out a faint chuckle. "It did."

"Thought as much." A grin brightened Tristan's voice. "He's not so bad, though, once you get past that."

"Did you know he's gay?" Joshua asked, then wished he hadn't when Tristan gave a sharp cackle.

"Didn't, nope. Can't say it matters to me, but you always did like it when people gave you a bit of lip, eh?"

Joshua exhaled, an impression of Leo's summer-bright, quick voice washing against the inside of his skull. It wasn't the point of his call, though, and it certainly wasn't why he'd asked for Tristan's opinion.

"That's not in any way relevant right now," Joshua said. "You know I've got bigger problems. I was just wondering what you thought of them, the whole team, since they're kind of... instrumental? And because of something Leo said to me, so it's—I'll tell you when I see you. I mean, you'll be at Mo's too, right? Can't promise I'll be good company, mind."

For once, Tristan didn't tease Joshua for rambling, just rolled with it. "We'll ply you with pizza and beer," he promised. "And yeah, I'll be there after I drop Kels off. Mo's worried about how we're all co-dependent, by the way. 'S adorable."

Seeing as they'd parted ways just last night, after a two-week holiday spent in each others' pockets, Mo might have a point. On the other hand, he'd been the one to suggest Joshua come over once the meetings were through. Mo did not have a leg to stand on.

"Thanks, T." Joshua exhaled. "I'll see you later, then."

"Hey," Tristan said quickly, before Joshua could end the call. "I got Leo's number, if you want it. Purely for crisis-related reasons, of course."

Oh. Well, Joshua had been planning to call James so as to give him the go-ahead on a subtle investigation, but... calling Leo would be easier. Less need for an explanation.

It would be convenient.

"Text it to me?" Joshua asked.

"Will do," Tristan replied, and if he sounded just a tad amused, Joshua chose to ignore it.

LEO'S PHONE rang during the one smoke break he allowed himself throughout the work day. Filthy habit, smoking. Nate had tried to wean him off it for the better part of a year, but Leo figured that he'd done much riskier things in life. Three cigarettes a day wouldn't kill him, at least not anytime soon. He planned to die young and beautiful anyway.

At the generic ringtone associated with unknown numbers, he blew smoke into the warm afternoon air and fished his phone out of his pocket. A string of unfamiliar figures flashed on the screen. All right. Call centre or a street kid looking for advice.

Leaning into the balcony banister, Leo picked up with a neutral, "Yes?"

"Hi, um." Deep, slow voice, slightly uncertain. No call centre, clearly. "Is this Leo?"

"Yeah, that's me." Leo softened his tone, smiled so that it would shine through and tapped some ash into a gap between two wooden boards. "Kylie give you this number? How can I help, love?"

A cough, followed by a pause. Leo waited it out by taking a drag of his cigarette, all too familiar with the inherent caution the street taught you quickly and efficiently, the kind of distrust in anyone but yourself that made it hard to ask for help when you didn't know what it would cost you. "You wanna tell me your name?" Leo asked when the silence began to drag and all he could hear was steady breathing on the other end. He deliberately thickened his accent. "Or I could talk a bit, if you want."

"It's Joshua," the voice said, gentle confusion clouding the words. "Uh. Prince Joshua?"

Fuck, fuck, *fuck*.

Leo dropped the cigarette and crushed it with the tip of his trainer, heat rising to his face. Shit. Prince Joshua, what do you know. Hopefully, he wouldn't make anything of the confusion.

"Joshua, hello." Leo fought to mould the greeting into something smooth and calm. Professional, that was it. "Sorry, didn't recognise you. Normal people state their names when they call. Didn't they teach that at royal etiquette school?"

Well, professional had segued straight into cheeky. Okay. To Leo's relief, Joshua huffed out a soft laugh. It shivered down Leo's spine like a warm gust of air. "Sorry," Joshua said. "I guess they did and I wasn't paying attention. You haven't been properly bored until you've wasted three hours of your life learning how to hold your tea cup *just so*."

Properly bored. Back at Eton, Leo might have spoken like that; now, he would be proper bored rather than properly so. "Posh," he commented. "It's true that the art of drinking tea is sadly neglected, though. You should do something about that. Funnel your royal influence into making a true difference to people's lives and all."

"Hey, it's not—we're not totally useless, you know? We can make a real difference in some areas, even if it might not always be obvious. My mum certainly does." Joshua sounded faintly irritated, and for once, Leo actually hadn't meant to offend.

"I was *kidding*, Princeling," he said quickly. Tilting his face up into the weak sunlight, he propped both elbows on the banister, phone wedged between cheek and shoulder. "I'm not a monarchy groupie, but I do acknowledge that you guys have a considerable amount of soft power. And that the Queen," *your mother*, holy shit, "uses it well. It's the idea of a few random lucky people being born into privilege that I object to. It's like you're playing FIFA at Amateur difficulty level while everyone else is set to World Class."

Goddammit, Leo needed to learn how to keep his mouth shut. It was a recurring challenge for him, but today had turned into a new low. Then again, he deserved some slack, what with how he'd been randomly thrown into close contact with the guy he'd fancied himself in love with several years ago. In another life.

Also, did Joshua even play FIFA? Did princes do things as mundane as playing video games?

"But is that different from being born into money?" Joshua's gravelly voice right by Leo's ear sparked the illusion of nearness, as though Joshua was leaning in for a private murmur. "Or into an academic household? Or with athletic skills or good looks? I mean, I get what you mean, and I do think it's important we keep working on equal opportunities, give everyone a fair shot at a good education, ensure that the same work gets the same pay, that sort of thing. Improve the scholarship system for those from poor families. But unless you want to bulldozer all differences at birth..."

Leo hadn't expected a serious answer from Joshua, and receiving one, delivered with an air of quiet sincerity—it was disarming. "I see your point," he admitted. "Doesn't mean I have to like it."

Joshua was quiet for the time it took Leo to draw a deep breath, then he gave a half-formed chuckle. "Well. They do say that a man who is not a liberal at twenty has no heart, and a man who is not a conservative at sixty has no head."

"Paraphrasing Churchill, eh?" Leo said.

"Well spotted," Joshua said. "Someone's been paying attention in school." It was an innocent statement that didn't press for more, but it made the muscles in Leo's stomach jump all the same. Joshua hadn't recognised him from the time they'd shared the hallways of Eton—of course he hadn't; Leo had been two years ahead of Joshua and moved in a different circle, had also looked like a twink—but Leo didn't want to supply him with clues that might stir up Joshua's curiosity and prompt him to dig deeper.

Not that Joshua would bother to look into the past of a guy who happened to run some errands for him. Jesus. Leo needed to calm his tits.

"Up until a certain point, yes," he said, sounding more bitter than he'd intended. He squinted into the sun, pale through a thin sheen of clouds. "Anyway, I doubt you called to discuss political views. So, how may I help you?"

"Oh, right. Yes." Joshua sounded almost surprised. "It's about what you told me earlier. Do you think you could do that? Ask Nate to look into whether he finds a trace, or... something like that? I don't exactly know how it would work, but please just make sure it won't trigger a panic reaction? I'd rather not be caught without..." He snorted. "With my pants down, like, *literally*."

To Leo's surprise, he found himself grinning. "As you wish. We've got until tomorrow morning, then? And you won't tell anyone, *anyone*, what we're up to. It'll be our little secret."

A palpable moment of hesitation, then Joshua sighed. "I won't. And you have my number now, so if there's anything you need to know..."

"I'll give you a call," Leo finished for him. Wow, fuck, he had Joshua's number. As a teenager, he'd have given his left arm for that—well, not *quite*, but maybe one of his kidneys. Living with one kidney was no problem, right? Also, embarrassing teenage infatuation aside... "How come you even have my number? Did you call James first?"

"I'm friends with Tristan Gleeson," Joshua said, and Leo needed a moment to place the name. Right—fun guy and son to the Marquess of Waterford, the latter ticking just about every box in Leo's book of prejudices. So Joshua was a friend of Tristan's, which definitely spoke in his favour, and so did the fact that he'd actually *listened* to Leo, had taken his input seriously enough to provide a time window for Nate to find out more. Not that it was a whole lot of time, but it was *something*.

"Tristan's a good one. Tell him hi from me, will you?" Pushing away from the wall, Leo turned to head back inside while they said their goodbyes in a mildly awkward shuffle. Jesus, Leo was normally much smoother than this; his ability to adapt had landed him this job in the first place. He hated feeling like this, out of his element, like some starry-eyed teenager. Stupid princes. It was worth keeping in mind that just because Joshua said 'please' and was willing to listen to someone like Leo, it didn't mean he wasn't a spoilt brat. He had yet to take a risk that wasn't strictly necessary, after all.

Right. To work.

The first thing Leo did once back inside was pull James out of his meeting with Atkin—with *George*, whatever—to fill him in. Then Leo barged into Nate's office and told him to work his magic.

After which he steeled himself to call Joshua back and ask for a list of people who were aware of Joshua's sexuality. Stupid. Really *bloody* stupid, fuck, Leo should have thought of that right away, should not have needed Nate to point that out.

It really hadn't been fair of Joshua to call without an advance warning, to act all nice and almost, well, *shy*. Not fair, no. Leo had been just fine talking to Joshua this morning, but that he had mistaken Joshua for a street kid in need of help had put them on uneven footing right away. Really, it had been like a kick to the kneecap before the conversation had even started. As someone who had been through that experience, Leo considered it a fitting analogy.

Well, not this time. This time, Leo was prepared, and he would play his role as a professional like a professional. A professionally professional professional, to be precise.

He would do James proud.

2

Joshua had only just settled into Mo's colossal sofa when his phone rang. Accepting a beer, he used his free hand to fumble the phone out of his trousers, surprised to see Leo's name flash across the screen.

It had been a mere twenty minutes since they'd talked. Surely Nate hadn't found anything quite this quickly? Oh God, *had* they found something? Was there a chance this nightmare was over before the sun set?

Tucking the beer between his thighs, Joshua picked up the phone and struggled to think of a casual opening, something that wouldn't make him sound too desperate. "Miss me already?"

Oh, great. Now he'd come across as a different kind of desperate.

If anyone had the skill to make silence seem loudly unimpressed over the phone, Leo Graham was that person. Joshua cringed. Sure, Leo had been a bit of a judgmental prick throughout part of their meeting, so it wasn't as though he could complain *too* much about Joshua skirting the edges of appropriate behaviour, but—uh. Two wrongs didn't make a right.

"Sorry," Joshua mumbled when five seconds had passed and Leo had yet to utter a word. Mo flicked Joshua a curious glance as he dropped onto the sofa next to Joshua, poking him with a foot.

"I *believe*," Leo's tone was as dry as the Sahara, "we're still at a stage in our acquaintance where I can go ten minutes without talking to you. In addition, I'm a strong, independent woman, and while you may have the curly locks of Prince Charming, I have yet to see you ride a white stallion. This is not that fairy tale."

"I've got a white mare," Joshua told him, and really, he should stop and direct this conversation back onto normal territory. "Surely that counts? Otherwise, it would be sexist."

To Joshua's surprise, Leo gave a quick, curling laugh. "All right, Princeling. I'm sure you're a fantastic rider. Far be it from me to question it. Them. Your, ah..." A tiny pause. "*Riding skills.*"

Had Leo just—*really*? How had they gotten caught up in a round of Innuendo Bingo? And how was Joshua supposed to think of a good retort when his brain was wiped blank, heat pooling low in his belly at the thought of straddling Leo's hips, holding himself up above him and—stop. Joshua needed to *stop*. There was a good chance he was reading more into this than he should.

He'd likely been silent for too long, because Leo spoke again, tone brisker than before. "Your collection of horses aside, I'm actually calling with a question. Can you give us a list of people who know you're gay?"

The way Leo said the words as though they meant nothing— *you're gay; the grass is green; look, it's a rainy day in London, now there's a surprise*—settled strangely in Joshua's chest. Leo made it sound so easy, so *natural*, when there were nights Joshua had fallen asleep wishing he'd wake up normal, would meet a nice girl and fall in love, get married in a splendid ceremony at Westminster Abbey and live up to expectations.

No such luck, of course. And while puberty had been hard, he'd mostly come to accept what he couldn't change. Hearing a near-stranger casually put it out there was new, though. Not necessarily in a bad way, just... new.

"Yes, of course." Joshua sucked in a breath to counteract the tight clench of his chest. "Not many people know, so it will be a short list. Give me five minutes, and I'll text it to you."

"Thanks, that would be helpful."

"Okay." Hesitating, Joshua wondered whether there was anything else, but he couldn't think of a reason to keep Leo on the line any longer. Leo had things to do anyway, and Mo was studying Joshua with an amused quirk to his mouth, wiggling his naked toes against Joshua's thigh.

"So, I'll call you if there are news," Leo said.

"Yes, please. And I'll send you that list." Joshua squeezed Mo's ankle before he reached for his beer, the bottle damp and cool against his palm. "You can call me anytime, okay? If you find something, please let me know right away?"

"You say 'please' a lot," Leo remarked, a glint of amusement to his voice. It was hard to tell whether it was criticism or a roundabout compliment, so Joshua went for a neutral tone.

"I wasn't raised by wolves."

"If you had been, I'd have asked for pictures. Talk to you later, Princeling." Again, Leo laughed quietly, and Joshua couldn't tell whether it was at or with him.

"Yes. Later." Another moment passed, then the connection was cut off, and Joshua lowered the phone, staring at it for a beat. *Princeling.* Huh. Leo was so... weird. Yes, weird. A confusing mix of cheeky and withdrawn, professional, dismissive and approachable; a whole world of adjectives to describe a person Joshua had only just met.

"If a guy calls me *Princeling*..." Joshua gave Mo a sideways glance and paused to sip at his beer. "Is he flirting with me? Or would you consider it an insult? Like, the historical context is nasty, but I don't think... I don't think he means it like that? More like little prince, or something?"

"Depends." Mo poked Joshua's thigh once more, for good measure, then tucked his cold toes in against the back of Joshua's knee. "Could be teasing, could be flirting, could be derogatory. I mean, Tristan and I call you that when you act all posh around us."

"You've known me for ages, though."

"How long've you known this one, then?"

"Met him this morning. He's part of James Boyle's team." Joshua slid a fingernail under the label on the bottle, began peeling off one corner as he continued. "We didn't have the best start since he's not a fan of... being born into privilege, is how he put it. But I think we have a truce now. Sort of friendly."

"Sounded friendly enough to me, from what I heard." Mo took a long pull of his beer and slid further into the cushions, his ratty, paint-splattered top rucking up over his stomach. Even so, his high cheekbones and classically beautiful face made him look more like a fairy-tale prince than Joshua did on his best days.

"He gay?" Mo asked into Joshua's thoughts.

"Yes. Out and proud." Joshua shrugged one shoulder and looked away, at the enormous telly they had yet to turn on. "He thinks I'm a coward for hiding."

"You're not a coward," Mo said, suddenly harsh. "Don't let anyone call you that, J. That's not *on*. It'd be harder for you than it would be for most." He frowned, touching Joshua's elbow. "It's not the same. Like, for me, it's not that tough, you know? First shot I did for Lagerfeld was all dripping with homoerotic tension, and if I officially come out as bi, no one will give a shit after the first excitement blows over."

"Are you thinking about it?" Joshua asked.

"At some point. I'm not in a hurry. It's not like there aren't rumours already." Mo paused before he went on, quiet and gentle. "For you, it'd be different. It'd come up again, and again, and again. It'd be tough, given the public interest in your life."

"Yeah. That's definitely part of it." Joshua exhaled on a sigh before he tilted sideways, into Mo's solid support.

Now that Joshua thought about it, they'd never really talked about the topic in any detail. Like Tristan, Mo had always seemed to get it without Joshua needing to squirm through an explanation. The closest they'd ever come to a discussion was probably after the first time they'd ended up in bed, and Joshua had felt incredibly awkward when he'd said, "You know, though, that it's not, like... I'm not looking to date anyone. Like, a guy. Our friendship's great, and I don't want things to get messy just because—this is good, yeah?"

Mo had thrown his head back and laughed around his cigarette, slinging an easy arm around Joshua's naked waist. "Don't worry, babe. This was fun, but I'm not looking to become your princess. Think we're both a bit young to settle down, yeah? Friends first, rest's a nice bonus."

And that had been that. Mo had gone through a string of lovers, with Joshua as a recurring one, and Joshua had gone through Mo. It worked for them.

"I love you a lot," Joshua said, apropos of nothing, and Mo laughed into his hair.

"Same, Curly. You're my very favourite royal."

"Don't let Emma hear you say that," Joshua advised.

"Far be it from me to offend your lovely and, frankly, scary sister."

Joshua took another sip of beer, the liquid cool and bitter on his tongue, before he tucked himself further in against Mo's side. "You know the whole... public scrutiny thing is not the only reason, right?"

Mo's attempt at an answer was cut off by the doorbell. "Hold that thought," he said, winding himself out from under Joshua's weight. Joshua's disgruntled noise and grabby hands were rewarded with a flick on the nose, then Mo left the room to buzz up either Tristan or the pizza delivery person.

Joshua took the opportunity to type up the list for Leo. By the time he sent it off, there was a mix of voices drifting in from the stairway—it seemed as though their food had arrived at the same time as Tristan and was now getting the bodyguard stamp of approval from Johnson. Hopefully, Mo would tip the poor delivery guy well.

Stuffing the phone back into his pocket, Joshua set his beer down on the floor and rose from the sofa to fetch some plates and cutlery. He ran into Tristan in the corridor and found himself pulled into an immediate headlock. With his face shoved into Tristan's armpit, he fought to free himself as he flailed his hands and muttered about deodorant and regular showers.

"Love you, bitch," Tristan told him, and let go.

Joshua stepped back and stuck out his tongue, then felt his mouth twitch up into his most genuine smile of the day.

With pizza, beers and a half-dozen fairy cakes Tristan had brought along to "commemorate the occasion", they sprawled out on the sofa, Joshua comfortably squashed between Tristan and Mo despite the fact that there was a football pitch worth of space available to them. Mo switched the telly on to some old episode of *The Simpsons*, and they talked about nothing much for a while: England and Ireland's chances in the World Cup and which matches they'd attend together; whether they could fit an additional week in Brazil into their agendas; in which ways the Church needed to chill and why; the tragedy of pizza never tasting quite the same after a day in the fridge. Even though Joshua was fully aware that Mo and Tristan were humouring him, giving him a chance to relax after the day's events, he appreciated their efforts.

His friends were the very, very best.

When he said as much, possibly with a slight thickness to his voice, Mo reached over to ruffle his hair. "Anytime, mate. You want to talk about those reasons now?"

"Reasons?" Tristan shifted to drape his legs over Joshua's thighs, pushing his plate closer to Joshua. From Tristan, it was practically a declaration of love. Helping himself to a slice of Tristan's pizza, Joshua took a bite, chewing carefully with his gaze on the telly. He had no idea what Homer and Marge Simpson were talking about.

"Reasons he's in the closet," Mo said in Joshua's stead.

"Oh, we're actually talking about that? Awesome." Tristan swiped his index finger through leftover cheese that had dripped onto his plate, nudging Joshua. When Joshua glanced over, Tristan gave him an expectant look while licking his finger clean. Against his will, Joshua found himself grinning.

"You realise that if you seek eye contact with a proclaimed member of the gay crowd while sucking on your fingers, it will come across as sexual innuendo, right?"

Waggling his eyebrows, Tristan let the finger slide out of his mouth with a wet pop. Mo snorted, and it took a second before

Joshua felt his own grin widen, tip over into a short laugh. It wasn't *that* funny, it really wasn't, and his mirth came with an edge of hysteria. He felt lighter all the same.

"Reasons," he said slowly. "Yeah. Like, Mo thinks it's mainly the public scrutiny that's holding me back, only that's not all there is to it." He frowned and put the half-eaten pizza slice back on Tristan's plate, hunger evaporated. "I can't believe we've never talked about this."

Tristan shrugged. "Figured you'd talk when you're ready."

"Same." Draping an arm around Joshua's shoulders, Mo pulled him close, fingertips snaking underneath Joshua's sleeve. "Guess you're ready now, so out with it."

Joshua tipped his head against Mo's shoulder, Tristan's legs heavy across his lap. Homer was performing some kind of shuffling dance on the screen, and Joshua's stomach wiggled with the motion, a hectic buzz under his skin. He'd made it a habit not to give the whole issue too much thought. In fact, he'd managed to tape off that section of his brain and declare it a no-trespassing zone—right up until this morning, when the threat of exposure had come crashing in with brutal immediacy.

"If I came out," his voice sounded deeper than usual, rougher to his own ears, "it could impact our relations with other countries. Uganda and India, for one. Or, I mean, our work on human rights? What if Mum and Emma are suddenly seen as biased, because of me? I just—there could be protests even here." Lungs tight, he remembered to breathe. "Like, the more conservative parts of the Church of England, the parts that prevented priests from blessing gay marriages. What if people take this as the reason to question all of it? Monarchy, us? I don't want to be the downfall of—of my family, kind of? The one to bring it all down."

"Jesus fucking Christ," Tristan muttered. He twisted a hand into Joshua's T-shirt, fingers warm through the fabric.

"*Josh.*" Mo's embrace tightened. "You ever asked your mum or Emma about it? Not that I've met them often, but seems to me they'd hate holding you back."

"They would. They love you a stupid amount, and they'd support you no matter what." Tristan's tone was confident, and unlike Mo, he knew both Joshua's mother and Emma well—most notably from those horrifying six months when he'd been dating Emma. Joshua had pretended to be oblivious; there were some things he did not care to know about his best mate and his sister. *God.*

"I don't want to be the weak link in the family." Curling further into Mo, Joshua took a deep breath, and another. With a pitiful noise, he stared at his beer, out of reach unless he moved from where he was comfortably settled between Tristan and Mo. Pinching Joshua's stomach, Tristan leaned forward to get it for him.

One day, when they least expected it, Joshua would make Mo a Knight of the Realm and gift Tristan with a castle or something. He could totally do it. There were many perks to being a prince after all, and most of the time, Joshua was very aware that he was lucky.

Just... not right now. Tomorrow, though. He'd be fine tomorrow.

THE LIST JOSHUA had texted was surprisingly short, contained just over a handful of names—his mother and sister (but notably not his father, who'd split from Queen Louise in a divorce that had been handled with quiet dignity some ten years ago), Tristan and Mo, George Atkin and, somewhat randomly, the musician Ed Sheeran.

Leo paused on the last one, sparing a wistful second for wondering whether he could get Joshua to introduce them. A happy coincidence had placed Leo in some bar with an open mike one night, browsing for clients, but he'd stopped the moment Ed had strummed his guitar and sung the first few notes of an unfamiliar song. Leo had listened to the entire set with a blank mind and a full heart, and then spent five quid he really didn't have on a demo album. Throughout the first few months of Leo starting to work for James, that album had been on repeat for Leo's tube rides to work, companion to his struggle to sink into a regular rhythm of rising early and going to bed before midnight. Not the issue at hand, though, and taking advantage of Joshua's connections would be a tacky thing to do anyway. Especially when Leo wasn't even sure he liked Joshua. Or vice versa.

Strolling into Nate's office, Leo sat down in a chair, then proceeded to bounce both himself and the chair around so he was next to Nate. In their early days of working together, Nate would have hated the disregard for boundaries; now his fingers didn't even pause on the keyboard. Boring. Leo would have to step up his game.

"Got the list," he said out loud.

"List?" Nate glanced up and blinked, his eyes clearing. "Oh. Give it here, then."

Bringing it up on his phone, Leo handed it over and kicked his feet up on Nate's desk, upsetting a pile of scribbled notes that might as well be written in an alien language. Nate huffed and moved to right the mess, then handed Leo's phone back. There was a pinched look to his face. "Does this list look weird to you?"

"Weird?" Leo looked down at the screen, then up at Nate. "Why, because of Ed Sheeran?"

"No, not that. 'Course Joshua would move in those celebrity kind of circles. He's friends with Mo Puri, right, and Puri is a pretty well-known model. Like the Armani campaign? The underwear one?'" There was a fascinating tinge of pink to Nate's cheeks. Leo could not recall seeing that particular Armani campaign, no, but maybe he should take a look. Based on Nate's reaction, it sounded worth the while.

"'Friends'." Leo lifted one hand to mime air quotes. "Yes, Joshua and that Mo person appear to be *very* good friends. Makes me wonder whether I need to rethink my own definition of friendship, since I'm clearly missing a certain element there."

Nate appeared to consider a rebuttal, then merely shook his head. "So you don't think there's anyone missing from that list?"

"His father?" Leo frowned and took another look, narrowing his eyes. Incomplete, how was that list incomplete? Who was missing? Apart from James' team, who should be on there and wasn't?

"It's so easy to forget the people in the background," Nate said softly. "The ones who are just there, and maybe you never tell them stuff, but they see so much more than you think."

Oh.

Oh.

"The people in the background," Leo repeated slowly, and for a moment, he was tempted to ask whether that was the kind of work Nate had done before this, whether he'd specialised in blending in with his surroundings, no one questioning his presence as he'd slipped in and out of rooms without anyone taking much notice, giving him a chance to sneak away and hack into computer systems. They didn't share stories from their past though; for all intents and purposes, their lives may as well have started when they'd joined James' crew. Leo had his suspicions, of course—Ben might have spent some time in prison, Nate showed traces of military training, and parts of Carole's story seemed to resemble Leo's own—but he'd never sought to confirm his theories.

They'd all been promised a clean slate. It was only fair he allowed others the same courtesy he expected.

"Don't ever forget the people in the background," Nate told him, a strange set to his mouth.

Leo nodded and didn't ask.

ONE OF JOSHUA'S bodyguards was in serious, *serious* debt.

Leo wasn't entirely certain how Nate had retrieved the financial status of everyone around Joshua, and he didn't think he wanted to know. What he gathered was that Tristan's family was filthy rich and didn't believe in placing restrictions on their son, that one of Mo's modelling gigs paid more than Leo made in a year, that Ed Sheeran must be the least millionaire-like multimillionaire, that leading the Royal Communications unit came with a decent salary, and that those in Joshua's immediate employ were rewarded for their discretion with generous pay cheques. *And* that one of Joshua's bodyguards had a problem holding onto that pay cheque regardless.

Which was why Leo had charmed his way into the good graces of a neighbour to that Johnson guy.

While Nate searched the man's flat and Carole stood guard, Leo had tea with wiry, old Ms Adams. Initially, she hadn't been too pleased at receiving an unannounced social call so late in the day, but by now, they were having a pleasant chat about the Royal Ballet's classic staging of *Romeo & Juliet* and the upcoming world premiere of *The Winter's Tale*. In between trying not to fuss with the starched collar of his button-up, Leo managed to steer the conversation towards Johnson's habits and the guests he tended to entertain.

All in the interest of a covert, royally sanctioned background check, of course. Because Mr Johnson Bales was in line for a great honour. Or in line for prison, whichever.

"He used to be *such* a nice chap," Ms Adams said. "A quiet neighbour, never any problems, really." After that, she faltered. Leo refilled her tea cup and smiled, resting his hands on his thighs. She continued while studying him carefully. "You told me you are looking for input into a nomination of Mr Bales for—what was it, dear?"

"The Order of Bath," Leo supplied, tone confident. "The Queen usually awards it for outstanding military service, but civilians may also receive it for acts of bravery. And she believes that someone who keeps her son out of harm's way would merit such an honour." In all honesty, he was relying on shaky memories of the Honours systems and could only hope that Ms Adams wouldn't be able to spot potential mistakes in his narrative. Leo was an ace bullshitter, though. It was how he'd caught James' attention in the first place.

When her indecisive expression held, Leo leaned forward just a little, looking up from under his lashes to make himself appear harmless and trustworthy. His tone was smooth like melted butter. "Provided, of course, that he is a role model in every respect, and that the candid opinions of those in his vicinity would recommend him for it. We will hold everything you say in strict confidence, I assure you."

"Well. I am not generally one to speak ill of anyone." Ms Adams chin lifted proudly, and wasn't it funny how that sort of statement was always, without fail, followed by its originator speaking very ill of someone?

"I wouldn't ask you to." Leo made his voice low and soothing. "I am merely trying to ensure that the Crown honours individuals who are deserving. True model citizens."

Another second passed in silence. Then Ms Adams set her cup down with a dainty clink, laced her fingers in her lap and pursed her lips. "Well then."

~

"Two nights before Joshua's trip to Spain, some guys forced their way into Johnson's flat." Leo dropped into the backseat of Carole's car and folded his legs up onto the upholstery. "Four of them, and the neighbour says they looked like the bad sort. Also says that Johnson's become increasingly curt and sketchy in the last few months."

"Shoes off the seat," Carole told him without even looking into the rearview mirror. She pulled off the kerb with a little jerk, her sad excuse for a car reluctant to launch into traffic. At one point, the old Fiat would turn to dust right under their arses.

"Caz, one of my shoes is worth more than this pile of trash," Leo said. "So what did you guys find?"

"Gambling." From the passenger seat, Nate handed his phone to Leo. The screen was open to a picture folder, overly bright in the darkness that was beginning to settle. When Leo enlarged the images one after the other, he made out slips of paper covered in a lazy scrawl, numbers and figures, ticket stubs. Oh, he *so* loved this part, gathering the puzzle pieces until everything came together.

He passed the phone back and undid the first three buttons of his shirt. "Did you copy his hard drive?"

"'Course. But if I had to *bet*," ridiculous as he was, Nate snorted, "it wasn't the guy himself. Doesn't seem the type, does he? Maybe he just gave them a tip to get them off his back. Or maybe he did set it up, but I don't think it was his idea."

"We shall see." Leo steepled his fingers together and beamed, wide and broad like a criminal mastermind. In his next life, he intended to become a supervillain. In this one, he was saving a prince from public exposure.

Not too bad.

JOSHUA WAS TIPSY.

Not drunk, mind, but a little blurry around the edges, loose-limbed and his lids heavier than they had any right to be. Made no sense in terms of, like, volume and weight... things. Lids were thin and not very large, right, so unless they had suddenly turned to lead, it couldn't possibly be this difficult to keep them open. Sniffling, he turned his face in against Tristan's shoulder and took a deep breath.

"Are you smelling me?" Tristan asked, sounding amused and far too sober for Joshua's liking. He needed everyone to be drunk and swimmy and unfocused. He needed this day to never have happened.

"Smells like home," Joshua muttered, and Mo puffed a laugh into his hair.

Tristan pulled Joshua closer by the sleeve. "Weirdo."

"You love me."

"Amazingly, I do," Tristan said.

Joshua was about to return the sentiment, go into a ramble about how he loved both Tristan and Mo a whole damn lot and was so, so grateful to have them in his life—maybe he was more than a little tipsy—when his phone buzzed against his thigh. He made a disgruntled noise and considered ignoring it. If this was George calling him about The Backup Plan, ominous capital letters and all, Joshua would rather saw off his own leg than deal with it at this very moment. Saw off his own leg with a *spoon*.

After three rings and an utter lack of reaction from Joshua, Mo dug into Joshua's pocket for the phone. He picked up with, "This is Joshua's phone, Mo Puri speaking. What's up?"

They were close enough that Joshua caught the lilt of Leo's voice.

Sitting up with a start, Joshua snatched the phone from Mo and uttered a quick, "Hi. Leo? *Hey.*"

"Sir Joshua," Leo acknowledged. "Making your non-boyfriend answer the phone for you, really? I take it this is the glamorous royal lifestyle the papers keep talking about."

Was this teasing? It felt like it, what with the spark of brightness to Leo's voice. Joshua tried to collect his skittish thoughts and wind them into a reply that made sense. "Sorry. Needed to wash down the caviar with some champagne. One shouldn't talk with a full mouth, you know."

"Given the circumstances, I'm strongly tempted to make a pun about you having your mouth full." As soon as the words were out, Leo seemed to regret them, his tone growing abruptly smooth and professional. "Never mind. There's an actual reason I'm calling."

And just like that, Joshua's stomach filled with ice.

"A reason?" he repeated softly. "What reason? Did you find something?"

Next to him, both Mo and Tristan stilled, then crept closer to listen.

"Might have," Leo said. "Who's with you right now?"

"Um." Joshua cleared his throat, tried to focus and speak around the rawness of his throat. "Mo and Tristan. But they're not—"

"I meant bodyguards," Leo interrupted, and oh.

"Johnson. Leo, what—"

Again, Leo didn't let him finish. "Thought so. Can you come to our office? Bring the bloke with you, please. And your friends if you want to, I'll leave that up to you."

Joshua's chest felt carved out from the inside, as though someone had removed all the blood and flesh and muscles and bones that should hold it together. "Okay," he whispered, and it hardly sounded like his own voice.

When the call ended, he lowered the phone, turned into Tristan's open arms and felt Mo curl up against his back. Breathe. He needed to *breathe.* And then he needed to pull himself together and act normal for the duration of their trip to Boyle's office, normal enough that nothing would seem amiss.

Johnson. Oh God. Was this—it had been implied, hadn't it? The way Leo had specifically asked which bodyguard was with Joshua, had told Joshua to 'bring the bloke' when he'd learned it was Johnson... It *had* been implied. Or not?

Why? *Why?*

Then again, did it even matter? Did it make a difference why?

Was Joshua jumping to conclusions?

"I think..." Joshua swallowed thickly and had to start again. "I think they found something. Maybe. Please don't make me do this alone?"

"Never," Tristan said, and Mo nodded into his hair.

IF LEO HAD HARBOURED any illusions regarding Joshua's acting abilities, he'd have been sorely disappointed. When Joshua arrived, flanked by Tristan and the dark-haired vision easily identified as Mo Puri, he was thrumming with barely suppressed nerves, face pale and eyes wide. He was the very epitome of discomfort. Johnson was trailing the trio with a neutral expression and tension etched into the line of his shoulders.

Following James' lead, the team had decided to play this fast and dirty, claim that they'd traced the original email back to its source (they hadn't) and that the source had named Johnson as the mastermind behind it all. Leo would need to sell it convincingly. He'd drop some details about the blokes Ms Adams had described, about the material Nate had found on Johnson's computer and in his flat, and hopefully, it would make it seem as though he knew what he was talking about.

Fuck, he was ready.

JAMES BOYLE CARRIED A GUN.

Although it was hidden underneath the man's jacket, Joshua caught a glimpse when James led them into the conference room. His team closed ranks just as Johnson wanted to position himself outside the door. Several moments of indecision passed, heavy like those thumping, throbbing heartbeats that sometimes pounded through movies.

Then Johnson said, "Joshua, I'll be outside as usual. Right?" There was a nervous twitch to his left eye.

Joshua forced himself to look away quickly. "Come on in with us. Please." He didn't recognise his own voice.

God, he didn't want to be here for this. Also, was James allowed to carry a gun? Joshua had heard rumours about their unorthodox working methods, something about connections in high places that led to the kind of leeway not usually allowed to civilians.

God, Joshua *really* didn't want to be here for this.

He dropped into a seat at the very end of the room, felt Mo and Tristan shuffle into place beside him. Under the table, Tristan's knee knocked against his, and Mo slipped a hand onto Joshua's thigh, squeezing in reassurance. "Game face," he whispered.

Joshua inhaled through his teeth, then nodded. By the time he regained a sense of control, draping it around his shoulders like a cloak, Johnson had been seated at the table with Nate standing behind him. Something about the way Nate held himself transmitted a clear warning. James had taken a seat at the head of the table, Ben was at the door, and Carole was flicking through some print-outs, pausing now and then to shoot Johnson an unimpressed look.

The tableau was completed when Leo hopped up onto the edge of the table, looking down at Johnson with his legs dangling, his cheerful attitude at odds with the thick tension that pressed in on the room. "So," Leo said brightly. "Let's talk about responsible gambling, shall we?"

Johnson made a sudden move. Immediately, Nate's hand came to rest on a spot that made Johnson groan and sag back into his seat.

"Ready?" Leo asked, just as brightly as before, perfectly unbothered by the interruption.

When Johnson sought out Joshua's gaze, Joshua swallowed and focused on Leo instead. Joshua's head was spinning, thoughts tumbling through empty space because *oh shit, oh no, it's true.*

Johnson had been with him for three years, had replaced Paul who'd wanted to spend more time with his kids 'instead of just this one royal brat here'. Joshua himself had helped pick Johnson from a long list of applicants, and he still remembered their first encounter, where it had taken four minutes of awkward small talk before they'd fallen into a heated discussion about video games.

Joshua should watch this scene unfold. He should. It would be a good reminder of just why he needed to be careful with his trust, but —fuck, Leo was ruthless. It was like someone taking apart a Lego castle, removing one brick, then another, almost lovingly. *You're done, man, just give it up. Better don't hold back because your trusted associates certainly didn't. Oh, and speaking of trust, of being in a position of trust, how do you sleep at night, hmm? How do you look into a mirror? By the way, does your little sister know just how fucked up you are? The debt you're in?*

Johnson's sister. Oh, shit, his *sister.* Joshua had met her a couple of times and found her a lovely girl. With their parents' early death, it had been left to Johnson, five years her senior, to raise her. She'd be devastated if she learned of this.

"How do you know about my sister?" Johnson asked, toneless. His eyes were wild.

Leo's grin was that of a shark who'd smelled blood. "Oh, we know a *lot* of things. In fact, I've got her number right here. What do you say, should we call her?"

Joshua hated him a little. He also couldn't look away from the tight set of Leo's jaw, the proud tilt of his chin, and the sharp blue of his eyes. The confidence he projected had Joshua feeling breathless and unhinged, deeply unsettled even though he wasn't the focus of Leo's attention.

The moment Johnson broke was the moment Joshua hid his face

in his hands, refusing to watch. If James and his team judged him for his weakness, he didn't care. He didn't give a shit. How could a single day feel like a decade?

Three deep breaths, a slow count to fifteen while Tristan and Mo rubbed his back. Then Joshua straightened and schooled his features into the closest imitation of composure he could manage. Blankly, he listened to Johnson's explanations and excuses, and while he could feel Johnson seeking out his gaze, he kept his focus on the wall, as whitewashed as his mind. He didn't move at all until James suggested Nate hack into the blackmailers' computers to erase all traces of the incriminating material, after which James would use his contacts at Scotland Yard to tip them off about illegal gambling practices.

"Please do," Joshua said, addressing James as much as Nate. With that, he dragged himself into a standing position and fought not to sway on his feet. "If you'll excuse me, please. Tristan, Mo, could we— is there somewhere we can wait?"

"What about me?" Johnson asked, more plaintive than demanding. The sound of his voice grated against the inside of Joshua's skull.

"What *about* you?" Tristan shot back, harsher than Joshua had ever heard him. "Don't think you're in a position to ask *anything* of Joshua, fuckwit."

Briefly, Joshua met Johnson's eyes, then blinked and looked away. His head hurt, and it felt as though the walls were crowding in on him, crawling closer each time he blinked. If he couldn't trust his bodyguards, couldn't trust *anyone* but his family and his two best friends—Jesus. How could he ever close his eyes with a time bomb ticking away under his pillow? How, *how* could he set one foot in front of the other without falling over?

"We'll keep him here for now," James said somewhere in the distance, and Johnson's protest was shut down with quick efficiency. There was more after that, something about the need to inform George and Queen Louise, about backup security before Joshua could leave the building. Joshua blocked it all out.

Steady and confident, Joshua. Smile. It's all about projection, about pretending you don't even notice the stares. You're above the scrutiny.

Hold the pose.

IT WASN'T the first time Joshua had misplaced his trust. There had been people before Johnson, false friends who'd wanted him for his status or his connections, for his family money. But this was the first time he'd been played with malicious intent.

In theory, Joshua should be on the phone right now. If he were stronger, he'd handle the calls to his mother and George himself. He'd be out there taking charge instead of hiding out in a tastefully decorated waiting room, trying to forget the last fifteen hours of his life while his stomach quaked at the mere idea of bringing in a replacement for Johnson. Just like Johnson, the other two bodyguards who sometimes worked for Joshua were bound to know things that Joshua had never told them, and just like Johnson, they might one day be tempted to twist that to their own advantage.

As long as Joshua kept his sexuality a secret—*as long as he was gay* —he was vulnerable. A liability to the Crown.

"D'you wanna talk?" Mo asked gently, sinking into the chair next to Joshua's.

Tristan dropped to the floor, crossed his legs and leaned back against Joshua's calves, one of his hands wrapping around Joshua's left ankle. "We can also shut our traps, if you prefer. Just, like. We're here, yeah?"

"I know." Clearing his throat, Joshua tipped his head back against the wall. His body felt heavy, heavy, heavy. "Never doubted it."

"You didn't? You never thought one of us might have... You know?" There was a hint of apprehension to Mo's tone, and Joshua was quick to shake his head. Tristan, still on the floor, twisted around to look up at them. His expression was uncommonly serious.

"No," Joshua said. He glanced from Mo to Tristan and back, repeated, "*No.* You wouldn't. I mean, I wasn't even supposed to tell you about the whole... investigation thing, like, Nate trying to find virtual traces and whatever they did. Leo told me not to tell anyone, and I told you both anyway. So."

Neither Mo nor Tristan replied, but Joshua could feel them shifting closer, wrapping him up. He was grateful for the second-hand warmth.

LEO HESITATED in front of the closed door. He'd moved past the waiting room a few times while hurrying back and forth between Nate's office and his own, and the initial murmur of voices had died down about an hour ago. Raising his hand, he knocked gently and waited for a response. None came.

Leaning around the Ficus tree Nate was fighting to keep alive, Leo peered into the room through a glass panel. Dimly lit by a single lamp, the room's occupants were cast in a bronze glow, asleep on the floor in a haphazard tangle of limbs, curled into each other with no space left between them. It was sweet, sparking a distant ache in Leo's bones.

He inhaled deeply before he went to open the door.

His steps were light on the wooden floor, not enough to disturb the sleepers. Leo crouched down beside them, and for a moment, he was caught staring at Joshua's face, features soft and lax in sleep, lips parted. Like this, Joshua looked painfully young.

"Princeling," Leo whispered. There was no reaction, so he reached out to touch Joshua's shoulder. "Joshua. *Hey.*"

Joshua woke up with a start, shooting into a sitting position and blinking, wide-eyed, at Leo. The sudden movement roused Tristan as well, had him roll over with a groan, while Mo mumbled something unintelligible and buried his face against his arms.

"I'm so sorry." Leo shifted away and sat back on his haunches. It was disconcerting to have all of Joshua's sleepy focus, made heat scramble up the back of Leo's neck and warm his cheeks, unsettling him further. He suspected his flush was obvious even in the weak light. "I wouldn't have woken you if it wasn't necessary."

With a soft exhale, Joshua ducked his head and scrubbed a hand down his face, then ruffled up his hair. The strands were long enough that a few curls hung into his eyes. "What time is it?"

"Nearing midnight."

"Any news?" Tristan asked.

Leo was glad for the excuse to look away from Joshua. "Yes, actually. That's why I woke you. Sorry again."

"Oi, Puri." Without missing a beat, Tristan pinched Mo's stomach just as Nate entered the room, stopping to take in the scene. He drew closer while Leo scrambled to his feet. Joshua followed suit, propped himself up against the wall. He looked drained, robbed of the self-assuredness he'd displayed that very morning.

When Mo made a protesting noise, Leo dragged his gaze away from Joshua's profile and caught Nate holding himself uncommonly still, as though transfixed by the tattoo that had become visible where Mo's T-shirt had ridden up. The black letters sitting above the waistband of Mo's trousers spelled '*Don't think I won't*' and reminded Leo of a tattoo he'd seen on Joshua while leafing through *Metro* earlier today —a '*why not?*' inked into a similar spot, clearly visible in the pap shots from Joshua's holiday in Spain.

Leo's attention hadn't lingered on those pictures. He wasn't that person anymore.

"What's the news, then?" Joshua asked once everyone seemed reasonably awake, even Mo having dragged himself upright. Sleepy and grumpy, Mo was still the most beautiful man Leo had ever seen up close. He could appreciate the aesthetics, but unlike Nate, he didn't feel a need to stare. His capacity for attraction had been on the back burner for years.

"It's good news." With a smile directed at Joshua, Leo spun a chair around and straddled it backwards, elbows on the armrest. "Looks like police got the guys, cleaned out their evil lair of sin and debauchery. They're in custody. And before that, Nate's virtual breaking and entering was successful."

"You can never be a hundred percent certain," Nate contributed, because of course he couldn't just omit some details in the interest of soothing a client. Sigh. "But chances are good. At least I managed to erase all traces I could find."

Well, yes. That, and he'd refused to let Leo have a look at anything before making it disappear. Leo's curious streak had been wildly offended at Nate squirming and blushing over something he wouldn't share. Bastard. Friends didn't kick their friends out of their offices.

"Thank you," Joshua breathed, and Mo sat up a little straighter to fix Nate with a look from underneath hooded lids.

"Same from me," he said. "Thanks."

Nate rubbed a nervous hand over the back of his neck and didn't reply. Wow, Leo had never seen him like this; he'd seen Nate on the prowl a number of times, but it had always been casual. This was... weirdly intense.

Up until now, Leo had been convinced that Nate considered sex a physical exercise rather than anything substantially important. Like scratching an itch. Leo understood all too well, although he didn't see the need to involve another person. Personally, he was fine wanking off in the shower whenever his body demanded attention, quick and efficient, head empty, mess-free with the evidence washing down the drain while he finished cleaning himself.

"You're welcome," Nate mumbled in Mo's vague direction, shuffling his feet. His stance didn't relax until Mo's focus had shifted off him.

"So we're... It's over?" Joshua's voice carried an edge of disbelief, and Leo lifted his shoulders.

"It's never really over until you wear your secrets like a crown, Princeling." In the wake of the informal address, Leo could feel Nate shoot him a surprised glance, and Tristan snorted while the corners of Mo's mouth twitched. Joshua on the other hand seemed cautious, even wary. His back straightened, gaze clear on Leo's face.

"You think there's more where this came from?" he asked.

"Hopefully not where *this* came from, but..." Leo maintained eye contact and didn't shift on his chair. "This was your bodyguard blabbing, Joshua. Unless you deny yourself completely, cut off your balls, so to speak," oops, inappropriate again, "there'll always be someone who could throw you for another loop."

Joshua pressed his lips together and looked away. He didn't argue, and Leo wondered if Joshua had already thought of it himself and Leo was merely putting it out in the open.

"Not a problem right now." Tristan's tone was defensive. He draped an arm around Joshua's shoulders. "Jay, you don't have to think about this just yet, yeah? Let it settle for a bit. Day's been shitty enough, just—let's go home, have some pints."

"Think I need stronger stuff," Joshua muttered. Again, he messed up his hair with both hands, twisted the strands into a wild tangle that made him look young and a little lost. Leo took too long dragging his attention away from Joshua's fingers.

Thank God this tango with the past was about to come to an end. It was playing tricks on his mind.

Mo stretched with a small yawn, rising to his feet. "I've got tequila and whiskey."

"Sounds about right," Joshua said.

"Just a sec," Leo told him, holding up a hand. "Sorry. If you want to leave without security, that's fine. I understand, and we won't stop you. Or," he cocked an eyebrow, "call your mum and tell on you. But there's still the matter of what we do with that Johnson bloke. We can't keep him trapped in the conference room forever, you know? In fact, we have no legal grounds as it is."

"Thought your unconventional methods are part of the package? Like, do unto them as they do unto you?" Tristan's grin gleamed white, but faded quickly—a commendable effort to lighten the mood. It was sweet, the way both Tristan and Mo had remained glued to Joshua's side, and Leo supposed it could be seen as an indirect assessment of Joshua's character.

It was possible that Leo had judged him too harshly. Not that he'd admit as much.

"Actually, we prefer to do unto them before they do unto us," Nate said.

"Pre-emptive strikes." Leo nodded. "Our specialty."

Nate cast a quick glance around the room. "Nothing too bad, though," he rushed to add, and, oh. They were in the presence of a representative of the Crown. Maybe not the best idea to brag about the, ah... very grey areas they exploited at times. "*And* it's for the greater good."

"The greater good," Joshua, Mo and Tristan intoned as one, a morbid chant that clearly doubled as an inside joke. Leo needed a moment to place it.

Right, of course: *Hot Fuzz*. As a self-appointed expert on Pegg/Frost movies, Leo should have recognised it immediately. Also, he wouldn't have pegged—no pun intended—Joshua as the type to watch black comedies; it was almost as though the Prince was a normal person. He just might do things as mundane as playing FIFA, which improved the chances that Leo's earlier comparison of privileged birth to an easier difficulty setting hadn't come across as gibberish to Joshua.

Also, Leo needed to stop wasting quite so much brain space on the Prince.

"Great film," he said. "But not actually an answer to my question about Johnson."

He regretted his insistence when all traces of cheer disappeared from Joshua's eyes, leaving them tired and helpless. Joshua's voice carried exhaustion. "I don't know. What options do I even have?"

"Fire his arse and leave it at that." Leo ticked off his fingers. "Fire his arse and burn his bridges. Have him arrested on made-up charges. Have him arrested on true charges, so accessory to extortion, only that would mean the story will get out. Or, lastly, keep him on as your bodyguard."

"Not an option," Mo bit out. "That cunt needs to be far away from Joshua."

Leo raised his hands in a placating gesture. "Don't shoot the messenger, mate. Joshua asked me for his options, so I gave him the complete list. It's not my call what he picks."

For an uncomfortably long second, Mo stared at Leo. Then he shrugged. "Fair enough."

"I think he needs therapy," Joshua said quietly. "Johnson, I mean."

"You're fucking shitting us." Tristan sounded both exasperated and thoroughly unsurprised. "Fucker betrayed you."

"Not to mention violated the non-disclosure agreement I'm certain he signed." Leo got up from the chair and stepped closer to Joshua, studying him. "This is your call, though. So what will it be?"

Joshua held Leo's gaze for a moment before he sighed and slumped further into Tristan's side, dipping his head down. The gentle light softened the contours of his face, evening out the sharp line of his jaw. "I don't know," he repeated. "I guess I can't have him work with me anymore, not after... this. And I can't have him work with anyone else either. What if he does the same thing to them? And I could have prevented it?"

"Not your responsibility." Mo's tone suggested it was a well-rehashed line of argumentation, but even so, Leo couldn't help but comment.

"I beg to differ. Joshua should factor in how his decision might affect others, so yes, I'd say responsibility does play a role."

If looks could kill, Leo would wither under Mo's glare. Fortunately, he was no fragile flower, so he stood his ground and met the disapproval radiating from Mo by raising his chin. He was right, damn it. And sure, yes, he could appreciate that Joshua had indeed had a bit of a shit day, was probably in need of another holiday already, but now was no time to coddle him. As Joshua's fuckbuddy, Mo was understandably biased.

Mo is my friend, first and foremost. We also happen to get each other off sometimes.

Christ, what did Leo even care? He shouldn't. He didn't. It was all a fragment of his past.

"Is there," Joshua's words were as hesitant as the steps of a night wanderer, "a way to get his license revoked? Like, there's a bodyguard association, right? Just—for now, that's the most important thing to me, I think. Is that all right?"

"'Course it's all right," Tristan was quick to assure him. He followed it up with a subtle, loaded glance at Leo. Either way, it was none of Leo's business. He really needed to shut his trap; it bordered on a miracle James was even letting him anywhere near Joshua after the disaster that had been their first meeting this very morning.

Well, their first meeting as far as Joshua was aware. There was also that one time they'd been on opposing teams in the Eton Wall Game. Even now, Leo felt a little queasy just at the memory—the tight press of Prince Joshua's body, shoved close together in the thick of the scrummage, and then Leo's horrifying realisation that he'd popped a boner. The experience had marked the beginning of a downward spiral. Maybe, if it hadn't been for that day, if it hadn't been for *Joshua*...

Anyway. Revoking licenses.

"That's definitely something we can do," Leo said.

"We'll get it sorted," Nate promised, suddenly present again. Sometimes, Leo envied him for his ability to fade into the background. Leo himself only ever came on too strong.

"Thank you." Joshua inhaled and lifted his head to look first at Nate, then at Leo. "Seriously, thank you all so very much. I owe you."

Leo refused to be charmed. "I am partial to diamonds and holiday trips to Jamaica," he declared—and promptly wanted to punch himself in the face. To his surprise, Joshua's lips tugged up into a smile. While small, it was the most genuine one he'd shown all day.

Leo smiled back without thought.

JOSHUA TRIPPED over his words of gratitude and shook everyone's hand twice before he left with Mo and Tristan. Leo turned away before the lift doors had fully closed behind them.

So. That had been the late and incomplete fulfilment of a teenage fantasy. All right, then.

Half an hour later, Johnson was informed that his Close Protection License had been revoked. Leo watched the guy's face crumble and didn't feel so much as a hint of pity. Gambling problem or not, the guy had got off lightly, and Leo rather hoped Joshua wouldn't leave it at this.

When Leo hinted that further retribution was yet to come, Johnson blanched. As soon as he was allowed to leave, he scurried off like a dog with his tail between his legs.

Good riddance.

IN THE END, they didn't get drunk. Just stumbled into Mo's bedroom and talked about absolutely nothing of relevance, long gaps between sentences, everything quiet and slow. It was exactly what Joshua needed.

And yet, when first Mo and then Tristan drifted off to sleep, Joshua's brain was still going fifty miles a minute.

The problem—the problem that wasn't really a problem *as such*— was that Mo and Tristan would always and irrevocably be on his side. They would pick what was good for *him*, personally, and might fail to see the bigger picture because of it.

Rolling onto his back, Joshua listened to Mo's deep, even breathing to his left and Tristan's quietly snuffling snores to his right. Distant brightness of a London city night filtered in through the curtains, light particles that sparked like glitter in Mo's dark bedroom. Joshua's limbs felt heavy, as though weighed down by countless of miniature anchors.

He trusted Tristan and Mo, trusted them beyond question. He just didn't trust them to be impartial in their advice.

The memory of Leo's voice flitted through Joshua's mind, foggy and bright like sunlight shining through milky glass. For all that Leo had been openly critical of Joshua, he'd also taken him seriously and had addressed him as a rational, sensible person. Leo hadn't shied away from attributing responsibility, yet he hadn't tried to dictate Joshua's decision. He'd emphasised that it was Joshua's call, just like he had earlier in the day, when they'd talked in the toilets and Leo had tried to wheedle a little time out of Joshua. Which had turned out to be the right decision.

Christ. Joshua couldn't pretend that Johnson's betrayal didn't change things. He needed to talk to *someone*. Figure out his next move.

Quietly, he slid out of Mo's bed. The air was cool on his bare chest, raised the fine hairs on his arms, and he stood still for a moment to study the way Tristan and Mo were sprawled under the duvet. God, he loved them so much. His brothers. He'd be a mess without them.

But they couldn't help him with this. Not really.

LEO WOKE from his phone vibrating on the bedside table. Blindly, he groped for it, his thoughts lagging like lizards in the winter sun as they limped through the following process:

Half one in the morning?

That was two quick buzzes, right? So, text messages. No emergency.

Fuck. Display too bright.

What's my code again?

Somehow, he managed to gather enough mental presence to unlock his phone and open the message. Which was from the number Leo had saved as *Bloody Prince Joshua WTF*. Okay. Except, what the hell? Leo hadn't thought they were at the stage in their relationship where it was appropriate to text each other past eight in the evening. Also, uh, anything about relationships needed to stay out of Leo's answering message.

What did Joshua even want?

Sinking back onto his pillow, Leo raised the phone above his face and squinted to make out the letters, his eyes still adapting to the brightness. *'Hi! Sorry, I know this goes beyond your job, but do you think we could talk? What you said about wearing it like a crown?'* A second message had followed right after. *'I'll pay for your time! Obviously.'*

I'll pay for your time. Thanks, but Leo wasn't in that business anymore.

Not that Joshua had meant it like that. Of *course* he hadn't, and if Leo hadn't been so bloody tired, his brain never would have flashed back to a period in his life when 'How much?' was an acceptable way to open a conversation. Really, it was quite inconsiderate of Joshua to send his text in the middle of the freaking night instead of waiting for a time when normal people with normal day jobs were actually *awake*. To be fair, normal people also silenced their phones at night, but after that one time Nate had come to fetch Leo for an emergency situation, Leo had disabled the night mode.

Slowly, he lowered the phone and blinked at the shadows that filled the room. Then he rolled out of bed and grabbed a T-shirt off the floor, padding over to the open balcony door. For late May, the night was chilly on his skin. It served to revive his brain.

'Why me?' he sent back.

'Oh God hope I didn't wake you,' Joshua replied immediately. *'Sorry if I did. Didn't expect you'd see this before morning.'* He sent a second message half a minute later. *'And there aren't many people in my life who are... impartial outsiders I can trust. And you said it's nothing to be ashamed of. And you know what it's like, maybe. So.'*

Yes, Leo did know what it was like. He knew what it was like to risk something and have his optimism backfire; he knew what it was like to hit rock bottom; he knew a lot of things Prince Joshua couldn't even imagine.

None of them were things Leo was willing to share.

On the other hand, if Leo turned him away... Fuck, he *couldn't*. Joshua had grown up rich, privileged and handsome, but at the heart of it, he was still just a person seeking advice.

Pulling his T-shirt tighter around his body, Leo sucked in a slow breath. All right, he could do this. Sitting down with Joshua for an actual conversation, just the two of them, might even provide Leo with some kind of closure. *'Food is my price,'* he wrote. *'Buy me break-fast tomorrow . Or lunch or whatever fits . Unless James needs me at the office I can work around your agenda .'*

'*Cheap date.*' Joshua's smiley made it clear he was teasing. '*Breakfast would be great, but are you fine with homemade? My place? Not the kind of conversation I want to have in public. But I make a siiick Full English breakfast, promise! And I'll pay for your cab.*'

Full English breakfast, homemade? Who even *was* this boy? This man. Man-boy. *Something.*

Maybe it was a joke. Or some cook would prepare the food and duck out just before Leo arrived. Yes, that sounded much more likely than Prince Joshua doing any actual cooking. For Leo, no less.

'*Tell me where and I'll be there at 9,*' Leo replied. Then blinked at his phone until he received an address in Camden.

After confirming, he leaned his elbows on the balcony banister and stared out into the night. The road below lay deserted, the bakery downstairs hours from opening. The sign of the bank on the street corner glowed in faint hues of blue, its brightness nearly swallowed by a nearby street lamp. He'd liked the rural feel to the area when he'd picked this flat, the quiet and peace, but right now, he wouldn't have minded traffic rush and music spilling out of clubs.

Anything to drown out the perplexed hum of his thoughts.

3

Leo was late, and Joshua was a bundle of nerves.

He'd slipped out of Mo's flat shortly after eight, while Tristan and Mo had still been out for the count and unable to ask uncomfortable questions. After picking up some fresh ingredients from the organic shop around the corner, Joshua had set to work. Now it was ten past nine, and everything was ready but the bread and eggs. He tugged at the knot of his apron and went to check that he hadn't forgotten anything when he'd laid out the table outside.

Even though he'd been waiting for it, the sound of the doorbell made him jump. Right. This was it.

Time to face the music.

The door viewer showed Leo looking out at the street, shifting from foot to foot. For a moment, Joshua was transfixed by the line of Leo's profile—hair sweeping across his forehead, the clear cut of his nose, a hint of stubble, and the curve of his thin upper lip which was offset by a more generous bottom lip. He was kind of stunning.

It wasn't the point of this meeting, though. At all. Leo's behaviour had not invited inappropriate delusions on Joshua's part. Mostly.

"Top floor," Joshua spoke into the transmission before he buzzed Leo up. He left the door open and went to place the bread in the pan, listening for the sound of movement in the stairway. The old wood creaked with each footstep.

"Hello?" Leo called when he reached the door.

"Kitchen," Joshua replied. "Come on in."

A second later, Leo poked his head into the room. He was barefoot, wearing a band T-shirt and tight jeans, looking like he'd hopped off a runway. With a start, Joshua realised he was still in his apron, the one Tristan had given him and which projected a woman's body onto Joshua's chest. Mortifying. Quickly, Joshua yanked it off.

The gleam of amusement in Leo's eyes made it clear he'd seen it. Fortunately, he didn't comment. "No bodyguard?" he asked, drawing closer. It was followed by, "Wait, you were actually *serious* about that homemade breakfast."

"Why wouldn't I be?" Joshua used a spatula to check the slices of bread. Another minute on this side before he could turn them over. "And I didn't feel like it. Security detail, I mean. Johnson was my main one, and he should have been on duty until this afternoon, but—you know. So." Avoiding Leo's eyes, he crouched down to peer into the oven; the sausages and bacon glistened with grease, the smell wafting through the kitchen.

"I get it," Leo said after a beat of silence.

Joshua exhaled and glanced over his shoulder for a quick smile. "Thanks."

"You're welcome." Leo's gaze swept over the space, lingering on a blackboard that contained some to-do's and a packing list for Spain, interspersed with Mo's doodles. Stepping closer to the fridge, Leo examined the photographs Joshua had put up there, random shots of things that had caught his attention. Leo's voice was absent as he asked, "You need help with anything?"

Joshua flipped the bread. "It's fine. Almost done."

Silence wrapped around them while Joshua prepared the eggs, the gas hob hissing gently, typical city noises spilling in through the open windows. It was quite possible that the mild awkwardness hanging between them was only in Joshua's imagination. For his part, Leo seemed content to amble around the kitchen, openly curious as he examined this and that. Without asking for permission to explore, he disappeared into the attached living room. Joshua should have expected something like this; after all, Leo had disregarded conventions from the moment they'd met, in spite of his familiarity with official protocol. It was as intriguing as it was frustrating.

Much like Leo himself.

While Leo appeared to venture further into the flat, Joshua piled the food onto two plates, nicely arranging bread and eggs, bacon, sausages, tomatoes, mushrooms, and black pudding. "Breakfast's ready," he called. "Out on the terrace."

Leo's vaguely affirmative noise drifted back from somewhere. Not that there was that much for him to explore—kitchen, living room, master bedroom, a guest room and a large bathroom was the extent of Joshua's flat. It was plenty of space for one person, of course, and Joshua wondered what Leo would make of it: a generously sized flat in Camden, overlooking Regent's Canal but off the beaten tourist paths, in a street lined with old, distinguished houses.

Joshua stepped into the sunlight and felt heat soak through his T-shirt.

"Nice place," Leo said when he joined Joshua on the terrace. At Joshua's questioning look, he elaborated. "Really. Less velvet and heavy drapes than I expected. It's all upscale hipster." His mouth curled up at the corners. "I like how your bed is built into the alcove. Nice work, that."

Joshua was *not* going to think about Leo casually strolling into his bedroom. There be dragons. "Velvet and heavy drapes? I'm gay, not sixty."

"Royal, though. In all honesty—" Leo shrugged and dropped into one of the outdoor chairs. "I didn't think much about what to expect. I'm not some monarchy groupie who religiously buys *Hello!* magazine to read your home stories and plans for baby princes and princesses." Then he grinned. "Guess your succession planning's on hold for the moment."

"That's Emma's duty to the Crown. I'm just the spare." Joshua put a plate in front of Leo and sat down himself, watching Leo bend over his food to inhale deeply. Leo's lashes were long and thick, sunlight turning their tips golden, and his cheekbones were prominent. Briefly, Joshua let himself drink in the sight. Then he pulled his focus away. "There's freshly pressed orange juice and tea. Or would you like coffee? Hot chocolate?"

"You're not sixty, and I am not six," Leo told him. "So no hot chocolate, thank you very much. I could go for tea, though." He helped himself to a cup without giving Joshua a chance to serve him. Only now that Joshua was looking at Leo's fingers did he notice a jittery quality to Leo's motions, and was it possible that Leo's decidedly nonchalant manner was designed to hide a case of nerves? Did Joshua have the power to affect him at least a little?

Or Leo might just be a naturally jittery person, and Joshua was getting ahead of himself.

Joshua sank back into his chair. "Well, go ahead and help yourself."

"Always." Leo sniffed the tea before he took a small sip and nodded his approval. Then he shot Joshua a sharp look over the rim of his cup. "You know what's interesting?" He didn't wait for a reply. "*You.* You let me snoop around your flat and call you Princeling, and you don't say a word in protest. But when it's about your friends or the institution of monarchy? That's when you become a baby lion."

"A baby lion," Joshua repeated flatly. It was the easiest part of Leo's comment to focus on.

"A baby lion," Leo confirmed. "It's a natural conclusion, what with that wild mane you call hair." He followed it up with a tiny roar that came out as more of a sad kitten meow, one of his hands coming up to claw at thin air, and oh, now that wasn't fair. Joshua didn't want to find him endearing.

To cover up the heat rising to his face, Joshua concentrated on his food, cutting a mushroom into even halves and spearing one with a bite of tomato. When he glanced up, Leo was squinting into the sun, his chair balanced on its hind legs. An old acorn tree rose behind him, shielding the terrace from view and granting the kind of privacy Joshua appreciated.

"Why is there a bed on your terrace?" Leo pointed his thumb at the wooden frame that was set against the wall, a canopy protecting the mattress from the worst of the weather.

"It's an outdoor sofa," Joshua said. Which wasn't a reply, of course, and he needed to get a grip and stop allowing Leo to unsettle him like this. "Doubling as a bed. I sleep out here sometimes. When it's hot in summer."

For some reason, that seemed to shut Leo up. He looked away and took a dainty bite of his bacon, wiped his mouth with a napkin afterwards before offering a polite, "This is really very good."

"Thank you," Joshua said. "And thank you for coming. I *really* don't mind paying you for your time, by the way. As you may have gleaned from your casual perusal of *Hello!* magazine, I'm loaded."

"No." Leo's tone carried a strange finality, and Joshua didn't understand him at all.

Leo was an enigma: obviously well educated, remarkably familiar with royal conventions, yet disdainful of nobility and what it represented. Had he dated a noble, maybe? Someone who'd disappointed him, had possibly even broken his heart? What if it had been someone who'd attended Eton? That would explain how Leo knew of College Chapel. It would explain a lot, actually.

Joshua spent too much time thinking about Leo, and not enough time thinking about the reason he'd asked Leo to come here. He needed to sort out his priorities.

Reaching for his orange juice, Joshua stared down at his plate. He wasn't particularly hungry anymore. "Okay," he said quietly. "Then I won't offer anymore, but please let it be known that I did. So, I guess that... Um. Like, why I asked you here. I guess I'd like to know your opinion. On me coming out. On why you think it would be a good idea."

Leo chewed carefully, and then swallowed. His eyes were clear and calm, focused on Joshua's face. "Let's do this the other way around. What's stopping you?"

Joshua should have been prepared for Leo to cut straight to the chase, but he hadn't been. His head felt oddly empty for the second that followed Leo's words. Nothing but blank space and white noise.

He realised he'd been holding his breath and exhaled. "It's not... It'd be easier if it were just about me and what I want. If it wasn't for the press and my... status." A sharp intake of air. "You know how Tristan and Mo scoff at the idea that I have some kind of responsibility? Well, I do. I grew up knowing that anything I did would reflect on the Crown, on my family. Even on the country."

"With great power comes great responsibility?"

Startled, Joshua looked up to find Leo smiling at him, almost kindly. So not only did Leo recognise a Churchill quote, no, he also cited Spider-Man, thus adding another piece to an incomplete puzzle. Unless he'd been thinking of the Voltaire version, that was.

Joshua cocked his head. "Thank you, Uncle Ben. Or were you thinking of revolutionary France? In which case... The opposite of thank you, I guess."

"Revolutionary France?"

"The quote dates back to Voltaire?" Joshua didn't know why he made it sound like a question. It was a habit his teachers had tried to rid him of—*don't ask; presume*—but Joshua still tended to slip up when he was nervous. Leo made him nervous. "So, you know, abolish the French monarchy. Kill them all because yay republic. Thought it might have been a dig."

"Relax, Princeling." Leo's fork scraped over his plate. "I'm not looking to have you beheaded."

"How reassuring."

Little shit that he was, Leo grinned wide enough for his eyes to crinkle at the corners. He assumed a gravelly tone of voice and a fantasy accent. "You're no good to me dead." A moment later, his amusement faded and he laid down his fork. "Let's be real, though. The British love their monarchy, and one gay prince won't change that. Some will disapprove, some will be delighted, most won't give a shit. What's the worst you think could happen? Both on a personal and a... broader level."

Now *this* Joshua could answer. There was a good chance that he'd spent several days of his life picturing various horror scenarios.

"Rumours will be, like..." Briefly, he considered his choice of words. This was a private conversation, though, and Leo was his age. "Rumours will have me fucking every guy I so much as talk to. People like Mo and Tristan will get a lot of shit just for being my friends." Joshua glanced over, waiting for Leo to make a sarcastic remark about Joshua's concept of friendship. To his surprise, Leo kept watching him, silent and serious.

After a few seconds had passed, Joshua continued. "And if I ever do end up dating someone—"

"*When,*" Leo corrected. "There'll be guys queuing up the moment you're considered available."

"Sure. Because I'm a *prince*, and that seems like the stuff fairy tales are made of. Just like all those girls who want to be my princess." Going by the way Leo's eyes narrowed, it must have come out more bitter than Joshua had intended. He shook his head. "But show me the guy who'll stick around once the media calls on the hunt. Once every past indiscretion is dragged out into the open, ex-boyfriends popping up to air the dirty laundry, telling stories that may or may not be true. Show me the guy who loves me enough to—"

Abruptly, he broke off. His silly hopes and dreams were not part of this discussion.

It took a short while for Leo to answer. When he did, he sounded uncommonly solemn. "I see the problem."

"Yeah. So." Joshua tipped his face up into the sun, closing his eyes against the blinding brightness. Behind his lids, everything was warm and peaceful, calm.

When he picked up his fork again, his food had cooled considerably. He still wasn't particularly hungry, but at least Leo seemed to enjoy himself, tucking in while a few minutes passed in quiet thought.

Leo ended the silence. "Did I mention that this is very good food?"

"You did. But thank you." Joshua gave him a smile which Leo returned.

"Back to the topic at hand," Leo said, and Joshua felt the smile slip from his face. "That's a valid concern in terms of how coming out would affect you personally. Of course, your alternative is not dating at all, or having to go to great lengths to keep it secret. Which..." He studied Joshua. "Maybe that's all right for you. Not everyone wants a relationship, right? Just like some people want marriage and others don't."

"I want to date." Averting his eyes, Joshua pressed his lips together. "I want to hold hands and kiss someone in public. I *want* that. But maybe it's just not in the cards for me."

For a long moment, Leo didn't respond. Then he nudged Joshua's foot under the table, the contact brief and light. "Or maybe it is, you never know. What about the bigger picture? What's keeping you up at night on a bigger scale?"

Joshua collected his thoughts. "I already mentioned how it might affect relations with other countries, right? And like, on top of that... We're a huge business factor, you know? The whole monarchy thing, it sets the country apart and draws large crowds of tourists. There are all those" —he made a vague gesture— "fan articles and books and things, and it's mostly made in China, but British companies are selling it. And there's the Royal Collection with, like, exclusive chinaware and linen sheets and Buckingham Palace jam. There are charities under our patronage. There's so much *stuff*."

Leo let it settle for a few seconds, then he nodded. "Again, I see your point." His voice was quiet and confident. "Let me reiterate, though, that the British love their monarchy. It's a national identifica-tion thing, and there've been scandals *far* worse than a gay prince. Even recently. Which," he frowned, "is not to say that being gay is a bad thing."

Except for how it was. In some people's eyes, it *was*.

When Joshua didn't react, Leo propped his chin on a fist and continued, watching Joshua. "Your parents' divorce, for one. That was a bit of a thing and didn't sit well with traditionalists. Neither did you allegedly dating a woman ten years your senior. Or your sister allegedly dating a guy four years younger and only just eighteen."

"That was such bullshit, though," Joshua cut in. "Not that Jessica and I ever even dated, but if it had been the other way around? Like, me at thirty rumoured to be dating a twenty-year-old girl? People wouldn't have cared half as much. Same for when Emmy dated Ashton. It's just unfair, isn't it?"

"Hey, you're a feminist prince." Leo's tone conveyed delight. His eyes were very blue. "I like it. And what I'm trying to say, Princeling, is that none of these things had much of an impact—if any. I highly doubt that a gay prince could break the economy. In fact, trust clever entrepreneurs to make the most of it, bring new stuff to the market." His grin was sudden and mischievous. "Like dildos which sing *God Save the Queen* when you turn them on. I should get that idea patented."

Joshua stared for a beat, then he exhaled on a laugh. Really, it was hard to stay pessimistic when singing dildos came into play. *Into play.*

"You should definitely toy with the idea," he said, fighting to keep a straight face.

Leo narrowed his eyes. "You didn't."

Joshua smiled a very toothy smile.

While Leo sighed, the brightness in his eyes betrayed amusement. "I fervently pray that someone else writes your speeches."

"You've met George, haven't you?"

"That I have." Leo helped himself to a ginger nut biscuit and washed it down with orange juice, all the while studying Joshua with a thoughtful expression. It felt as though he was trying to figure something out, and when he spoke, it was entirely devoid of humour. "One thing I want to know, though... Has anyone ever told you that the public isn't owed your perfection? That you don't have to conform to their standards? Being forced into a role that doesn't suit you just because of your DNA, that is every *inch* as wrong as the idea of privilege as a birth right."

"Just as much of a reality, though." Joshua hesitated. "The truth of the matter is that I'm not supposed to be gay. It's... an inconvenient plot twist."

"It's not a fucking flaw," Leo said sharply.

"It is, in some people's eyes." Joshua went on quickly, before Leo had a chance to argue. "Look, I've had to hide this for years. I guess it's easier for you to be confident and proud." Or was it? Vaguely, Joshua recalled something Leo had said about costs, about knowing the costs, so he amended to, "Maybe, I wouldn't know. But I've been hiding this since I was sixteen. Like a dirty secret, something to be *ashamed* of, and you can't expect—it leaves a scar or two, you know?"

Twelve seconds passed until Leo replied; Joshua knew because he counted them out in his head. "I think it's hardly ever easy," Leo said slowly. "But yes, I see how it may be harder for you than for most."

Given Leo's initial disdain, it was more than Joshua had expected. "Thank you," Joshua told him. It came out a little stiff.

"Of course." Leo raised a brow. "I'm not an arse, you know. I do try to understand."

"Could have fooled me," Joshua muttered. At Leo's silence, he realised how that must have come across and looked up quickly. "Sorry. I mean, not now. I appreciate you being here, taking the time. But you were a bit of an arse the first time we met."

"The first time we met, yeah." There was a strange lilt to Leo's voice, something almost self-deprecating that Joshua couldn't read. "Sorry about that, I guess. The whole thing caught me by surprise."

While Leo had apologised before, it sounded as though he actually meant it this time. So Joshua took a deep breath and nodded, reaching across the table to touch the back of Leo's hand. "It's fine. Let's forget about it."

Just as Joshua was about to retract his hand, Leo grasped it for a quick squeeze. Still, he let go sooner than Joshua would have liked. "Clean slate, then?"

"Clean slate," Joshua confirmed.

They smiled at each other for a long beat that shivered in Joshua's bones, warm and bright. Then Leo sat up straighter and clapped his hands.

"Now, with that out of the way? Let's get down to business." He tipped an imaginary hat at Joshua. "We're going to make a list of pros and cons. Structured, rational, irrefutable. Like proper adults. Adults who get a biscuit for each good argument they find."

A list. A list of pros and cons that might tip the scales in favour of a coming-out. Joshua's stomach clenched around nothing.

Okay. He could do this. It was why he'd asked Leo over, after all.

He *could* do this.

Hoping that his momentary freak-out had gone unnoticed, Joshua saluted Leo. "I accept your terms, dear sir. Will we require vodka for this undertaking? Desperate times and all."

"No vodka before five in the afternoon." Leo's grin was wide, almost manic. "What about sparkling wine? That's acceptable any time of the day."

"I like the way you think," Joshua told him. With that, he rose from his chair and went in search of alcohol. As soon as he was inside and out of view, he stopped for a second, one hand against the wall, his heart beating high up in his throat.

Okay. *Okay.* He could absolutely, totally and definitely do this. He was ready.

He was not ready at all.

But he was going to do it all the same.

Pushing away from the wall, he continued on his way into the kitchen and ignored the gently swaying motion of the floor under his feet.

ONE BOTTLE of sparkling wine and a package of biscuits later, they'd jotted down thirteen arguments to support a coming-out, and eleven reasons to stay in the closet. Not altogether helpful, really.

Leo could tell that Joshua was growing increasingly more frustrated and confused, when the goal had been to achieve the opposite. They'd moved over to the outdoor bed—*sofa*—a while ago, and Joshua was stretched out on his stomach, glaring down at the piece of paper as though personally offended by how it didn't provide a clear answer. Briefly, Leo considered suggesting that they weigh the different arguments, rank them by importance and likelihood of occurrence. But Joshua needed additional complexity like he needed another Johnson in his life.

Speaking of needing things, Leo wouldn't mind another glass of sparkling wine. Except for how his blood was already sizzling like a well-shaken fizzy drink, on the verge of spilling over. More alcohol would be a bad idea.

Leo excelled in those, though. See: agreeing to spend the last two hours in Joshua's sole company. Fuck. It had been *years* since he'd been truly attracted to someone, but right now, his body was in a muddled state of yes-yes-no, perplexed at his past colliding with his present. He really wanted to twine his hands into the mess of Joshua's curls. He also wanted to dance his fingers down the curve of Joshua's spine and slide them underneath his top.

What the fuck was *wrong* with him?

Shifting a little further away, he crossed his legs and tugged at the collar of his T-shirt, the day heating up with noon drawing close, warm air wrapping around him like a heavy cloak in spite of the canopy which protected them from direct sunlight. Warm air, yes. It was the only reason he felt restless and buzzing. Nothing at all to do with his teenage crush right there, within easy reach.

"This is useless," Joshua announced suddenly. "It's not helping at all." He dropped the pen onto the floor where it landed with a clatter, rolling into a gap between two wooden boards. For once, he seemed every bit like the spoilt brat Leo had expected when Joshua had come into James' office—and Christ, had that really only been yesterday?

"I never promised a fucking miracle, little prince," Leo said.

Immediately, Joshua twisted to look at him. His expression was stricken. "Not how I meant it, Leo. I'm so sorry it came out that way. I just meant—*not* that our talk was useless. Or this, you coming over." His lips parted for a deep sigh. "I'm just annoyed with myself, I think. Like, I have all the pieces right here, so why can't I just look at them objectively and figure out what the hell I should *do*?"

And just when Leo had thought he might win back a shred of healthy irritation, of *distance*, stupid Prince Joshua disarmed him by acting all lost and vulnerable. Who'd given Joshua the fucking right to be... *this*? This mix between the pretty boy Leo's teenage self had obsessed over and the young man who was no less attractive. Oh, hey, and since Leo was asking questions already, who'd declared it okay for Joshua to cook Leo a full English breakfast, and have it taste *good*? Who'd allowed Joshua to be the kind of person that struggled with wanting to do the right thing, the kind of person that chose words slowly, as though each one deserved undivided attention? Was there some higher deity Leo could appeal to?

He must have been fucked in the *head* to agree to this meeting. This was the opposite of getting closure.

Leo drew his knees up to his chest and took the list from Joshua, skimming through the items. *Kiss someone in public* had been underlined, as well as *Wouldn't need to fear outing by someone I trust.* In the contra column, Joshua had added an exclamation mark behind *How will this affect mum and Emma? What if this is the thing that breaks us?*

"Are you really worried that a coming-out could end the monarchy?" Leo asked. "Don't you think that's a bit dramatic?"

"I don't know." With a groan, Joshua rolled onto his back and threw an arm over his face. His voice came out muffled. "I don't *know*. Maybe I'm too scared, or maybe it'd have the people storm Buckingham Palace and declare everything public property and then my whole family will be executed at the gallows and it'll be *my fucking fault.*"

"You realise the death penalty's been abolished, right?"

"Exceptional circumstances. One-time reinstitution."

"Joshua. That will *not* happen." Leo fought the temptation to combine his words with a touch to Joshua's elbow, anything that would get Joshua to look at him. "People love the whiff of scandal, and if it's carefully planned, it could even increase your popularity. If we make it clean and innocent, spin it into a sweet love story, maybe..." A sudden idea occurred to Leo, and he turned it over in his head. It just might work. "Mo could pose as your boyfriend for a while. You'd make a gorgeous couple, and there's the friends-to-lovers narrative that never fails to attract. *And* he's already a public figure, so it wouldn't be quite as much of a shock to him."

"Throwing other people under the bus?" Joshua peeked out from behind his arm. His eyes held the faintest glint of humour. "Not the act of a gentleman, is it? Shouldn't you recklessly offer up your own person? You could be my boyfriend. For God and country and all that."

You could be my boyfriend.

Leo's chest felt abruptly tight. "It won't be me," he snapped, blinking away the cobwebs in his brain.

"I was *kidding*. Jesus." Joshua sat up, moving away. His posture was tense, muscles coiled tightly as his gaze flickered to settle on a spot behind Leo. "I know you don't like me, but there's no need to—"

"That's not what this is about," Leo interrupted. "It's really not that."

Fuck. *Fuck.* Why did he keep putting his foot in his mouth when Joshua was around? Of *course* Joshua had been joking, blissfully ignorant to how there was no way, absolutely *no way,* Leo could put himself in a position where past and present might become even more tangled. Or—*worse*—where people might be tempted to dig into his background.

"What, then?" Joshua sounded sceptical and hurt. "You've got a boyfriend already? You won't be publicly associated with a noble? You took a vow of celibacy, and holding my hand in public would be a breach?"

Leo shook his head and took great care in smoothing the list out on his thigh. "Nothing like that. I'm simply not boyfriend material, trust me."

"You're not any kind of *material*," Joshua said.

"You're missing the point."

"I'm really not." The edge of anger to Joshua's voice was strangely unsettling. "*You* are."

Their gazes caught and held, each second chipping away at Leo's defences, tugging at his nerves like strings pulled to the point of tearing in two. Fucking Prince Joshua, though. He didn't know a single *thing*.

Leo looked away first. It felt like defeat.

"Okay. Moving on." He held up the piece of paper and strove for a calm, even tone. "What it really comes down to, I think, is that you have three choices."

"Leo—"

"First off," Leo spoke right over Joshua's attempt at an interruption, "you can come out at your own pace. Secondly, you can stay in the closet and date guys in secret, running the risk that someone will out you and you have no control over how it happens. Thirdly..." He glanced up to find Joshua watching him intently, and it had him miss a beat. "Thirdly, you can dig yourself so deeply into the closet that there is no gay behaviour to discover. In other words, you can completely deny that part of yourself."

Joshua's throat moved when he swallowed. "I don't think I can do that." He sounded deeply unhappy, gaze skittering away. "I don't think I want to."

"Well, I'm glad. You shouldn't." Folding up the list, Leo placed it between them and waited for Joshua to meet his eyes. Only then did he continue. "All that aside... Joshua, just imagine the *impact* someone like you could have. You told me it's taken its toll on you, having to hide this thing. If you came out, don't you think it might encourage some young people, show them that it's nothing to be ashamed of? Even make it easier for them to find acceptance when they have such a prominent patron?"

For a heart-lurching moment, Joshua held himself perfectly still. Then his chest swelled with a rough breath. "I can't decide this on my own," he said softly. "This affects my family as well, and I can't make a decision without them."

"Then maybe you should talk to them."

"Yeah." Joshua's voice was quiet, almost as though he was thinking out loud. "Maybe I should."

⌐∿

LEO HELPED Joshua clean up the table before saying his goodbyes, leaving Joshua sprawled on the outdoor bed, quiet and withdrawn, still poring over the list of pros and cons. There was a distinct chance it was the last Leo would see of him.

Jesus Christ, he'd spent several hours alone with Joshua—in Joshua's *flat*, no less. Leo's younger self would have had a heart attack.

Well, thank God he wasn't the smitten teenager anymore. These days, he was able to talk to Joshua like an adult, like an *equal*, and he was able to let things go without obsessing over whether he'd ever hear from Joshua again. Maybe he would, maybe he wouldn't. If Joshua decided to come out, Leo hoped that James' team would be in on the action.

That was a big if. Leo wasn't holding his breath.

It was just past noon by the time he made it to the office. When he tried to duck past Nate's open door, his attempt to sneak past was foiled by Nate spinning his chair around. Nate's grin was huge.

"I hear someone's been fraternising with princes."

Why did Leo even try? All he'd told James was that something had come up and he'd be late to the office, but Nate had probably tracked Leo's every move via GPS and security cameras. With a sigh, Leo leaned his hip against the doorframe and crossed his arms. "There's a thing called privacy, you know?"

"It was accidental," Nate said immediately. At least he looked faintly contrite.

"How can you *accidentally* tap my phone?" Leo asked. "Or whatever it is that you did."

"I didn't tap yours. I tapped Johnson's. Guy made a stop at Joshua's flat, must have dropped something off, and I was scrolling through some footage when Joshua popped up." Nate waggled his brows. "About forty minutes before you did."

Wait, Joshua had spent the night somewhere else? With someone else?

That wasn't actually the issue at hand, and also none of Leo's goddamn business. The rest of what Nate had said was though, and

Leo straightened. "What do you mean, Johnson dropped something off? Did you check what it is? What if it's—"

"I sent Carole," Nate cut him off, "since I didn't spot you there until after. I thought, you know, it'd be best if we didn't trouble the Prince unless we had to."

"He's a fully functional person, you know." Exhaling, Leo crossed the floor and plopped into the chair in front of Nate's desk. "As in, capable of rational thought and processing information. No need to coddle him."

"Is that so?" Nate twisted it into something suggestive. "Funny how you couldn't stand him just a day ago."

"It wasn't personal," Leo said. The protest sounded weak even to his own ears, and Nate's snort proved that he agreed.

"In that case..." Nate ducked down to fish something out of a drawer, then slid a small parcel towards Leo, barely larger than a letter. "How about *you* fill Joshua in, mate? Turns out it was an apology, also a USB stick with another copy of the video. If we're lucky, it's the last one."

"An apology?" Leo reached for the parcel and turned it over in his hands, frowning. "That's not good enough. I think the guy deserves much worse than just having his license revoked."

"He's left the country."

"He what?"

Nate shrugged. "He went to Heathrow right after stopping by Joshua's place, destination San Francisco. James said to let him go, so I did. Might be better for everyone involved, don't you think?"

"I suppose it is." Shaking his head, Leo rose from the chair but was stopped by Nate's question.

"So what was it you and Prince Joshua had to talk about in such detail? Pretty long conversation for two literal strangers, mate."

"Surprised you didn't hack my phone to listen in," Leo said. At the flash of hurt in Nate's eyes, Leo sat back down and gave him a small smile. "Sorry, that was... I'm just a little out of it, is all. He's thinking about coming out, wanted an outsider's opinion."

"And he asked *you*?"

"Harsh."

"It's just..." Nate lifted a shoulder. "You guys got off to such a bad start, I'm surprised he was able to look past that. Speaks in his favour, doesn't it?"

Nate had a point. Leo hesitated before he replied. "To be honest, it's not like he had much of a choice. His friends are too close to be impartial, and I take it he doesn't know a lot of gay men. Especially not gay men who know about him. We both saw his list."

"The communications dude is gay."

"I'm not going to ask how you know that," Leo told him.

"Subscription to *Attitude*," Nate said anyway. "And his email password is *More Dicks 4 Me*."

Leo honestly, sincerely hoped that Nate never had and never would use his powers for evil.

"George might also be too much of a friend. Or too professionally affected." Leo got back up, waving the parcel. "And with this, I'll leave you to do your thing while I go check on the tragic state of my inbox. I'll sneak this back into Joshua's mail on my way home."

Nate looked as though he considered making some kind of joke. In the end, he merely nodded and turned back to his computer. Leo watched him for another second before he turned and left the office.

Maybe Leo would confess to knowing Joshua from before—not now, but in a few weeks. When it wasn't quite this fresh in his mind. Nate was a good listener, and entrusting that particular piece of the past to him... Yeah. That one piece, Leo might be willing to share.

He would still hold on to the rest.

APPROXIMATELY THIRTY-SIX HOURS after the proverbial bomb had dropped on Joshua's head, he was back at Clarence House. This time, it was only his mother and Emma, and Joshua cringed through Emma's rant about all the ways she wanted to see Johnson suffer. In reply, he offered vague promises that he'd think about it, *really*, just *please* not now, can't we just have dinner? Please?

"You can't let him get away with a slap on the wrist," Emma said around a bite of salmon. "That's fucked up, Shrimp. Twat deserves to be deported to a Siberian labour camp. Or worse."

"Language," Mom reprimanded, but she didn't sound as though her heart was in it. "Also, political correctness. Also, table manners."

Emma set down her fork and raised her head. "That arse fucked with my baby brother. *No one* gets to fuck with my baby brother. And it's just us, anyway."

It was, actually; Mom must have asked for a private meal since the servants had come in only once, right at the beginning, to bring in a range of choices before leaving them alone.

Maybe you should talk to them.

Taking a deep breath, Joshua wiped his mouth with a napkin and folded it into a neat triangle. The smell of the fish filets turned his stomach. He kept his gaze on his hands, his voice barely loud enough to rise over the gentle jazz music his mother had recently come to enjoy. "Mum, Emmy. If I—I think that I want to come out. Maybe. What do you think?"

For a horrible, *horrible* moment, the world tilted and lurched on its axis.

Then Emma jumped up, napkin falling to the floor, and went to hug him, their faces pressed together. "Been waiting for that, Shrimp."

His mother got up more slowly, taking the time to set aside her napkin before she bent to give him a kiss on the cheek. Her voice was warm, and when Joshua dared look up, he found her watching him with a proud shine in her eyes. "Of course I approve, darling, but it will take a lot of courage. Are you quite certain?"

"No. I'm not certain at all." Joshua struggled to breathe around the sudden lump in his throat. "But I think, like, maybe? Probably. You really would approve?"

"A million times over." Mom made it sound like a foregone conclusion.

"But you never *said* anything."

"I didn't want to push you." She frowned, a crease appearing between her brows. "Why, what did you think?"

"I..." Another intake of air, easier this time. "I thought you would maybe not approve. Because it might be a problem for the country. Or our family."

Her frown deepened, but her voice was gentle as she rested a warm hand on Joshua's shoulder. "Baby, that is *not* the kind of duty to your role that I tried to teach you."

"I think this could even have a positive effect," Emma said. "It makes us seem modern, doesn't it? Shake off the dust. Welcome to the 21st Century!" The last part was said in the tone of a sports announcer, and she spread her arms, beaming. With her aubergine hair and loose-fitting T-shirt, nothing suggested she stood to become the reigning monarch of sixteen nations one day.

"I am all in favour of a bold move," Mom said, much more sedate. "We're an old institution, but that doesn't mean we can't set a precedent, give society a little nudge. And if this causes a Commonwealth state to break its ties, then that would not be a country I want to represent anyway."

Joshua felt like crying. Instead, he clambered to his feet and pulled both his mother and Emma into a tight embrace. It felt like he was constantly clinging to people these days—Tristan and Mo, his mother and Emma, seeking reassurance in their closeness. If he did this, he couldn't use them as his crutches; he'd have to hold himself up on his own. Be strong all by himself.

With a quiet sniffle, he pulled back and wiped at his eyes. His smile might have turned out a little watery, but he decided it was the effort that counted.

At this point, Leo would equal the appeal of porn to that of curdled milk. Yet it was only his conscience that stopped him from checking out the contents of the USB stick. Pesky thing, conscience.

True to his word, he swung past Joshua's place on the way home, checking to find the windows of Joshua's flat dark. The lock of the building's door wasn't worth much. It took less than a minute for Leo to pick and, if they were friends, he would have some choice words for Joshua about taking safety more seriously.

As it was, he snuck inside, shoved the parcel into the mailbox labelled '*Top Floor*' and slipped out undetected. He didn't let himself wonder whether it had been his last contact with Joshua.

LEO'S PHONE rang just as he was about to climb into bed. *Bloody Prince Joshua WTF* the display announced, and these late-night conversations were becoming a bit of a habit, weren't they? Did two days in a row constitute a pattern?

Falling onto the sheets, Leo picked up with a cheerful, "Little Prince. Calling about those diamonds and holiday trips to exotic locations?"

Joshua's chuckle rasped like fine sandpaper. He sounded exhausted, yet somehow relaxed, at ease in a way Leo hadn't heard him before. "That reminds me that I never actually paid for your taxi."

"I didn't take a taxi."

"I told you to take one," Joshua protested, and Leo sighed.

"I'm perfectly fine using the tube, mate. Tends to be faster anyway. Maybe you should give it a try sometime, see how the other half lives." That had come out slightly more provocative than Leo had intended. Still, in for a penny, in for a pound. "Or the other ninety-nine percent."

Joshua was silent, the faint rhythm of his breathing disconcerting, too intimate with the phone pressed to Leo's ear. He put the call on speaker, placed the phone on his pillow and wondered whether he should apologise for his comment. It had been the truth, nothing more and nothing less. But fine, all right, *maybe* he could see how it might be tricky for Joshua to take a bus when the country's entire population recognised him on sight. And thirty percent wanted to marry him.

"Sorry," Leo said quietly. "That was a bit dickish, right? I guess you'd cause a mob scene if you ever hopped on the tube."

"Yes." Joshua let the word hang between them for a moment. When he spoke again, there was a rough edge to his voice. "Johnson left me a message, like, saying goodbye. He had another copy of the video. Left that, too."

"Did he, now." Leo didn't strive too hard to feign surprise. "Just so you know, the guy has sailed off to the Americas. Figuratively speaking. Took a flight out this morning."

Another pause trailed Leo's declaration, long enough for him to grab the phone and roll out of bed in search of a glass of water. "I guess that's for the better," Joshua said eventually.

"You're glad you don't have to do anything, aren't you?" On his way into the kitchen, Leo bumped into the doorframe. He hit the light switch and waited for the lamp above the table to flicker to life, wondering briefly what Joshua would make of his flat. It wasn't anything special, nothing like Joshua's tastefully decorated loft with its custom-made furniture and view over Regent's Canal—but it belonged to Leo.

Well, two thirds belonged to the bank. He was steadily paying off the mortgage.

"Whatever I could have done wouldn't have affected only him, you know? His sister is very nice." Joshua's voice carried a trace of challenge. "It's never just about the direct consequences. There are usually implications beyond that."

"Is this" —Leo switched the phone off speaker mode and brought it back to his ear— "your roundabout way of saying that you've decided to stay in the closet?" He fought to keep his tone even, not let his disappointment show. It was Joshua's call. And he did have valid reasons, Leo could admit as much.

Just... he'd thought that maybe Joshua would make a bold statement. Have some of those bloody traditionalists choke on their breakfast when they unfolded the morning paper. Leo's parents included.

He swallowed around the bitter taste in his mouth. This wasn't about him.

"No," Joshua said. The word came out quiet, but calm. "It's my roundabout way of saying I've decided to come out."

Leo's head jerked up. He took a deep breath and reached for a glass of water, filling it to the brink before he said, "Okay, wow. I did not expect that. *Damn.*" He cleared his throat. "Good on you, man."

"You really think so?" Joshua didn't sound convinced.

"Yeah." Even though Joshua couldn't see him, Leo nodded. "I really think so. This is *massive.*"

"Hey, I was wondering..." Joshua hesitated, then continued. "I mean, George does regular PR for us, but his specialty is managing what is thrown his way, not so much hatching out grand schemes. Which is what you guys are known for."

Leo chugged down some water and set the glass down with a decisive clink. He felt a smile twitch around the corners of his mouth, grow and brighten, until he was grinning at his own reflection in the windowpane. "Are you asking whether we will take on the biggest story of the year? If not the decade? I don't need to check in with James when I say *hell yeah*. This will be brilliant."

A small puff of breath, not quite a laugh. "Sound more excited, please."

"Sue me." Leo rolled back his shoulders. "If you ask me, this is the best thing to happen to the monarchy since... Queen Elizabeth's patronage of Shakespeare, possibly."

Now Joshua did laugh, soft and warm, fleeting like a ghost touch. "You just pulled that out of your arse."

"Why, Your Royal Highness. I am *shocked* at this outrageous accusation. And the use of profanities." In contradiction to the words, Leo was still grinning, and he was certain Joshua could hear it in his voice.

There was another, very short gap before Joshua asked, "Can it be you? My main contact with James' team, I mean. It's kind of..." He snorted. "You're a little shit sometimes, but you're honest and clever. And I'm comfortable with you. Talking about... things."

A little shit, eh? Yeah, Leo could sort of see how Joshua had drawn that conclusion. He decided not to take offense, instead went for a dry, "Eloquent, Princeling."

"Shut up," Joshua muttered.

"So sorry, really not my area of expertise. Shutting up, that is."

"You're not sorry at all."

"No. I'm not." Leo felt his amusement fade and make room for something sweeter, almost wistful. "I'm really not. Got you to listen to me, didn't I?"

"Yeah. You did."

The silence that trailed Joshua's admission wasn't awkward, but it still felt heavy, clasping a tight band around Leo's chest. So he'd be spending more time with Joshua. Much more time. He didn't think he was in any way ready to face the memories it would drag up, but at the same time, he couldn't imagine letting anyone else handle this. He *wanted* to be in on it, have Joshua call him up late at night to share ideas and ask for advice; he *wanted* this odd push-and-pull between them, the challenge it held.

He hadn't felt this alive in years. Which was really fucking scary.

Shoving the thought away, Leo leaned back against the fridge and felt its vibration hum in his bones, thrum in his stomach. A cool breeze shivered down his arms. "So," he began. "Do you already have an idea of how you want to do this? You *could* ease into it by first announcing that you're bi. That seems to have worked well for a number of celebrities."

"I'd be lying, though." It was hard to read Joshua's tone, his low, deep voice not giving much of a clue how to interpret the statement, so Leo waited. After several seconds, Joshua went on with more confidence. "I don't want to lie. That's my condition. Whatever the plan, I don't want to tell lies."

"A little white lie here and there might make things easier," Leo said carefully.

"Still." Joshua exhaled. "It's a no."

No lies. It seemed like such an outdated concept, the kind of honourable behaviour more commonly found in tales of old. Leo had grown so accustomed to selling lies for breakfast he didn't even stop to think about it anymore.

He would have, back then. Younger and less jaded, the lies hadn't come so easily.

"No lies," Leo agreed.

If Joshua had noticed the delay in response, he didn't point it out. "Thank you," he said instead, gentle and sincere. "I'll let you catch some sleep now, okay? Sorry for calling so late."

"Anytime," Leo told him. "Thank *you* for trusting me with this." It came out too intense, and he quickly shaped his tone into something much lighter. "Promise I won't stop being a thorn in your side."

"I'd expect no less." Joshua's words were laced with gentle humour, and Leo needed to end this conversation before he said something stupid. Something like, *I used to have the most embarrassing crush on you.*

"Sleep well, little prince," he managed, bordering on affectionate, and yes, he did need to end this conversation right the fuck now. "I'll call you tomorrow with some options on how to do this thing, all right?"

"All right," Joshua echoed. He sounded cautiously excited, a little disbelieving.

"Hey." Leo softened his voice. "I mean it, you know? I think this is bloody fantastic. And I'm proud to be part of it, however small."

Joshua was silent for the time it took Leo to stumble back into the bedroom. Then he inhaled sharply. "Thank you, again. I'll talk to you tomorrow."

"Good night," Leo said. He listened to Joshua wish him the same, then a click and the dial tone, abruptly real after the previous minutes that had felt like something out of a lucid dream. Just to make sure, Leo pinched the skin at the crease of his elbow.

Okay. So this was happening.

He crawled into bed with his heart beating in his fingertips, restless energy itching under his skin. The clock had long since struck midnight by the time he finally fell asleep.

.

4

J oshua woke to a phantom hangover.

Disregarding that he'd had but a glass of wine with last night's dinner, his head throbbed in time with his heart. He'd slept fitfully, jerking upright from dreams where he'd been shot and it had sounded like tolling bells and barking hounds, like a hunting call.

He didn't have to do this. No one was forcing him to come out. Right now, it was a theoretical exercise. If he called Leo this very instant and told him to drop it, he'd never have to deal with the reality of it, would never even have to consider the possible scenarios. Sure, he'd seem a coward, and his mum and Emma would be disappointed. Tristan and Mo, on the other hand, would respond with the same, "Whatever feels right to you, bro," that had been their reaction to Joshua telling them he was maybe, quite probably, going to come out.

But it wasn't about others, was it?

Well, it was. In part. But also not.

Joshua's brain was trying to claw a way out of his skull. Time to dig out that list of pros and cons again, then. After a shower, and tea, and checking when he'd be expected at the children's hospice to christen the new wing.

~

It was quiet around lunchtime, everyone having gone out, with Nate and Leo the only two left in the office. They'd commandeered the conference room, Leo pouring over notes while Nate tapped away on his laptop. Since it was Friday, Nate had decided to go all out on the casual part and shown up in baggy jeans and a snapback, more unbuttoned than Leo had ever seen him before, and that included their standing appointment for pints at a random pub each Saturday. Leo hadn't bothered holding back his delight at Nate turning into a frat boy.

It was a good change, though—made Nate look younger, less like a stuffy manager and more like a twenty-something who knew how to have a good time. Maybe Leo would even compliment him on it before the day was done.

First, though, he'd have to bring some order into the mess of notes he'd taken during his earlier discussion with James.

"Your boy's on the telly," Nate said all of a sudden, and Leo glanced at the muted TV in the corner of the room. He found Joshua beaming back at him and everyone else in the UK who happened to be watching. Joshua's eyes were tired.

Leo dragged his gaze away and continued reviewing the questions James had fired at him. "Not my boy," he corrected. Never his boy. Not in this universe.

"He made you breakfast."

"Only because I refused to take his money for a little advice," Leo replied, a little more harshly than he'd intended. "Did you forget the part where he's already got a supermodel for arm candy?"

Nate frowned. "I really don't think it works like that between them."

"Uh." Leo let his pen still on the paper, shooting Nate a pointedly incredulous look. Because seriously? "Aren't you the one who watched the video? 'cause I'm pretty sure that yes, it very *much* works like that between them."

"I didn't watch it." The tinge of pink to Nate's cheeks was impossible to miss. "Not the entire thing, I mean. Just enough to... make sure it was what we were looking for."

Leo gave him a shark-like smile, drawing the word out. "Sure."

"It's not what I meant anyway. I just meant they're not..." Nate lifted a hand and dropped it again. "Romantic. Or exclusive or anything."

"Why do you even care?"

"I don't."

"If you say so," Leo said flatly. His open disbelief was met with a moment of silence, then Nate sighed.

"Don't be a dick, okay?" Reaching for the remote control, he turned the volume up just enough to make out some presenter's voice, infused with professional warmth, something about charity work and donations and the royal family. "Why," Nate began a moment later, "did you refuse to take his money anyway?"

Flicking the telly a quick glance, Leo found Joshua surrounded by kids, kneeling to be on their level, his smile not quite as bright, but kinder, sweeter. "I wouldn't take money from anyone else asking for advice on this kind of thing. So why take it from him?"

"Because you were spitting expletives the first time you met him?"

Not the first time.

Leo almost, *almost* let it slip. He caught himself at the last second, swallowed it back down and gave an indifferent shrug. "I'm open to revising a first impression."

"Fine, whatever. Don't feel like you need to explain a damn thing."

"I don't."

For a short beat, they stared at each other. Nate was first to look away, a sad tilt to his mouth. Leo bit the inside of his cheek and focused back on the task at hand. "Care to go through my notes once I put down a few ideas?" he asked, striving for a casual tone. "Tell me whether I'm making sense?"

Nate's answer came with a small, but noticeable delay. "Yeah, okay."

"Okay," Leo echoed.

In the background, Joshua was talking about rare diseases and research and the braveness he'd witnessed in the kids, about one girl in particular that had clearly left an impression. "'If I'm sad,'" he quoted her, "'it'll only make my dad sadder. And I don't want him sad.' Isn't that amazing? She's eight, and she's dying, and that's how she handles it." His voice grew quieter. "If I even have half her courage one day, I'll be proud."

Leo looked up just in time to see Joshua blink a little too rapidly, smiling through it—always smiling. Then he reached up to ruffle his hair, and a few days ago, Leo would have considered it a prattish move, something intended to charm his audience. Now, he recognised it as a tell-tale gesture that revealed insecurity.

If you go through with this, Leo thought, *you should be proud of yourself. I would be proud of you.*

He pushed the thought away and went back to his notes. James had put him in charge, and Leo wasn't about to let him down. He wasn't about to let Joshua down either.

THEY HAD a brief chat on the phone early in the afternoon, Joshua's voice bright and firm as he called to ask how things were going, whether Leo needed any kind of input. He sounded more determined than the night before, almost impatient, when Leo had feared that things would look different to Joshua in the light of the morning. It seemed as though Joshua was someone who stood by his decisions. Rare, that.

Leo suggested that he and Nate show up at Joshua's place later in the day, meet up with Joshua and his trusted sidekicks to form the Small Council—and, by the way, Leo demanded to be named Hand of the King in spite of the inherent risk to his life. To Leo's disappointment, Joshua didn't catch the *Game of Thrones* reference. Really, any self-respecting royal should be intimately familiar with sinister plays for power. How was Leo supposed to trust a leader who'd exposed such a shocking gap in education?

"Good thing I'm not first in line," Joshua said around a laugh when Leo expressed his misgivings.

"Better get your sister a taster, then," Leo told him. "To sample her wine. Wouldn't want this country to end up in your incapable hands."

Again, Joshua didn't catch the reference. "*Someone*," Leo told him, "desperately needs to bring you up to speed. This is embarrassing. How do you last through any social gathering with your astounding lack of knowledge?"

"Is that an offer?" Joshua asked.

The question pulled Leo up short. "Maybe," he said after a delay that had likely been noticeable, and Joshua didn't probe for more.

JOSHUA HAD ORDERED enough food to sustain a small army. On the way home from the hospice, he'd also looked up what exactly the Small Council was and had then considered dressing his living room table in red brocade and picking up some antique candle holders and wine cups from his mum. Atmosphere was important, after all. He'd been running late, though, and by the time he arrived at home, he had just enough time left to hop under the shower.

He wandered out of the bathroom, towelling off, to find Tristan perched on the work surface in the kitchen. He was surrounded by food that had arrived at some point between the start of Joshua's shower and now. "Put some clothes on," Tristan said in lieu of a greeting. "No one needs to see that. Or are you reconsidering a career in the porn industry?"

Joshua spread his arms and twirled. When he came to a stop, Tristan looked decidedly unimpressed, and Joshua snorted, not hurt in the least. He draped a towel around his waist and glanced around. "Did you come with the food?"

"Good timing, eh? What if they'd turned around 'cause you didn't open?"

Joshua nodded. "A tragedy in the making."

"We'd have to eat Mo," Tristan said. "Or Nate. Not as scrawny."

"Too much muscle, though."

"And Leo is tiny. Guess it'll have to be you."

"Thanks for calling me fat," Joshua said.

"Eh, you're pretty scrawny too. But among all those subpar choices, you're my best bet for survival."

Joshua ambled over to look into the casserole that had been left on the hob. Au gratin potatoes that smelled like heaven. Only now did he notice he'd barely eaten all day. "I'm the best cook you know," he said over his shoulder. "Cooking the cook is a bad idea."

"You don't know about Leo and Nate. Maybe they're decent cooks, could take over from you."

"Why are we talking about cannibalism again?"

Shrugging, Tristan hopped to the floor and flicked one of Joshua's nipples. "Put some clothes on, cunt. Mo and I might be used to it, but the other two aren't. Don't want to scare them away, do we? Or—" he waggled his brows "—seduce them?"

The bell rang just as Joshua was about to reply. Tristan looked disappointed to see his investigation cut short, but went to open the door while Joshua dashed into his bedroom to pull on a pair of shorts and grab a T-shirt out of the closet. He was still tugging it on, wet hair dampening the fabric, when he went back outside and arrived just in time to catch Leo's light tenor, addressing Tristan. "Are you supposed to be Joshua's bodyguard? Because mate, I'm not convinced."

"It's all about dedication and loyalty," Tristan replied, perfectly unperturbed. "I'd help Joshua hide the body. Any body."

"By eating it," Joshua supplied. Which probably sounded weird to people who hadn't been around for his and Tristan's earlier exchange. Glancing up to gauge reactions, Joshua found Nate watching him with a vaguely amused expression. Leo, on the other hand, was staring fixedly at Joshua's hip, at the tattoo there, not yet covered by the hem of T-shirt. Joshua stilled his efforts in tugging it all the way down, holding his breath.

Leo blinked and snapped out of it. "I smell food," he said, voice a little slow. "Baked cheese, praise Jesus our Lord and Saviour. But real talk, Joshua, still no bodyguard?"

Oddly disappointed, Joshua pulled his T-shirt all the way down. "Worried about me?"

"Hardly." Leo raised a brow. "More like making plans to return with a ski mask and rob the place. Just let me know where you keep the crown jewels."

"You couldn't keep your mouth shut long enough to stay incognito."

"Good point," Nate said.

"Hey," Leo protested. "You're on my side, remember?" He kicked off his shoes beside the entrance, Nate following suit while looking around curiously. Leo's shoes came to land a marked distance apart, while Nate arranged his in a neat parallel.

"This way to the kitchen," Joshua told them. "There's beer and wine."

"Also food," Tristan added.

"Also food." Joshua nodded. He turned to lead them into the kitchen, speaking over his shoulder. "And I'm not usually... I'm not *always* surrounded by bodyguards. Or, I decided that I don't want to be. Johnson was the one who did most of the day-to-day surveillance, and now it's like..." Not thinking about Johnson, Joshua was *not* thinking about Johnson, no. He pushed on. "I do have some leeway in deciding when it's necessary. Official appearances are enough, right? And if I go out, or something."

"Might need to step it up after this story drops," Leo said. "At least for a bit."

The thought didn't sit well with Joshua. He didn't care for someone else trailing his every step, seeing things Joshua had never intended to disclose—but of course, once he was out, his biggest secret would already be public knowledge, making him less vulnerable and any betrayal exponentially less damaging. *Wear your secrets like a crown, Princeling.*

"I'll cross that bridge when we get to it," he told Leo.

Whatever Leo might have said was interrupted by steps on the staircase, just before a tell-tale rhythm of three sharp knocks sounded on the door. Like Tristan, Mo had a key, but unlike Tristan, Mo had the decency to give Joshua a warning before barging in. Bestowing upon others the same courtesy he expected, that was how Mo put it.

"That'll be Mo," Joshua said.

Nate, closest to the door, caught Joshua's eye before he went to open. There was something a little stiff about him when he stepped aside to let Mo pass.

Mo shot him a smile, then uttered a quick hello at no one in particular and announced, "Bloody underwater shoots, man. Have me reeking like chlorine, and I don't know what the fuck's so sexy about, like, mermen with scales and fishy tails. Explain?"

With some amusement, Joshua noticed that Nate was openly gaping. Mo tended to have that effect on people. At least Leo seemed largely unruffled, a grin tucked into the corners of his mouth as he glanced from Mo to Nate and back. Joshua refused to acknowledge the relief that settled in his blood.

But. Fact was: Leo wasn't staring at Mo as though he wanted to devour him, yet he'd been pretty captivated by Joshua pulling on a T-shirt. No one could blame Joshua for reading something into that. Not much, just enough to boost his self-confidence a smidgen.

"You've got make-up on your brow," Tristan pointed out. Mo raised a hand to rub at the spot. He looked deeply unamused, which was about his usual level of disdain for the pretentious artifice that often came with his job. Experience suggested he'd be fine after a shower and with a cold beer in hand.

Joshua felt a smile twitch around his mouth. "Hey. Do you think mermen compare the size of their tails?" he asked.

"Or the size of their scales," Leo put in, and Joshua was startled into a short laugh. Leo responded with a smirk, and yes, all right, it was possible Joshua liked him rather a lot. Even if it turned out to be one-sided.

THE FIRST TIME Leo had been to Joshua's place, he'd taken only a quick peek into the bathroom. He hadn't noticed the freestanding bathtub behind the door. Now, it made him halt in his steps.

White porcelain enamel and clawed feet, a mounted faucet, just like with—with René, that's what he'd called himself. Really, he'd probably been a Peter or a John. Either way, he'd been one of only two regulars Leo had had, and he'd liked to wash Leo in a tub just like that, *dirty boy, let's get you clean for me, clean for daddy.* He'd rub Leo down with vanilla-scented soap, and then he'd make him get out, still dripping water, to bend him over the sink and fuck him in quick, sloppy strokes, pulling out just in time to discard the condom and come all over Leo's back. After which Leo had tugged on his clothes over the mess and left. Clockwork, really. Pun intended.

It had been all right, though. No bruises, never any dispute over using protection, and the reliability of a bi-monthly appointment had played a big role in his decision to rent a shitty place in Lewisham.

Also, René's tub had come with white feet. These were bronze and looked more expensive. And even if they had been white, it didn't matter. Leo had been stupid back then. He wasn't stupid anymore.

Turning away, he peed without casting the tub another glance. Joshua's soap smelled of lavender and citrus, and Leo washed his hands twice until the scent was clinging to his skin.

His stomach was still strangely light when he re-joined the others, all of them spread around the terrace. Outlined by the dim glow of fairy lights, Joshua was on his back on the floor, Tristan and Mo were sprawled on the sofa bed, and Nate had appropriated two chairs for himself. In theory, Leo and Nate could have called it a night once they'd reviewed the options and settled on a rough plan, but then Tristan had made a remark about the English national squad that Leo had not been able to leave uncommented, and before he'd known it, they'd been in a discussion about zombie football, of all things. Then there had been more beer, and some ice cream, and suddenly, the church bells nearby had struck ten, and it had been too late to pretend that this gathering was still of a professional nature. Leo had found it almost too easy to sink into it.

Sitting down beside Joshua, Leo crossed his legs and counteracted the mild unease in his stomach with a firm, "Now, Princeling. Let's talk *Game of Thrones*. And why everyone in line for a throne needs to watch it."

"I thought it was a series of books?" Joshua asked, blinking up at Leo. The shadows turned his lashes to charcoal dust, and Leo was tempted to reach out and trace the bow of his upper lip.

He curled his hands into loose fists and rested them in his lap. "The books are for nerds."

"Maybe I am a nerd." Joshua sent Leo a tiny grin.

"You're a prince," Leo told him. "You can be eccentric, but never nerdy. It's just not in the cards."

Joshua chuckled, low and private, too quiet to carry. "I take it you're an expert on princes."

"Clearly," Leo said lightly, very much a joke, nothing that had ever been even remotely true. At all. "Know thine enemy, right?" To show that he wasn't serious, he nudged Joshua's hip with his knee, and Joshua's grin grew, the darkness not quite enough to conceal the dimple pressing into his left cheek.

"Keep your friends close and your enemies closer. Makes sense." Joshua nodded.

Nate chose that moment to get to his feet, steadying himself with a hand on the frame of the sofa bed. He'd shared a bottle of wine with Mo, and much to Leo's amusement, the effect was starting to show; it was the tipsiest Leo had ever seen him. Quite a change for someone who clung to control just as much as Leo himself did.

"Gonna take a piss," Nate announced. "Anyone need something?"

"How is you pissing and someone needing something connected? Are we talking golden showers?" Leo asked, tipping his head back for a smirk.

"Twat." Nate flushed, his forehead wrinkling unhappily. "From the *kitchen*. Like beer, or stuff."

"Fruit, please? There should be cubed ones in the fridge." Joshua waved a hand.

Tristan snorted. "'Course that's what you want. 'nother beer for me, yeah?"

"I'll come with," Mo said. He slid off the mattress and headed on inside. For a moment, Nate stood awkwardly suspended, staring at the bright rectangle of the doorway before he followed. He hit his hip on the doorframe and cursed, glancing back over his shoulder with a pained expression.

As soon as he was gone, Joshua propped himself up with his arms behind him, stomach dipping in, his T-shirt straining around the chest. His tone was thoughtful. "Is Nate always that clumsy?"

"Not at all." Leo paused and selected his next words carefully, studying Joshua's features for any sign of discomfort. "Is this weird?"

"Why would it be?" Joshua asked, and Leo was about to wonder whether Joshua had somehow missed Nate's obvious infatuation when Joshua gave a short laugh and added, "It's kind of funny, actually. I mean, Mo is supremely oblivious, and Nate is way too subtle for him."

"This is subtle?" Leo asked.

With a cackle, Tristan rolled off the sofa bed and landed with his head on Joshua's stomach, making himself comfortable while Joshua made a disgruntled noise, yet didn't move to push him off. "Subtle for people interested in Mo," Tristan said. "Joshua, remember that party at George's place? When Mo got five blowjob offers in less than an hour?"

"That was a good one." Joshua sounded delighted with the memory, no trace of jealousy. Well, he did keep insisting that he and Mo were friends first and foremost, and while Leo couldn't quite wrap his head around the concept of friends with benefits... Maybe it worked for some people.

"Josh here," Tristan said, directed at Leo, "had just as many offers, of course. Mildly classier, mind, but the intent was the same."

"Why am I not surprised?" Leo muttered.

Joshua shifted, taking a deep breath that had his stomach rise, Tristan grumbling at the disturbance: "Bad pillow. Lie still, you fucker."

Not even blinking at the insult, Joshua patted Tristan's head and said, "It's just people who are into the prince thing. Like, girls. Well, and even if it had been boys, it's not like I could have done anything about it without risking exposure."

So chances were that Joshua hadn't been with anyone but Mo. Even factoring in some girls he might have fucked before he'd come to acknowledge his sexuality, it was so... vastly different to Leo's past. So innocent.

Leo envied him for it.

"Well," he said out loud. "Don't worry, little prince. Once we get this show on the road, you'll have plenty of offers. You'll be positively drowning in them. Mr Supermodel inside will be jealous of your game."

"Mo doesn't do jealousy," Joshua said evenly, giving Leo a strangely blank look before he dropped back down. His next words were directed at the sky. "How often do I have to tell you we're friends until you believe it?"

"To be fair," Tristan put in, "you're friends plus. It's like a bottle of tequila that comes with an extra shot glass, like, special offer. You and me, on the other hand, we're just a standard bottle."

All right, so Tristan was pretty damn fabulous. Not that Leo hadn't suspected as much. "I like the way your brain works," he said, while Joshua gave a low hum before replying.

"But that'd imply that you and me are less. That's not true."

Tristan appeared to consider this. "We can be a slightly bigger bottle," he decided. "A bigger bottle of the really good stuff. To make up for the missing shot glass."

"Works for me," Joshua said. "But if we've got two bottles and a shot glass between the three of us, what about the lime wedge and the salt?"

"Nate and Leo can battle out who's who," Tristan decided, and really, they were both ridiculous. Leo could easily see himself being friends with them; he could see all five of them being friends.

Jesus, he couldn't be thinking like that. This was temporary. A job, something James had entrusted to Leo, and Leo wasn't about to fuck it up just because at the moment, he couldn't tell left from right.

Conversations about *Game of Thrones* and zombie football went beyond his job, though. He'd crossed the line already, and it wasn't a problem, was it? Not as such. He just needed to keep his wits about him, hold on to his sense of objectivity—it was what had brought Joshua to him in the first place.

Leo shifted a little further away from Tristan and Joshua, leaning his back against the banister. The fairy lights were twinkling above him, like miniature stars, and he wasn't drunk, but possibly a hint tipsy. Maybe. It was at the stage where it was mostly pleasant. "My bite stings," he remembered to say. "Thus, I claim the title of lime wedge. Because Nate is nicer than I am. And his talents are widely applicable, just like salt."

"Not another bottle with a shot glass, then?" Joshua sounded decidedly casual, yet the sharp look he shot Leo from underneath his lashes gave him away. Who—Leo and Nate? Ha. Why would Joshua care though?

Leo was about to ask when he heard laughter from inside the flat: Nate's abrupt cackle and then Mo murmuring something that didn't translate. Okay, there was a chance that Joshua was looking out for Mo. Seemed likely, in fact.

"Nate's a great guy," Leo said, weighing each word before he put it out there. "Great friend, but definitely no shot glasses for us. We're pretty happy to drink straight from the bottle. Personally," he wiggled his fingers, "I believe that shot glasses are overrated."

That might have been a little too much information.

"Overrated?" Tristan sounded offended. "Not possible."

"I don't know. Like, in society, maybe a bit." Joshua's voice was slow, his gaze sliding away to settle on the night sky. "I think I'd kind of like... I don't know. I'd like it to mean something, I guess."

Okay, so they were talking about sex. As in attitudes about sex. As in Joshua was sharing.

That was cool. Leo could totally handle it. No biggie.

When I was young and stupid, I dreamed about making love to you.

Haha. Yeah, no.

Admittedly, he had brought this on himself, although he hadn't been the one to initiate the thing about shot glasses, but—this wasn't just teasing, was more than just joking around. Joshua had sounded quite serious, and Tristan might have heard this before, but Leo hadn't. He needed more beer.

"It's better when it means something," Tristan agreed easily, and Leo opted out of a conclusive statement by twitching his shoulders.

"Never really thought about it, I guess," he said.

He was immensely grateful when Nate and Mo chose that moment to emerge again. They brought with them the blessed miracle that was beer, as well as a bowl with fruit that Joshua accepted with a delighted noise, sitting up and dislodging Tristan in the process.

Rolling a cold bottle against his cheek, Leo tilted his head back against the banister, closed his eyes and let the others' voices wash over him. Everything was fine, and the entire mess that was his past could go fuck itself—he'd put it so far behind by now that it might as well be on a different continent.

Things were good.

IT WAS WELL past midnight by the time Tristan offered to drive Nate, Mo, and Leo home. "And then I'll share a bed with my lovely girlfriend instead of you tossers, for a change," he added, and Leo decided not to ask.

They dropped Mo off first, barely a mile from where Joshua lived, the area equally posh. No surprise there. Mo seemed half-asleep on his feet, managing no more than a vague mumble as he climbed out, and Leo took note of Nate gazing after him for longer than was necessary. Or polite.

Leo was next, and he made arrangements to meet Nate for their typical round of pints before he left the car. When they invited Tristan to join, Tristan declined on the basis of needing to spend some quality time with his girlfriend. "Not all of us are single Pringles, bitches."

"But some of us like it that way," Leo told him. He offered a high-five to Nate, and Nate moved into it with a hint of hesitation.

Interesting.

"See you soon," Tristan called after Leo. He'd said the very same thing after their pub night, and then months had passed.

"You better," Leo replied. After a rap of his knuckles on the car hood, he made his way to his building. With a honk that was bound to disturb the neighbours, Tristan sped off.

Ignoring the sudden silence that followed in the wake of the car's departure, Leo unlocked the front door and climbed the stairs to his flat. His head felt empty, limbs leaden. As tired as he was, he still counted two tolls of the bell before sleep finally claimed him.

THE WEEKEND STARTED with the usual tour of various company canteens to collect leftovers. It was a pretty decent haul, and Leo was in a good mood when he and Kylie made for the construction site they'd pirated for three weeks in a row. They should probably move soon; now that summer was in the air, the garden parcels around their spot were coming alive, and word travelled.

A few stragglers were already hanging around when they arrived, and Leo ordered them to help with laying out the food. *No sneaking, minions. If I catch you, I will give you a hard slap on the arse, and you won't like it. Buffet opens at noon, and that's for everyone.*

Structure was important. As was authority.

More kids trickled in while Kylie returned the rental van, and by midday, they amounted to about forty, some of them new faces who mostly kept to themselves, others comfortable as they told Leo about their week. Word on the street was that the day centre near Victoria Station had a new social worker who took 'personal interest' a tad too far. "Just the vibe, man," Shayna said, fiddling with her brand-new watch. Leo decided not to ask where she'd picked it up, but he did make a note to look into that worker, check out the bloke's background.

"New place next week," Kylie announced as the first few kids were about to scuttle away. "We'll send the location to Kev and Stacy, so hit them up for info."

"That aside, anyone up for a game of footie?" Leo asked, and a weak cheer went up from the usual suspects. Seven against eight, not too shabby when not that long ago, he'd have considered a handful of players a good turnout.

From personal experience, he knew that trust was hard to gain and easy to lose out here. More than a year in, he figured they were doing all right.

∼

IF LEO WERE to keep a list of his busiest days ever, the following Monday and Tuesday would be at the top. True, there was also that time they'd handled a kidnapping and sleep had consisted of a couple of hours here and there, curled up under his desk with a jumper for his pillow—but he'd been following James' lead. This time, Leo was the one who had to hold it all together, juggle preparations and check the boxes, work out the narrative, revise it, and then revise it again.

If Joshua's coming out went to hell, it was Leo who would be accountable. Even more so as he'd played a role in Joshua's decision to go through with it.

Sleep was for the weak.

∼

"Ten," Leo said.

Joshua sagged back in his chair and stared at the screen of Leo's computer. The displayed article, written by James' regular contact at *The Sun*, insinuated just enough to get the rumour mill started and test the waters without having to commit. Citing a fictitious source 'very close to the Prince', it was illustrated with a picture of Joshua and Mo, heads bent together as they laughed at something.

Leo cleared his throat. "Nine."

"Maybe not with the picture of me and Mo?" Joshua asked, then groaned and slid further down. "No, fine. I know they need something that works with the text. *Fine.*"

"Better Mo than some random shot of you with a bloke, and then the poor sod won't know what hit him." Leo waited three seconds. "Eight."

"Seven," Joshua said.

"Six." For some reason, Leo's chest felt tight. "Promise you'll stay away from the internet and keep a low profile after this hits, at least for a few days. No Google until Monday."

"I'll try."

"Good enough, I guess." Leo moved the mouse to hover above the button that would send his email, the message consisting of a simple, *'Okay.'* He watched Joshua's face for a reaction. "Five."

Joshua looked pale, but determined. "Four."

"You're not going to pass out, are you? Need a minute outside, some fresh air? A cup of tea?"

"Three," Joshua replied. "Two."

Leo inhaled and held the air in his lungs. He felt weightless and ready to burst, radiant as though the very veins in his body were filled with light. "One."

The smile Joshua gave him was wobbly. "Zero," he whispered. "Go."

Leo sent the message.

They were both silent while the recall option was displayed, counting down the seconds from ten, nine, eight, seven, six, five, four, three two one. And over. Joshua folded into himself, smaller than Leo had seen him before, stripped of his usual cheer. His voice was tone-less. "Oh God."

Leo hesitated. Very carefully, slowly, he reached out to give Joshua's shoulder a gentle pat.

It was Joshua who closed the gap between their chairs. He slid to the edge of his seat, their knees knocking together as he pulled Leo into a tight hug, burying his face against Leo's neck and taking huge breaths that shuddered through his body. For a beat, Leo sat frozen, all thoughts screeching to a halt.

"Sorry," Joshua mumbled, the word rough and thick. "Sorry, I just needed—sorry."

He was about to pull away when Leo finally jolted out of it, bringing his arms up around Joshua's back to keep him close. Pressing his nose into Joshua's hair, he registered something that smelled sweet and light, like apples and mint. It was probably wrong on several layers that he even noticed in a situation like this.

"Hey, little prince?" Leo moulded it into a low murmur. "I'm really proud of... I'm so proud to be part of this. And I hope you're proud of yourself."

Joshua hitched in some air. He relaxed back against Leo, and it took a short while before he answered. "Don't know how I feel. Just kind of numb right now, to be honest."

"Do you want me to call Mo?" Leo tightened his hold. "Or Tristan? Tell them to come get you?"

Joshua's sigh shivered over Leo's skin. "In a minute, yeah. Just give me a minute."

"Of course," Leo told him, and if it came out too soft, too quiet... then no one but Joshua was around to hear. It scared Leo how much he didn't want to let go.

TRISTAN WAS the one who picked Joshua up. They waited at Mo's until he returned from a fitting, then left for the country home Tristan's family owned in Buckinghamshire.

It was a quaint old house made from orange bricks, removed from time and overgrown with ivy. When the news hit on Thursday, Mo confiscated Joshua's phone, and Tristan changed the password to Joshua's tablet. They spent the day lounging around the pool and playing snooker, getting drunk on fancy wine from the cellar that only Tristan knew how to truly appreciate, whereas Joshua and Mo made up random things about bouquets of honeyed mead and chocolate frogs, about harvests conducted under the light of a full moon.

They got back Friday afternoon, in time for Mo to pack his bags for a fashion show in Paris, and for Tristan to get Kelsey and himself to a family reunion in Ireland. Joshua's schedule, on the other hand, had been deliberately cleared until Monday.

His phone conversation with Leo ended with Leo joking about how Joshua could always fall back on a career in porn—"Heard two girls on the tube this morning saying it'd be hot be to see you and Mo snog, and then an old lady gave them a scandalised look." Shortly after, George came over to sit Joshua through a first run-down of reactions. Not unexpectedly, the article had received broad attention in the tabloid press and other gossip channels, George's phone ringing off the hook as he declined all comments. The quality press was holding its collective breath, although George had received a couple of off-the-record inquiries from regular contacts.

"So. Fairly neutral, all in all. Some jokes about how this country can have only one queen, but mostly, it's still too speculative to treat it as serious news. Ball's in your court."

Still and again. It felt as though ever since that morning after his return from Spain, Joshua had been thrown into a parallel universe where he was constantly expected to make decisions that *mattered*, far beyond what bowtie he'd be wearing to some appearance and what field he would study when he would never have to apply for a real job.

He thought back to Anna, the girl in the cancer wing, and the childish clarity in her voice. "Well, of course I could be sad. But that's not very helpful, is it? Like, if I'm sad, then my dad will be even sadder, and then he'll cry, and that'll only make me sadder too. If I'm gonna die, I don't want to—" She'd smiled and blinked away a few stubborn tears. "I don't want them to remember me as sad. 'Cause I'm not."

Joshua had given her the leather wristband he'd been wearing and told her he wanted to be a bit like her. He doubted she'd understood what he'd meant, but her smile had widened, become this real, bright thing as he tied the band around her dainty wrist.

Ball's in your court.

"I'm not a coward," he told George. It sounded more certain than he felt. "It's not going to go away if I ignore it, right? I am gay, so I might as well... be brave about it."

George toasted him with his beer and easily accommodated Joshua changing the topic to new music they'd discovered, to the old classics and the guilty pleasure that was Britney Spears. They made plans to attend a Metallica concert later in the summer, and neither of them mentioned that it could be at a time when Joshua's life would be in turmoil and public appearances might not be an option for him.

Once George had left, Joshua flicked through the bundle of printouts. It consisted of candid headlines and tongue-in-cheek articles which claimed that rumours about the royal family flourished like weeds, never a dull day, so here was a new one, enjoy. Unless George had provided a skewed perspective, the reactions seemed amused, entertained rather than scandalised—mildly disbelieving, as though the idea was laughable.

It would be a mistake if Joshua were to google himself. Even on normal days, nasty comments were easy to find, and he had a tendency to let the negativity affect him. Resisting temptation, he went to bed fairly early and managed to fall asleep within minutes.

He woke up at five in the morning on Saturday, incapable of going back to sleep. His head was filled with murky remnants of dreams about runaway trains and crowds chanting for his head. It would be a horrible idea to get up and check what people were saying about him.

Truly just a horrible idea.

5

The day Joshua checked his Twitter mentions was the day he washed up at Leo's flat. At seven in the morning.

When Leo opened the door, vision hazy with sleep, Joshua brandished a paper bag like a peace offering. Blinking rapidly, Leo shook his head. The apparition persisted, so, yeah, all right. There was a prince on his doorstep. A prince with red eyes and a paper bag clutched to his chest.

Okay.

Except *what*?

Some of Leo's sleepiness evaporated. "Joshua?" he asked. The name came out softer than he'd intended. "What are you doing here?"

"I'm sorry I didn't... Mo and Tristan aren't in London, and I needed to—and Tristan gave me your address, hope that's okay." Following the verbal equivalent of a nosedive, Joshua tried for a smile that turned out wrong and twisted, close to a grimace. For someone who must have been trained to smile through anything, it was a remarkably poor performance.

Cold dread pooled in Leo's stomach. "What's wrong?"

"I just—that thing you said? About how it's not a flaw?" Joshua lowered the bag, avoiding Leo's eyes. "Like, there are all these *comments*, on, like, online, and—I think I need to hear that right now?" He hiccupped, then his face crumpled and he burst into tears.

Oh God, oh God, oh *shit*.

Tugging Joshua into the flat, Leo kicked the door shut and did his best to wrap himself all around the other man. His chest ached with the need for air, only there didn't seem to be enough in the room, not enough in the flat or in the *world*. All he could do was hold on until Joshua sagged into him, making Leo stumble into the wall with their combined weight. Joshua's cheek was damp where it rested against Leo's temple.

"You're all right," Leo whispered. What a lie. What a *lie*. "You will be. This is just a temporary glitch, okay?"

He wasn't sure he believed it himself, but the tension in Joshua's muscles lessened, one arm coming up around Leo's back. Leo felt his own anxiety recede just a little.

"I just don't want them to hate me." Joshua sounded small and lost, and bloody hell, Leo wanted to punch everyone who'd dared to hurt him. He could totally do it too, make Nate track down the people behind the comments and then travel the country on a quest for revenge, show up at people's doors with some choice words, an ugly grin and a wooden bat. Or maybe a fly swat, but it would get his message across.

It wouldn't accomplish anything. It wouldn't bring a genuine smile to Joshua's face right this very moment.

"Babe." Quickly, Leo pushed past a flare of discomfort at letting that endearment slip. "People couldn't hate you if they *tried*. Trust me. I mean, *I* tried, and now look at me."

Joshua gave a hoarse laugh that got stuck in his throat. "Maybe you just didn't try very hard."

"Excuse you, I was president of a club called *10 Things I Hate About Joshua*."

"Really?" Joshua lifted his head to look at Leo, eyes wet, but brighter now, a very distant spark of amusement in them.

"No," Leo grumbled. "I am not obsessed, thank you very much."

Liar, liar, pants on fire. Then again, was it a lie if teenage-Leo would have been much more likely to preside over a group called *10 Things I Want to Do to Joshua's Body*? Jesus, he'd been ridiculous, wrapped up in an illusion of his own construction. In a way, he'd been every bit as blind in his demonstrative dislike for Joshua upon meeting him again. It hadn't been about Joshua at all. How could it have been, when they'd been strangers to each other?

They weren't strangers anymore.

Okay, fuck. This wasn't helping.

"What's in this thing?" Leo asked, drawing back to peer at the bag still clutched in Joshua's left hand.

"Oh." Joshua flushed. "Fairy cakes? I didn't want to come empty-handed."

"You could have," Leo told him. "But I'll take them just the same. You want some tea with those? Because I sure as hell do."

Taking a step back, Joshua wiped at his eyes before he nodded, his smile still watery, but much more convincing than before. He cast a curious look around, and Leo realised that this was Joshua's first time seeing how Leo lived, a glimpse into Leo's life that went beyond what little Leo had been willing to share. Shoes were piled up in one corner of the corridor, and through the doorway into the kitchen, Leo spotted dirty dishes and an empty pizza box. He also realised that he was wearing Superman boxers and a ratty T-shirt that sported a large hole under his left arm.

Jesus, he hadn't stopped to consider what it meant, letting Joshua into his flat—nothing had mattered but Joshua himself, fraught and fragile on Leo's doorstep. Leo refused to examine his reaction too closely.

"Sorry I didn't clean up," he said. "Or put on my best suit. Would have, if you'd called ahead."

Joshua rubbed a hand over his nape. "Sorry for, like, barging in."

"It's absolutely fine," Leo told him. "Anytime, Joshua."

He wondered if Joshua realised just how true it was. Hopefully not.

THEY HAD breakfast on the balcony, tea warming them against the chilly morning breeze. While Joshua was perched on a rickety chair, Leo sat on a pillow on the floor even though Joshua had offered to switch places. "I'm no brute," Leo had told him. "I won't let my guests sit on the floor just because I never got around to buying a second chair."

He could tell that Joshua was curious, was probably wondering just how lonely Leo's life had to be when one chair was enough for him. But in the end, all Joshua said was, "Thank you."

"For?"

"Not making this into a royal thing, but into a guest thing."

"Well." Leo took a small sip of his tea and swallowed it down before he continued. "See, it's a bit hard to remember the royal thing when Her Majesty the Queen is regal and elegant, and you're really kind of ridiculous. In a good way, mind." He winked. "Are you quite sure you weren't switched out at birth?"

Joshua's laugh pearled like beads of condensation on an ice-cooled water bottle—and that was a rather clumsy comparison, wasn't it? Leo felt mildly drunk, but it was all down to sugar and chocolate sprinkles and hot tea. Nothing at all to do with the company.

"I really don't think this is that story, L." The nickname rolled off Joshua's tongue with ease. Joshua didn't even seem to have noticed, and Leo found himself staring at Joshua's mouth, bitten red and a hint too generous to fit conventional standards of male beauty.

Leo had kissed a lot of people, and it had always been a prelude to something, a step in between; some clients had liked it, and Leo hadn't minded. Honestly, he couldn't have cared less about some arbitrary rule installed by a romantic comedy, of all things. But here, with Joshua soft and close, Leo thought he would enjoy kissing him just because he could—not as a means to an end, but as simple human contact, comfort and closeness.

He broke a piece off his fairy cake and chewed thoroughly, gaze on a slice of road that was visible between the bars of the banister. The city was beginning to wake. In less than an hour, Leo was supposed to pick up the usual rental van. After that, he'd need to collect Kylie, who'd scouted out a new location for them—the backyard of an office which was deserted on weekends.

Leo couldn't ditch Joshua, though. It would be a shitty thing to do, especially when Joshua had specifically come to him. Joshua still appeared smaller than usual, quieter, a sad curve to his mouth.

Fuck, he'd brought fairy cakes so Leo wouldn't turn him away. As if. *As if.*

"Listen, Princeling." Leo drew both knees up to his chest and glanced over to find Joshua looking at him already—searching, almost intense. "There's stuff I have to do in a little bit."

"Oh. Yes, of course. I'll just... be on my way, then." Joshua ducked his head and exhaled, then set his cup down and made to rise from the chair. Without thinking, Leo reached for his ankle, fingertips grazing warm, bare skin where Joshua's jeans ended.

"*Hey,*" Leo said sharply. "How about you let me finish?"

After a brief moment, Joshua sunk back into the chair. Leo's fingers were still clasping his ankle, and Joshua made no move to extract himself.

"As I was just about to say before your rather rude leap to conclusions..." Leo loosened his hold. "I've got stuff to do. Which means I'm giving you a choice: either you'll let me drop you off with some nice person who gets to enjoy your company for the day, or you'll tag along. Fair warning that there's a bit of trespassing involved. And that you're not allowed to ask questions."

"No questions?" Joshua picked his cup back up. His grin was small, but real. "At all? Why? When are we leaving? Are we there yet?"

"Funny," Leo said dryly. And... well, damn. Only now did the full implication of his offer catch up with him. Even with sunglasses and a wig, there was no way Joshua would go unrecognised, and hanging out with a bunch of street kids was precisely the kind of thing that he shouldn't do without a bodyguard. Yet the presence of a bodyguard would scare away the kids, thus putting a dent in the trust Leo and Kylie had managed to build over the course of the last fourteen months.

"Another thing." Leo turned to face Joshua fully, giving him a frown as he retracted his hand. "I cannot guarantee that it's entirely without risk for you. I don't *think* it'll be a problem, but it'd probably be breaking about seventeen rules of royal safety protocol for you to go without a bodyguard. Only a bodyguard would be... out of place."

"That's all very cryptic, you know?" Joshua paused to study Leo, a thoughtful weight to his gaze. He smiled suddenly, brightly. "I'm very curious now. And I trust you, so if you say you don't think it will be a problem..."

"It shouldn't be. Probably." Leo flicked his fringe out of his eyes. "I've never exactly taken a prince along for the ride."

"Not lessening my curiosity," Joshua told him.

Leo waved a hand before he broke another piece off his fairy cake. Taking in Joshua's designer jeans and flower-patterned shirt, most likely tailor-made, Leo sighed as he stuffed the bite into his mouth. Jesus, why hadn't he kept his mouth shut? He'd never taken anyone along before. Even Nate knew only the barest minimum about how Leo spent a good part of his Saturdays.

This was a bad idea. But there was also no getting out of it now, and really, Leo didn't want to get out of it. He didn't want to leave Joshua alone for even a minute, not when he was this... vulnerable. Not when he'd come to Leo for support.

God, this was a mess.

He'd need to warn Kylie away from any comments that might betray too much. The kids didn't know enough to give Leo away, but Kylie had been the one constant, Leo's only bridge between this life and his old one.

"You'll need to borrow some clothes of mine," Leo said. "Some band T-shirt and a beanie, I think. Won't keep people from recognising you, but at least you'll fit in." The idea of Joshua wearing his clothes started an itch under Leo's skin, unsettled him in a way it absolutely shouldn't. Yeah, very much a bad idea. Very much the *worst* idea, really. "Are you sure you want to come? Again, I can drop you off with someone."

"I do want to come." Joshua gave Leo's hip a gentle nudge with his toes. "Also, I'm not a puppy. I am capable of being on my own."

In retaliation for the nudge, Leo stole a bite of Joshua's fairy cake. Banana, huh. Not Leo's favourite kind of flavour, but to each his own. "I never said you weren't. But" —he gave Joshua a pointed look— "this is an exceptional situation, and you shouldn't have to deal with it on your own. And I don't..." *Want you to.* Leo swallowed it back down, replaced it with, "Can I just say I told you so?"

"Told me so?" Joshua asked, and then darted out a hand to snag the entirety of what remained of Leo's fairy cake. Well, well. Turned out the Prince was a filthy little thief.

"I was going to eat that," Leo said.

Joshua swallowed and grinned, looking much more at ease than he had earlier. "Sorry for your loss."

"Robbing your subjects is how revolutions are born."

"Let them eat cake. And what was it that you supposedly told me?"

"To stay away from the internet," Leo replied. When Joshua's features twisted back into something quietly sad, Leo wished he'd swallowed his self-righteousness. If it had been him, he would have found it just as difficult to stay away. "Anyway," he added quickly, "never mind. Let's do something about your outfit, and then we can walk to pick up the van. Better not take the tube with you in tow."

"Better not," Joshua echoed. He sounded wistful, but as soon as he caught Leo's gaze, he moulded his expression into something smooth and cheerful, only his eyes giving him away.

"Don't do that," Leo told him.

Joshua's smile dropped, and his forehead wrinkled with his frown. "Do what?"

"Put on a persona. Like..." Leo motioned at Joshua's face. "It's like you're pulling on a mask, and it's creepy. Don't do it. Aren't we past this?"

Joshua was silent for the time it took a group of excited teenagers to amble past on the road below, shouting about an upcoming class trip and all the things they needed to pack, the booze they'd smuggle wrapped up in their clothes. Then he exhaled, sliding off the chair to sit beside Leo on the concrete floor, his back against the building. "It's something like an automatism by now," he confessed lowly. "Tristan and Mo kick me when I do it." His voice was slow and quiet, melting into the air, nearly lost amongst the typical noises of an urban morning. "I guess you can kick me too."

"Don't think I won't," Leo warned.

This time, Joshua's smile was true. "I'll hold you to it."

Surprisingly, Joshua wasn't stopped once on the way to the car rental agency. He blamed the fact that he looked like a bum, curls peeking out from under a beanie knitted in the colours of Jamaica, dressed in a frayed, black *The Clash* T-shirt that smelled like Leo and was a little too tight on Joshua. Most gazes slid right over his figure without even taking in his face, and those who looked more closely did a double take, met his eyes—and left it at nods and smiles. It was *awesome*.

They picked up a van with minimal hassle, Leo obviously well-known to the person behind the rental desk. Joshua slid into the passenger seat and immediately flicked on the radio while Leo adjusted the driver's seat, then fiddled with the rear-view mirror. He really was on the short side. Shapely legs, though, and nicely muscled arms, his eyes narrowed against the glare of the sun, arched brows giving him a constant air of mischief.

"Something on my face?" Leo asked, and Joshua flushed and looked away.

"No. Just wondering where we're going. Since I'm not allowed to ask questions."

Leo breathed out a soft snort. "That's going to be tough for you, huh? Just wait and see, Josh. Patience is a virtue."

"That is such a piece of fortune cookie wisdom. Waiting for something hardly ever makes it better, you know?"

Backing the van out of the parking spot, Leo didn't reply until they were on the road. He sounded distracted, quickly checking his phone for messages. "Beg to differ. I do remember that the anticipation was the best part of Christmas. My little sisters always—" Abruptly, he cut himself off.

"Your little sisters always...?" Joshua prompted. Relaxing into his seat, he watched Leo's eyes cloud over, followed by an impatient headshake.

"Never mind." Leo's fingers were tense around the wheel, words quick and combined with an oddly calculating glance. "So here's a question for you: we're about to collect some leftover food from a number of places. And I usually have a friend who's helping, but she just texted me, said she's not feeling too great. So if you don't mind getting your princely hands a bit dirty, some light lifting, nothing that will fuck up your nails—"

"I'm not completely useless, you know?" Joshua interrupted. It came out terse. Fuck, he'd thought Leo had moved past his prejudices, and here they popped up again. "I do have two arms, so yes, I can lift things, and I don't have a weekly manicure or whatever you think is part of my... role." He let his voice dip lower. "Hey, remember how we're totally past this?"

Leo dipped his head. His smile was sweet, bordering on apologetic. "I remember, yes. Sorry. All right, then. Gladly accepting the help, and thank you."

The whiplash change in demeanour was odd, and Joshua stared for a moment. What the hell? Wait, had that been—*ah*. Leo had effectively changed the topic, hadn't he? Yes. Yes, he had. And while Leo had been the one to mention his sisters in the first place, it would be awkward if Joshua were to bring them up again now, after this change of course in their conversation. He'd seem as though he was snooping even though he'd agreed not to ask questions.

Leo was good at controlling conversations. Something to keep in mind.

"You're welcome," Joshua said, after a pause that might have dragged on a hint too long.

LEO MOVED among the street kids like someone who belonged.

No, that wasn't quite right. He moved like a leader, like someone who provided others with a sense of direction and knew they would listen, hang on to his every word. And they did. For all that there were some kids who tried to project an air of danger—snapbacks and tattoos, skulls decorating their tops—they all orbited around Leo. They trusted him. A simple, "Yeah, so we got a special guest today, but anyone bothering him will answer to me," had been enough to stave off any problems.

Joshua wondered if Leo realised the power he had.

Who even was this guy? What drove him? And where were those little sisters he'd mentioned? He'd never even hinted at his family before, hadn't offered anything about his past in spite of the many hours they'd spent together. Had he somehow lost touch with his family, and this was his way of replacing them, by surrounding himself with a whole bunch of troubled kids and making certain they ate their fill at least once a week?

And why, *why* had Leo agreed to take Joshua along? Why was Joshua allowed to witness this side of him? Pity? Was there a part of Leo that wanted Joshua to see him like this, wanted Joshua to learn more—a tiny part of Leo that was starting to tire of putting up walls?

Bloody hell. Joshua had several dozen questions, and he'd promised not to ask so much as one.

Nothing stopped him from striking up a conversation with some of these kids, though—teenagers, really, ranging from thirteen to twenty or so. God. They were so *young*. Yet most of them looked old beyond their years, dark circles under their eyes, tired and distrustful when they caught him looking. How had they ended up like this, without a family that protected them? Had they run away from homes that seemed worse than life on the street? Had they been orphans, and the system had failed them somehow? Had they landed themselves in a spot of trouble, something involving drugs or alcohol? Before he'd met Leo, Joshua had rarely ever felt this out of his depth.

There was a girl who'd been eyeing him with curiosity rather than hostility. When her friend got up to fill another plate, leaving her alone, Joshua sat down beside her on a dirty patch of grass, beside some rubbish bins that were mostly filled with paper. "Hi," he said softly. "I'm Joshua."

"I know." She tilted her head. "Shayna. But Leo said not to bother you."

Joshua glanced up to find Leo in a quiet, intent conversation with some boy who had a bruise on his jaw. Turning back to Shayna, Joshua tried for a smile. "I came to talk to you, didn't I?"

"Guess so." Her gaze skimmed over him, assessing, then she propped one leg up and wrapped her arms around it. A colourful watch hung off one thin wrist, her tank top torn, revealing the straps of her bra and the sharp cut of her collarbones. She gave him an assessing smile. "You know, I'm not, like, working until later, but I'd make an exception for you. I'm a patriot, like."

What—oh. *Jesus.* She couldn't be older than sixteen. Joshua swallowed around the lump in his throat and gently shook his head. "I'm not interested in that. I just want to talk to you a little. That's all."

"Talk," she repeated carefully.

"Talk." Joshua nodded.

She narrowed her eyes and took him in, a different kind of interest in her eyes now. "Is it true how they say you're gay?"

Wow, all right. This no-bullshit approach was becoming more and more familiar. Joshua inhaled and met her gaze. "I am. But I haven't made an official statement yet."

Yet.

It echoed in his head, bounced from one side of his skull to the other. Yet, yet, yet.

"Okay." The confirmation seemed to relax her, and she shifted to sit cross-legged, turning to face him. "We can talk. But if you want to know about Leo, I don't know much. And I wouldn't tell you anyway 'cause that's not, like... 'Cause I just wouldn't."

Joshua hated himself for the muted curl of disappointment in his belly. It hadn't been his primary reason for approaching her, it really hadn't been. "That's all right," he told her. "I'm curious, of course. But I wouldn't want the story from anyone but him. That would be cheating."

"Right." She seemed satisfied with his answer.

"So this is... slightly unfamiliar. To me." Joshua gestured at their surroundings. The kids were spread out in the backyard of what appeared to be an office building, their voices echoing off the concrete walls, blank windows staring down at them. One boy had turned on music, some rap tune spilling from the tinny speakers of his surprisingly new mobile phone. Turning back to Shayna, Joshua gave her another smile. "If you don't mind me asking, I take it you live on the street? And so does everyone else here?"

She hesitated before confirming it with a tiny shrug. "Yeah. Like, there are worse places. If you know where to go, got some friends to rely on... 'S not so bad."

"It was worse, then? Where you came from?"

Again, she hesitated. Then she raised her chin, gaze direct as she looked at him. "I broke my left arm when I was three. Right when I was four, got a concussion out of it, too. Dislodged my shoulder a couple months later, bruises down my back most of the time. D'you need me to go on?"

His stomach twisted. Slowly, he inhaled, his voice coming out rough. "No. Not unless you want to."

"I don't mind," she said, firm with only the tiniest hint of a quiver. "I've learned to wear it like armour, you know?"

The words were so familiar that Joshua fought not to react. "That's good. That's... admirable, really."

"Admirable," she repeated, openly sceptical.

"Admirable," he confirmed.

Her smile flashed like sunshine. It was gone too soon, but it made Joshua's chest feel lighter all the same. He was about to say more when Leo's loud voice cut into their conversation.

"Everyone," Leo called. In a threadbare vest and black skinnies rolled up to the ankles, he would have fit right into this crowd if it weren't for the handful of years he had on them, and how he was less rugged than the kids. "Minions and ladies and princes! No football match today. I'll make up for it next week, yeah? Same place, same time, unless you hear from Kylie or me. Now *scatter*. Sir Prince and I gotta clean up after your arses."

Leo spread his arms in a blessing gesture, all theatrics, and Joshua bit down on a laugh.

"Well, that's my cue." Shayna climbed to her feet and, after a second's consideration, leaned down to give Joshua a half-formed hug. Her, "You're kinda all right, Prince Joshua," made him swallow, then reach up to squeeze her hand.

"Thanks. You too."

"See ya." With that, she turned away to collect her friend, the two of them linking arms before they marched off together.

Once the area had cleared out, leftovers distributed among the kids, Joshua helped Leo with the empty boxes and plastic cutlery. They piled everything back into the van, erasing all traces of their presence. By half past two, about three hours after they'd arrived, they were ready to go.

"I feel like a ninja," Joshua said, settling into the passenger seat once more. "Or Robin Hood. Feeding the poor."

"You realise there's an inherent problem with the narrative, right?" Leo twisted to look over his shoulder before he backed out onto the road. The motion emphasised the line of his jaw, sharpened it, and if Joshua were to reach out and run his knuckles along its curve—would Leo lean into it?

Joshua needed a moment to avert his eyes. "You mean that I can't be the rogue when I'm part of the establishment?"

"Accurate." Leo grinned over at him. He seemed lighter than he had before, and Joshua wondered just how worried he'd been about showing Joshua this particular aspect of his life. That he'd done it at all was... surprising.

Joshua really shouldn't mistake this for more than it was.

He switched the radio on in time to catch the tail end of the half hour news, updates on the national squad's stay in Brazil. It reminded Joshua that he still needed to sort out which match he'd attend with Mo and Tristan, and whether there was time for a bit of a ramble around the country afterwards. The last match of the group stage sounded like their best bet.

As soon as the news segued into music, Joshua lowered the volume and sat back, turning his attention to Leo. "You're different with the kids," he said. It didn't count as a question, did it? "You speak more like them."

"That a bad thing?" While Leo's tone was off-handed, he took a bend with slightly too much momentum.

"Just interesting." Since Joshua was pretty certain he wouldn't get more out of Leo on that topic, he changed gears. "I wouldn't have minded staying around for a football match. You didn't have to cut things short on my account."

"Let's just say that I remember how dreadful of a player you are." The moment it was out, the corners of Leo's mouth tugged down into a frown. He looked distinctly uncomfortable when really, his assessment hadn't been too far off the mark. Although, wait...

"Not that you're wrong, but when did you see me play?" Joshua asked.

A red light forced the van to a halt. Tapping his fingers against the wheel, Leo was staring at the car in front of them, presenting Joshua with only his profile. "I saw a documentary on Eton a while ago. Included some footage of you playing." He shot Joshua a quick smirk. "Bloody awful, mate."

Joshua hadn't known such a documentary existed. Had George cleared it? Probably. He did love to embarrass Joshua, disguising it as a vested interest in making 'Your Royal Brattiness' seem human and approachable. "I'm not *that* bad anymore," Joshua said. At Leo's sceptical glance, he laughed and splayed his fingers. "I mean, I'm still pretty bad, just not as bad as I used to be. Tristan's been teaching me some."

"I thought your lot didn't do torture anymore." In spite of a lingering tightness around Leo's eyes, the statement was laced with humour. Joshua decided they were at the stage in their relationship where it was acceptable for him to punch Leo's arm, so he did.

Leo moaned and pretended to collapse from the pain, but quickly righted himself when the car behind them honked. "Hold your horses," he muttered, flipping off the other driver in the rear-view mirror.

Joshua shouldn't be charmed by Leo acting like a dick. He shouldn't be charmed at all.

Tugging off the beanie, he ruffled his hair before he moved to pull off Leo's T-shirt. "What are you *doing*?" Leo asked, sounding frazzled, and Joshua gave him a confused look, pausing with his fingers on the hem.

"Taking off your T-shirt?"

"You can't just strip naked while I'm *driving*."

"I've got something on underneath," Joshua said—which Leo would have known if he hadn't pointedly left the room as soon as Joshua had begun unbuttoning his shirt earlier. Shrugging the T-shirt off, Joshua folded it into a neat square that he placed on the dashboard. Only then did he stop to consider the near-panic that had coloured Leo's voice. Why would Leo be quite this invested in Joshua's state of undress?

Was there some interest? At least a little?

Joshua studied the way Leo was tightly focused on the road. Even if Joshua had mustered up the courage, ignored the whole no-questions promise he'd given and actually asked it—*Are you attracted to me?*—he knew that Leo would evade an answer. Like he did with all things personal.

Adjusting his posture into something casually at ease, legs splayed and head tipped back, Joshua kept his tone light. "Can I ask a logistical question?"

The tension in Leo's shoulders relaxed. "Yeah. I may or may not answer."

"Why switch locations? Wouldn't it be easier to stick to one place?"

"Of course it would be easier." Leo nudged the volume of the radio down. His gaze seemed to linger on Joshua's left shoulder, where Emma's initial was inked into Joshua's skin. "But then we'd have to find somewhere that's not illegal, probably pay rent. We'd have to fill out the necessary paperwork." The mere thought seemed to disgust him. "We just want to help, quick and efficient, not waste money on things we don't need. Or waste energy on filling out three copies of forms."

That... was such a logical response that Joshua wondered how he hadn't thought of it. Probably went to show his naivety with real life matters.

"Fair enough," he murmured. They were both silent for a short while after that, long enough for the song to fade into another one, and Joshua thought about asking Leo what kind of music he listened to, about favourite songs and bands. Would that be too personal?

In the end, Joshua settled for, "So what's the plan now?"

"The plan is to get rid of the trash and return the van. Then meet Nate for some pints later, if that's all right with you."

Joshua rested both hands in his lap. "You don't mind me intruding?"

"Wouldn't have offered otherwise." Leo shot Joshua a smile, one that crinkled the corners of his eyes and teased with the faintest notion of a dimple.

Joshua wanted to kiss him.

He bit down on the inside of his cheek and hoped his expression didn't give him away. "That sounds really good, then. And thank you for today. And also in general. You've just been really great about this."

Leo was quiet for a beat. When he replied, his voice was soft. "You're welcome, Princeling. For the record, it's an honour."

Princeling. It was strange how quickly it had come to sound like an endearment. Joshua wanted to hear it murmured into his ear, wanted to hear Leo rasp it out with his hand on Joshua's dick.

Reign it in.

Clearing his throat, Joshua dragged his gaze away from the other man. Christ, this wasn't a good idea. Leo had given him no clear indications that he was interested, and Joshua needed to drag his mind out of the gutter. It was just... a bit raw, all of it—the bleak morning and Leo's unexpected sweetness, and then seeing him with those street kids, the way he was able to provide them with a temporary focal point. If Joshua were smart, he'd call it a day.

"Mo's getting back from Paris in an hour. I could call him." He shot Leo a sidelong look. "Ask him to join, if that's fine?"

"Moonlighting as a matchmaker?"

"Just a night between friends." Joshua smiled and crossed his legs at the ankle. Without even trying, his voice dipped just slightly, bringing in a note of suggestion that he hadn't quite intended. Or maybe he had. "If you and I happen to become third wheels, I am certain we can find a way to entertain ourselves."

"I'm sure we can think of something." Leo sounded neutral. His thumb twitched to the beat of the music, eyes fixed on the road. "That aside, your place is pretty much on the way. How about I drop you off? Then we can meet up later at the pub."

"You trying to get rid of me?" Joshua followed it up with a grin. He might as well have saved himself the effort; Leo wasn't looking.

"I need to pop to the shops and do some laundry. Boring things." Leo's forehead wrinkled. "Not everyone has servants at their beck and call."

Joshua stiffened. "I do my own laundry and shopping." Most days, anyway. "It's not like—do we really have to do this again?"

It took several seconds before Leo ducked his head. "Sorry," he said, so quiet is was almost a whisper. "That was thoroughly uncalled for. Feeling a bit irritated, took it out on you though it's none of your fault." He continued before Joshua could interfere with a question. "Thank you for today. You really pulled your weight, and I'm grateful for the help. And" —the shortest of delays— "the company too. It was a real pleasure having you along."

If not me, what's got you irritated? No questions, though. Joshua had promised, but it seemed to get harder with each moment they spent together, with each tiny, fractured puzzle piece Leo nudged his way. Uncrossing his legs, Joshua hesitated with his gaze on Leo's profile. "You were glad to have me around?" he asked eventually.

Leo glanced over, so briefly that Joshua almost missed it. "Yes. You're decent company, little prince. Considering."

From Leo, that must be close to a declaration of friendship. Joshua would take it. "You're decent company as well," he told Leo.

"Glad to hear it. Feeling a bit better, then?" This time, Leo didn't look away immediately, a smile lingering in his eyes. Joshua's breath stuttered in his throat, heat wiggling in his stomach.

When Leo's smile dropped, Joshua realised he'd been silent for too long, simply staring. He jerked his gaze away. "Not necessarily better," he replied. "But I guess more... grounded. There was this girl who, like, offered herself to me? And that kind of—that must be a rough life. Having to do that. Definitely worse than getting some internet hate. I wish I could do something to help."

"Don't make this into a saviour thing." All of a sudden, Leo's tone was carefully clipped. "Shayna—that's who you talked to, right?—she's not a victim, Joshua. She's not an illegal immigrant enslaved by some pimp or anything like that. I'm not saying those things don't exist, but her situation is nothing like that." His intake of air was audible. "She's not a damsel in distress waiting for someone to save her."

Joshua sat up, all warmth flushed away. He was getting really tired of playing emotional pinball. "I just wanted to *help*," he asked sharply. "Like you do. Or am I not allowed to feel empathy?"

Leo opened his mouth to respond, then shut it again. The silence that wrapped around them was heavy like a steel jacket, and Joshua refused to break first. This wasn't on him. Sure, he'd been a bit of a mess this morning, but Leo was the one who went from hot to cold in seconds, turned defensive as though he'd been personally insulted.

Why? What was it to him?

He had fit in well with those kids. They'd treated him like one of their own.

When Leo finally spoke, his eyes were fixed on a red light, the hum of the idling engine almost swallowing his voice. "No. No, that's not what I'm saying. What I'm saying is that you shouldn't pity her. She wouldn't want your pity, not when it's choices she's made for herself. I'm not saying they're good choices, but they're hers."

Exhaling in a rush, Joshua worked through Leo's words before he replied. "Well, okay. I get that. You're still trying to save them."

"I'm not." Leo put the car back into gear, and when Joshua glanced ahead, he glimpsed the tower of the Greek church, just a couple of minutes from his flat. He focused back on Leo in time to see him reach up a hand to push back his hair. "It's not about saving them. I want to give them a chance to fill their stomachs at least once a week, without having to lie, steal or sell anything for it. And if someone asks me, I give advice. I help them see the alternatives. They're the ones making the choices, but it should be informed choices. Very often, they're not."

"So you help them save themselves."

"I try." Leo turned left onto Pratt Street. "If that's what they want."

"That's very..." Leaning back, Joshua shook his head. The only term he could come up with was, "Good. That's so good of you."

"Good," Leo repeated flatly. His eyes brightened by a fraction, though.

"Good. Yes." Joshua nodded to himself, then reached across the gap between their seats to touch Leo's shoulder. "Thank you, again, for taking me along." He didn't move his hand. After a moment, Leo leaned into the touch, the corners of his mouth tugging up.

"Yeah, well. It wasn't a hardship. You can be a bit of a charming bastard."

Joshua gasped dramatically. "Beg your pardon, I am one hundred percent legitimate. I could have you *hanged* for that."

"You really couldn't," Leo told him dryly.

Joshua hummed, considering. "Tower of London?"

"Still a no."

"This gig sucks," Joshua said. "Curse these modern times. Can't even have people drawn and quartered anymore."

"It is a tough life." Leo's tone was all fake sympathy, and Joshua gave him a tiny shove and withdrew just as they crossed Regent's Canal. Leo pulled the van to a halt. His smile had widened into a small grin, and Joshua grinned back, a little lightheaded with exhaustion. Too little sleep, too many things on his mind—and then there was Leo.

Three hours apart would give Joshua a chance to clear his head.

"Are you sure you don't mind getting rid of the rubbish by yourself?" he asked anyway.

"*Princeling.*" While mostly exasperated, the word held a hint of fondness. "I've done this many times before Your Royal Helpfulness came along. I'm sure I'll manage."

"Fine. Just want it to be known that I am willing to get my hands dirty."

For an instant, Leo's grin grew into a smirk, then dimmed again. "Noted," he said simply.

Joshua cleared his throat and swallowed, the air tasting thick on his tongue, the vibrations of the idling van buzzing in his stomach. He grasped the door handle while Leo continued watching him with that odd half-smile. "So I'll see you at the pub? You and Nate?"

"And Mo, if he's up for it." Leo looked away, but his smile persisted. "I'll text you when I know the details."

"Sounds good. Yes." Joshua grabbed the T-shirt Leo had lent him and held it up. "I'll wash this and return it to you after."

"Don't be ridiculous. I'll just throw it in with the rest."

Oh. Well, there went Joshua's plan of possibly keeping the T-shirt for a while longer. It was *comfortable.* "If you're sure? I don't want it to be a bother."

"Told you, I'm doing laundry anyway." Leo's tone left no room for doubt, so Joshua gently set the T-shirt back down on the dashboard.

"Okay. Then I'll see you later."

"Absolutely." Leo smiled at him, hands loosely clasping the wheel. Joshua stalled for another moment, waiting for—for *something.* Leo didn't offer anything more, though, so Joshua finally opened the door and hopped out onto the sidewalk. With a little wave, he nudged the door shut and made himself turn away, did not allow himself to glance back.

He'd see Leo again in three hours. By then, he'd better have managed to begin untangling the mess in his head.

~

NATE PAUSED with his beer halfway to his mouth. "You took him along to your street kid thing."

"That's what I just said. Don't make it sound like I murdered someone." Leo checked the pub entrance, Joshua having texted that he and Mo were running twenty minutes late due to some security thing. No sign of them just yet. Once they showed, it would be interesting to see just how long they'd manage to stay without being mobbed.

Shit, there might be people trying to take Joshua's picture while Leo was in the frame. He'd need to duck out. Not that anyone would care about a blurry person in the background, not as such, but they probably would if one of Leo's old clients were to recognise him and go blabbing to the papers—the Prince with a rent boy, holy shit, that story would *sell*. Especially if Joshua went through with his interview on Tuesday, two days before the opening match of the World Cup in Brazil.

The timing was perfect. It would give the public one day for hysterics, and then football would take over the headlines. Hopefully, by the time the World Cup was done, the sexuality of Britain's second-in-line would be old news, printed on paper just good enough to wrap some fish 'n' chips.

Nate kicking his foot brought Leo out of his thoughts. He jolted. "Sorry, what?"

"I *said*" —Nate used the back of his hand to wipe away a beer moustache— "that after you started the street kid thing, it took you six months to even tell me about it. You've never invited me along. And I'm, like, one of your best mates."

Nate's tone didn't give away much, but his eyes betrayed hurt. It prompted Leo to reach across the table and squeeze his hand "Not one of," he corrected gently. "My best mate. That's you."

"Still you never took *me* along." Again, Nate sounded painstakingly neutral. Leo tightened his grip, then let go.

"I'm sorry. It never really occurred to me."

Nate took a minute to respond. When he did, it was with a sigh, shoulders slumping. "I get it, I guess." He set his beer down and leaned back in his chair. "It's connected to your past, right, and that's not something we ever talk about. Your past. Or mine."

Leo grappled for a tentative smile. "True."

"And yet," Nate said. "The moment Prince Joshua saunters into your life, you invite him in?"

Looking down, Leo ran a finger along the condensation gathered on his glass. "He was quite upset, and his closest friends were out of the country. Plus I encouraged him to do this. I couldn't exactly tell him to turn around and cry at home. I owe him that much."

"He gets under your skin," Nate said. It wasn't a question, and Leo kept his hands steady and his gaze off Nate's face.

"Well, Mo gets under your skin. Joshua is bringing him, by the way."

Nate sucked in a breath, then relaxed again. "Nice try, mate. But I know your little tricks, and you're not changing the topics just like that." He raised his glass and frowned over the rim. At the table next to theirs, a group of tourists broke into excited shouts over something on the telly—ah, the Italian national squad—and Nate waited for the excitement to die down before he said, "What I want to know is what makes him different. It's not just the prince thing, is it? Probably never was."

Leo stopped to consider it. Back at school, Joshua being a prince had been fodder for Leo's obsession. Now it was an afterthought. More than that: it was an inconvenience.

Movement by the door drew his attention, a burly bloke entering first to tax the room's occupants with a narrow-eyed stare. From their background checks, Leo recognised him as another one of Joshua's bodyguard, Zach—married, paying off a reasonably sized flat, no expensive gambling habits. Behind the man's bulk, Joshua seemed dwarfed, an unbuttoned shirt in blues and reds hanging off his shoulders. He turned to hold the door for Mo.

Leo shot Nate a warning look. "Look, this thing with Joshua, it's complicated. And they're here, so let's just—let's just not."

"They're here?" Nate twisted around in his chair, the motion so abrupt he spilled beer down his front. While Nate cursed and dabbed at his stomach, Leo fought to stifle a laugh.

"Smooth, Nate," he said. "Do you need me to hold your hand, or do you think you'll be fine talking to him on your own?"

"Shut up," Nate hissed just as Mo pulled out a chair and sank into it. He held himself with the kind of effortless coolness that Leo would despise if he hadn't see Mo erupt into giggles at the idea of zombies lumbering around a football pitch and groaning, "Goooooooal," in morbidly strangled voices.

"All right?" Mo asked. His gaze lingered on Nate's bicep for a beat too long—not that Leo was judging; Nate's biceps were impressive. As was his eight-pack. Sometimes, he tried to share his disgusting protein concoctions with Leo. They smelled and tasted like mud, and if that was the price for killer abs, Leo wasn't man enough to pay up.

"All good," Leo said. He glanced around to find Joshua stuck taking pictures with a bunch of people. "How was Paris?"

"Paris?" Nate tried to subtly dispose of the soaked napkin.

"Oh, yeah." Mo shrugged. "Just a day trip, pretty much. Never get to see much of the city with those, you know?"

No, Leo did not know. He figured it would be mildly bitchy to point that out, so he didn't. While Nate asked about the Louvre—as far as Leo was aware, Nate had zero interest in art—Leo watched as Joshua posed for another picture, then one more, his smile wide and practiced, empty. Past the flash of a camera, Joshua caught Leo's eyes. His smile shifted into something more authentic, softer.

Had Leo done that?

Once Joshua had completed his duty, bodyguard looming nearby like a menacing shadow, he excused himself to finally make his way over, arriving in the middle of Nate and Mo discussing an exposition of Marvel concept drawings that Mo had not yet managed to attend. Which—now wait a minute, this was Leo's jam. How had he missed the shift in topics? And did he want to get into the middle of it, or should he leave Nate to his awkward courtship dance?

Leo decided to leave them to it. Mostly because Joshua finally made it over. Kicking out a chair for him, Joshua grinned. "Hello again. So you're fine chilling with a bunch of homeless kids, but you need a minder for a round of pints. Explain?"

"Hi." Dropping into the seat, Joshua rubbed a hand over the back of his neck. His smile was sheepish. "Well, just, there hopefully won't be pictures from earlier, so no one will ever know. But there'll be pictures of this, and my mum would have my head."

Joshua's mum, the motherfucking *Queen*. Leo needed a moment to process the reminder because holy shit, yeah, right.

"We could have met at someone's place," he said out loud. "If that'd been easier."

"No, this is nice." Joshua turned his head to study the blackboard listing beer options, the distant glow from the bar reflecting in his eyes and turning the wispy ends of his curls an electric blue. "And you told me you and Nate do this every Saturday, different pub every time, so I didn't want to break the habit."

"How generous."

Joshua threw Leo a bright look. "I can be. If the situation calls for it."

Leo was quite, *quite* certain he hadn't imagined the suggestive note to Joshua's voice. There had been a few moments just like that earlier in the car, when Joshua had seemed to be flirting and Leo had told himself to keep his cool. Although that boat might have sailed already.

Maybe he just needed to get it out of his system. A one-time thing. Closure.

No. *Fuck* no, that would be a horrible idea—not only because it had been a while since Leo had been with anyone, but also because he had no clue where Joshua stood, whether there was true intent behind his teasing, what he wanted from the world in general and Leo in particular.

It spelled trouble. In capital letters and with several exclamation marks.

Leo drew a deliberate breath and leaned over to bump his

shoulder against Joshua's. "How about you go get us another round, then? That would be highly generous of you."

"I can do that." Nudging back, Joshua got to his feet again. He wiggled his fingers to attract Mo and Nate's attention, the two of them startling apart where their heads had been bent close together. "Drinks," Joshua told them. "What do you want?"

For a beat, Leo found himself looking at Joshua's long, slender fingers. There was a good chance Joshua could clasp both of Leo's wrists in one hand, and Jesus, no, Leo couldn't go there.

Inviting Joshua might have been a mistake. Leo was sure he'd made worse mistakes than this, though, and he'd always come out with his head held high. This would be no different.

He'd coach Joshua for his interview with David Dimbleby, then it would be recorded and broadcasted. While they handled the aftermath, Leo would make sure to stay behind the scenes, and then, sooner rather than later, Joshua would fade from Leo's life because people like him were friends with social winners like Mo and Tristan, not with misfits like Leo and Nate. So Joshua was bound to melt away, slowly and steadily.

He'd go back to his world, back to where he belonged, leaving nothing but a sweetly bitter taste at the back of Leo's throat.

ABOUT FORTY MINUTES LATER, the pub started filling up with notably more people, with their whispers and stares. Zach ushered them out through the backdoor. "It's like clockwork," he explained in reply to a question from Nate that Leo hadn't caught. "*PrinceWatch* tweets his location, and then we've got about ten minutes."

"*PrinceWatch*?" Leo mouthed at Joshua. Out of all the ridiculous things that cluttered Joshua's life, this must be near the top.

Joshua's flush was delightful. The discomfort in his tone wasn't. "They're a bit... intense."

"They stalk him," Mo supplied. "Proper obsessed with figuring out his every move, where he goes and who he talks to. They found his flat a couple years ago. Got about half a million followers and posted just enough details that there were people showing up at his door 'round the clock."

Joshua stared straight ahead at the car that was waiting for them, the light of a streetlamp edging his profile in orange. "I had to move."

Jesus fuck. Leo was taking it back; this wasn't even a little bit funny, and instead veered straight into creep territory. Half a million followers. Half a *million* followers. They'd be scattered all over the world, of course, but some must be right here, in London. What if they were already puzzling over grainy shots of Leo from the bar just now? What if someone made the connection, *what if*—stop.

Stop.

It had been six years. He'd changed a fair bit since then. A lot of his clients had been drunk, or it had been a rushed thing in a dark alley or a shabby hotel room, insufficient time, illumination and sobriety to leave much of a memory. Most clients hadn't been interested in his face anyway. René would be able to identify Leo, though, and so would the only other regular Leo had had, a nervous bloke by the name of Jake who'd got off on coupling vanilla sex with verbal abuse. But neither of them had seemed particularly interested in Prince Joshua, so—fuck, okay. *Okay.*

Leo forced another breath. Even though there were no cameras around, he ducked behind Nate's broad frame. When Joshua shot him a confused look, Leo countered it with a shrug and a waggle of his eyebrows that could mean anything.

Fortunately, they made it to the waiting car before Joshua had a chance to ask.

LEO HAD BEEN NOTABLY distant throughout the car ride, but Joshua could sense him relaxing once they had made it back to Joshua's flat, spreading out in the living room. Popular vote demanded the second *Iron Man*, and when Mo and Leo realised they both knew it by heart, they spent several minutes exchanging lines of dialogue from the first one.

Joshua sat back, grinning and sipping at his beer, watching. When Mo nailed a particular monologue, it earned him a smile from Nate that was oddly sweet, lingering, and Joshua felt something twist in his stomach that wasn't quite envy, wasn't quite something else either. *There'll be guys queuing up as soon as you become available;* that was what Leo had said. Joshua didn't think he wanted guys queuing up, though; all he wanted was for someone to look at him like that: with undivided attention and a genuine smile.

Turning away, he rose from the sofa to find them some snacks. He was digging through his cupboards when Leo ambled into the kitchen, beelining for the sink to fill up a glass with water. Joshua watched him from the corner of his eye, but didn't offer a comment.

"What's wrong?" Leo asked into the tension spanning the space between them.

Stilling with two bags of crisps clutched in his hand, Joshua glanced over. He found Leo watching him, leaning against the sink with one hip popped out, a hand on his waist and an expectant look on his face.

"I could ask you the same," Joshua replied.

"I'm perfectly fine."

"You weren't when we left the pub. You went all quiet."

Leo arched a brow, and Joshua shouldn't be attracted to that. Neither should he be attracted to the hint of stubble dusting Leo's chin, or to how Leo had been all soft and dishevelled this morning, clad in a ragged T-shirt and boxers with the Superman logo. The silence between them extended for another few seconds, the sounds of the movie drifting through the open door, mixing with Mo erupting into sudden laughter.

After emptying the glass in one go, Leo set it down on the work surface, then wandered over to the fridge to examine a betting list for the World Cup that Joshua had pinned up just yesterday. His tone was casual. "Tell you mine if you tell me yours."

"Mine's silly," Joshua said. "Probably."

Leo shook his head and smiled. "I doubt that. Come on. You're not thinking of those idiot people on Twitter again, are you? Because they know nothing, Jon Snow."

"What?"

"Never mind. Another *Game of Thrones* reference. Which you really need to watch, by the way. Have I mentioned that?"

"You might have. Like, two or three or fifteen times."

"I should probably sit you down and make you watch it with me. Doing my duty to the country." Leo fingered the edges of the betting list, but his gaze was on Joshua. "Now spill. What's got you frowning at nothing?"

Joshua exhaled through his nose. "Just, like. Thinking about what I want, I guess."

"What you want?" Leaning his hip against the wall, Leo waited for a moment before he added, "From life? For breakfast? Under the Christmas tree?"

Against his will, Joshua found himself smiling just slightly. "When it comes to a relationship. That I don't need a queue of guys. That I'd be happy with just one person who looks at me with stars in his eyes." He shook his head." I told you it's silly."

"And I told you it probably wouldn't be, and it isn't. 'Fraid I don't have anything useful to offer, though. Very limited experience myself." Leo lifted one shoulder. Under his thin T-shirt, his collarbones shifted with the gesture. Joshua wanted to lick them. He wanted to press Leo back against the fridge and kiss him until they were breathless and stupid with it.

Not going to happen.

"You haven't dated much?" Joshua asked.

Another shrug. "Try 'not at all.'"

"But you—*why*?" Joshua was staring; he knew he was staring. "I mean, you must have tons of offers? You're, like, gorgeous, and clever, and—" And Joshua needed to shut his mouth. "I don't get it," he finished lamely.

"Thanks for the vote of confidence. But there's really nothing much to get." Leo's smirk had a strange twist to it, but Joshua didn't think it was directed at him. Touching his chest, Leo's next words sounded like a recital. "Sometimes things just happen."

Meaning he wasn't willing to discuss it. All right, then. Joshua should have been used to running into Leo's invisible walls, but he'd felt like Leo had opened up today, as though maybe...

Maybe nothing.

"So what was up with you earlier?" Joshua asked instead. A deal was a deal.

"Oh, that." Leo's smirk made room for a frown. "I didn't realise people are quite that bad when it comes to stalking you. Had me a bit blindsided, that kind of disrespect for your privacy."

"You get used to it."

"Well, you bloody shouldn't. It's none of their business where you live, or who you hang out with. They need to mind their own fucking business instead of living vicariously through Twitter." Leo shoved away from the wall, messing up his hair with one hand. His fringe stuck up a little and gave him a frazzled air, a mad genius in training. In spite of it all, Joshua gave a soft laugh.

Leo fixed him with a wry look. "It's not funny."

"No, it's not." Joshua inhaled and sobered. "But it can't be changed either, so I prefer not to think about it. Things just happen sometimes, right?"

"Did you or did you not" —Leo crooked his fingers into a pistol— "just have the audacity to quote my own tattoo at me?"

"Your tattoo?"

"'Sometimes things just happen. Other times you make them happen.'" Tugging at the collar of his T-shirt, Leo brought it down just enough to show the upper curves of small black letters scrawled across the left side of his chest. Fuck, that wasn't fair. Joshua didn't have a tattoo kink or anything, but he itched to touch this one, was starting forward already by the time he caught himself. He attempted to turn it into a casual thing by moving past Leo to reach for a bowl. Crisps, right. The crisps needed to go into a bowl, and Joshua needed to get a grip.

"Looks nice," he told Leo in what he hoped passed for a nonchalant compliment. "Is there a story behind it?"

"There is," Leo said, but he didn't go on to explain. Instead, he slapped his hand over the betting list and asked, "This is for the World Cup, right? What are the stakes?"

"Your honour is at stake," Mo answered for Joshua, walking into the kitchen with Nate just a step behind.

"Obviously." Leo tilted his head. "What else?"

Mo grabbed the crisps from Joshua and ripped them open, offering the bag to Nate who declined with a polite shake of his head. Shrugging, Mo helped himself and said around a mouthful, "We were thinking your soul and five litres of blood. Blood can be yours or someone else's, up to you."

"Plus a bottle of wine," Joshua added. At Leo's surprised look, Joshua tilted his head. "What did you expect?"

Leo hesitated. "Something like a few thousand quid. Unless by wine, you mean some crazy expensive stuff."

"It's not about the money," Joshua told him, a little miffed.

"Sorry," Leo said softly. "It honestly wasn't intended as a dig. But people typically bet money, and you guys are rich."

It was Mo who broke the tension. "Look, we've done this since we met at uni. Always the same thing for World Cups and European Cups, and Champions League past the group stage." Taking the list off the fridge, he passed it to Nate, who examined it with a serious expression while Mo continued. "I was a piss-poor student then, totally depended on a shitty job in a café and bargain deals at Tesco's. That's why we settled on a bottle of wine. Difference being that I always bought whatever was on sale, and Joshua and Tristan raided their parents' cellars."

Joshua went to empty the second bag of crisps into a bowl. "You say that like we didn't take a personal risk. I think Tristan narrowly escaped being disinherited once."

"What did he do?" Leo asked, glancing up.

Mo grinned. "Accidentally gifted me with a bottle of some fancy French wine that was pretty much irreplaceable."

When Leo gave a small laugh, Joshua found himself staring at the

6

I f Leo were to count only his waking hours, there was a chance that over the last ten days, he'd spent nearly as much time at Joshua's place as he'd spent at his own. What had started with that very first breakfast on Joshua's terrace had evolved into strategy sessions in Joshua's living room, into rambling conversations and clicking with Joshua's friends over beer and movies, exchanging glances while Nate laughed a little too hard at Mo.

Throughout those early mornings and late nights, Leo had come to find traces of himself scattered about. There was his name on the betting list pinned to Joshua's fridge, there was Mo's sketch on the blackboard which showed a cartoon version of Leo and Nate giving each other high-fives, and there was a teacup that Leo had claimed as his own because he strongly identified with the words printed onto the ceramic. A litany of *'tit twat wanker tosser fuckwit arsehole'* helped him wade through a small but vomit-worthy portion of the online speculation about Joshua's sexuality. In the absence of an official statement from Buckingham Palace, rumours were running wild.

Well. That statement was about to happen.

"So people are mostly worried about two things, yeah?" Sprawled on the floor in shorts and a tank top, Nate waved a printout of some fancy graph that linked the frequency of certain key words to topics. Leo had blanked out a minute into the explanation of how Nate had grabbed the data, and tuned back in for what it meant. "There's those who think you'll hit every club in town—"

"Every dick in town, more like," Tristan put in with a bright grin.

"Only fair, isn't it?" On his back with his head on Joshua's thigh, Mo didn't even bother opening his eyes. "Our boy's got to make up for lost time." His drawl was lazy and amused, and Leo liked him, he really did, but something about the words didn't sit well. They shouldn't be joking about Joshua running wild with meaningless flings, not when Joshua would need to sell the very opposite to the public. Not when he had told Leo that he wanted something steady, seeming almost embarrassed by it.

Show me the guy who'll stick around once the media calls on the hunt.

Leo had done his best not to linger on that early admission, yet his mind kept replaying it at odd moments, *show me the guy, show me the guy.* He was about to protest Mo's careless treatment of the topic, but Joshua beat him to it.

"I don't think I can make up for lost time by, like, fucking my way through—just, never mind." Joshua shook his head. "I wouldn't do that. And not only because it would look bad."

"You've always been a bit of a romantic," Mo said, blinking his lids open for a small grin at Joshua. Some kind of private joke was tucked into it, and Joshua smiled back just like that, warm and intimate, his fingers hooked into Mo's sleeve.

Objectively, they were beautiful together. At the same time, it was strange to watch them like this, knowing that their... arrangement had been the catalyst, the first domino to topple over and set off this chain of events. Leo wondered whether they'd done anything since that morning when Joshua had walked into James' office. There'd been no hint of them crossing the line of friendship while Leo had been around, and each time the five of them had called it a night, Mo had left with Leo, Nate and Tristan.

In any case, it was none of Leo's business. He made himself look away.

"We can easily counter that fear by Joshua emphasising how much of a family guy he is. If we make it clear that casual flings aren't his style at all." Shifting to pull both legs under his body, Leo leaned his back against the sofa table. The telly, on mute, showed a commercial in which a woman was slathering salad oil all over a guy's well-developed chest. Leo assumed that it was so tasty she wanted to lick it off him. Okay. "He's looking for something serious, and the reason he's coming out isn't because he wants to run amok in gay clubs, but because he hates lying to the country. To his people."

"Minions," Mo corrected. In spite of the humour woven into his voice, he shot Leo a quick glance which conveyed respect.

"Minions, underlings, smallfolk. *Semantics.*" Leo nodded at Joshua. "You said you wouldn't tell lies. This is largely accurate, isn't it?"

Joshua blinked prettily. "Me having minions?"

"The rest," Leo said. He leaned over to poke Joshua's stomach. "Do try to keep up, little prince. Being cute is no excuse to slack off."

As soon as it was out, Leo wanted to take it back. Flirting just for the hell of it, joking around, no strings attached—that was so far in his past that it felt like part of an entirely different person. He'd shoved it into a box, closed the lid and sealed it, left it to collect dust. And it had worked just fine, right up until Joshua had come back into his life and stirred up memories of an easier time. It carried the scent of fresh grass in the spring, a whiff of the musty smell that had clung to the books in Eton's library, and a hint of the wax that had made the staircases shine, smooth with centuries of use. Last night, for the first time in half a dozen years, Leo had dreamed of hurriedly pulling on his school uniform, leaving his room on bare feet and running to make it to the Chapel in time.

A gentle nudge of his hand jolted him out of the thought. With a start, he realised he'd been looking at Joshua without really seeing him, and it was Nate who'd brought him out of it. Nate's expression was questioning, and Leo shook his head incrementally. Later, he'd explain later. Maybe.

No, he would.

The expectant silence informed him that he'd missed something, most likely Joshua's reply to his comment. "Sorry," Leo said. "Blanked out for a moment there. Just remembered that I need to call James about the interview slot. Did you say something?"

Overcompensating — a beginner's mistake, offering an explanation where none was needed. He knew better.

"Never mind," Joshua told him. "It wasn't important." He angled himself away, looking distinctly uncomfortable. "Nate, what else are people saying?"

While Nate went back to consulting his graph, Leo kept studying Joshua's profile for a few seconds longer. He couldn't help but feel that he'd missed something.

～

ALL RIGHT. So that had been awkward. And kind of strange as well—after all, *Leo* had been the one to call Joshua cute; he'd started it. So why had he frozen up at Joshua countering with, "But I think you're cuter?"

Leo was the epitome of mixed signals.

Tangling a hand in Mo's shaggy hair, Joshua forced himself to pay attention to Nate. Main concerns of the public, right. Potential effects on foreign relations and how to counter those concerns, yes, *that* was what this was about. It was all about preparations for Joshua's interview.

Oh God, the interview. Joshua didn't think there was any way he'd be ready by Tuesday; two days wasn't enough. A year wasn't enough.

Fuck that, though. Fuck those doubts and fears. Joshua wouldn't back out now, and two days would have to do.

Being ready was a choice, wasn't it?

～

THEY FINISHED a rough outline for Joshua's replies to predetermined interview questions by five in the afternoon. By six, they'd done a couple of run-throughs; Mo, Tristan and Nate watching while Leo took the role of the interviewer and fired off question after question until Joshua's ears were red and his eyes were wide and unhappy, curls mussed up from how often he'd been running his fingers through them. Leo could tell he was growing more anxious with each minor stumble, with each answer that didn't come out quite the way it should.

Maybe this wasn't a good idea. Maybe they should go with the usual, scripted speech instead of an interactive exchange between Joshua and David Dimbleby. It had seemed like a good idea at the time, something lively and engaging rather than a dull monologue, but... maybe this wasn't working.

Leo lowered his sheet with questions and sat back, shaking his head as he tried to find the right words. Joshua pre-empted him.

"This isn't working." Joshua sounded dejected, and fuck, Leo wanted to hug him, tell him it would be fine, that they'd work through this together.

"Joshua, I was much harsher than Dimbleby will be. Let's not give up just yet." Leo set the sheet aside and rose from his chair. Settling next to Joshua on the sofa, he draped an arm around Joshua's shoulders because if there was one thing he'd learned, it was that Joshua responded best to physical contact. Joshua came easily, pliant and quiet. A moment later, Tristan and Mo joined their huddle, crowding close. Nate hovered until Leo snagged his wrist and dragged him down as well.

With Joshua pressed all along his front, Leo could feel him take a deep, shuddering breath. Joshua's fingers curled into Leo's T-shirt. Someone's knee was digging into Leo's side, but he barely noticed, too focused on Joshua's solid warmth, the weight of his body and his curls tickling Leo's chin. Good God, Leo was so in love with him.

Wait.

Wait, what the—no. *No.* Leo wasn't. He couldn't be. There was no way, *no way,* he could be in love with Joshua. It was his past getting all tangled with the present, and if only he'd had a chance to take a step back and think, this would never even be an issue.

Slowly, Leo loosened his arms around Joshua's frame, pulling away just slightly. At the movement, the others shifted back to give him some space while Joshua's grip on Leo's T-shirt tightened.

"Love," Leo told him softly, and his heart skipped a beat. There was no doubt that the others had caught his slip, that *Joshua* had caught it. Leo needed to get a fucking grip. He needed to continue. "You've had enough. Let's call it a day. Eat some ice cream and veg out in front of the telly? Fresh start tomorrow."

"Please?" Joshua cleared his throat. When he raised his head, there was a wet sheen to his eyes, and Leo wanted to kiss it better.

"I'll get the ice cream," Tristan announced, sliding off the sofa.

"Bring the vodka too," Mo told him, and Tristan gave a thumbs-up.

Joshua's smile was wobbly, but it was there. Past the point of rational thinking, Leo skimmed his fingertips along the line of Joshua's jaw, quick and light, while Joshua held perfectly still for him. His gaze was fixed on Leo.

What are you doing?

Leo dropped his hand. He shuffled further away, up against Nate's side, and when he finally looked around, it was to find both Nate and Mo watching him curiously. How much had they seen? Had it all been plain to read on his face, right there, exposed? Had Joshua picked up on it? Leo didn't dare glance at him.

He took a deep breath. "Let's watch *Game of Thrones*," he said loudly, his own voice jarring in his ears.

"Is that the one with the incest?" Mo asked.

"It's the one with the boobs," Tristan called from the kitchen.

"There's male bums too," Nate supplied helpfully, and Mo's gaze snatched to him with open interest.

"You into that?"

Seriously? It seemed Joshua and Tristan hadn't been kidding when they'd called Nate too subtle for Mo. Leo glanced at Joshua just as Joshua glanced at him, and they shared a tiny smile. Since Nate seemed at a bit of a loss, Leo answered for him—because Leo was an awesome friend, thank you very much. Also because it helped distract him from the carbonated liquid bubbling in his stomach.

"It's safe to say that in this flat, Tristan is the only person with an exclusive interest in boobs."

Returning with a bottle of vodka in one arm, and five spoons and ice cream in the other, Tristan set everything but the ice cream down on the coffee table, then plopped himself down on Joshua's lap. "It's a tough job," he confided. "But someone's got to do it. And I'm up for the challenge."

Joshua wrapped an arm around Tristan's waist. "*Up* for it," he said, heavy emphasis and a quiet giggle tagged onto the end. Jesus. He was positively ridiculous and Leo was so charmed, so very out of his depth.

"That's a sad attempt at a pun," he told Joshua. "If that is the best you can do? I weep for this grand old nation."

Joshua's smile showed a lot of teeth. "No one here to judge me."

"I'm judging," Leo said.

"No." Slowly, sweetly, Joshua shook his head. His smile softened, and Leo wanted to touch him again—always, always. "You're not, really. Not anymore. Thank you."

There was no good response; nothing Leo could say that wouldn't betray the unease sizzling in his veins. He was still all wrapped up in Joshua's space, and for the sake of his own sanity, he should move back. He didn't want to, though. Wrestling his gaze away from Joshua, he found the other three watching him with varying degrees of curiosity, waiting for his reply. Leo drew a blank.

Nate narrowed his eyes at him. Leo widened his own eyes in response.

Sooner rather than later, he would need to talk to Nate. He didn't owe him an explanation, didn't owe anyone anything, but... he wanted to. He needed at least one person to understand.

"Ice cream?" he asked, breaking the strange silence that had cloaked the room. On the edge of his vision, he noticed how Joshua's smile dropped, and—yeah. Calling for ice cream was an inadequate response to Joshua's honest expression of gratitude, could suggest that Leo was uncomfortable with it, uncomfortable with Joshua trusting him, relying on him, considering him a friend.

Could they be friends? Would Leo ever be satisfied with having Joshua as a friend, *just* a friend, when he was struggling to quench emotions from the past?

What if this had nothing to do with the past?

Leo tried to crush the thought as soon as it had occurred.

"Ice cream," Tristan confirmed loudly. "And someone please find a semi-legal streaming website so we can watch some boobs."

"Semi-legal?" Joshua sat up a little straighter and released an audible breath. His arm was still wrapped around Tristan's waist, their physical proximity easy and casual, as it always was with them. It drove home the point that all those times Joshua had sought out Leo's touch, it really didn't mean anything.

Which was good. Much safer for everyone involved.

Leo looked away, just in time to catch the probing glance Nate sent his way—yet another time Nate had caught him out. Jesus, Leo really wasn't subtle when it came to Joshua, was he? He needed to try harder.

Nate scrambled off the sofa to collect his laptop. "Don't worry, I'm on it."

"Make sure we don't have police knocking down His Royal Highness' door, will you?" Leo asked. Nate's response consisted of a flat look.

Tristan popped open the carton of ice cream, and Leo wasn't surprised that it was the homemade kind, not the industrial stuff that could be bought in stores. He wondered if Joshua himself had made it, wouldn't be entirely surprised to find him mixing swirls of liquid chocolate into the creamy substance, concentration written into the crease between his brows.

Leo needed to stop. And he needed to put some distance between himself and Joshua. *Now.*

He didn't move an inch.

"Who wants the first taste?" Tristan asked. Before anyone had a chance to reply, he quickly added, "Me, obviously," and dug his spoon into the mass. In retaliation, Joshua shoved him off his lap, and Tristan tumbled to the floor, bumping into the coffee table with the carton clutched protectively to his chest.

"Serves you right," Mo told him.

"Just for that comment," Tristan said, "you won't get any. Joshua won't get any either."

"But I made that," Joshua protested.

Tristan righted himself, tipping up his face with a broad smirk. "So?"

Over Tristan's head, Leo met Nate's eyes. Leo raised his eyebrows, and Nate grinned and nodded, then crawled across the floor to dig his fingers into Tristan's side, making him jolt. Leo used the distraction to pluck the carton from Tristan's hands.

Grabbing a spoon off the coffee table, Leo ignored Tristan shouting insults in between trying to squirm away from Nate's tickle attack. Leo held both items out to Joshua and received a slow, surprised smile in return. "Thank you," Joshua said, and this time Leo was ready with a reply.

"Anything for you, Princeling."

Joshua's smile widened. Their fingers brushed over the carton, Leo's cold from the ice cream and Joshua's warm and dry, a gentle touch to the back of Leo's hand as he accepted the spoon.

Leo held his breath and counted to three before he smiled back.

THEY'D INTENDED to watch three episodes, give Joshua and Mo a taste.

Halfway through the first episode, Joshua had sat up a little straighter at a conversation between the Dwarf and the Bastard, glancing at Leo. It had taken Leo a moment to understand that it had been in reaction to the Dwarf's words—*wear it like armour, and it can never be used to hurt you.* Leo sent Joshua a private smile and lifted one brow.

At the end of the third episode, Joshua had turned to Leo with wide eyes, voice soft with apprehension. "But what happens to the little boy? He can't just—they can't just leave him like that, wishing he was dead. Can they?"

"It's *Game of Thrones*, love. You ain't seen nothing yet." Leo shook his head and slotted his fingers into the gaps between Joshua's, retracting his hand after a quick squeeze.

So they'd watched another episode. And then another. By the time the King had died and his son was delightedly preparing his own coronation, Mo had sagged into Nate's side, his head on Nate's shoulder, only just awake enough to make a displeased noise each time Joffrey made an appearance. Nate was sitting very still, his gaze fixed on Joshua's enormous flat-screen TV, as though any movement could endanger the fragile state of things.

Leo knew the feeling. Lack of room on the sofa had pushed him all up into Joshua's space with their shoulders pressed together, arms bumping each time one of them moved. Light from the screen flickered over Joshua's face and tangled in his hair, and Leo wanted to chase each spark with his hands and his mouth. Everything felt like a giant cliché, and yet he couldn't bring himself to move away. Fuck, when had he agreed to star in a romantic comedy? He wanted out.

He really didn't want out.

But he should.

When the end credits for the seventh episode filled the screen, Joshua gave a little sigh and raised his arms above his head, stretching. The motion exposed a slice of his stomach, black letters inked into pale skin, and Leo was too tired not to stare just a beat longer than he should. Time to go home, probably.

"Hey, you guys want to crash here?" Joshua's words dripped like slow-motion rain. "Like, you'd all be back here tomorrow anyway, so it just makes sense, right?"

Stay here. Leo shouldn't, he really, really shouldn't; things were already so muddled and the time away would do him some good. Not that he'd be sleeping in Joshua's room, in Joshua's *bed*, but it was still too damn close.

Mo lifted his head by about an inch. "If I'm sharing with you and

Tri, you take the middle. He kicks in his sleep. Don't know how Kels puts up with it."

"She loves me," Tristan said. "You should try it sometime."

"Try what?" Mo asked, his head dropping back down to rest on Nate's shoulder. "Loving you? Sorry, bro. You're like a hundred percent too much twink for me."

Tristan's tone was offended. "I've got some muscle, bitch." By means of demonstration, he flexed his left arm. In the background, the series' main title was just fading out.

"You're scrawny as fuck. Now *this*," Mo lazily gestured at Nate's bicep, eyes half-lidded and voice sleepy, "is what I call muscle."

Even in the dim glow of the screen, Leo could tell that Nate's cheeks were flushed. He was rather proud that he didn't burst out laughing, although the impulse became nearly too much when he found Joshua biting down on his bottom lip to stifle a grin, eyes bright. God, Joshua was lovely.

Leo's distraction was to blame for how he agreed easily when Nate suggested they share the guest room. It did make sense, after all. Especially since the tube had stopped running about an hour ago, and Leo didn't feel like dragging himself to a night bus or calling a taxi.

It made sense. Really.

He was weirdly charmed to learn that both Tristan and Mo kept toothbrushes at Joshua's place. The obvious closeness between them, the way they didn't seem to have any secrets from each other, it was... nice. Really just nice.

For Leo and Nate, Joshua dug out two new toothbrushes, still in their plastic wrapping, and then went to find them sleep shirts. He returned with two that looked soft-washed and well-worn, lingering in the doorway of the guest room to ask whether they needed anything else.

"I think we're good, man," Nate told him, while Leo looked around the room that contained a queen-sized bed along with a desk cluttered with various papers and what looked like printouts of articles. Stepping closer, he caught headlines all related to speculation about Joshua's sexuality. A shelf with books sat beside the desk, and Leo's gaze slid past spines that looked well-worn, lingering on a few familiar names—Franzen and Pamuk, Machiavelli, Goethe. Some of those had been on the curriculum at Eton, others not. There were children's classics as well, and he didn't let himself linger on those.

Leo turned away to give Joshua a smile that had to be edged with tiredness. "Thanks, Princeling. We'll be fine. See you tomorrow, all right?"

"Okay. Good night." Still Joshua hesitated for another few seconds before he nodded and left, gently closing the door behind himself. The silence that settled in his wake was noticeable, and Leo shot a glance at Nate to find Nate already watching him.

"Think he was waiting for you to take off your top," Nate said, a sudden grin twitching around his mouth.

"Not funny." With a sigh, Leo sat down on the bed, the mattress giving under his weight. He hoped it wouldn't be too soft; he'd slept on a camping mat so often that he'd come to find the floor more comfortable than one of those beds that felt like sinking into a marshmallow.

"Wasn't meant to be funny." Nate crossed over to the windows, drawing the curtains. Halfway through, he paused to take in the view, and after a moment, Leo joined him. Regent's Canal lay beneath them, water reflecting the distant brightness of the city; most of the houses on the other side were still and quiet, their windows dark. Leo propped both elbows on the windowsill and set his chin on his hands.

"This is so nice," he said softly. "Imagine waking up to this view every day. Think Joshua'd notice if we just never leave?"

"Probably." Nate's tone was dry. "Not sure he'd mind, though. He seems to love having people around."

Leo had been like that once—the life of every party, happiest when he was in the middle of a crowd. He kept his voice deliberately light. "Imagine what that's like."

"Yeah, imagine." A significant pause followed Nate's statement. When he spoke again, it was laced with caution, like someone treading on thin ice. "D'you realise that we've been mates for ages, but this is the first time we've spent the night together?"

Fuck. So they were doing this. They were going to have an actual, serious conversation when Leo already felt as though his thoughts were weighed down with exhaustion. Somehow, he worked up a cheesy grin and nudged his feet against Nate's. "Aw, darling, you just had to ask."

"Not what I meant, dickhead." Without sparing Leo so much as a sideways glance, Nate shoved away from the window and went to change into one of the shirts Joshua had given them. It was snug on Nate. Leo moved to do the same and found that the other shirt was loose on him, comfortable. The faint scent of detergent triggered a sense of familiarity.

When he crawled into bed, Nate was already stretched out on the other side, a thin blanket pushed down to his waist, staring fixedly at the ceiling. The lamp on the bedside table showed the unhappy line of his frown, and all of a sudden, Leo felt drained.

He didn't even know why he was still fighting. At this point, it had become a reflex.

"I know what you meant," he said softly. Settling on his side and tugging his own duvet up to his chin, he waited for Nate to look at him before he continued. "Sorry. I'm adjusting, you know? Feels like everything's changing right now, and it's all going so quickly. Like... It's as if Joshua walking into our office started off a chain reaction. I mean," he snorted, "you've started wearing tank tops, for fuck's sake. What is even *happening*?"

"I like what's happening." Nate's shrug turned out awkward with the way he was lying down. "You're a bit different, you know? Not like you're a whole other person, but you're starting to become more... open. Brighter, kind of. I like it."

Somewhere in the flat, Tristan was singing a pop song that Leo vaguely recognised. Then a thump, and he fell silent. The toilet flushed, followed by running water, and a door clicking shut. Everything was quiet after that, and Leo wondered how Tristan and Mo had settled in next to Joshua—whether they were all up in each other's space, legs tangled, sharing one duvet for the three of them. When Leo had wandered into Joshua's bedroom the first time he'd been here, he'd seen only one duvet, spread out over the large bed that had been built into an alcove. Maybe Joshua kept spare blankets somewhere, just for occasions like this.

Leo shouldn't care if Joshua shared his duvet with others. Or maybe he needed to give up trying to fool himself. Rolling onto his back, he punched his pillow into shape, Nate's words ringing in his ears. *You're different. More open.*

"When I was younger. Like, sixteen or so." Leo cleared his throat. "I had the worst kind of crush on Prince Joshua. It was embarrassing. You'd have laughed until you cried if you could have seen me back then."

Nate made a noise that was trapped halfway between amusement and surprise. "Is that why you were such a twat to him? When you met him for real?"

"Yeah." Glancing over, Leo tried for a grin, but it might have turned out as more of a grimace. "Well. We went to school together."

"You bloody what?" In the stillness of the night, Nate's voice carried, and he looked contrite right away. "Sorry," he added, much more quietly. "You and Joshua? You went to school together?"

Leo raised a hand towards the ceiling and let it drop again. His chest felt a little tight, heavy, as though there was a weight pressing down on it. "Eton. I was a couple of years above him, though, and also very much a twink. I've changed quite a bit. Not surprised he didn't recognise me."

A short gap followed Leo's words, then Nate raised himself up on his arms, studying Leo with a quiet half-smile. "You know, that's more than you ever told me about your past. I can see it, mate—little twink Leo, swaggering about the place as though the world was at your feet, being a little shit to your teachers, sneaking glances at everyone's favourite prince in the hallways and during lunch in the dining hall." Nate paused. "Does Eton even have a dining hall, or would that be too, like..."

"Proletarian?" Leo finished for him. He snorted and shifted to get more comfortable, the mattress not quite as soft as he'd feared. At least he wouldn't wake up from dreams where quicksand was about to swallow him up. "There is a large dining hall, yes, and half the houses eat there. Students are organised in different houses, you know. Like at Hogwarts."

Nate chuckled, but stayed silent otherwise, gaze curious even as he clearly held back his questions. Wading through his thoughts, Leo tried to bring them into a semblance of order. "It's all very posh—black tailcoat, waistcoat, stiff collar, although we were allowed our own clothes over the weekend." He felt his lips twist into a tiny grin. "I had a colourful trousers phase that I would like to bleach from my brain, but I suppose there's nothing to be done about it now."

"Do you," Nate said, still with that quiet half-smile, "realise that your voice gets more upper-class when you talk about Eton? Your accent, maybe a bit the words as well. Not quite enough to give Joshua a run for his money, mind. But, yeah."

"It does?" Leo considered it, and yeah, that made sense. God, what a posh, sheltered twat he'd been back then. "Anyway, so Joshua was in a different house, one that had its own dining facilities. Guess they didn't see it fit to have the Prince mingle with the masses. He also had a bodyguard with him at all times, a burly bloke who lived in the room next door. Not Johnson, but someone else."

"That must be so weird, living like that. Like, having someone else shadow your every step. He turned out all right, considering. Didn't he?" Nate didn't wait for a reply, settling back down on his stomach as he turned to face Leo, his voice thoughtful. "Doesn't it suck that you know all this stuff about Joshua, and he doesn't have a clue? You ever thought about telling him?"

"About my utterly embarrassing teenage infatuation? *Hell* no." Leo inhaled, and all of a sudden, he felt lighter, almost giddy with relief. He'd done it. He'd shared this slice of the past with Nate, and it had been close to easy. Painless. The world hadn't come to an end, and Nate was watching him with warm eyes and didn't press for more than Leo was willing to offer.

"Well." Nate grinned. "Obviously not that part. Just about Eton in general, I guess. Pretty sure he'd like to know, and it's sort of like you're holding out on him. When you have all these memories and he's in them, but he doesn't even know you guys have crossed paths before. Doesn't really seem fair, does it?"

"Life isn't fair. Didn't they tell you?" Leo was careful to keep all bitterness out of his tone. "And you're right, it doesn't seem fair, I guess. But I wouldn't want him to ask follow-up questions. Like what happened to me after."

"Or why you changed your last name."

Leo stiffened. "How did you—"

"Educated guess," Nate interrupted. "Jesus, don't get your knickers in a twist, yeah? It's just that early on, you always took a bit long to react to the name, you know? You don't do that anymore, mind."

Oh. Yeah, okay, Leo could see how Nate would have drawn that conclusion. When Nate had joined James' team, about six months after Leo had, each 'Graham' had sounded strange to Leo's ears, had tasted sour and unfamiliar on his tongue. By now, he'd long since made it his own; it was *his*. An integral part of who he had become.

"So you didn't, like..." Leo hesitated. "You didn't look into my background?"

Nate's brows pulled together. "I wouldn't do that. Friends don't spy on their friends, right?"

The words were interwoven with hurt, and Leo touched his shoulder, trying for a smile. "Sorry. I know that you wouldn't, it's just... stupid paranoia. Please don't take it personal."

"No, I get it." Nate was quiet for a moment, then the corners of his mouth tugged up into an answering smile. "So, like, I know you're a bit prickly about physical stuff, but I think this warrants a cuddle, yeah?"

Leo exhaled on a chuckle and shifted closer, sliding up his hand to rest between Nate's shoulder blades. "All right. If you must, I suppose that we can have a cuddle. Just don't cop a feel, okay? I know it'll be hard to resist, what with my ace body and all, but I'll have you know—"

Nate's laugh cut him off, and then he was pulled into a tight embrace, his face shoved against Nate's shoulder. "Suffocating here," Leo managed weakly, which only served to make Nate tighten his grip until Leo sighed and relaxed into it. All things considered, this wasn't too bad.

Pressing his nose into Nate's chest, he took a deep breath, caught the lingering scent of lavender soap and detergent that was carved into his memory as belonging to Joshua. Leo could get used to the whole cuddling thing. "Thank you," he mumbled.

"Anytime, mate." When Nate loosened his hold, Leo didn't move away. Honestly, he was comfortable where he was. It reminded him of tucking his sisters into bed, reading them a bedtime story while they'd burrowed in close, listening with rapt attention as he moulded his voice to fit the characters—the little blue fish all happy and optimistic as it begged for one of the rainbow fish's glittering scales, or sweet Miss Honey in a back-and-forth with Matilda's high-pitched, energetic tumble of words, both of them offset by ill-tempered Miss Trunchbull.

Fuck, it had been years since he'd let himself think about any of that. He wondered how the girls were doing, whether they thought about their brother at least once in a while.

Swallowing around the knot that had lodged itself in his throat, Leo pulled back and scrubbed a hand down his face. He was fine. He was *fine*.

Nate watched him with his mouth twisted into a gentle downwards curve. "So I guess it's my turn, right? Tell you something about my own past." For all that he clearly strove for a casual tone, it didn't quite work; Leo could hear the discomfort underneath.

"You don't have to," he said. "We're not playing tit for tat. That's not how friendship works."

"It's not that I don't trust you, yeah?" Nate rested his chin on a fist, the dim brightness of the lamp softening his frown. "It's more that it's a long story, kind of. And kind of not, but I don't really like to think about it. You know?"

Yes, Leo did know. He hadn't offered anything past the fact that he'd attended Eton, and Nate hadn't asked—had known not to ask, probably. Because he understood Leo in a way that people like Joshua, or Mo, or Tristan, never would.

"I get it." Leo paused to study Nate's face. "No need to tell me, okay? Just wondering, though... Did you get into trouble with the law? Like—I think Ben did. But not you, I don't think so."

"I didn't. My missions, they were" —a tiny hitch— "officially sanctioned."

Missions, Leo thought. *What did you do, what happened? Does it have anything to do with how you never drive, but always insist on taking the passenger seat?*

He forbade himself to ask, simply nodded.

"What about you?" Nate asked a moment later. "Did you break the law?"

Well. There'd been a few instances of shoplifting, and the first time Leo had accepted money in return for sex, he'd been seventeen. It had been early November, an unusually cold one with night-time temperatures dropping towards freezing, and a warm bed for the night had been his original goal—a bit of a fumble in exchange for a roof over his head and maybe, if he was lucky, even a cup of tea for breakfast. Instead, he'd found himself back out on the street an hour later with fifty quid in his pocket and his heart lodged in his throat.

Fifty quid for a hand job and some dirty talk. The bloke had been generous, seriously decent as well, even if Leo had been too bewildered to appreciate it at the time. He'd been fortunate.

"Nothing that would have landed me in jail," he replied, slightly delayed. If anything, the underage component would have landed his punters in jail and him back with his parents. Which—thanks, but no thanks.

Outside, a motor boat chugged past, then everything was quiet again. They should get some sleep, especially seeing as tomorrow would see them jumping right back into coaching Joshua for the interview. Yet Leo felt wide awake, his thoughts skittering about like ants in a tizzy.

Nate had accepted Leo's response with a faint smile. He'd only just moved to flick off the light when Leo asked, "What's going on with you and Mo, then?"

The room was plunged into shadows, lit only by the distant brightness that trickled through the curtains and turned the windows into rectangular shapes. It took a few seconds for Nate to sink back into his pillow, and when he spoke, he sounded mildly confused. "I don't actually know. He's really hot, obviously. And much nicer than I thought. A bit of a dork, which I think is cool, you know?"

"Holy fuck, you sound like you're ready to propose." Leo grinned and rolled onto his side, closing his eyes. He could feel his pulse slowing down, less erratic in his ears. "Honesty hour, mate: did you or did you not wank off to that underwear shot you told me about?"

Nate breathed out a snicker. "I am under no obligation to answer."

"That's a yes," Leo decided.

"Shut it, Grammy." A brief silence followed Nate's words, and while it wasn't awkward as such, Leo wondered whether Nate was pondering how the nickname was based on a lie. If Nate was bothered, he didn't show it and instead went for a light, teasing tone. "You know, that whole flirting thing you and Joshua got going on—"

"Flirting thing?"

"You call him Princeling and little prince," Nate said, matter-of-fact and thoroughly unperturbed by the warning Leo had tucked into his tone. "And maybe you meant to mock him at first, but now, you just sound fond. You know, I think Joshua would go for you."

Leo inhaled slowly, carefully. "So this is what we've come to now? A pair of gossiping teenagers chatting about boys we like?" Much more quietly, he added, "But really, it's not an option."

"Because of your past." It wasn't a question. Leo answered anyway

"I couldn't—yeah. I could never be there with him, you know? Not really. He wants something steady, like a real boyfriend. I can't be that." The space behind his lids was of a deep, velvety black, and he let it soothe his thoughts, felt them slow down to a crawl. *I couldn't be what he wants, needs. What he deserves.*

"Leo—" Nate began, and Leo interrupted before this could

deviate into a conversation he wasn't ready for, not yet. Maybe not for a long time.

"Let's just sleep," he said.

Three seconds trickled past, then Nate exhaled around a yawn. "Sleep," he agreed.

In an unspoken show of gratitude, Leo gave Nate's shoulder a quick squeeze before he turned to face away, tucking the pillow under his shoulder. He fell asleep to the rhythm of Nate's deep, even breaths, to distant images of empty sidewalks and headlights streaking past, of tangling his hands in dark hair and squeezing his eyes shut, head tipped back for a kiss that never came.

JOSHUA'S NOSE TICKLED. There was, like, hair? In his mouth? And God, what, it couldn't be later than seven, but they'd forgotten to close the curtains last night, so it was too bright, and it was too warm, and also, *also*, there was *hair* in his *mouth*. Sharp, spicy cologne. Mo.

Joshua shuffled back only to bump into Tristan, who made a disgruntled noise and flapped his arm without waking. Astonishingly, he managed to hit Joshua square in the jaw. Cheers.

Rubbing at the spot, Joshua slid out of bed and stood at the foot for a few seconds, trying to blink the haze from his brain. A glass of milk, yeah. Then maybe catch another couple of hours of sleep because it was—ugh, really? Just past six? Too early, yeah.

It promised to be a warm morning. He didn't bother putting on a T-shirt when he left his bedroom, taking care to be quiet so he wouldn't wake Leo and Nate. Remembering why they'd stayed the night prompted the thought that Joshua would have to go through another round of interview preparations today. He'd sucked yesterday; there was no way around it. If he didn't gain a sudden burst of inspiration...

God, how was he supposed to pull this off? Could he?

He found the kitchen empty and poured himself a glass of milk before he stepped out onto the terrace—and spotted Leo perched on the sofa bed, sipping from a cup of tea as he stared at the large tree shading the house. He jolted at Joshua's approach, then stilled, his slow gaze dragging down Joshua's body and back up. Was he—he was checking Joshua out. Wasn't he?

Lashes, Joshua thought, a little nonsensically. *Lashes, cheekbones, blue blue eyes.* Fuck, Leo was gorgeous, all sharp angles and soft curves, a synthesis of contradictions. Did that even make sense? Joshua didn't know. There were a lot of things he didn't know, and as if to illustrate, Leo snatched his attention away and pressed his lips together. Irritation was written into the stiff set of his shoulders, and Joshua couldn't tell who was the target—Joshua, Leo himself, Monday mornings, or the world in general?

Leo's voice was quiet and airy, blending in with the serenity of the early hour, with a city only just beginning to wake. "Morning. I didn't think anyone else would be awake for at least another couple of hours."

"Me neither." Joshua approached carefully and settled on the very edge of the mattress. "Sorry if I startled you."

"You didn't. Also," Leo snorted, "it's your bloody flat, mate. Hope it's okay I helped myself to some tea."

"You know it is." Sliding fully onto the sofa bed, Joshua took a sip of milk and glanced at Leo's profile, its precise cut, the way his unstyled hair swooped down over his ear, a little tangled from sleep. He was bundled up in Joshua's T-shirt, its hem falling well below the waistband of Leo's boxer shorts. The way he was sitting, reclined against the wall of the building with his knees pulled up to his chest, drew attention to the thick muscles in his thighs. Joshua wanted to smooth the palm of his hand down Leo's spine as he drew him into a kiss, Leo falling into it without hesitation.

He might.

Joshua wrestled his gaze away. He was sharply aware that he was wearing only a clinging pair of boxer briefs, and while he wasn't shy about his body, he was growing chilly with the breeze that stirred the leaves of the tree. Grabbing a crumpled afghan off the floor, he wrapped it around his chest, leaving only his shoulders bare.

"Couldn't sleep?" he asked, softly so as not to disturb the tranquillity that surrounded them.

"Not particularly used to sharing my sleeping space. Got some things on my mind as well."

"Anything in particular?" Joshua strove to make it sound unobtrusive, an invitation rather than a request.

Over the rim of the cup, Leo gave him a long look. His lashes trembled when he took a sip, throat moving as he swallowed. When he spoke, his words were as translucent as the steam rising from the tea. "Family things, mainly. I had a look at your books—was a little amused by picturing your mum reading you *Ronia, the Robber's Daughter* as a bedtime story."

"Hey, Ronia's the daughter of the chief, so technically, it's about a ruler's child. I consider it perfectly appropriate." Grinning, Joshua tugged the slipping afghan back up. "And my mum and Emmy took turns, actually. At least for the easier books, the ones Emma could already read."

Again, Leo was silent for a moment. His smile was soft around the edges, distinctly wistful. "That's a nice thought, you know?"

This was the point when Joshua had come to expect that Leo would close off. Right now, with the day still hazy and gentle around them, Joshua wondered whether just this once, it would be different. He kept his tone light. "Did you not get bedtime stories as a kid?"

Leo's sharp look conveyed that he was perfectly aware of what Joshua was doing. Joshua countered it with an innocent smile, hoping it would be rendered even more harmless by how he probably sported a milk moustache. His efforts earned him a snort from Leo.

Focusing on his tea, Leo tucked his naked feet under one corner of the afghan. "Only got them if I read them myself, or if the babysitter girl was there." He paused, and when he continued, his voice was so quiet it was hard to understand him. "Did read some of the classics to my sisters, though, that's how I got to know them. Like the *Rainbow Fish*, I saw that on your shelf as well. *Willy Wonka* and *Matilda*."

Joshua shifted closer, enough so as to provide Leo with better access to the blanket. With a little smile, Leo wrapped it around his calves. It was clear he wouldn't elaborate further on reading to his sisters, so Joshua went with, "First time my mum read me *The Witches*, I was so scared. She did all the voices, and her Grand High Witch was quite terrifying." He raised a brow. "You don't want to mess with my mum, trust me."

"Wasn't planning on it," Leo deadpanned. His eyes were amused, bright, and that was what prompted Joshua to push for just a tiny bit more information.

"So your parents, they didn't read you things?"

"They weren't that type of parents." It was a wry statement, very matter-of-fact, one corner of Leo's mouth quirking. "In fact, they were more the type of parents who host fancy dinner parties and show off their kids like pieces in an art exhibition."

No love lost, was there?

Joshua thought back to Leo with those street kids, the way he'd fit right in and had seemed to naturally adapt to their manner of speech. They'd treated him like someone they respected—but not with the kind of respect one would bestow upon an outsider.

How long had Leo been with James? How had he ended up there? What had come between his parents' fancy dinner parties and working for James? Come to think of it, just how fancy had those dinner parties been? And why did Leo know so much about royal protocol when it was the kind of knowledge one would expect from a noble rather than a commoner? How, why, what, where?

"Do you miss them? Your family?" Joshua watched Leo from the corner of his eye. "I mean, I take it you don't really talk to them very often. Or do you?"

Several seconds dragged by before Leo replied. "I miss my sisters sometimes. It's been a while, though." While gentle, his tone didn't invite further questions. Nudging his toes against Joshua's ankle, he moved right on to ask, "What about you? What's got you out and about at this hour?"

Chapter closed. All right, Joshua would take this at Leo's pace.

"Woke up to a mouthful of Mo's hair. Which was followed by Tristan's flailing limbs hitting me in the face." Joshua smiled into his milk, then eyed Leo's cup with sudden interest.

"Poor baby." Leo sounded supremely unsympathetic, and just for that, Joshua did indeed set down his milk, then pried the teacup from Leo's fingers. Leo made a disgruntled noise and tried to scuttle away, but the wall limited his movement, and the element of surprise was on Joshua's side. With a triumphant grin, Joshua took a huge gulp, nearly burning his tongue, then handed the cup back. Leo accepted it with a narrow-eyed glare and a quick squeeze of his fingers around Joshua's wrist.

"Thief," he muttered. "Robbing your subjects, honestly, I can't *believe* you, Princeling. Where's Robin Hood when you need him?"

"That's my cup, my water, and my tea," Joshua said.

"I put in all the work, and this cup has been annexed. It is mine now. Customary law."

So Leo did consider himself the rightful owner of that cup. Joshua had suspected as much after Leo had slapped away Nate's hand when Nate had tried to pick it up at some point yesterday. Tristan had bought it from a charity shop in Maidenhead, shortly after Joshua's initial breakdown over his sexuality. The list of insults was faded by now, contours washed out with years of being in Joshua's possession, and the rim showed a chip. Still Joshua didn't think he would ever bring himself to discard it.

If Leo wanted to fool himself into believing Joshua would give it up, well. It wasn't going to happen.

"Don't even think about trying to squirrel it away," Joshua told him. "I'd have to send the Secret Service after you."

"Over a tired old teacup?" The left corner of Leo's mouth hitched up. "Talk about an overreaction, love."

Love. It was the third time Leo had directed it at Joshua, and it had come with a teasing note twice, once in an attempt to comfort Joshua. Around the street kids, Leo had used it frequently, and he'd also let it slip that very first time on the phone when he'd mistaken Joshua for —*oh.* When he'd mistaken Joshua for a kid calling for advice, obviously. That made a lot more sense now.

Either way, Leo used the term quite casually, so it didn't justify the bright spark of hope shivering in Joshua's belly. But it was a sign that Leo's walls were thinning, gathering cracks.

"That cup means a lot to me." Joshua hoped that the slight delay hadn't been obvious. "I don't share it with just anyone."

"Did you imply that I am 'just anyone'?" Leo moulded it into a show of affront, and Joshua absolutely couldn't resist drawing him into an impulsive, one-armed hug, snickering.

"You're the most anyone I've ever met."

"That's such rubbish," Leo grumbled. "Doesn't even make sense. And what do you think it is that you're doing? Will you just—okay, be careful, there's *tea* in my hands. Hot tea. *Scalding* tea." In spite of the protest, he tucked himself into Joshua's side, his breath fanning out over Joshua's naked shoulder.

Joshua held himself quiet and still, and after a few short seconds, Leo relaxed further into his hold.

"So, little prince..." Leo's voice was hardly above a whisper. "Are you ready for another go today? Fresh start?"

"I'll just have to be, don't I?" Joshua didn't mean for it to come out quite this plaintive. He stole Leo's cup for another sip of tea, but it didn't quite soothe the faint quiver in his stomach at the thought of forcing himself through another round of rapid-fire questions. The warmth and solidness of Leo's weight against him helped, if only a little.

This time, Leo had easily surrendered the tea. When he took it back, their fingers brushed over the warm ceramic, and Leo let his touch linger for a moment, turning his head to meet Joshua's eyes. "You can still call it off. Right now, that's still possible. If you've come to realise that you don't actually want to go through with it, then the time is now." The corners of Leo's mouth tugged down, barely enough to be noticeable. "No one would blame you for it."

"*You* would," Joshua said softly. They were so very close, a scant few inches separating them. It felt as though the morning was holding its breath, all noises falling away, a fragile standstill.

Gently, Leo shook his head. Breaking the connection, he ducked over the cup of tea, blowing across the surface. Steam briefly obscured his face. "I wouldn't. Not anymore. If you've changed your mind, if it isn't what you want anymore, if you think it isn't *good* for you..." He trailed off, chewing on his bottom lip, looking down so that his lashes hid his eyes.

Joshua's blood thrummed with distant need, the images in his head shadowed like out-of-focus photographs. He exhaled, some of the haze melting away. "I don't want to back out."

Leo glanced up. "You're sure?"

"I'm sure." It came out surprisingly confident, and once Joshua had put it out there, he realised just how much he meant it. There was a chance he'd come to regret his decision, but if he didn't do this now, there was no doubt that he'd never forgive himself. "I'm *sure*," he repeated.

Leo's smile started in his eyes and grew, brightened, until it took over his face. Joshua swallowed and smiled back, everything slow and radiant. He felt as though he was standing on the edge of a cliff, ready to fall.

If he kissed Leo now, now, *now*—

Leo straightened up and moved back by a few inches, enough to bring one hand up and rub his thumb over the black '*L*' inked into Joshua's left shoulder. "For your mother?" he guessed. "And the '*E*' on the other side is for your sister?"

Joshua nodded and didn't dare move. After a stretch of time that might have covered a couple of seconds or the better part of a century, Leo retracted his hand. He shuffled further back, out from under the afghan, and crossed his legs, but his entire body was still turned towards Joshua. "Do you think," Leo began, voice thinner than normal, "that it would be easier if you didn't have to do the interview by yourself?"

Was there a tinge of red to Leo's cheeks? Joshua couldn't tell. He caught his breath. "What do you mean?"

"Your mum and sister." Leo raised the cup to his lips, but didn't drink. "You told me they're supportive, and you obviously trust them.

What if they did the interview with you? Present a united front to the public. Do you think that would make it easier?"

It took Joshua several moments to work through Leo's words, like puzzling together the pieces of a dream, like waking up and becoming aware of his surroundings—the morning breeze cooling his skin, a car passing by on the road below, the bitter scent of Leo's tea. The tight knot of disappointment in Joshua's stomach.

Pulling the afghan tighter around his body, Joshua nodded. He couldn't quite bring himself to meet Leo's eyes.

FOR ALL THAT Leo had been blatantly disrespectful when he'd first met Joshua, he was the very epitome of correctness with Louise and Emma. He inclined his head in a flawless execution of protocol, was polite without being deferential, charming and funny, professional. Joshua was slightly relieved and very impressed.

When he caught Leo's gaze, Leo winked at him, a hint of a smirk curving his lips. A moment later, he answered Louise's question about how he'd ended up with James Boyle with an entertaining tale about a chance meeting in a bar, Leo's ability to weasel free snacks out of the bartender the reason he'd landed his job. It was possibly the truth, but more likely just a fraction of it.

They settled down to discuss the questions and what their responses would need to cover. The first run-through was shaky—although better than any of Joshua's solo attempts—whereas the second one was decent already. The third one, though...

It was good. Really good. Joshua's smiles came naturally, and his words felt easy and smooth, his confidence bolstered by his mother to his left and his sister to his right. Emma jumped in to address how she was now solely responsible for continuing the family line, and she did so with verve and humour. After Louise had fielded the question about how Joshua's sexuality might impact foreign relations—"
Have people truly forgotten that Germany had an openly gay foreign

minister, and the country hasn't fared worse for it?"—Tristan bounced to his feet for a spontaneous round of applause.

Again, Joshua caught Leo's gaze. Leo was beaming at him, happy and open, and Joshua felt his own grin fade, melting into something much too soft and private.

Leo blinked, turned away, and went to join Nate to review the video they'd recorded. It took Joshua several moments to move. Draping himself over Tristan's back, he demanded a piggyback ride that resulted in both of them toppling to the floor while Mo laughed and Emma declared them idiots, Louise watching with a gentle smile.

"Don't break him," Leo told Tristan. "I might have some use for him yet."

"Really?" Joshua asked, tipping his head up to watch Leo from where he was sprawled on the floor. "What kind of use?"

Leo snorted and didn't reply. Joshua was certain that this time, he wasn't imagining the flush to Leo's cheeks.

He also wasn't imagining the way Leo kept a careful amount of distance between them for a while. He didn't relax until Louise and Emma had left and the five of them were spread out on the floor of Joshua's living room, shouting their way through a FIFA tournament. Leo's shoulder was pressed against Joshua's arm, and Joshua had never met anyone who confused him more. He'd never met anyone who fascinated him more, either.

IF CIRCUMSTANCES HAD BEEN DIFFERENT, Leo would have scoffed at the opulence of Buckingham Palace. He'd have passive-aggressively praised the heavy, gleaming fabrics, the sparkling chandeliers and polished gold frames of enormous mirrors, might have considered trying to smuggle an ornate candle holder out, just for the hell of it. He could have pawned it off for a hefty sum too, money that would come in handy if he ever had to bail a kid out of jail.

As it was, he was too focused on the omnipresence of cameras, the heat of the spotlights. James was talking to David Dimbleby, both of them seeming perfectly at ease, but Leo had seen how the bloke had gone completely still when he'd taken his first look at the questions he was supposed to ask. Finally, Dimbleby clapped James on the shoulder with a jovial expression, then went to take his seat in an armchair which had been moved to face one of the brocade sofas, waiting for the Queen and her children to appear.

Slipping into the space Dimbleby had just vacated, Leo lowered his voice so that only James would hear him. "Did you tell him to stick to the damn questions?"

"He will." James' tone was warm and confident. "Relax. We can always do a second take. Or a third. And we'll approve the final cut before it airs tonight."

"I know." Leo did know, was the thing. But he wanted the first one to go off smoothly, without a hitch, so that Joshua wouldn't have to go through it twice, wouldn't start doubting himself the way he'd done after their first practice runs. Leo had hated seeing Joshua so small and uncertain, and if it happened again today... Please, no. It didn't help that neither Mo nor Tristan had been able to make it. Nate had ducked out as well, tending to avoid gatherings of too many unfamiliar faces.

Just Leo, then.

"*Relax*," James repeated. His smile was kind. "That's an order."

Stiffly, Leo nodded. Right, okay. He needed to chill. Chill, chill, chill. He was an iced tea, a frozen cucumber, a tub of Ben & Jerry's. He was so totally cool, no one had been this cool in the history of forever.

Fuck, if *he* was a bundle of nerves already, he could only imagine what it must be like for Joshua.

When the flurry of activity in the room ceased for an instant, then picked up again with an almost frantic quality to it, Leo knew that the Royal Family had arrived. He turned, immediately seeking out Joshua where he was shielded by his mother and sister. Walking with his head held high, he was in a black, tailored suit that fit him beautifully, emphasising his broad shoulders and slender hips, clinging to his thighs.

As soon as Leo got past the sheer loveliness of Joshua's body to focus on his face, he felt his own muscles lock up. Joshua's eyes were glassy, his skin pale.

Oh, fuck.

JOSHUA WAS GOING to throw up. He would open his mouth to answer the first question—*Good evening, how are you?*—and instead of words, his breakfast would hit the floor. It would be an excruciatingly dreadful experience for everyone involved.

Setting one foot in front of the other, he did his best to block out the hectic buzz of activity, people swarming around them, his mother addressing someone in a clear, sharp voice. Emma's arm was linked through his and he tried to focus on that. Left foot. Right foot.

"Baby, are you all right?" Warm concern, and Joshua needed a moment to understand that it had been his mum, a question directed at him, and fuck, he was so far from all right that there were continents, entire universes, that set him apart.

He swallowed around the bile rising to the back of his throat and managed a nod. "Just need a second to—I'll be right back, please excuse me. I'll be—gents. Right back."

With that, he unwound himself and turned, took quick steps for the exit, *keep your shoulders straight and your head high, you look up to no one.* He thought there might be someone calling after him, but it merely prompted him to pick up the pace.

He made it out of the room, rounded a corner, leaned his back against the wall. Blessed quiet surrounded him. He tipped his head back and closed his eyes.

Breathe.

Huge, gulping intakes of air. Exhaling in a rush.

Repeat.

An unexpected touch to his shoulder made him jump.

"Joshua," Leo said, "*Princeling*," and then he drew Joshua in for a rough embrace that shocked a gasp out of Joshua. "Hey," Leo murmured, quiet now, right by Joshua's ear. "Hey, hi, *breathe*. Breathe with me."

"I—" Joshua coughed. His ribs were pressing down on his lungs, and the backs of his lids were drenched in red. "I can't. Leo, I can't do this."

"Yes, you can." Leo sounded so *confident*, and where did he take that confidence from when he'd been there for Joshua's practice runs, had heard him mess up and stumble over his own words? When he'd seen it all?

"I can't," Joshua repeated, and Leo was silent for a beat before he pulled back. Both his hands remained on Joshua's shoulders, heavy through the fabric of Joshua's suit, heavy like expectations, heavy like disappointment. Joshua refused to open his eyes.

"Josh." Leo's tone was imploring. "Look at me."

Squeezing his lids shut, Joshua shook his head.

"Joshua." This time, it came out as a command, and it only made Joshua take a blind step back and collide with the wall, still shaking his head. He couldn't. He *couldn't*, could *not*.

"I *can't*."

For a moment, Leo's grip loosened, and Joshua thought that he'd leave, that he would walk away from this pathetic mess. Leo had been right all along: Joshua didn't deserve any of the privileges life had thrown his way, not when he couldn't even hold himself together long enough to be honest for once.

Then Leo crowded right back into Joshua's space. Their bodies pressed together from head to hip to toe, the leather of Leo's jacket whispering over Joshua's skin. Joshua's thoughts stuttered to a halt.

"Joshua. *Josh*." It came out soft, reverent. Leo slid one of his hands underneath Joshua's suit jacket, his palm flat against the small of Joshua's back. Bringing them even closer. "Don't do this. Don't bring yourself down. You're lovely, okay? You're so, so lovely, and I just—you can do this. I know you can, because I've seen you. Take that fear and shove it where the sun don't shine, okay? Or" —his hand was rucking up the back of Joshua's dress shirt— "wear it like a crown."

Joshua's stomach swelled with a deep breath. He didn't dare

move. With his eyes still shut against the world, there was no way to escape Leo's warmth, the faint whiff of his cologne, the damp brush of his lips over Joshua's jaw.

Blinking, it took Joshua a few seconds to bring Leo's face into focus. They were so close that Leo's features seemed blurred. "What do you—Leo?"

Leo was staring back at Joshua with a strange kind of intensity, holding himself perfectly still. So *close*, God, and Joshua was desperately aware of all the places where they were touching, heat radiating outwards from Leo's hand against Joshua's back, shivering through his veins. Somewhere far, far away, a voice was calling Joshua's name.

Leo startled. His gaze flicked away, then back to Joshua. Eyes wide, it was as though his expression had broken open, a desperate edge to his whisper. "I really want to kiss you."

Oh God.

Oh God.

Before Joshua could find words or even just his voice, before he could so much as *move*, Leo had wrenched himself away. Two feet of space suddenly gaped between them, and it felt like a mile.

Joshua was about to reach for him—*please, please, yes*—but Leo had already taken another step back. Then Emma barrelled around the corner, aubergine hair streaking behind her. She nearly collided with Leo, spared him an absent, "Sorry, excuse me," and was gripping Joshua's shoulder by the time Leo nodded. It turned out shaky, his gaze linked with Joshua's for another instant before he looked away.

"It's showtime, Shrimp," Emma announced, and—wait. Shit. The interview. Joshua had just about forgotten.

He did want to go through with it. And he would.

Finding Emma's eyes, Joshua worked up a grin, or something that should pass for a grin, anyway. Showtime. "Okay. Let's do this, then?"

"Let's do this," she confirmed, tugging him into motion. By the time Joshua remembered how to move, Leo was already several steps ahead, his spine straight, his shoulders stiff. He did glance back over his shoulder, though, and when he did, it was to direct a reassuring smile at Joshua.

It was enough for Joshua's chest to loosen.
You can do this.

~

THERE'D BEEN A MOMENT—LIKE balancing on a tightrope, like flipping a coin—when Leo hadn't known which way he'd turn. All he'd known was that Joshua needed *something* from him; a push or a pull, a kick or a kiss.

Leo had almost taken a verbal swing at him. He'd been so close, had already tasted the taunt on his tongue, wondered whether Joshua would have believed it just long enough to rise to the challenge. *So you're just the kind of coward I always thought you were. Not sure what I expected. Not like you ever had to fight for something, eh, Princeling? Go on, then. Protect your pathetic little lie of a life. Hope the gold makes for a pretty cage.*

And then Leo had gone for honesty.

Even now, he could feel his heart beating in his fingertips, pulsing out echoes of his own words; *I really want to kiss you.* Each time he blinked, he saw the shock written into Joshua's features. Before, Leo had thought Joshua might be at least a little interested, but now... Well. Guess not. At least Leo's words had served their purpose. Job done.

From the sideline, he watched as Joshua smiled at Dimbleby, easy and sweet, ducking his head a little to avoid the brightness of the spotlights. His voice held a bashful note as he talked about how he wanted a family one day, wanted to get married and have kids, really not very different from the kind of things a heterosexual man might aspire to.

He was beautiful, and Leo still wanted to kiss him.

Wanted so much more than just that.

~

THE FIRST TAKE of the interview had been as close to perfect as these things ever were. Dimbleby requested they do a second one anyway, just to be certain they had options, and Leo could see Joshua swallow, lips tightening briefly, before he nodded.

Halfway through the second take, Tristan arrived out of nowhere, sliding into the space next to Leo. With the way Leo had been solely focused on Joshua, Tristan's sudden appearance startled him. He fought to disguise his reaction by cocking an eyebrow, voice low so it wouldn't interrupt the recording. "How did *you* get in? Security's really shit at this place, isn't it?"

"I could totally run this show," Tristan said with a grin. "I always wanted to be—like the Master of Whispers in *Game of Thrones*? The spider guy pulling the strings in the background? Dream job."

"Varys," Leo supplied. "The bald eunuch. I'm sorry, but you're not creepy enough. Or discrete enough. Or castrate enough. Or sticking-to-the-shadows enough."

"I'm wounded." Tristan's grin didn't dim at all. He leaned his shoulder against the wall next to Leo, glancing over at where Joshua was perched between his mother and his sister, the three of them presenting a strong, united front. As it should be. Even Joshua's father, estranged from his children to the point that Joshua said they talked maybe once a month, had found words of encouragement when Joshua had called him earlier in the day.

Leo was glad that Joshua could fall back on the support of his family.

"You'll live," Leo remembered to tell Tristan.

Together, they watched the rest of the interview. Everything went smoothly, Joshua stumbling over a response only once, and then laughing at himself in a way that would win him every heart in the country. Well, every heart that wasn't made of stone. Or wrapped up in homophobic hate or anti-monarchist prejudices.

God. Jesus fucking *Christ*, Joshua was doing this. In five hours, at seven p.m. sharp, the interview would air as a special, short-notice programme change on *BBC One*, and it would drop like a bomb. Every single British newspaper would yell the story from its cover tomorrow. International newspapers would do the same—and while many would applaud his courage, some would paint it as a sin. People he'd never met would hate him for no reason other than his sexuality. He'd be at the centre of a storm, and for all that they'd mapped out the consequences, it had been guess work. What if reality proved them wrong?

Leo wanted to call it off. He wanted to grab Joshua and get him out of this room, out of this city, hide him where the world couldn't touch him.

It wasn't in his power.

The moment the interview was over, Tristan shoved away from the wall and was the first person to wrap himself bodily around Joshua, smothering him in an embrace. Joshua sagged into it. Over Tristan's shoulder, he found Leo's gaze. Joshua's smile was all in his eyes, a warm gleam that made Leo's heart perform a drunken lurch. He grinned through it, gave Joshua a thumbs-up.

Tristan released Joshua to make room for Emma, and then Joshua was suddenly swarmed by people, like moths to a flame. Everyone wanted a piece of him.

Leo snuck out of the room without catching Joshua's eye again. He pulled out his phone to send him a quick message—*'You did fantastic !! I have to take care of some stuff at the office , see you tonight for the broadcast?'*—and left the Palace without looking back. He felt like someone fleeing the scene of a crime.

7

Leo spent the next few hours buried in work, finalising things. Carole and George had joined forces to select wholesome pictures of Joshua that went with the I-want-to-be-married-with-kids narrative, complementing pre-written articles that would be distributed as soon as the interview aired. Online portals in particular would gratefully gobble them up — anything for a speedy release.

Controlling the first wave was key to smoothing the entire ride.

At six, Leo shut down his computer. While he felt vaguely guilty about leaving the rest of the team to field the immediate aftermath, he and Nate had promised Joshua they'd be with him. Handling the client was part of the job, wasn't it? Sure was. Even if their main task consisted of keeping Joshua away from the unfiltered fallout by distracting him.

They rode the tube in silence, Nate fiddling with his phone and Leo staring blankly at an advert for an Open University course. *Uncover your potential.* Surrounded by tourists, they got off at Camden Town, emerged into a grey evening and walked the rest of the way to Joshua's flat, Leo with his hands shoved deep into the pockets of his jeans.

"You nervous?" Nate asked, just before they rang the bell.

"It's not my future that's at stake," Leo told him.

"No. But you care about him." Nate's tone was unassuming, and Leo didn't bother with an answer. Of course he cared. More than he should.

He pressed down on the doorbell, released it, then rang again, just to be a git. Normal, right. This was just like any normal day, nothing out of the ordinary. After watching the interview, there'd be beer, there'd be football talk, there'd be teasing and video games. Just a normal lads night.

The door buzzed open to let them in. With a deep breath, Leo led the way up the stairs.

THEY WATCHED the interview in utter stillness—no one moved, no one spoke. At times, Leo wasn't convinced he knew how to breathe. Next to him on the sofa, Joshua was frozen, not so much as a twitch of a muscle.

After Tristan had flicked the TV off and plunged the room into silence, Leo counted to ten in his head before he turned to look at Joshua. Face pale, Joshua's skin was damp with sweat, his pupils so wide they reduced his irises to slim rings of green. When Leo nudged their fingers together, Joshua jolted.

"I'm fine," he squeezed out.

Yeah. Nice try.

Leo bit the inside of his cheek and nodded. "Let's play some FIFA, all right? Have another beer, order pizza."

"I'd like that," Joshua said, barely audible, and Leo longed to touch him, run gentle fingers through his hair until the tension in his muscles evaporated. By the time Leo dragged his gaze away, Tristan was already on the phone to order food and Nate had jumped up to fetch another round of beer. Mo had curled further into Joshua's other side, his head tipped against Joshua's shoulder.

Just a normal evening, yes. They'd try.

THEY DID TRY. It was a valid effort to project normalcy. Except Leo's stomach felt sick with unease each time he received an update on his phone that he checked as subtly as he could; except for the weighted glances they exchanged behind Joshua's back and the way they all orbited around him, hugging him at random, petting his hair, slinging an arm around his waist or squeezing his hand. Leo shouldn't let himself get this close, but Joshua seemed so small and fragile even as he tried to put on a brave front. The need to reassure him overrode Leo's sense of self-preservation.

Once in a while, Leo could feel Joshua staring at him for several beats too long, a question in his eyes. Because Leo was a coward, he was quick to look away, and he also made sure that he wouldn't find himself alone with Joshua.

He wanted to kiss Joshua so badly that his throat ached with it. But that didn't make it a good idea.

Maybe, if they kissed once, just *once*, to satisfy the current of tension running between them... They'd kiss, and it would be nice, but nothing more than that. They'd separate, would grin at each other with a hint of bashful embarrassment, and Leo would say, "Friends?" with a chuckle that Joshua would echo.

One kiss. One tiny, little kiss, and Leo would realise that he wasn't in love. *Surely.*

It was just after eleven when Tristan called it a night. After tackling Joshua to the floor, then uttering a hurried goodbye, he dashed out the door, late in picking up his girlfriend from the airport. Shortly later, Leo clambered to his feet as well, legs numb from being crouched in front of the TV for half an hour, battling it out with Nate.

"Let's call it a draw," Leo declared, and Nate frowned up at him.

"I was winning."

"That's what you tell yourself," Leo said comfortably. Offering a hand to Nate, it took a moment before Nate accepted it with a shake of his head.

"You're unbelievable, you know that?"

Leo gave him his widest, toothiest grin. "Thank you, darling. Such flattery, how very kind." Turning to look at Joshua, Leo felt his expression settle into something much too soft. "Listen, Princeling. I need you to stay away from the internet, as well as from the telly. Don't go out. Basically, grab yourself a good book and sit tight for a couple of days, at least until the World Cup starts or Bieber lands himself in some kind of mess. Got it?"

"You're leaving?" Apprehension was plain to read in Joshua's eyes, and fuck, Leo wished he *could* stay. Nothing was fair.

"It's back to the office for us. Time difference means the US are just waking up, so this is the beginning of our night shift."

"I'm sorry." Joshua dropped his gaze.

"Joshua, it's our *job*." As soon as it was out, Leo wanted to punch himself in the face. Joshua meant so much more than a job. He meant *so much*.

He meant everything.

Before Leo could add anything else, Nate had stepped on his toes —since they were both barefoot, it didn't hurt, but it drove the message home. "It's also an *honour*," Nate said pointedly. "At least in this particular case."

Quickly, Leo nodded. "It really is."

While Joshua didn't reply, he lifted his gaze, glancing from Leo to Nate and back, then forced a tentative smile. "Thank you for everything, you know?"

Nate didn't hesitate to pull Joshua into a hug, and Leo spared a momentary thought for how two weeks ago, Nate wouldn't have been nearly so quick to do this—not only because Joshua had been Prince Joshua, but also because Nate had been more restrained with physical affection, more restrained in general. The same was true for Leo. Spending time with Joshua, Mo and Tristan really had done a number on them, catching like an infection. In the best way.

Squeezing into the middle of Joshua and Nate, Leo inhaled deeply. The faint trace of Joshua's cologne made him want to cry.

Fuck, Joshua had done it. He'd *done* it.

"You did it," Leo whispered just as he felt Mo joining the group hug, grumbling about not wanting to be left out. Nate angled closer to Mo, a seemingly unconscious move that took him slightly away from Joshua and Leo, and suddenly, Leo was all too aware of the press of Joshua's body, the sharp jut of one hipbone against Leo's stomach. When Joshua's lips brushed over Leo's cheekbone, Leo held very still.

"Thank you," Joshua repeated, so quiet it was meant for Leo's ears only.

Leo took a measured breath and stepped back. His smile felt like a foreign entity. "You're welcome, little prince. Really." Another breath. "As Nate said, it is an honour."

With that, he nudged Nate, who startled, then made to ease himself out of Mo's embrace. Mo held on for several moments longer, a tiny grin quirking the corners of his mouth. They were ridiculous. If Leo weren't wrought out of barbs and wires, he'd consider it sweet.

A quick glance proved that Joshua was still watching him, confused and maybe a little hopeful. Fuck, Leo needed to get away before he did something he'd regret.

After another round of goodbyes, he and Nate were tripping down the stairs, whereas Mo had announced he'd stay the night to keep Joshua from the news. It made sense, and Leo was glad Joshua wouldn't be alone. He wasn't sure how he felt about it being Mo, but... he held no claim. He couldn't.

"So what's up with you and Joshua?" Nate asked once they'd made it out of the building, the night like velvet. The road lay deserted, and they descended another flight of stairs to follow the footpath beside Regent's Canal. Distant lights reflected off the water.

Leo took his time coming up with a reply. He didn't have one, really, because whatever was going on—it couldn't happen. Joshua wanted steady and long-term, someone who'd be by his side in public, and that person couldn't be Leo. If the media caught so much as a whiff, they wouldn't rest until they'd dragged the sordid mess of Leo's past into the open, and Leo didn't—he couldn't—*fuck*.

What if Joshua looked at him differently after he found out? All of Joshua's warmth twisting into disgust? Or—God. What if Joshua stuck with Leo, and the public would judge him for it? What if they cast Joshua as a sleazy, sex-driven creep?

"Nothing," Leo said slowly. He felt cold and small. "Absolutely nothing is up with Joshua and me."

Their steps echoed hollowly on the path, the boats they passed swaying gently, a few portholes painting bright circles into the night. "Hey." Nate's tone was offhand, contrasting with a quick, probing glance he directed at Leo. "Are you bothered by Joshua and Mo spending the night together? Just the two of them?"

Against his will, Leo's shoulders tightened. "Are you?"

"I asked first," Nate said. They walked several paces in silence, past a houseboat where three blokes were camped out on deck, sipping their beers with barely a word being spoken in the time it took Leo and Nate to leave them behind. When Leo turned to look at Nate, Nate's head was ducked, gaze on the ground. "I don't think," Nate started quietly, carefully, "they're like that anymore. Mo mentioned he didn't get laid since Spain."

What the fuck?

"Okay, now I am worried." Leo's voice was too loud, travelling in the tranquillity of the night.

Nate looked up. "You're worried?"

"Not *worried* worried." Leo tucked his T-shirt into the waistband of his black jeans and pulled his leather jacket tighter around himself. Soft with use, it was the only piece of clothing he'd kept from his time on the street, and when he'd found it again a couple of days ago, it had taken him a minute to wrestle down the onslaught of memories stitched into its seams. "I'm merely a concerned third party. Joshua is very vulnerable right now, after all, and so Mo really shouldn't—"

"You think Mo would take advantage of him?" Nate interrupted, a rare note of sharpness to the question. He stopped in the middle of the path, shrouded in shadows. "Fuck, Leo. They're friends. And Mo wouldn't."

"I'm not saying he'd take advantage, that's not what I meant. I just meant, maybe..." Leo exhaled. "I don't know what I'm saying."

Nate was quiet for a beat, studying him. Then he shrugged. "You're jealous. For the record, it makes you act like a dick."

Something in Leo sagged, like a rollercoaster tipping over a drop. "I have no right to be jealous."

"Doesn't mean you're not."

"I know they're not romantic. Joshua and Mo. I know that, but I don't want..." Leo's voice sounded weak to his own ears, brittle. The night got tangled around his words. "I don't want anyone else touching Joshua. No one but me." *Fuck.* "Fuck, I can't—"

"Hey, guess what?" Nate cut in, sounding strangely delighted. "I really think Mo told me that for a reason, the whole not having had sex. Like, to make the point that he and Joshua aren't fucking around anymore. That they're strictly friends now."

It took Leo a few seconds to work through Nate's meaning. Then his shoulders dropped, breath escaping him in a long rush. "Biggs, you fucker." He started walking again. "You played me. You totally played me. You tricked me into admitting that I'm..." Jealous as hell. "Worried."

"Learned from the best, didn't I?" Nate skipped a couple of steps to catch up. While clearly proud of himself, an edge of concern had seeped into his voice, and when Leo glanced over, Nate was watching him carefully. With a sigh, Leo nudged their shoulders together. Camden Lock was just up ahead, the branches of weeping willows brushing the water's surface, and they crossed the bridge to the other side of the Canal, everything calm and peaceful safe for the scattered tourists leaning on the banister. It could have been any normal night.

"Let's make a detour past the Palace," Leo suggested. "I want to see how bad it is."

Nate didn't reply, but he shifted a little closer, unspoken reassurance in the repeating bump of their elbows.

BUCKINGHAM PALACE WAS UNDER SIEGE. Floodlit, it stood like a beacon in the night with flocks of reporters in front of the gates, curious onlookers mixed in with them to create the impression of a feeding frenzy. Leo and Nate stood side by side, overwhelmed, Leo's sense of equilibrium oddly shaky. God, if he hadn't encouraged Joshua, this would not be happening. The media wouldn't have called on the hunt.

It had been Joshua's decision. Still, Leo had played a part in it. What if he'd been wrong, what if they'd *all* been wrong and this would end horribly?

Once again, he fought down the impulse to grab Joshua and run. He'd never been more grateful that the location of Joshua's flat wasn't common knowledge.

"Let's go," Nate said after what might have been minutes, might have been hours.

Leo nodded and made himself turn away, move.

THE TIP of Mo's cigarette sparked orange, smoke curling up towards the dark sky. Joshua fanned the smell away from his face, then fell onto his back. "Can we sleep out here?" he asked. He hated how it came out: lost and thin. "I think I need to remind myself that there's a normal life out there."

"'Course." Mo's cheeks hollowed around the last drag, then he dropped the stub and extinguished it with the bottom of his beer bottle. Rolling into Joshua's side, he tucked an arm around Joshua's waist, and they lay quietly for a short while, breathing together. The gentle, regular rhythm of their rising and falling chests eased the tension behind Joshua's forehead, his muscles loosening gradually.

He turned his head to press his nose into Mo's hair—cigarettes and hair spray, spicy aftershave Joshua would always, always connect to him.

"Hey, Mo?" Joshua laced their fingers together. "Leo said he wanted to kiss me. Earlier today. Before the interview."

"Did he now?" Mo didn't sound surprised. There was a smile tucked into his voice.

"Yes." Joshua closed his eyes and imagined he could watch the word float into the night. "I mean, we didn't. No time, and, I don't know. It was so out of the blue that I couldn't even react. Maybe he just said it to shock me. Like, because I was really nervous?"

Mo's response consisted of a low hum, which honestly wasn't helpful.

"I think" —Joshua inhaled on a sigh— "he avoided me tonight. Or, not like he avoided me as such, but like... avoided being alone with me. And earlier, he left as soon as the interview was done."

"Does he know you want to kiss him too?" Mo asked. "Along with other things you want to do to his body, I'm sure. Did you clarify that?"

Grabbing a pillow, Joshua shoved it under his head and thought back to that moment outside the White Drawing Room—the slow sweep of Leo's lashes, the husky quality of his voice, the way he'd been pressed all along Joshua's front. How Joshua hadn't got in so much as a word before Emma had startled them apart.

"I'd never reject him," Joshua whispered. It felt heavy in a way he didn't quite understand.

"Well, yeah." Mo twisted a little closer, raised his head and bit Joshua's chin, then moved back with a soft snicker. "Like, the thing is, you and I and Tristan know that. Question is, does Leo?"

After flicking Mo's nose, Joshua rubbed his chin while he considered the question. Joshua had been pretty obvious, right? But Nate had probably thought the same, not factoring in Mo's astonishingly thick skull. Maybe Leo was on a Mo level of oblivious? He didn't seem the type at all, always so aware of everything, but you never knew.

"Maybe not," Joshua admitted. "But I can't exactly corner him when he's avoiding me, can I? And I don't want to do it over the phone. That'd be weird."

"We'll just have to create an opportunity for you, then." Mo sounded positively gleeful, as though he was scheming already. Joshua wasn't sure he approved; Mo's plans had landed him in trouble more than once, more than twice. A particularly shining example was that time they'd ended up in a drunk tank even though they'd been completely sober. Johnson's predecessor had bailed them out before the press had caught wind of it, and the lecture Joshua had had to endure in return had been a small price.

The press. Not thinking about that, no.

Burying a hand in Mo's hair, Joshua used his other hand to tug on Mo's arm until they were pressed together, one of Joshua's legs slotted between Mo's thighs. It was comfortable, and only when they'd both settled in did Joshua think to ask, "Should this be weird? I mean, with the way we—you know. And now talking about Leo and me?"

"Mate. Sometimes, I find it hard to believe you were ever trained in eloquence." Mo lifted himself up to grin at Joshua. "And nah, don't see why this should be weird. Up to us, isn't it?"

Joshua grinned back. "Exactly. Just, some people don't seem to get it. Us. Like, Leo keeps asking me, and I think—maybe he gets it now. What about Nate?"

Dropping back down to rest his head on Joshua's chest, Mo reached for the afghan to cover them both up. Only then did he reply. "Yeah, pretty sure that he gets it. But it's still like... Feel like I'm out of my depth with him, you know? Being friends when there's always this thing where we could be more?"

"*I'm* your friend," Joshua said, "and we did plenty more." To illustrate, he cupped Mo's bum and gave it a friendly squeeze. Mo reacted with an exaggerated moan that echoed strangely in the quiet night, making both of them snicker.

A month ago, they might have taken it from there, playing around until one of them moved in for a kiss, just to test the mood. A month ago, Mo hadn't met Nate, and Joshua hadn't met Leo.

"Except" —Mo slumped into Joshua's side, tone wistful— "you were always my friend first, and anything else was just... you know. Whatever."

"Hey," Joshua protested, pinching Mo's bicep. "Have a little respect for my ego, thanks."

Mo snorted. "Not like you're not a good lover, babe. Taught you some of those tricks myself, didn't I? It just wasn't ever key to our relationship, more like a very nice bonus."

It was true. Somehow, their friendship had never been questioned, and only now did it occur to Joshua that they might have been extremely fortunate in how they'd always been on the same page. He pondered it for a moment before he asked, "Did you ever wonder how come... Why we never fell in love? With each other, I mean. If you look at us, all the ingredients should be there, but it just never happened."

"Yeah, I wondered about that." Mo's tone was thoughtful. "Think we might have been a bad match, probably. We're both pretty easygoing, yeah, and that makes us a great fit as friends, but maybe not so good romantically. Missing that spark of fascination, like."

"The challenge?" Joshua asked, and yes, that made sense. He chuckled at the mere idea of them lobbing insults at each other in passionate anger. "We'd never fight, would we?"

"Nah, we wouldn't. You and Leo, on the other hand..." Amusement shining through, Mo trailed off.

You and Leo.

Joshua found himself smiling. Shifting a little, he turned to study Mo's face, its details shrouded in shadows. "What about you and Nate? Do you think you've got that spark?"

"He's... complicated." Mo paused. "I think there's a lot more than meets the eye, and I think... With him, it could be..."

When a few seconds had passed without another word from Mo, Joshua finished for him. "You want to *date* him. Make sweet love under the moonlight."

"Smug doesn't suit you," Mo muttered.

"I'm not smug." Joshua considered it. "Okay. Maybe a little. I mean, you're the one who always called me a ridiculous romantic, like, with my dreams of something steady and exclusive. And now look at you." He bit back the urge to coo at Mo—mainly because Mo's knee was dangerously close to his groin, and Joshua valued his ability to reproduce. Even if he wasn't quite certain about his options just yet.

"Fuck off." Belying that, Mo inched closer, his exhalation escaping him in a sigh. Draping an arm around his waist, Joshua hummed a little. For a short while, they remained like that, the night breathing around them. Somewhere not too far off, a car honked, offset by the stuttering engine of a boat on the Canal below.

Ordinary sounds. So easy to forget that in this very same city, hundreds of people were bound to be dealing with the consequences of Joshua's interview—Leo, Nate and the rest of their team, George and his staff, reporters for newspapers and TV, bloggers, people discussing it online. Everyone who had an opinion would itch to put it out there, for London to see.

No. This wasn't just London. This was global.

"Hey, Mo?" Staring up at the sky, Joshua tried to make out individual stars and couldn't. Light pollution drenched everything in a gentle orange glow.

He remembered how, when he'd been thirteen and anxious about living at Eton, Emma had claimed that all boarding schools were like Hogwarts. He'd arrived expecting a big lake and an enormous dining hall with a ceiling littered with stars. Instead, he'd found himself in a school that was by no means in a remote Scottish location, had joined a house where pupils ate in a smaller common area rather than in the central dining complex where many other houses gathered, and the proximity of London had eliminated all chances of a splendid nighttime sky. On the other hand, he'd got Tristan out of it.

"What?" Mo asked when Joshua had been silent for a moment.

Joshua cleared his throat. "Do you think me weak for hiding right now? Should I be out there? Listening and reading what people are saying?"

"No." Mo's voice was sharp in a way it hardly ever was. "There's bound to be some nasty stuff mixed in with the good, because you're rich and a public figurehead, and some people are jealous shitheads. They don't deserve your attention. And I think..." He paused, one of his hands nudging underneath Joshua's T-shirt. "You already said your piece. For now. Anything else wouldn't improve the message, you know? Think it might cheapen it, even. Time to let the professionals do their thing and not give a fuck about what some stranger on the internet says about you liking dick. It doesn't matter."

"I'm trying to get there," Joshua said softly. "Not caring so much what people think, separating what matters and what doesn't. Getting better at it, I think. Incrementally so." Briefly, he weighed his next words. For some reason, he hadn't shared the specifics of the time he'd spent with just Leo on Saturday. It had felt private somehow, but then again, Leo hadn't asked him to keep it a secret. So. "Three days ago, that morning I went to Leo's place because you and Tristan weren't around?" Joshua frowned at the too-bright night sky. "Leo does some kind of volunteer street worker thing, and he took me along. Those kids are—I can't imagine what it would be like, that kind of life. Scavenging for food, sleeping with someone for a little bit of money. *That's* rough."

"Joshua." Mo's fingers curled against Joshua's stomach, knuckles digging in. "You'll never have to find out. That'll never be you."

"That's not what I meant. I just meant..." Another boat stuttered past, and an echo of the humming engine buzzed behind Joshua's forehead. "I meant that compared to that, it's really—the things I'm worried about, they're quite marginal. Unless the Commonwealth breaks apart, but as Leo so kindly likes to point out: if a little gay prince is all it takes, the foundation must have been weak already."

"Not funny," Mo said.

"I don't think it's meant to be funny." Joshua followed it up by tightening his arm around Mo's waist. "Hey, you were never... I know there were times when money was tight, but with your job, and the scholarship, you always made it work, right?"

It wasn't the first time Joshua had wondered about it; he and Tristan had even discussed it a few times when they'd all still been at university. They'd never dared ask an outright question, though, well aware that Mo had grown uncomfortable each time they'd so much as tried to broach the topic. Maybe it would be different, now that Mo had easily paid off his academic debts and a spacious flat on top of it.

For an instant, Mo's body tensed against Joshua's. Then it went lax again. "It was never anywhere near that bad for me," he said quietly. "Yeah, there were times I had to—like, when I shopped for groceries, and it was always picking the cheapest jam, and maybe no yoghurt because it was the end of the month and toast was cheaper. Some-times, the luxury still hits me now, you know? Just the simple fact I can pop to the shops and grab whatever jam looks best, that I don't have to keep track of what's in my basket."

Jesus Christ. Joshua couldn't even imagine what that would be like—always counting, calculating. It sounded horrible, a constant weight to carry.

Instead of voicing those thoughts, he pulled Mo even closer, burying his nose in Mo's hair. "When Tristan and I asked you along when we went out," he began, low and careful, "you said no some-times, right, because you didn't have the money. We thought as much. But you also hardly ever let us invite you, or allowed us to skip you when it came to paying for a round. We kept trying, and you wouldn't let us. Why?"

Mo was quiet for so long Joshua thought he wouldn't answer. Just as Joshua was about to give up, Mo spoke, tone hesitant. "I didn't want your pity, you know? Or worse, if you had thought I was using you. I know it's happened to both you and Tristan, people hanging on for the money or the status, and I never wanted you to see me as that person."

Oh. That was so... so *Mo*. And it made much more sense than Tristan and Joshua wondering whether Mo had been ashamed, or felt he couldn't trust them with his problems.

"You could have said as much," Joshua told him, nose still buried in Mo's hair. "We could have worked out something."

"Joshua." Mo's smile showed in his voice. "There was nothing to work out. I wouldn't have accepted money from either of you. *Espe-cially* not from you. With us screwing around sometimes, it'd have been wrong. I didn't ever want you to feel like you were paying for my company. 'Cause mutual fun and all."

There were so many things Joshua could say. He settled for swal-lowing around the lump in his throat and curling his fingers into the hem of Mo's T-shirt. "Very eloquent, darling," he commented. "Remind me why they didn't appoint you as my coach?"

"Fuck off, love."

Joshua grinned. "Love you, you know?"

"'Course you do." Mo lifted himself up for a wet smooch to Joshua's cheek before he dropped back down. "You should," he said around a yawn, "go get us an actual duvet."

"Why don't you get it?" Joshua asked. "You're a model, you need to stay in shape. Some physical exercise would serve you well." The urge to yawn had transferred from Mo to him, and he fought it for a moment, just on the principle of it, before he gave in. Raising a hand to cover it up, he was already sliding out from under the afghan, Mo releasing him with a brief delay.

On bare feet, down to boxers and a T-shirt, Joshua padded inside to grab one of the duvets off the guest bed. He imagined it smelled like Leo.

Fuck, Joshua was ridiculous.

When he returned to the terrace, Mo was blinking at him with a sleep-heavy smile, barely visible in the shadows. Joshua tucked him in like a child, pinched his cheek and called him Mo-bee, earning himself a half-hearted grumble of complaint.

Still Mo lifted the duvet for Joshua to slide in with him, and they drifted off tangled and warm, comfortable. Familiar. Vaguely, Joshua wondered what this would look like to someone who didn't under-stand them—a potential boyfriend, maybe. If someone didn't get the closeness between him and Mo, between him and Mo and Tristan... Joshua couldn't ever be with a guy who didn't fit in with all of them, even less with someone who would object to their easy physical proximity.

He tried not to think of Leo.

Failed.

LEO WENT HOME at around three in the morning, took a quick shower and slept for a small number of hours. He was back in the office by eight.

Around noon, just as Leo was smoking his one allotted cigarette of the day, Joshua called him for a status report. Leo was glad that he didn't have to lie because all things considered, it was a fairly positive reaction. Granted, there were some low blows—the likes of the Westboro Baptist Church had jumped on the news, salivating as though they'd caught a case of the rabies—but the echo in the relevant European, American and Commonwealth papers ranged from neutral to positive, and many of the customary jokes in talk shows revolved around suitable husbands for Prince Joshua. Alan Carr was planning to introduce a section to his show called *Who Wants to Marry the Prince?*, where two male celebrities were pitted against each other.

"And guess who wrote about half of all those jokes?" Grinning, Leo tapped some ash over the balcony banister and didn't wait for Joshua's answer. "Yes, that's right. *Me.* I do hope you appreciate that I got Ian McKellen onto the list of your husband candidates. Classy bloke. Out of your league, if we're being honest."

Other names Leo had put on the list were David Beckham (already married to a posh one), the guy playing that vampire (creepy and too much sparkle even for a gay prince), the Pope (celibate), and Justin Bieber (probably on the way to rehab or prison). The fact that all of them were unfeasible candidates... well, that was down to the simple logic of comedy.

"Don't you think Ian is a tad outside my age range?" Joshua sounded bright, his voice airy with relief, and Leo wasn't even going to think about how Joshua was on a first-name basis with one of Britain's greatest actors. Nope.

"He's *Gandalf*," Leo said. "And age is just a number, love conquers all, yadda yadda."

Joshua snorted. "Repeat that, but with conviction."

"True love," Leo went for a smarmy, overly dramatic tone, "conquers all. But if that doesn't do it, how about some hard, honest work?"

"Not much of a romantic, are you?" While Joshua's tone was still easy, Leo thought he detected an underlying hint of seriousness to it. Which—shit, no. If this was Joshua steering the conversation towards

Leo's line about wanting to kiss him? Then Leo needed to head it off right this very moment.

"Honestly?" he said. "Hard to get in the mood when there's a Royal Communications guy with a quiff camped out in your conference room and remarking on your bum each time you walk past."

"Wait, George is—sorry, he can be a bit inappropriate, especially when he's stressed out. I'll tell him to stop." Joshua sounded upset when Leo had intended for it to be a joke. Really, he wasn't that bothered. He and George would never be friends, but over the last few days of being forced into close collaboration, they'd found a common ground built on mutual bickering. No harm, no foul.

"Don't worry about it," Leo said quickly. "It's in good fun, and I'm perfectly capable of taking care of myself. No need for you to bring your white mare." He paused to take a drag of his cigarette before switching gears. "Speaking of royal employees, I thought you might want to know that your Johnson bloke is now working as a doorman to some nightclub in San Francisco. Really looks like he's trying to build a new life for himself, and as far as we can tell, it doesn't seem like he's about to sell you out to the press."

Joshua was quiet for the time it took Leo to squish the cigarette, pinch it between thumb and forefinger and drop it into the chipped cup Nate had set out for him, to keep Leo from snipping the stubs over the banister. When Joshua spoke, it was slower than before, deep and calm.

"I'm glad."

Squinting into the blurry brightness of the sun, veiled by a semi-translucent cover of clouds, Leo bit his lip. "I still think you were too easy on him, just so you know."

"People deserve a second chance," Joshua said. "I mean, you of all people, with your street work thing... You believe in that, don't you?"

Wait a second.

Leo strove for an even tone. "Are you comparing living on the street to someone maliciously abusing your trust? You can't be bloody *serious*."

"That's not how I meant it. You know it's not, so don't take my words out of context, all right?" Joshua rushed to continue. "But a few of those kids have probably done questionable stuff, right? Shoplifting, breaking into a car to get at some money, doing drugs..."

"So every street kid is a lowly criminal or junkie, is that what you're saying?"

"*No*. Jesus, Leo." Joshua sighed, sounding tired all of a sudden. "Stop twisting my words. I just meant that some of them are bound to have broken the law. And a lot of that is probably just... trying to survive, or, like, scavenging for food or a place to stay. It doesn't make them bad people, just... desperate people. And I think Johnson was, too. Desperate, I mean."

The bitter taste of smoke lingered in Leo's mouth and made him swallow twice, in rapid succession. "What do you know about desperation?"

"I never said—"

"No, really," Leo interrupted. "Can I just ask—do you have the faintest idea what the price would be for a cup of coffee? Doesn't have to be Starbucks, just a normal cup of coffee at some café."

Joshua's hesitation was palpable. When he replied, it was edged with unease. "I do my own shopping, you know? Most of the time. I bought you fairy cakes, remember?"

"So how much were they?"

Again, Joshua took a moment to speak. "They, um. They kind of told me they were on the house. At the bakery. I gave them a tenner, though."

Ten quid for two fairy cakes. *Seriously*.

"I think you just proved my point," Leo told him. Joshua remained silent, and several seconds stuttered by before Leo felt abruptly cold. God, that had been out of line. Yes, of course, Joshua was naive about so many things, but he didn't deserve Leo's scorn. Not like that.

Leo was about to apologise when Joshua beat him to the point.

"I think you're being rather..." Joshua cleared his throat, voice quiet. "Rather unfair, really. I didn't mean to put those kids down. I said that I didn't know what it was like, living that kind of life. It must be tough, and I didn't mean... I'm not *judging*."

"I know." It came out gentle, and Leo drew a deep breath. "I'm sorry, Joshua. I just feel very, very protective of those kids, you know? To the point where I may overreact just a little. Or a lot. Especially when I'm tired. So, yeah. I'm sorry. It isn't you."

"I understand. To the extent someone like me could possibly understand, anyway." Hurt shone through Joshua's response, and Leo braced both elbows on the banister and rested his forehead on his arms.

Fuck, he needed to stop being a dick.

Tomorrow. He'd apologise tomorrow, when they'd all gather at Joshua's place to watch the opening match of the World Cup— already a glorious event in its own right, it was made all the more relevant since they were counting on it to take precedence over Joshua's coming out. Yes. Leo would apologise again tomorrow, in person. He'd give Joshua a hug and promise to be less of a dick in the future.

For now, he left it at, "Joshua, seriously, I am sorry. All right? Don't take it to heart. Let's just... I should get back to work, but I'll see you tomorrow night for the match, okay? We can talk then."

"You'll be there?" Joshua asked, and Leo hated that Joshua even thought to question it.

"Wouldn't miss it for the world," Leo told him. "I'll bring the beer, and I fully expect to win my first three points in our little betting game. Take the lead right away, you see? There's a fancy bottle of wine from the Palace cellar with my name on it."

Joshua's laugh seemed slightly forced, as did his, "Keep dreaming, darling."

Darling.

Leo bit down on the inside of his cheek and raised his forehead off his arms. "See you tomorrow," he said. "Stay away from the internet. And the telly. And the radio."

"You're basically telling me to become a recluse."

"Aren't Mo and Tristan keeping you company?"

"Tristan should be here any minute, I think." Joshua's tone had reverted back to something lighter, easier, and Leo felt his own mood lift. They were fine, then. Joshua wasn't holding grudges, it seemed.

"Tell him hi." Making his way back into the office, Leo found himself smiling and hoped it would translate. "I'll see you tomorrow, Princeling. Chin up, okay?"

"Okay," Joshua echoed.

"*Okay*." Leo nodded to himself and shit, this was ridiculous. He was meant to be smooth and eloquent. "Tomorrow," he repeated, then tagged on a quick goodbye and ended the call. He stood in the corridor for a moment longer, phone clutched in his fingers, before he took a calming breath, shoved aside all non-professional considerations, and made himself move.

Back to work.

It HAPPENED before Leo had a chance to react.

One minute, he and Joshua were arguing about the match result, with Leo maintaining that of course, of bloody *course* referees could be bought—in order to appease the political climate, the FIFA would do anything in its power to ensure that Brazil would come far in the tournament. The next minute, Nate, Tristan and Mo were calling out goodbyes, already halfway out the door, and Leo looked up and found himself alone with Joshua.

Well. So that had seemed like a well-executed plan. *Et tu, Nate?* Leo was impressed.

He was also *alone with Joshua*.

A moment of awkward silence stretched between them, the telly waffling on in the background, too quiet to make out single words. They started speaking at the same time, Joshua mumbling, "I really don't think—" just as Leo said, "So, about yesterday." Both of them fell silent once more.

"About yesterday?" Joshua asked after a gap that was even more awkward.

"Right." Leo exhaled and glanced at the TV. He was overly aware of how, in spite of the space now available, he and Joshua were still shoved together on the sofa, their thighs pressed together. "I just wanted to apologise. Again. You're a good person, really good, and yeah, there are some things you don't know, but that's not really your fault."

"I—" Joshua began, and Leo shook his head and sent him a tiny smile.

"No, hey, let me finish. Okay?" He waited for Joshua's nod before he continued. "Look, the thing is, I am a bit of a cynical arse at times. And overly defensive when it comes to certain things. And I don't deal well with feeling vulnerable, so I tend to lash out. It's a bit of a reflex at this point, one I'm trying to master." Too general, it was all too general; Joshua deserved more than that. With a sigh, Leo bumped their shoulders together. "Thing is... I know you don't mean to, but you do make me feel quite vulnerable. Which means that you are in the unfortunate position to have enjoyed a taste of me being a dick. More than once. Definitely much more than you deserve. So, I'm sorry about that."

Pulling both legs up onto the sofa, Joshua turned to face Leo fully. "I make you feel vulnerable?"

In for a penny, in for a pound. Leo forced himself to hold Joshua's gaze and responded with a nod. Unease was crawling along his skin, but he ignored it.

His reward came in Joshua shooting him a tiny smile. "Did you mean it?"

"My apology?"

Joshua's eyes were calm, all his contours mellowed out in the dim flicker from the telly. "When you said that you wanted to kiss me."

Oh God.

Leo swallowed. "It doesn't matter. I'm aware you're out of my league, thank you very much."

Hurt flashed over Joshua's face. "That's stupid, and you know it. It isn't—you don't usually treat me like a prince. I thought you didn't care anymore. That it's not..."

"It's not why I'm here tonight," Leo finished for him. He needed to shut his trap, needed to get out of here before he made a mistake, but —Joshua was so close, and he was just... so lovely. So very, very lovely. All green eyes and pale skin and unfairly red lips.

I always want to kiss you.

"Then why?" Joshua asked softly, and why what? Oh.

"Because you're my friend," Leo told him. "That's why I'm here. Not because you're a client of ours, or a prince, or some crap like that."

Another smile flashed over Joshua's face. Leo wanted to see him smile all the time; he wanted to be the reason for it.

Jesus, Leo was in too deep. Quicksand dragging him under.

When Joshua spoke again, it was with the quiet confusion of someone attempting to solve a riddle. "We are friends, but I also... I feel like I know so *little* about you. I don't even know how old you are." He frowned. "I know something happened with your family, and that you miss your sisters, but I don't know where you grew up. Whether it was in London, or if you came here to study. Whether you even did study."

Leo's skin felt brittle, transparent, his bones hollowed out from the inside. Sitting up straighter, he was about to get the hell away, already had the right words on the tip of his tongue that would remove him from this situation. Joshua was watching him with caution etched into the curve of his mouth.

With a measured intake of air, Leo forced the words back down.

Another breath. He loosened his posture and met Joshua's eyes. It felt as though the room was expanding around them, walls shrinking away like cockroaches that feared the light.

"I'm twenty-seven." Even this small piece of tangible, concrete truth tasted like sour grapes, foreign and acidic. "Born on the twenty-fourth of December. Wouldn't recommend it."

Drawing his knees up to his chest, Joshua folded his hands over them and set his chin on top. His smile was timid. "I take it Baby Jesus stole your thunder?"

I always want to kiss you, Leo's brain echoed, *always, always.*

So he reached out to fit his fingers around Joshua's jaw, leaned in and waited three slow, anxious heartbeats for Joshua to stop him. Instead, Joshua's lips parted on a soft exhale, warm air shivering over Leo's skin. He made no move to extract himself.

Leo kissed him.

The gap between a flash of lightning and the rolling of thunder. That's what it felt like, waiting for Joshua to respond.

Leo kept the pressure light, a gentle brush of his mouth over Joshua's, coaxing—and then, suddenly, Joshua turned into it, fingers tangling in Leo's hair to pull him in. Their noses bumped, and Joshua giggled softly even as he nudged closer, *closer*, mouth open and inviting. Christ, *yes*. Leo was vaguely aware of Joshua's knees digging into his chest. Mostly, he tasted salt and a hint of fruity sweetness, felt his own breath stutter around the realisation that he was kissing Joshua and Joshua was kissing him back; *they were kissing*.

He inhaled through his nose, glorious black flooding the space behind his lids and soothing his thoughts. The playful touch of their tongues, kitten-rough, and when Leo pulled back for a quick, gentle nip to Joshua's bottom lip, Joshua gave a tiny moan that was more a rush of breath, really. His thighs fell open.

Leo slotted into the space between them, cupped the back of Joshua's head as they sank into the cushions together. The world tilted with them, lurching on its axis. Or maybe it was Leo's heart lurching in his chest, like a drunkard trying to grapple for purchase.

Did that make sense? Nothing made sense. Everything made sense.

The buttons of their jeans caught as Leo pressed down, and Joshua exhaled on a breathy laugh that gusted over Leo's chin. Why was he laughing? Was he laughing at Leo, with Leo? Was it normal for Joshua to laugh during sex?

"What's so funny?" Leo asked, the words shaped against Joshua's throat, and Joshua's laugh cut off abruptly.

"Just," he began, but fell silent when Leo slid a hand underneath his shirt, palm flat against Joshua's stomach. Holding him down. "Just happy," Joshua finished.

Leo's lungs constricted around a hollow ache. He took a deep breath and claimed Joshua's mouth for another kiss, Joshua's fingers still tangled in his hair, their tips light against Leo's scalp, grounding.

One kiss. One kiss, that was all it should have been, all Leo had wanted, but now—*God*. With Joshua warm and solid against him, moving in incremental shifts, restless and responsive... Leo wanted to learn everything there was—which touches would make Joshua gasp, what would have him squeeze his lids shut, how he'd rock into Leo's fist, into Leo's mouth, Leo's body. Whether Joshua liked it slow and deep, fast and rough, or anything in between.

Leo skidded his mouth along Joshua's jaw, then pressed his nose into the spot below Joshua's ear, curls tickling his forehead. "Hey," he murmured. His voice sounded foreign in his ears, husky and thin. "What do you want? Tell me what you want, and I'll do it."

Joshua's fingers tightened in Leo's hair, one hand sliding down Leo's back to settle above the waistband of Leo's jeans. "You," Joshua said simply.

It should have been cheesy. Instead, it made heat crawl up Leo's spine and pool low in his belly. He lifted his head, certain that his cheeks were flushed, and waited until Joshua's eyes slid open. Their green was no more than a faint suggestion, a little hazy, pupils large in the glow of the TV.

"That's such a line," Leo reprimanded, but he couldn't help the twitch of a smile around his mouth.

"True, though," Joshua told him. "I just want you. Whatever you want." His pinkie dipped below the waistband of Leo's jeans, brushed over bare skin and came to rest on the bump of Leo's tailbone. The implication had Leo's thoughts stutter to a halt. Fuck, yes. Yes, he wanted that. Wanted to feel Joshua any way he could, wanted—so much, too much. Had never wanted anyone quite like this.

Rocking his hips down, he watched Joshua's lids drift shut, could feel the outline of Joshua's cock even through the denim. Joshua's lips parted on a hitched intake of air. Leo dipped down to suck on Joshua's bottom lip, and his ribcage felt split open, like the crater of a volcano which... No, okay, that made no sense at all, what even *was* this tangled mess in Leo's head? Thoughts spinning like dust moths, catching random rays of light.

He pulled back enough to form words, words that he had to drag up from the tips of his toes. "Want you inside. Can I ride you? Can we do that? I want—in your big, fancy bed, make this so good for you. *Josh.*"

Joshua's hips rocked up, and he turned his face away, into the backrest of the sofa. His body shuddered on a slow breath, seeming so *overwhelmed* that Leo wrapped him up in a hug, their chests aligned, no space left between them.

Leo didn't ever want to let him go.

He pushed the thought away and hid his face against Joshua's neck. "Can we?" he repeated, barely above a whisper.

Joshua's response consisted of tumbling both of them off the sofa. He bore the brunt of the fall, muttered a softly surprised, "Ouch," that had Leo chuckle against his jaw.

"Smooth, little prince. Gravity is such a confusing concept, isn't it?"

"Shut up." In spite of it, Joshua was grinning, straining off the floor to rub their hips together just once, cheerfully, before he pushed at Leo's chest. "Up, up. Naked in my bed. Want you very much, please."

Leo's chest hurt with how lovely he was.

He scrambled to his feet and offered a hand to help Joshua up. Their fingers fit; *they* fit. But Leo couldn't afford to think like that.

With a little tug, Joshua led the way to his bedroom, and Leo stumbled after him, vaguely disoriented. The moment they were inside, Joshua shed his shirt without any hesitation, messing up his hair as he pulled it over his head. His jeans followed suit, and he bent over to peel them down his thighs along with a pair of skimpy boxers briefs, then toed off his socks. Leo swallowed dryly, staring. Fuck, he wanted to map out every inch of Joshua's body with his mouth and his teeth. Leave a mark. Leave several marks.

Never like this. Never wanted anyone the way I want you.

"Your turn," Joshua announced, stepping into Leo's space to undo the button of Leo's jeans, tug down the zip. Leo rid himself of his T-shirt and gave an involuntary shudder when Joshua wedged a hand into his trousers to cup him through the fabric of his boxers. Joshua's mouth found his again, and for a short while, they stayed just like that, kissing, with Joshua completely naked and moulded to Leo's front, Leo's jeans unzipped, Joshua's thumb rubbing slow circles around the head of Leo's cock. The tendrils of slow, burning heat that twisted in Leo's belly had become a tangled mess of *want* and *more* and *you.*

He bumped Joshua towards the bed, the sheets gleaming in the golden glow of a reading lamp. The window at its head was open, letting in a rush of night air, and there was a curtain to section the alcove off from the rest of the room, the rest of the world.

Joshua went down easily. One of his hands wound around Leo's bicep to drag him along. Leo paused to take it all in: Joshua sprawled on the sheets, staring back at him with dark eyes and his expression so open. Leo wanted to give him everything, everything.

He lowered himself to straddle Joshua's hips and ducked in for another quick kiss. At this point, he'd lost count of how many there'd been. "You've got lube? Condoms?"

"Yeah." Joshua sounded a little breathless, gaze sliding down Leo's body before it returned to his face. He blinked a couple of times, then smiled and stretched underneath Leo to reach the bedside table.

"Do we need to" —Leo dug his knuckles into the tattoo on Joshua's hip, right next to the curve of one hipbone— "close the shutters? Neighbours?"

"Big tree." Joshua dropped lube and a tinfoil package onto the sheets, his smile widening. "Just us."

Now that Leo was listening, he could hear the whisper of leaves outside, stirred by the same breeze that cooled his flushed face. He pressed down against Joshua's cock, caught the way Joshua's lashes fluttered and his body stilled.

Reaching for the lube, Leo snicked off the cap, then paused. This was—how did—okay, he hadn't done this in a while, couldn't even remember the last time he'd opened himself up with someone else watching. Did Joshua expect a show? Or would he prefer that Leo make it quick and efficient—the sooner Joshua could push inside, the better? Jesus, it had been years since Leo had needed to read a sex partner, interpreting small clues to make it good for them.

No. Stop, this was nothing like that.

Joshua couldn't be *further* from a client. Leo had never had sex with someone he trusted without question, but he did trust Joshua. Wanted him so much. Was stupidly, impossibly in love with him. His own desire was hopelessly entwined with Joshua's, all muddled up, making it difficult to tell things apart. Blood rushed in Leo's ears, everything just a little new and overwhelming.

A touch to his mouth brought him out of it.

"Can I?" Joshua thumbed at Leo's bottom lip, smiling as he nodded at the lube. Leo needed a second to understand the question.

"You want to do it?" he asked, just to be certain. "Like, open me up?"

The corners of Joshua's mouth curled up into a full-blown grin, dimples pressing into his cheeks. Leo wanted to lick whiskey out of them. "I want to lick whiskey out of your dimples," he said, hardly aware of his own voice, utterly trapped, and Joshua's eyes found his.

Joshua's giggle was bright and happy. "Only if you let me drink tequila from your belly button."

Leo grinned back without thought, felt a giddy laugh buzz behind his ribs. Seemed *Leo* was the kind of person who laughed during sex. Who'd have thought. "Deal."

He passed the lube to Joshua, a little gel dripping onto his fingers. For a moment, he hesitated, then took a deep breath, felt his lungs widen with it, and shoved his sticky hand into Joshua's curls. "Dirty Princeling," he muttered.

Joshua retaliated by rolling them over, a brief sense of vertigo, and then Leo found himself on his back, sprawled out under Joshua. Naked skin, so much of it, and Leo ran his hands down Joshua's back. Another kiss. Joshua's weight anchored Leo, kept him from floating away.

By the time Joshua moved down Leo's body, stopping to nip on his

Adam's apple, then again to suck on a nipple, Leo's muscles had loosened. "Is there," Joshua asked quietly, mouth brushing over Leo's ribs, "a story behind your tattoo? *Sometimes things just happen.* Sounds like there's a story."

"There is." Leo tucked his fingers into the crook of Joshua's elbow and inhaled deeply. "But it's a sad one, and I'm not sad right now."

"Happy," Joshua mumbled, dipping down to kiss Leo's belly button.

"Very happy," Leo agreed without thought. He felt another laugh bubble up, a little desperate, and this time, he exhaled around it, bright in the shadowed space of Joshua's bedroom. His focus narrowed to the tickle of Joshua's hair on his skin, the light, teasing touches and small bites that marked Joshua's path—as though Joshua intended to lay claim to Leo's body, erasing all those that had come before.

In all the ways that mattered, he already had.

At Joshua's prompt, Leo parted his legs and lifted his head off the pillow to watch. His heart throbbed like an open wound.

Joshua glanced up through his lashes, and his smile was mischievous. Fuck, he looked *obscene* like this, crouched between Leo's thighs with his hair a wild mess, naked and unabashed. When he ducked his head, it pronounced the bony juts of his shoulder blades, and Leo could have easily counted the bumps of his spine and catalogued each one, committed them to memory so he'd never lose this. So he wouldn't lose even a second of tonight.

Leo twitched when Joshua blew warm air over his cock, hips rising off the mattress. Pushing Leo's body back down, Joshua's fingers came to grip the base of Leo's cock. Joshua's voice was bright. "Careful there, darling. Relax, lie back and think of England."

Leo was startled into another laugh. He choked on it when Joshua's lips opened around the head of his dick, gentle suction as Joshua circled the tip of a finger around Leo's hole, teasing. He seemed to get a kick out of Leo's stuttering groan.

Jesus fucking *Christ,* Leo was so in love with him. He was so, so in love with Joshua. But there was nothing here for them.

For one night, though, Leo could pretend.

His pulse skipped a beat, then resumed its hectic pace. He closed his eyes, head falling back into the pillow, and when Joshua nudged the tip of his finger inside, Leo exhaled and opened up for him.

LEO ROLLED the condom on Joshua using only his mouth. Yep, Joshua was ruined for anyone else.

His expression must have given him away, because Leo straightened with a smug little smirk, a contrast to those instances of uncertainty he'd shown at odd moments—instances which had made Joshua wonder just how much experience Leo actually had. Enough, clearly.

Joshua dragged him in for a kiss, and Leo stopped with his mouth just inches from Joshua's. "I taste like latex," he warned. Ignoring him, Joshua closed the gap between them.

Leo did taste like latex. Joshua kissed him anyway, licking into Leo's mouth until the lingering hint of latex had faded, until they tasted like each other, pressed together from head to toe. The sheets rustled with each shift of their bodies.

Eventually, Leo shuffled up onto his knees, thighs on either side of Joshua's hips, caging him in. He was gorgeous, Jesus Christ—all sharp angles. Joshua reached up to trace the curve of one arched eyebrow.

"Love your lashes," he said. It came out too honest. Since it made Leo's face relax into a smile, Joshua couldn't bring himself to regret it.

"Flattery..." Leo grasped the base of Joshua's cock and lifted himself up. "Will get you everywhere."

With that, he sunk down.

Oh God, oh dear sweet mother of *Jesus*, holy—*oh*. Joshua squeezed his eyes shut and struggled to stay still, to not drive his hips up before Leo was ready to take him fully inside. The tight drag, excruciatingly slow, had him clench his hands into the duvet.

"Joshua." Leo's voice was quiet, but there was a hint of authority to it. "Look at me."

Sucking in a breath through his teeth, Joshua pried his lids open. Leo was watching him. His skin was awash in bronze, and Joshua took in the sight—Leo's flat stomach and the sharp curve of his collarbones, his eyes so very blue, clear and focused. The moment their gazes met, Leo twisted down, took Joshua all the way in, and Joshua couldn't control the tiny, desperate twitch of his hips.

"Sorry," he forced out, "sorry, sorry."

Leo's smile was brilliant. He clenched around Joshua, still watching him intently, and Joshua felt his stomach muscles flutter with it. "Good?" Leo asked, leaning down until their noses touched.

Joshua fought to form words. "Like you have to ask."

"Tell me." There was a curious edge of urgency to Leo's voice, a need for reassurance etched into the line of his shoulders. "I need to know how you like it."

By way of a response, Joshua rolled his hips up at the same time as he jerked Leo into a kiss, the angle awkward and strained. Still so, so good. Leo's mouth opened for him. He shifted to meet Joshua's thrust, bouncing a little before he steadied himself with a hand on Joshua's shoulder.

When they parted, Leo's eyes had lost their focus. He sat up with one hand still flat on Joshua's chest, the other reaching down to lace their fingers.

Joshua squeezed back. "Your show," he whispered. "Any way you want it, I'm game."

It took a moment while Leo studied him, something almost reverent in his eyes. Then Leo nodded, dipping down just long enough to steal another kiss, and sat up straighter, leaning back just slightly as he raised himself a few inches up and sank back down quickly. His chest rose with a breath, fell as he exhaled, and still he was staring at Joshua. Joshua couldn't have looked away if he'd tried.

Again, Leo lifted up. This time, when he bounced down, he clenched around Joshua, a little twist to the motion. Joshua didn't succeed in biting back his groan.

Leo used his free hand to flick his fringe out of his eyes. Tightening his hold around Joshua's fingers, he changed the angle, rising up onto his knees. When he lowered himself back down, Joshua met him halfway. Leo's lips parted around a sigh, lashes trembling, a tinge of red to his cheeks and a thin sheen of sweat glistening on his forehead. Holy fuck, he was just... He was incredible. *Incredible.*

"Want to stay inside you forever," Joshua told him. As soon as it was out, he wished he could take it back. Too much, too soon, too bloody intense.

Leo blinked and focused back on Joshua. Before he could ask a question Joshua didn't know how to answer just yet, Joshua wrapped a hand around Leo's cock. He gave it a tight stroke in counterpoint to Leo's next bounce, just one, just enough for a little friction, before he let go again.

Eyes sliding shut, Leo dropped his head, chin against his chest. "Want you to," he mumbled, scarcely intelligible, and—oh.

Oh.

Joshua clenched his free hand into a fist, dug his own nails into his palm to keep from coming. His hold on Leo's fingers never loosened.

8

Leo woke in a cold sweat. Grey brightness cut into the space behind his lids, and as soon as he moved, he felt a twinge in his muscles, a soreness that was mostly pleasant, his body loose and relaxed.

Oh. Oh, fuck.

He'd spent the night with Joshua.

Slowly, Leo turned his head. Joshua lay sprawled next to him, cheek smushed into a pillow, lips parted in sleep. He was naked, the duvet having slipped down to pool around his waist, and a shiver of arousal zipped down Leo's spine.

He stamped down on it.

Shit. *Shit.* This shouldn't have happened. None of last night should have happened. Not that first time they'd fucked, Leo riding Joshua, deep and steady until his thighs had quivered with each shift and Joshua had flipped them over, thrusting into Leo with quick strokes and a hand on Leo's dick, too good for Leo to last much longer. Not the second time either, in the tub with Leo's fingers tangled in Joshua's curls, little tugs as he'd fucked Joshua's mouth, water rushing all around them, clumping Joshua's lashes together. Joshua had sounded wrecked afterwards, voice raw, and Leo had pushed him down into the tub, had crawled on top of him and kissed him while wanking him off, had still been kissing him when Joshua had spilled over Leo's fist. They also shouldn't have fallen asleep facing each other, hands laced between them, one of Leo's ankles trapped between Joshua's calves.

In the harsh light of the day, it seemed like a beautiful, impossible dream. And Leo was no less in love with Joshua than last night.

He'd made a mistake.

But there was also no way to undo this, no way to go back. There was no way forward either.

Leo shuffled down to the foot of the bed and slid out from underneath the duvet, grabbed yesterday's boxers off the floor and snatched up Joshua's plaid shirt. He stood silently for a moment, watching the rise and fall of Joshua's chest, the twitch of his lashes that suggested a vivid dream. Quietly, clothes bundled in his arms and bare feet noiseless on the wooden floor, Leo crept out of the room.

As much as he wanted to, he couldn't make a run for it. He also couldn't stay in Joshua's bed for even a second longer, not when he'd be fooling himself, would be fooling Joshua as well.

Want to stay inside you forever.

Leo's foot caught on the kitchen door. He stumbled into the room, pausing just long enough to pull on the boxers and Joshua's shirt, before he went to put the kettle on. Automatically, he moved to reach for the mug he'd claimed as his own, then stopped himself as he realised there were traces of himself scattered everywhere. His glance flickered to the blackboard, the one with Mo's sketch of him and Nate, then moved on to the betting list pinned to the fridge.

He chose a different cup, one that came with a blue flower pattern on a white background, delicate porcelain that looked as though it would break if you dared handle it with anything but the utmost care. It was the kind of cup Leo's mother would have kept in her cupboards, to bring out only on Sundays after church, or for very special guests.

Maybe she still did. Maybe she laughed her high, pearly laugh whenever someone inquired after her only son's well-being and changed the topic to a more agreeable one.

Maybe she missed him.

No. She wouldn't—not with the way she'd turned to ice, voice like cold-wrought iron, when she'd told him that homosexuality was an abomination, was *wrong*, and that those who lived it were rightfully shunned in polite circles. She hadn't lifted a hand to defend him against his father, had watched in silent agreement as he'd shoved Leo into the edge of a door and made him choose between the honour of their family and the misconstrued path he had set out for himself.

Well, Leo had made his choice. The bruises had faded after a week; it had taken a year for the streets of London to become his home. It had taken longer until he'd stopped listening for his sisters' voices when drifting off to sleep.

Charlotte and Rosalind. Had they moved out by now, built lives for themselves? Did they attend university, maybe even nearby? Did they keep in regular contact with their parents, or had they found a way to escape the tight clutch of expectations, of rules and commands?

Leo flinched when the kettle whistled.

It was glaringly loud in the quiet flat, and while he jumped to turn it off, he wasn't quick enough; barely a minute later, he caught the sound of movement, feet whispering over the wooden floor. Shit, he wasn't ready to face Joshua. Busying himself with measuring out tea into a pot, he kept his back to the door.

"G'morning," Joshua mumbled, consonants soft-washed with sleepiness. Leo's stomach clenched around nothing and he glanced over his shoulder to find Joshua lingering in the doorway, naked and dishevelled, eyes hazy and greengreengreen. God, this wasn't *fair*.

Somehow, Leo managed to work up a smile. He returned his focus to pouring boiling water into the pot. "Morning."

Joshua padded closer, swaying in indecision for an instant before he hooked his chin over Leo's shoulder. Nuzzling in, he tucked his face against Leo's neck, a smile brightening his voice. "Make me a cuppa as well?"

Everything was awful. Leo fought not to lean back into Joshua's warmth, overly aware of how he was wearing Joshua's shirt—it had been a thoughtless move when he'd grabbed it off the floor, a betrayal by his own subconsciousness that Joshua was bound to read as an unspoken confirmation. An invitation. Leo's throat felt raw as he swallowed, and he settled for a simple nod.

Gently, he unwound himself from Joshua under the pretence of grabbing a second cup, then fetched milk from the fridge. On the edge of his vision, he caught the way Joshua's posture stiffened, a mild awkwardness to it when he scrubbed a hand through his hair.

"So, um. Last night was, like..." Hesitation coloured Joshua's words. "Really nice?"

Leo took great care in pouring milk into the cup he'd chosen for himself, added a few drops to Joshua's cup as well, just the way Joshua liked it. Leo's hands shook just slightly, but his voice didn't. "Yeah, it was fun," he said, and didn't give in to the confessions scraping against his palate, tickling his gag reflex.

I've never laughed with anyone during sex. I've never touched anyone like that, never kissed anyone like that. Never wanted to.

I'm stupidly, blindly, impossibly in love with you.

"Well, good." Joshua sounded emboldened, and Leo was too weak to resist glancing over just quickly, just for a blink of an eye, to find Joshua still unfairly naked. He was half-hard, completely casual about it, and Leo snagged his gaze away.

No. Not again. Falling into bed with him once had been one time too many.

How did Joshua not feel vulnerable? Or did he? Either way, he drew himself up straight, head tilted as he stared at the side of Leo's face until Leo couldn't ignore it, had to meet his gaze. Only then did Joshua continue, the hopeful tilt to his mouth so very painful. "So, I thought that if you want... It could be more? *We* could be more. You're really—I think we could be great together."

In a kinder, happier world, Leo could have been the lucky guy by Joshua's side.

This wasn't that fairy tale, though. Joshua wasn't Prince Charming, and Leo wasn't a damsel in distress, wasn't a cursed blue-blood or a wronged stepchild locked away in some dungeon.

Averting his gaze, he stepped around Joshua to check on the tea. It hadn't been three minutes yet, not even close, but time was crawling. "You don't even know me, Joshua." It came out flat, toneless. "You said so yourself."

"Not true. I said there are a lot of basic *facts* I don't know about you." Joshua sucked in a breath, loud in the overwhelming silence that loomed wherever Leo turned. "I did not say I don't know *you*." Crossing his arms, Joshua appeared smaller, confidence stolen. Leo wished Joshua would put some clothes on.

For a long while, silence reigned. Joshua ended it.

"I know what you taste like," he said softly. "I know that your eyes go all soft when you drink tea in the morning. That you miss your sisters even though you barely talk about them. That those street kids look up to you like you're their hero. And I know that there's something..." He paused, daylight sharpening the lines of his frown. "I know that there's something you're not telling me. Like, something about your past. And you're so defensive of those kids, almost like you know what it's like, and I think—"

No.

"Don't," Leo cut in, harsh and jagged. "I'm not some bloody project, okay? There's no need for you to fucking save me."

"I don't want to save you. I just want *you*." Joshua dropped his arms. Hurt was obvious on his face, and Leo wanted to take it back, wanted to mould himself to Joshua's front. He wanted to kiss Joshua, touch him, take him apart inch by inch until Joshua's breath came out in tiny gasps and he wouldn't know how to form a sentence anymore, until he was pliant and loose, smiling at Leo with happiness bright in his eyes.

Leo inhaled. "It's not going to happen, all right? Us." He gestured between them and hated everything about this, about himself. "It's just not."

For much too long, Joshua remained silent, still. Then he took a step back, bumping into the work surface, and shook his head. His eyes were too wide, his posture too vulnerable. God, Leo wished he could wrap him up in a blanket and apologise, say he hadn't meant a word. He wanted to scream.

Instead, he went to pour the tea.

"So this is it?" Joshua asked from behind him. "Are you really —*look* at me. The way we clicked, did you really not... I've never clicked with anyone like that."

Leo gave a hollow laugh that shuddered down the length of his back. "You've only ever had sex with Mo."

Joshua didn't reply. When Leo glanced over, a quick, stolen look from the corner of his eye, he found Joshua staring at him.

Another breath. Leo gathered his composure around him like a leaden cloak, and somehow, he managed to meet Joshua's eyes. "I'm sorry. I didn't mean to make you think—this doesn't have to be awkward, right? You and Mo have been doing this for ages."

"You're not Mo," Joshua snapped, the first hint of irritation in his voice. Leo should be glad for it. If Joshua was angry, it would be so much easier to put an end to this before it could spiral out of control.

Before it could spiral out of control? Christ, it was too bloody late for that; Leo had lost control the moment he'd kissed Joshua. This was the aftermath of his personal apocalypse.

"I know I'm not Mo." Tea. There was tea, and Leo was meant to be pouring it. He continued evenly. "I just meant that sex doesn't have to fuck up a friendship, right? We're still friends."

"Are we?" Irritation had thickened in Joshua's voice. "Are we friends when you won't tell me *anything*? You're so... How do you bloody live like that, with all these walls?"

It felt like a punch to the throat, and Leo exhaled around the impact.

Grabbing one of the cups, he offered it to Joshua, and their fingers brushed over the porcelain as Joshua went to accept it. It seemed like an automatic reaction, and afterwards, Joshua stood in the middle of the kitchen with both hands clutching the dainty cup, blinking at Leo before he swallowed and turned away. Leo allowed himself one second, one tiny, insignificant second of memorising the line of Joshua's back, the gentle swell of his bum.

Then Leo picked up his own cup and took a sip. The liquid was too hot, almost burned his tongue. He focused on the bitter taste of herbs rather than the sour bile that sat at the back of his throat. This was bloody awful, and Leo needed to say *something*, offer some small measure of truth.

"I had a crush on you. When I was a teenager." It was out before he had a chance to think better of it. There was no way but down. "And that was confusing as hell at first, and I took it out on you more than I should have. But now I just... You're..." *Everything.* "Last night was brilliant, all right? But there's not—we just can't. It would never work."

Not a lie. Not quite the truth either. Leo felt the sour taste rise, and he washed it down with another mouthful of tea that burned behind his sternum.

Joshua set his cup down with a clank, tea sloshing over the rim. "So you used me?" he asked sharply. "Like, living out some teenage fantasy, getting it out of your system, and now you're just—*fuck*." His chest rose on a deep breath, and wait, what?

What?

Before Leo could interrupt, Joshua rolled his shoulders back, voice rising. "Well, okay, fuck you. I thought that you were—I thought you were different. That *this* was different, like, I thought you saw *me*. But you're just like everyone else. Aren't you?"

"Joshua," Leo began, and then he didn't know how to continue. How the fuck could he set things right without exposing all of himself? His heart was trying to claw a way past his ribs.

"I want you to leave," Joshua said, fierce and rough.

So. Okay then.

Leo's entire body shrunk down to skin and bones. With Joshua's words clanging around his skull like skeletons rattling their chains, Leo put down his cup, turned away and moved towards the bedroom.

"Where are you going?" Joshua snapped from behind him.

"Grabbing my things. I can't very well leave like this." Each word scraped against the inside of Leo's throat, leaving a raw, bloody mess in its wake.

Joshua made no attempt to stop Leo. He didn't follow either.

One step, another. And another. Leo glanced around Joshua's bedroom—the sheets they'd messed up last night, Joshua's jeans a crumpled heap on the floor, tangled up with Leo's own. His hands shook when he bent to pick them up. He pulled them on, then scooped up his T-shirt.

He should change into it. He had no right to keep Joshua's shirt, had no right to *anything* that belonged to Joshua.

Leo didn't change. Patting his pockets for his keys and his wallet, he kicked his own T-shirt under the bed and left the room, moved past the kitchen and hoped that Joshua would call out—but Joshua didn't. Of course he didn't.

When Leo stepped out into the stairway and shut the door, it sounded like the lock of a prison cell clicking into place.

THE MOMENT THE DOOR CLOSED, Joshua sagged into a chair. He felt cold all over, ice running through his veins. Anger buzzed under his skin, but it evaporated within seconds, made room for something bleak and heavy, a nauseating pressure that originated in his chest and radiated outwards.

Leo's tea still sat on the work surface. The scent turned Joshua's stomach.

He clambered to his feet and went back to his bedroom. Everything smelled like sex and sweat, disgusting and dirty, and he started by pulling the sheets off the bed and throwing them in the wash along with last night's clothes. His shirt wasn't there; Leo must have taken it.

What an arse. What a bloody fucking *bastard*. How dare he?

Joshua almost, *almost* called him. He'd already reached for his phone, fingers numb, then opted to send a quick text to Mo and Tristan instead. *'So L is a proper dick.'* Dropping the phone on the bedside table, he considered putting fresh sheets on the bed. He couldn't be bothered. The bare mattress stared back at him, like an accusation.

A shower, that was what he needed. Wash off Leo's scent and the memory of last night, flush it all away and start this day from scratch. He left the bedroom without a backwards glance.

Beside the tub, a small puddle still sat on the tiles, a reminder of last night. Joshua stared at it for too long, remembered water streaming down his back and Leo's fingers in his hair, the helpless little sounds Leo had made as he'd worked himself into Joshua's mouth. Thoughtless words of praise, *so good, best I've ever had, no one else, no one else.* Leo spilling with a ragged sigh, slumping a little, supporting himself with a hand on Joshua's shoulder. Using that hand to push Joshua onto his back, even though it was crowded in the tub. Leo kissing him until Joshua couldn't taste anything but Leo, Leo, Leo.

BY THE TIME Joshua left the bathroom in loose pyjama bottoms, Tristan had arrived. "Mo's bringing the vodka," he said in lieu of a greeting, then dragged Joshua into a hug.

Joshua took what felt like his first breath in years. "How did you know?"

"We know you. You wouldn't call someone a dick unless they'd acted like the biggest fuckwit in the universe, so..." Pulling back, Tristan poked at Joshua's collarbone. Glancing down, Joshua noticed the prominent lovebite, glaringly obvious, a bruise. "Take it he spent the night?" Tristan asked.

"Yes." Joshua exhaled through his nose. The two cups were still on the work surface, and he peeled himself away from Tristan to empty the cold tea into the sink.

Tristan watched him, frowning. "Take it he didn't spend much of the morning?"

"Let's wait until Mo gets here. Don't think I want to tell the story twice." Leaning back against the sink, Joshua crossed his arms. "Fuck, I hate being cooped up in here. Do you think... The paps are probably stalking Windsor Castle and—I mean, they're probably stalking everything that's royal property, but do you think we could maybe go to your country home? Just for bit? Bring Mo and Kels?"

"She's got some fashion thingy tomorrow," Tristan said. "But we could spend today there, definitely. And the night. I'll make some calls."

"I love you," Joshua told him, completely honest. Just the idea of getting out of London calmed his blood so that it was no longer rushing in his ears like a waterfall, like water pouring down on him as he kneeled—*no*.

While Tristan went to make arrangements, Joshua busied himself with breakfast preparations. Mo arrived in the middle of it, pulled Joshua into a hug and didn't ask any questions while he fell into Joshua's rhythm, helping him fill the plates and carry everything out into the grey light of an overcast day. The vodka bottle took a spot of honour at the centre of the table, even though the sight turned Joshua's stomach. It was the principle of the thing.

"So am I right," Mo asked around his first mouthful, "that you got your hands on Leo's dick, yeah? And it turns out he's little more than that? Like, a dick?"

"Well fucking said," Tristan congratulated.

Joshua put down his fork. He hadn't been hungry in the first place. "Something like that. It was... The sex was really good. Like... I mean, I just never..."

"Careful there," Mo warned, but his smile was kind, and beneath the table, he pressed his foot against Joshua's.

Joshua managed to return the smile. "I'm not going to stroke your ego. We both know you're adequately competent."

"Do I have to be here for this?" Contradicting his protest, Tristan raised his glass of spiked orange juice. "Either way, here's to damn good sex, everyone."

"I don't know. Damn good sex, yes, that's brilliant. It's just... I didn't expect the emotional connection. Someone should have warned me." Joshua's throat felt dry when he swallowed. He squinted at the clouds, and they seemed to be frozen, no movement at all. Like the world had come to a standstill. It heightened the impression of being trapped, removed from reality, and Joshua was really fucking sick of it.

Leo had told him to stay away from all news channels. But Leo was also a massive twat, so why should Joshua listen to anything that came out of his mouth?

Tristan's voice brought him back. "Let's be real, the emotional connection is the best fucking thing about it."

"Not if it's all a lie." Again, Joshua swallowed. "Like, if *you* think it's real, but the other person is just living out some teenage fantasy. And then ditching you afterwards, like yes, thanks, glad I got that out of my system."

"I'll fucking kill him," Mo muttered.

Tristan was quiet for a moment, staring at Joshua. Then he shook his head, very slowly, and scrunched up his nose. "No. That doesn't make sense. Way he looks at you, that's not—no. Mate, when he watched you record that interview, that didn't look like a teenage crush to me. And he's prickly, yeah, but he's also... His face goes all soft around you. Like when we did those trial runs and you were upset, and he's the one who—"

"Please don't," Joshua interrupted. No. *No.* He couldn't allow Tristan to confuse him further, not when Joshua was still struggling with the realisation that he'd been wrong about Leo, all wrong. He'd thought the rough-cut exterior was protecting a sweetness underneath, was a defensive wall to hide the real Leo—the one who helped street kids and showed flashes of vulnerability, the one who kissed Joshua like he meant it, who built Joshua up and engaged him in serious discussions, the one who laughed with his eyes reduced to small slits, crinkled at the corners.

Joshua could have fallen in love with that Leo. Had been halfway there already.

Only it had been an illusion.

"I'm just saying it doesn't add up." Tristan paused, frowning.

"Doesn't give him a right to be an arse to you, mind. Mo, what do we do with the body?"

"Eat it," Mo said, tone perfectly flat. "Use his bones for bread."

Tristan nodded. "I like the way you think."

Even though Joshua's muscles felt heavy, he made himself smile at them. "Cannibalism is not the solution, didn't they tell you? Alcohol is. And I'll feel better once we get out of here. On top of everything else that's going on, it was just... a bit much."

Without a word, Tristan got up to hug Joshua from behind, cheeks pressed together. Leaning into it, Joshua blinked away the wetness in his eyes. He wouldn't cry. Not over Leo, and certainly not over how his private life had become a dramatic installation for all the world to see, and he was the only one missing the spectacle.

Enough of that. In fact, he'd done enough hiding for the rest of his life, hadn't he?

He cleared his throat and tucked his toes against Mo's instep. "Anyway, I'm done with this. I should have known better and didn't, and that's that. Can we talk about something more fun? Like Mo's date with Nate?"

There was a stretch of silence, Mo studying Joshua's face while Tristan held on. Then Tristan straightened, Mo's expression relaxed, and Joshua could breathe just a little easier.

"Not sure it was a date," Mo said. "We just walked and talked, you know? Was nice, though. He's sweet." A pause, then he snorted. "Fuck, I have no idea what I'm doing."

On the way back to his chair, Tristan clapped Mo on the shoulder. "You'll figure it out. Insert part A into slot B—"

"Piss off," Mo told him.

Joshua's grin felt like a foreign entity, not quite fitting onto his face. Stubbornly, he clung to it. "Cool, okay. I guess I'll have to live vicariously through you guys. Since this relationship thing isn't really working out for me."

"One twat doesn't make a..." Tristan trailed off and pursed his lips. "Well, fuck. I was going for some variation of 'one swallow doesn't make a summer,' but all I can think of now is a flock of bums. Not a pretty sight."

"Says you," Mo put in. "Also, mate, that saying doesn't even make sense in this context. There's no flocks here, just the one twat."

"Which," Tristan said, "means it's no summer, because it's just one swallow. Makes perfect sense. I don't know what you're talking about."

Joshua had watched their exchange with distant amusement, not quite enough to brighten his thoughts, last night's memories too fresh. Tomorrow would be different, though. Glancing down at his plate, he found his appetite diminish even more.

"Hey, Mo?" he asked. "Do you ever feel like Nate is holding back?"

Mo's reply came with a delay, his brows drawing together. "Yeah. Don't know much about his past, really. Just told me that if you're with James, it pretty much means you got a second chance. Like a clean slate or something. Didn't want to push him too much."

A second chance—just like what Leo hoped to achieve for those kids. Was it an attempt to recompense for his own fortune, paying back the favour? There was no doubt Leo was hiding *something*. How bad was it, though? Bad enough that he couldn't face the public scrutiny that was intrinsically tied to Joshua's life and affected anyone who got too close?

All Joshua had were fragmented pieces of a puzzle. Was Leo worth the effort of trying to piece them together? Did he even deserve it, when he'd pushed Joshua away?

It would never work.

Joshua found it hard to remember Leo's precise words. The thing he'd said about his teenage crush—had Joshua jumped to conclusions? He'd been quick to accuse Leo of acting out some fantasy of the past, and Leo hadn't corrected him. But did that mean it was true? Why had Leo stolen Joshua's shirt if he didn't care at all?

God. Joshua's head was a mess.

He must have blanked out of the conversation for a moment, because when he focused back on the present, Mo was telling Tristan that no, he was not a coward for refusing to invite Nate along on their trip today when Nate was *working*.

"Well, he won't be working tomorrow, right? At least not the full day. It's the weekend." Tristan lifted his brows. "So invite him over for the England match."

"Ed's coming, too," Joshua said. A moment later, he didn't know why he'd considered it relevant to the discussion; as far as he was aware, Nate had no particular interest in Ed. It was Leo who'd sat up straighter each time Ed's name had come up, although he'd never asked.

"Ed is in town? Awesome." Tristan speared a piece of tomato and waved it in the air. "Wanted to ask him for input about my new guitar, should keep me entertained if the English squad doesn't do its job."

"*Excuse* you," Joshua told him primly. "The Three Lions are a national institution, and I will not have you sully them on my watch. Just because you insist on supporting Scotland for nostalgic reasons..."

Under the table, Tristan kicked him, and Joshua kicked back. He told himself this was just like any other day, but somehow, he could still feel the ghost of Leo's hands on his skin. He hated it. *Hated* it.

THERE WAS A STRANGE, sickening weight in Joshua's stomach, as though his intestines had shrivelled up into a tightly compressed ball.

He might come to regret this, but he was so very, very tired of receiving information in easily digested bites. He was an adult, for fuck's sake, and it was time he acted like one. Nudging his readily packed bag aside, he glanced at his watch and guessed that he had about half an hour before Tristan would be over to pick him up. Plenty of time.

Joshua grabbed his tablet off the coffee table and unlocked it while he made his way out onto the terrace. *The Sun, The Mirror* and *The Guardian*, along with a brief look at his Twitter mentions—that should give him a good idea of the discussion in the country. He dropped onto the sofa bed and called up the first page.

Football at the top, but right below, there was an article on him. *'Prince Joshua's supermodel: more than friends?'* Predictably, it went on to speculate about his relationship with Mo and combined it with pictures of the two of them from Spain and other occasions. The comments were what really interested Joshua, and he skimmed through them with his heart beating high in his chest, bits and pieces jumping out at him.

Scorching hot together. Who cares. I'd do both. Disgrace. Sex tape please. Shameful. Commend his bravery.

With the words a quiet, low-level buzz in his head, he navigated to Twitter.

Twenty minutes later, he emerged blinking and a little disoriented. So that had been... not too bad. Right? There'd been some hate mixed in, yes, of course—homosexuality as a sin, inherently wrong, and those who practiced it doomed to burn in hell—but somehow, it couldn't quite touch him. It hadn't been *personal.* He'd been the peg to hang the prejudices on, nothing more.

A week ago, he might have taken it to heart. A week ago, he might have gone running to Leo.

Now, Joshua was fine. Some of the comments had made him swallow, yes, had made his hands shake, but... Overall, he was fine. Maybe the morning's events had rendered him too numb to feel the impact just yet. He didn't feel numb, though; he felt wide awake, as though for the first time, he had a clear view of the things that mattered, and the things that didn't.

The opinions of strangers on the internet didn't matter. They couldn't hurt him. They couldn't use him, betray his trust, make him fall for an illusion. They couldn't walk out on him.

Thanks, Leo.

∾

IT WAS noon by the time Leo made it to the office.

After leaving Joshua's place, he'd wandered aimlessly for... a while. He didn't quite know how long it had been, only that it was long enough for Nate to try calling him twice. Leo hadn't picked up. Instead, he'd drifted with the crowds. For some reason, he'd expected to stick out in Joshua's plaid shirt, but so far, no one had pointed at him and exclaimed, "He's wearing the Prince's clothes!" No one had taken notice of Leo at all.

There'd been no clear direction to his mindless movement, but when he'd found himself in front of Kylie's bar, he'd halted in his steps. At this hour, the place had still been closed, its windows shuttered. Seven years ago, it had been one of Leo's usual haunts, had been where he'd met Kylie and found a constant in the cheerful bartender. It had also been where he'd met James.

Leo had turned away, deliberately so, to finally make his way to work.

Now, he paused in front of Nate's office and gathered his courage. Everyone else seemed to have gone out for lunch, but the quiet sound of clicking keys hinted that Nate hadn't joined them, and... Shit, Leo needed to talk to *someone*. Kylie would have been the obvious choice, but while Kylie knew Leo's past, she didn't know Joshua. Nate did.

Taking a deep, measured breath, Leo entered without knocking. Nate glanced up sharply and relaxed when he recognised Leo. His smile was wide. "Oh, hey. Been wondering when you'd show up."

"Yeah, well." Leo shrugged one shoulder and moulded his expression into an approximation of normal and composed. He lowered himself into the chair facing Nate's desk. "Some things on my mind. I kind of—"

Nate interrupted him with, "So I think I was on a date with Mo."

Whatever Leo had been planning to say escaped him. Nate looked so happy, all bright eyes and beaming grin, perched on the edge of his seat as he looked at Leo. A date. Yeah, that's how these things should go: meet, date, fall in love and into bed.

"That's..." Tentatively, Leo returned Nate's grin. "Great. That's really great. What happened?"

"After we left. Yesterday, I mean, when Mo and Tristan said that we should leave you and Joshua to talk. And then Tristan ditched us, so, yeah." Nate picked up a pen and twirled it between his fingers, restless in a way that contrasted with his usual calm demeanor. His voice was soft. "We walked through Camden, just talking, basically. It was... nice, you know? Think I really like him a lot."

"I'm happy for you," Leo said. He meant it. Fuck, he did; if anyone deserved good things, it was Nate. That didn't fully cancel out the spark of envy, though. Why couldn't Leo have this one thing, too? Why didn't *he* get to keep Joshua?

Joshua had been so quick to assume that Leo didn't want him, that Leo didn't care—as though Joshua hadn't expected any better. How did he not see just how stupid Leo was for him? But then, that was all on Leo, wasn't it? He hadn't been very open about the fact that he thought Joshua brilliant and lovely. He hadn't been open in general.

Well, he'd paid a price.

"Hey," Nate said suddenly, dropping the pen. "Isn't that Joshua's shirt?"

Leo snapped back to the present. "I borrowed it."

"Oh?" Nate's eyes narrowed, and his tone was openly curious, gaze clear on Leo's face. "Last night? This morning? Is that why you were so late to the office? Wait, and what did you guys have to talk about, anyway?"

This was it. Leo's opening.

"Nothing," he said slowly. His stomach was churning around empty air, and right, he hadn't actually eaten anything today, just a few sips of tea. "Just stuff. Shit, though, I totally forgot—we had that heads-up for some sketch on the Late Show. How did that go last night?"

For a moment, Nate didn't move, his focus still sharp. "Are you sure you're all right?" he asked eventually.

No. "Yes," Leo told him.

Nate sighed and looked away, shuffling through some papers before he retrieved a transcript that he passed over. "It went well," he said. "They faked a royal gay wedding, so really, fit right into our narrative. Made Joshua's character look solid to the point of being endearingly boring and wanting to spend his honeymoon knitting socks and doilies. Link to the video is in your inbox."

"Thank you." Leo sat staring at the transcript blindly, willing himself to *bloody say something already.*

After half a dozen years of avoiding all mentions of their pasts, the words wouldn't come. When he glanced up, Nate was watching him carefully. With a smile, Leo got to his feet and turned to leave. A little more time, that was all he needed. He'd work up to it.

By late afternoon, Leo's lack of sleep had him blinking at the screen, unable to concentrate. Each time he closed his eyes, he saw Joshua staring back at him. Leo needed to clear his head, but how could he possibly get away when Joshua was his client as much as his... his... *Fuck.*

There was no getting away.

The smart thing would be to leave all direct communication to Nate, but that would mean admitting to what had happened, explaining why Joshua wouldn't want to talk to Leo. Why they weren't even friends.

Numbing his mind to that particular thought, Leo grabbed his phone and stepped out onto the balcony. His cigarette was down to a sad stub before he found himself capable of selecting Joshua's entry from his contacts.

Bloody Prince Joshua WTF. Leo would laugh if he didn't feel so very much like crying.

Five rings. He'd almost given up, had resolved himself to a neutral voicemail greeting, when Joshua picked up. His voice was devoid of inflection. "Can I help you?"

"I, um." Smoke burned in Leo's eyes, so he squeezed them shut, blindly stubbing out the cigarette. "Hi. Joshua, hey. I just called to give you the daily status update. Like we agreed."

"I don't think that will be necessary." Joshua sounded painfully professional, completely out of reach. "I had George brief me earlier, and I went to check some online sources myself."

He'd—oh, bloody hell. Joshua had waded into an unfiltered version of the public's reactions? It wasn't so bad, all things considered; the way they'd shaped the narrative had soothed most of the common concerns, and football provided a welcome distraction. There were always some hateful comments, though, and the last time Joshua had made the mistake of seeking them out, he'd washed up on Leo's doorstep with red eyes and fairy cakes.

"Are you okay?" Leo asked, fingers clenching around the phone.

"I'm fine," Joshua said curtly. He didn't offer anything else, and the realisation made Leo's breath hitch in his throat.

Joshua had locked him out.

"Are you sure?" Leo asked. "If there's anything I can do—"

"I think you've done quite enough, thank you." It wasn't a compliment, each word flat and cold. There was no trace of the beautiful, open man who—the man Leo had fallen in love with. That Joshua had been replaced by a stranger, the equivalent of a smooth, slick wall that offered no purchase. Was this how Joshua had felt each time Leo had shut him out? Small and helpless, inadequate?

A taste of his own poison.

"Joshua." Leo swallowed around the sting of metal in his mouth. "Please don't. This isn't like you."

Joshua's laugh was an abomination of itself. For the first time since he'd picked up, his words weren't completely blank, exposing jagged contours. "Maybe it is, though. Maybe it just isn't like the teenage me that you used to fancy."

If Leo hadn't been paying close attention, he'd have missed the tiny, near-inaudible quaver in Joshua's voice. Slumping back against the wall, Leo slid down to sit on the tiled floor, pulling his knees up to his chest. He'd *hurt* Joshua. He'd really, truly hurt him, and yes, of course he had, and he should have realised as much, but... But nothing.

He should have told Joshua the truth. Not all of it, but enough for

Joshua to understand that it was circumstances which worked against them, that it wasn't—that Leo was—just, fuck. Joshua needed to know that Leo would never discard him like that. Never, never, never.

Leo needed to see him. He needed to talk to him.

Laughter on Joshua's end of the line cut into whatever Leo had intended to say. Someone called out for Joshua, a female voice, bright with some kind of challenge. "I need to go," Joshua said into the phone. "I'm with," a deliberate pause, "*friends* right now, so this is not a good time."

The implication cut deep and true. The last time Leo had cried, he'd been on a train to London with two-thousand quid in his backpack and his father's voice ringing in his ears. *I'd rather you be dead than gay. It would be less shameful.*

Right now, Leo felt like crying.

"Okay," he said softly. "So when's a good time for you tomorrow? It should be fairly quiet in the British media, what with our match coming up, but I'd still like to give you a run-down of the international development."

"Don't trouble yourself." Joshua had reverted back to a polite stranger. "As far as I can tell, your team did a great job with the initial surge, and it's going well. I believe George can handle it from here on."

Leo tucked his face into the crook of his elbow and forced himself to take a deep breath. Joshua's shirt didn't smell much like Joshua anymore; it smelled like smoke and Leo. "So this is goodbye?" he asked.

"No, goodbye was this morning." Joshua's intake of air was audible. "This is cutting the majority of our remaining ties, I believe."

Leo squeezed his eyes shut tightly enough for sparks to bloom behind his lids. "The majority?"

"Well, there's still, you know." Briefly, Joshua sounded unsettled, then he regained his footing. "There's still Nate. So I guess we might bump into each other on occasion."

Right. Of course that's what Joshua had meant. Not emotional ties, nothing like that.

"I'm sorry," Leo managed. It came out quiet and desperate, and the silence that followed let hope flare—hope that Joshua would get it, that he'd see through Leo's layers and understand everything without Leo ever having to explain.

"So am I," Joshua replied, and while it didn't sound quite as firm as his previous words, it still didn't invite further comment from Leo. A moment later, Joshua ended the call, and Leo was left sitting on the floor, phone pressed to his cheek, nose buried into a shirt that didn't even smell like Joshua.

He counted to three while he inhaled, waited a beat and exhaled again, counting to three once more. Repeated it. The regularity soothed his thoughts. With each cycle, his lungs felt marginally wider, his throat not quite as raw.

Nate's voice jolted him out of it.

"Leo?" Shock was clear in the name.

Leo hadn't heard him approach, so it took him a second to gather his wits about him. He lifted his head and blinked his eyes open, the daylight painful. How long had he been out here? Couldn't have been more than a few minutes.

He had yet to reply, had probably taken too long already because when Nate crouched by his side, gripping Leo's shoulder, the concern on his face had heightened. "What's wrong?"

Everything is wrong. The whole fucking universe is a bloody joke.

Leaning into the touch, Leo cleared his throat. "I'm in love with Joshua."

"Oh." Of all things, Nate sounded relieved. "I thought it was something awful. You only just realised?"

"This *is* awful," Leo told him. "Like, there's absolutely no chance there. At all. And I just—Jesus fuck." There was so much more he should say, but right now, he couldn't. The words just wouldn't come.

Instead, he tugged on Nate's wrist, and it took only a second before Nate got the hint. He moved in for a hug, and Leo sank into it. While he was holding on too tightly, Nate was kind enough not to complain.

For a short while, they stayed like that—sitting on the dirty tiles, the afternoon grey and milky around them. Eventually, Nate shifted into a more comfortable position. "Did something else happen with Joshua?" he asked quietly. "Last night, I mean. Something that's got you all twisted over a phone call."

Leo burrowed into Nate's T-shirt, voice coming out muffled. "You already know, don't you?"

"I didn't pry, if that's what you mean." Nate sounded careful, and Leo shook his head, but didn't move away.

"Not what I meant. Just meant that you knew the moment you asked if I was all right. Earlier."

"Suspected. You're wearing his shirt," Nate said. One of his hands slid up Leo's back to tangle in the hair at Leo's nape. "You're also obviously not okay, so, yeah. Something happened."

"Sex happened." Leo sighed and closed his eyes. "Best I ever had, hands down. I didn't think I was even able to click like that with anyone, but... yeah. Here's to learning something new, I guess."

"Huh. Always thought you weren't interested in sex." There was no judgement in Nate's tone, just easy acceptance. If Leo could have crawled into Nate's body—like, platonically—to hide out there for a bit, he would have done so. He settled for twisting both hands into Nate's T-shirt instead.

"I..." Leo's throat constricted. Now. He was doing this *now*. "I overdosed for a bit. On sex. In a manner of speaking. Lost my appetite."

If Nate was in any way surprised, there was no physical evidence of it. His posture didn't change at all, and neither did his tone. "Until Joshua?"

"Until Joshua." Blindly, Leo nodded. "We fought, though. This morning. My fault, mostly, and it was..."

"Stupid?" Nate suggested kindly.

"Inevitable," Leo said. He swallowed around the aftertaste of the word. "But also somewhat stupid, yeah. I told him I fancied him as a teenager, wanted to give him something honest, and when he thought that was the reason we'd fucked—the only reason, just because of my teenage crush—I didn't correct him."

"Shit, Leo. Why not?"

"It made sense at the time? Like, a reason why we couldn't work, without having to tell him... everything."

"So now he thinks you're just like everyone else who uses him for his name? But that's awful." Nate gave a little tug on Leo's hair. His thumb pressed into the back of Leo's neck, a grounding kind of pressure. Leo lifted his head and felt Nate's words like a punch to his gut. *That's awful.*

Yeah. It was. It *was.* So why had Leo walked out without even trying to correct it? Jesus fucking Christ, he was an *idiot.*

He sat up. "I need to talk to him. Joshua. I really need to talk to him, but I don't think—Fuck, he'd probably close the door in my face."

Serves you right.

Nate didn't say that, though. Instead, he dropped his hand to Leo's elbow, giving it a gentle squeeze. "Well, maybe. But I know you, so I think you could make him listen. If you really wanted to."

"I'm not even sure what I'm ready to tell him." The pressure behind Leo's forehead was like a physical being, weighing down his every thought. It got marginally more bearable when he closed his eyes. Jesus, he was sixty shades of pathetic. "I'm pathetic."

Three beats of silence, then Nate punched him. There was no force behind it, his fist barely even making contact with Leo's shoulder, but it was enough to have Leo's eyes snap open. "Careful," Nate told him, frowning. "That's my best mate you're talking about."

Unplanned, Leo felt his mouth twist into what had to be his first genuine smile for the day. "Your best mate's a bit of an idiot," he said quietly.

"Sometimes, yeah." Nate smiled back. "But since Joshua isn't actually in London today, my idiot best mate's got until tomorrow to figure out what to say."

"How do you know that?" Pausing for just a beat, Leo answered his own question. "Oh, wait. Mo told you?"

"Yeah. Talked to him a bit earlier, and he invited me to the England match tomorrow. He also, um." Nate's smile dropped, his hesitation palpable. "He, like, specifically asked me not to bring you. Seemed like he expected me to get it, so I acted like I did."

Leo's stomach relocated to some lower level.

"I told him I'd need to check with you first," Nate added quickly. "Your plans and stuff. It's our usual pub night, after all. But I thought... If you need to talk to Joshua, but he's maybe not so keen to listen? That's probably your best shot, if you just come with me. Always easier when there's a bit of a buffer, right?"

Slinging an impulsive arm around Nate's waist, Leo tilted sideways to rest his head on Nate's shoulder. His voice came out rough. "It's not going to be easy, no. Not when the buffer is Tristan and Mo."

Nate hummed and took his time replying. "Well, maybe it isn't meant to be easy. You know?"

Yeah, maybe it wasn't.

"You'd do that?" Leo asked. "Bring me along, even though Mo asked you not to?"

"He'd do the same for Joshua." While the statement was firm, Nate's muscles tensed up enough to be noticeable, and he shifted his position against the wall. "So he'll just have to understand. If he doesn't... It's not much use then, is it? You're part of my life."

Leo's body felt small and heavy. "But you want him to be part of your life, too."

"Yeah." Nate exhaled slowly, steadily. "Means I need you and him to be compatible."

"You really are my best friend, you know that?" It came out complacent, and Leo tightened his hold on Nate. The late afternoon was quiet around them, broken only by the low-level rumble of traffic and, distantly, the purr of a helicopter that buzzed in Leo's stomach. "One day, in the none-too-distant future, you and I will get spectacularly drunk together. And then we'll talk about how we ended up here."

"I'm ready when you are," Nate said, his tone not quite as decisive as he'd likely intended.

"Working on it," Leo told him.

Nate's response consisted of a quick smile which Leo returned.

For all that his body was still heavier than it should be, the memory of Joshua's cool voice like a fresh wound, he did feel better than he had all day. He'd need to tell James that they were off the case, and then he'd go home, take a nap to catch up on sleep, maybe meet up with Nate to watch one of the matches that were on tonight.

And then, tomorrow, he'd figure out what he'd tell Joshua—if Joshua could even be bothered to listen. If he was willing to give Leo yet another chance, when Leo had already used up more than his fair share.

9

After a full day of being surrounded by people, Joshua's flat felt disconcertingly quiet.

He dropped his bag just inside the door and moved on to the kitchen, pouring himself a glass of water that he chugged in one go, stomach churning around it. The dirty plates and glasses from yesterday's breakfast with Tristan and Mo were still sitting in the sink, along with two delicate teacups—the ones with the blue flower pattern that Joshua hardly ever used. His gaze skipped over them, returned only to skip away again, like a flattened stone bouncing off water. Eventually, he picked them up for a clean, then dried them off before putting them back into the cupboard. Out of sight.

The flat was still too quiet. He stopped by the living room to switch on the telly without even checking the programme, then turned towards his bedroom. The others would be over in a few hours, just before kick-off. There was plenty of time to squeeze in a nap.

His bed was just the way he'd left it, naked without its sheets.

Joshua stood in the doorway for several seconds before he

entered. Heavily, he sat down on the edge of the mattress and felt it give under his weight. Just one body, though. Just the one.

He set both elbows on his thighs and lowered his head, briefly closing his eyes. It was all right. Or it would be. Leo had been a momentary glitch in the system, and Joshua would get over him in a little while. Starting today.

When he raised his head again, he caught sight of black fabric, shoved halfway underneath the bed. With his toes, he tugged it out. Leo's T-shirt. Joshua exhaled a rough breath.

Fuck. This wasn't fair.

Why had Leo left it? To mock? Or was this what he considered adequate compensation for the shirt he'd stolen from Joshua? Joshua still didn't get why Leo had chosen to dress in Joshua's shirt in the first place. It spoke of an attachment that didn't exist. Or had Leo kept it to—*no*. Joshua shoved the idea of Leo keeping it as a trophy away. Surely he wouldn't be that cruel. But then, did Joshua know him at all?

Someone saying his name snapped Joshua out of his thoughts. What...? Oh, of course, the TV.

He jumped up and followed the sound back into the living room. It was some gossip show, a smiling presenter with stark blond hair and her face caked with make-up, features oddly static as she talked about his disappearance act, no trace of him since that truly *astonishing* interview. With the nation juggling its attention between football and a game of hide-and-seek that Prince Joshua had clearly won, wasn't it time for him to show himself? Explain where he wanted to go from here?

Joshua disliked her instantly. Even more so because her words hooked into his skin and wouldn't come loose as he tried to shake them off.

Leaving the telly on, he stepped out onto the terrace, fell back onto the sofa bed and closed his eyes. The low hum of the city buzzed around him, ever-present yet distant, and he felt strangely removed from it, as though he occupied a parallel universe. Orbiting.

Imagine the impact someone like you could have.

Fuck Leo. Fuck him, *fuck him* for having managed to lay claim to every cell of Joshua's body, for thoroughly embedding himself into Joshua's life. How utterly ironic when Leo played all his cards close to his chest.

It didn't mean Leo was all wrong, though. Not when it came to Joshua's ability to make a difference. Joshua would never be able to offer the kind of practical, one-on-one advice Leo did, probably didn't possess the kind of life experience to pull it off in the first place—but if he stopped hiding, if he manipulated the public attention rather than the other way around...

Maybe, if he put his weight behind it, he could make a difference.

NATE WAS RUNNING LATE, and Joshua was amused by how Mo was growing more nervous with each minute that passed. Since Joshua was a good friend, he resisted teasing Mo about how he'd spent an inordinate amount of time in the bathroom earlier to get his hair *just* right.

When Mo checked his watch for the third time in less than five minutes, Joshua leaned down to where Mo was perched on the carpet in front of the sofa, his back propped against Joshua's calves. "You look brilliant," Joshua said, quietly so as not to interrupt the heated discussion Tristan and Ed were having about guitar strings, of all things. "Nate will be here any moment, and he won't know what hit him. Now relax, please? You're making *me* nervous. More nervous. I don't need that when we're about to go up against Italy. Even if it's cute."

"Suck it," Mo muttered back. "I am not cute." He combined it with twisting around to brush a kiss against Joshua's bare knee, right where Joshua's shorts ended.

"But you are," Joshua told him. "Very. Let me revel in your glow, please."

Mo shot him an unimpressed look and was about to comment when the bell rang. With a brief glance at the countdown, Joshua nudged Mo aside and jumped to his feet. All right, fifteen minutes till kick-off. Crisps, tonic water and gin were readily available, and they'd all dressed in national jerseys. Well, except for Tristan, who'd stubbornly painted the Scottish flag onto his cheek even though Mo had greeted him with, "Mate, did your team even make it into the group stage?" They were all set for a successful match; the English team had better shape up.

The viewer showed Nate looking straight into the security camera downstairs, the darkening road deserted behind him. Joshua buzzed him into the building and waited at the open door, most of his focus on the sound of a squabble in the living room; Ed was ribbing Mo about how a non-swimmer had become the face of the *Acqua di Giò* campaign. The distraction was to blame for how Joshua didn't notice that there were two sets of footsteps—not until he caught movement on the edge of his vision.

No.

Fuck no.

Half-hidden behind Nate, Leo climbed the final steps. His red jersey hung loosely on him, posture betraying discomfort as he stared at Joshua with apprehension written into his careful smile. His hair had been styled into a swooping fringe, but underneath, his eyes looked tired. Still beautiful, though. Always fucking beautiful.

That bastard.

"Joshua, hi." Nate's quiet voice cut into the silence that had settled around them, with Joshua blocking the doorway, Nate on the landing and Leo a step below. Leo was still staring at Joshua.

Deliberately dragging his gaze away, Joshua frowned at Nate. "Hey, glad you could make it. But I thought Mo told you the invitation didn't extend to others?"

To Joshua's own surprise, it came out reasonably composed, although he didn't achieve the clinical coolness he'd managed to cling to during his phone conversation yesterday. It had been easier when he didn't have to see Leo flinch out of the corner of his eye. Seriously, though. Had Leo expected Joshua would be *happy* to see him? Why was he even here? He probably just wanted to meet Ed.

"Yes, right." Nate sounded wildly uncomfortable. "I'll just... If you just let me pass, I'll leave the two of you to—um. Discuss this. Yeah?"

"I don't see how there is anything to discuss," Joshua said harshly, directed at Nate rather than at Leo. He did step aside to let Nate in, though, and moved right back to block the doorway.

"I'll be inside?" Nate made it sound like a question. While Joshua wasn't sure whether Nate had addressed Leo or Joshua himself, he didn't bother glancing back to check. He nodded jerkily instead.

"Right behind you. Just need to take out the rubbish." The moment the words were out, Joshua hated himself for them. This nasty, vengeful person that took delight in the way Leo's eyes widened in hurt—Joshua didn't want to be that.

This isn't like you.

"Joshua," Leo said, very softly. "Please don't."

Swallowing, Joshua leaned his hip against the doorframe and crossed his arms. He inhaled through his nose. The nauseating pressure behind his forehead made it hard to think. "Sorry," he muttered. "That was out of line. My point stands, though. You're not invited, and you've got some nerve showing up here."

"I..." Leo cleared his throat, blinked and lowered his gaze to the floor. "I really need to talk to you. Set some things straight."

Like how Joshua had been a bloody fool for believing they'd had a connection when Leo had never made a single promise? Thanks, but no thanks.

"Not interested," Joshua said.

Leo's gaze skimmed up Joshua's legs, over his torso, briefly clung to his face and then skittered away. "Please, little prince. You should know that I never—"

"Don't *little prince* me," Joshua interrupted. He felt sick to his stomach. "And save your excuses 'cause I don't want to hear them. So let's just... stay out of each other's life."

Leo was quiet for a short while, his shoulders drawn tight and lips pressed into a firm line. He'd never seemed less self-assured. The light in the stairway flicked off automatically, plunging them into sudden shadows. How delightfully symbolic. Joshua fumbled for the switch, and Leo squinted into the brightness, seeming momentarily disoriented before he collected himself and met Joshua's eyes.

"Nate is my best mate, Mo is yours. I don't think Mo is playing with Nate—I will fuck him up if he is, but... Yeah, I don't think so. Which means that you and I *will* be in each other's life. Whether you like it or not." Leo's voice had gained an edge of confidence. "This would be my usual pub night with Nate, remember? We're overlapping already. D'you really want to spoil this for them?"

It was a low blow. In fact, it was downright manipulative, and while Leo had a point, Joshua wouldn't be played like this. He stood up straight and glared at Leo. "I would *never*. That doesn't mean I have to let you into my flat."

"Well," Leo said, tilting up his chin. "But things would be much easier if you and I agreed to a truce, don't you think so?"

No. No, Joshua did not think so.

He was about to say just that when Mo's laughter drifted out of the living room, mingling with the sound from the telly, with Tristan's shout and Ed's bright voice, then a chuckle from Nate. The words died in Joshua's throat. For a long second, he merely stared at Leo, his skin stretched too tight over his bones.

"Why are you here?" Joshua asked eventually.

"To talk to you. And to watch the game, but mainly to talk to you." Leo's answer came out low and sincere, and Joshua didn't know what to believe anymore.

"So you're not just here for Ed?"

Leo's brows pulled together. "Ed?"

"Ed Sheeran."

"Shit, he's here?" Leo released a rush of air, then shook his head. "No, that's not—that's cool, but it's not why I'm here."

While Leo was a good actor, his reaction had seemed genuine. God, this was all just so... stupid. So messed up and tangled, and Joshua didn't know; he just didn't *know*.

"I'm not ready to talk to you."

Leo glanced away and shifted his weight, tugging at the hem of his jersey. "Okay," he agreed softly. "Then I'll stay out of your way until you are. But please don't make our friends choose."

Manipulative bastard. Why did he *care* so much about Joshua letting him in? Was it really just so he wouldn't miss out on a football night with friends, or was he serious about his need to talk to Joshua? Was he desperate enough to use Mo and Nate as an excuse to stay in Joshua's life? Joshua swallowed against the sour taste in his mouth.

"Don't talk to me," he said, the words rough and scraping over his palate. "Not unless I talk to you first."

He didn't wait for Leo's reply. Just turned and left the door open, didn't look over his shoulder as he made his way back to the others. He imagined he could feel Leo's gaze lingering on the nape of his neck—like a phantom touch, like cobwebs brushing over his skin.

So this would be every bit as difficult as Leo had feared.

Lingering in the dimly lit entryway, he took his time toeing off his trainers and told himself he had no right to feel hurt. Really, he should be grateful Joshua had let him in at all, even though it had taken Leo using their friends as a weapon to make it happen. Jesus fuck, how was Leo supposed to undo the hurt he'd caused without giving away too much? How could he convey what was at stake—for both of them—without telling Joshua the worst of his past? The pretty apology Leo had wanted to offer seemed painfully inadequate after he'd had to fight dirty just to get inside the flat.

He'd figure it out. He'd have to.

Shoulders squared, he moved towards the light spilling out of the living room. On the threshold, he took in the scene—the flicker of Joshua's enormous telly, Mo and Nate sprawled on the floor, Joshua on the sofa, squished in between Tristan and Ed Sheeran. Holy shit, *Ed Sheeran*. Three weeks ago, Leo would have had a heart attack. Now, the spark of excitement was blanketed by cold dread weighing down Leo's stomach.

It took three thundering seconds before Mo glanced over, noticed

Leo, and sat up sharply. The narrow-eyed surprise proved Joshua hadn't bothered to announce Leo's presence. "The fuck are *you* doing here?" Mo asked, the question slicing through the chatter of the TV.

Almost in sync, Tristan and Ed looked over, while Joshua stared fixedly at the line-up of the Italian players. Nate blinked and turned to frown at Mo. "Hey, please don't."

Everything was awful.

"I take it that's Leo?" Ed asked, carefully neutral, so he was obviously aware of the story. Of course he was; Joshua didn't hold back with his friends, did he? Maybe Leo should take a leaf out of his book.

With measured strides, Leo went to offer his hand for a shake and worked up a smile. "I'm Leo, yes. Pleasure to meet you. Big fan."

Christ, he sounded like an idiot. If he'd bothered picturing a meeting with one of his favourite musicians, it would have started with Leo saying something witty, Ed laughing at it and offering to buy him a pint, and they'd be best mates by the end of the night. The way Ed accepted Leo's hand for a curt shake and said, "Ed," in a cool voice, no trace of the easy-going smile he sported in most pictures...

Yeah, this wasn't that fantasy.

"Pleasure," Leo repeated, quite uselessly. He glanced at Joshua just long enough to memorise the clean cut of Joshua's profile and the way his hair curled against his temple, then forced himself to turn away and sit down on the floor, close to Nate.

Mo was still glaring at him, and a quick look confirmed that Tristan didn't look pleased either. Well, Leo had known they'd be irrevocably on Joshua's side. He'd expected it, felt grateful for it even because Joshua deserved friends like that. It hurt all the same, just a little. Pulling his legs up to his chest, Leo tried to make himself as small as possible.

"You haven't answered my fucking question," Mo said. He shot Nate a look. "I told you not to bring him."

On the telly, the teams lined up for the national hymns, and Leo's chest hurt with the need for air. He was about to come up with some kind of reply, justification, *anything*, when Tristan spoke up.

"You got some bloody fucking nerve, Grammy. Not cool." He didn't look quite as murderous as Mo, but there was a clear message in the way he draped an arm around Joshua's shoulders to pull him close. Joshua came easily, naturally—just the way he'd used to sink into Leo's embrace. If Leo could touch Joshua just a little, run his fingertips along the instep of Joshua's foot and up his bare calves...

He wrestled his gaze away and stayed silent. What could he have said, anyway? *It's all a misunderstanding*? No, it wasn't; it hadn't been. Not really. Leo could have corrected Joshua as soon as he'd realised how Joshua had misread that tiny bit of truth Leo had offered—only he hadn't, because it had seemed like as good an excuse as any for why he and Joshua could never work out. He'd need to come up with a better reason, something that didn't make Joshua feel quite so used.

Or maybe he needed to stop lying.

"Look, everyone," Nate began. "I know this isn't ideal, but—"

"The match is about to start," Joshua interrupted, uncommonly rude for his standards. "I'd rather not spend it watching my friends fight, which does include you, Nate." The way Joshua refused to so much as glance in Leo's direction clearly excluded him from the term. "Let's just declare a truce, all right?"

A truce. Just what Leo had suggested. So Joshua still paid attention to him, still listened. It wasn't much, but it was a start.

Leo felt the tension in his spine loosen slightly, and then a little more when Tristan agreed, Mo grunting his assent a moment later. The kick-off whistle couldn't have come at a more opportune time.

THROUGHOUT THE FIRST HALF, Leo's gaze kept straying to Joshua. Not once did he find Joshua looking back.

Tucked in between Tristan and Ed, with Mo leaning against his legs, Joshua was more out of reach than he'd ever been. He kept chewing on his bottom lip, clutching his drink and twisting the fabric of a red jersey which matched the ones Mo, Ed and Leo himself wore.

His eyes were fixed on the game, and each time Italy so much as crossed the centre line, he tensed up, gripping Ed's thigh.

Leo needed to slow down on the gin and tonic.

When Italy drew ahead half an hour in, Joshua sagged into himself and released a long breath. Leo wanted to kiss him so much that he almost missed Sturridge evening the score two minutes later.

Jumping to his feet a second later than the others, Leo found himself in the middle of a celebratory huddle that included Nate and Tristan, Mo bumping into them. Then Ed and Joshua were there as well, elbows knocking together, Tristan yelling about English bastards and their goddamn luck while Joshua laughed, free and open and beautiful. Leo had never wanted anyone like this. He didn't think he ever would again.

There was a moment of awkwardness when they all separated, Joshua's grin flickering as he caught Leo's eye. He turned away quickly, pointedly, and Leo was left with his heart beating in the very tips of his fingers. All he could do was sit back down on the floor and watch as Joshua leaned into Ed's side and gave him a kiss on the cheek, received a smile in return.

Their interaction was easy and friendly. Casual.

Frowning, Leo turned to look back at the telly. Nothing about Joshua and Ed suggested an undercurrent of sexual tension. Even if it had, Leo had no right to be upset. Really, they were *friends*, just like Joshua and Tristan, Joshua and Mo—although that was probably the wrong parallel to draw, fuck. Either way, there was no reason why this was in any way different.

Except for how Ed was an outsider to the bubble the rest of them had formed while planning Joshua's coming out; Ed was a reminder that Joshua was slipping away. A reminder that Leo had never been meant to keep him.

Not that Leo hadn't known that already. It was just... God. The gin bubbling in his veins made him feel restless.

He shot another glance at Joshua, and this time, Joshua was looking back. As soon as their eyes met, Joshua's mouth drew tight and he faced away. Leo kept watching him for several seconds longer, but Joshua's gaze never strayed from the telly again.

Taking another sip of his gin and tonic, Leo tried to focus on the game. At any other time, he'd be fully consumed by it, would find it hard to concentrate on anything but the Italian players pressing in on the English penalty area, keeping tight possession of the ball as they sought out gaps in the defence. But with Joshua just a few feet away, with the way Joshua draped his legs over Ed's lap, gripping Ed's arm each time the Italians came near the goal... Leo took another sip and didn't bother looking away when Joshua finally glanced over again. This time, Joshua maintained eye contact for a slowly pulsing heartbeat, then his brows pulled together and he frowned. Almost deliberately, he tilted further into Ed's side, a challenge in his eyes.

Pressing his lips together, Leo directed his attention back at the TV. Maybe he shouldn't have come. Whatever he'd been hoping to accomplish—well, he was ready to declare it a failure.

The last few minutes before halftime break were torture; two Italian chances, one cleared on the line, the other by the goal post. When the whistle provided them with temporary reprieve, Leo realised he'd somehow emptied his glass, and his body felt like a tightly coiled spring. He got to his feet with a sigh, stretching, and countered Nate's worried expression with a half-smile.

"Anyone want a smoke?" he asked no one in particular, already moving towards the terrace. Usually, Mo would have jumped at the chance to join in, but Leo wasn't surprised when obstinate silence was the only response he received.

All right, then.

Leo answered Nate's unspoken offer to join with an incremental headshake. He didn't mind a few minutes to himself, some fresh air to clear his head and get the sad weight in his chest under control. It constituted a breach of his one-cigarette-a-day rule, but fuck, he'd bloody well earned it.

He'd only just lit up, was taking his first drag with his elbows on the banister and staring down at the Canal, when footsteps sounded behind him. He glanced over his shoulder—and swallowed smoke when he recognised Joshua. Coughing, he turned fully and tried to read Joshua's expression in what little light spilled out of the living room. He didn't succeed.

"Hi," he said quietly, stifling another cough, smoke burning in his throat. Then he remembered Joshua had told him not to address him first and added a quick, rushed, "Sorry. You told me not to—"

"Thought you only smoked in the afternoon," Joshua cut in. His voice was sharp and precise, and Leo's body felt heavy all over. Heavier.

"One per day, yeah." Leo cleared his throat. "Exceptions are made when I'm nervous or angry. Or sad, I guess."

Stiffly, Joshua drew forward to lean against the banister. He was looking at the velvety evening sky rather than at Leo when he asked, "Why do you keep watching me? And with Ed, why do you—"

"Because I'm jealous," Leo interrupted, and the words echoed in his head, *jealous, jealous, jealous.* Maybe he shouldn't have said it; he had no right, no right at all. If he'd felt just a hint tipsy before, he was fully sober now, cold from the shadows that surrounded them and pressed in on his chest.

Joshua gave a snort that didn't turn out quite right, his breath hitching. "Fuck you," he muttered, face still tipped towards the sky. "You're such a dick, seriously. I can't *believe* you." One of his hands closed around the banister, and Leo fought to stay where he was, to keep from shifting closer—just a little, just a tiny bit, just enough that he would be able to soak up the imagined warmth of Joshua's skin.

He took a deep drag of his cigarette and remained silent, staring at Joshua's profile.

A few moments passed before Joshua spoke again, rough around the edges. "I seriously just can't believe you, Leo. You just—you can't not want me, then be upset if someone else... And Ed isn't even into dudes. That's not—and even if it were, then that'd be none of your bloody business. You don't get to ask anything of me."

"I know." It was barely above a whisper. The inside of Leo's chest hollowed around the knowledge that it was true, that he'd had his chance—only it hadn't ever been a chance at all. Not really. He continued after a beat. "And I never said I didn't want you."

Joshua made a sudden, abrupt move, not quite a flinch and not quite anything else. "It was clearly implied." For all that his tone was harsh, Leo caught the hurt that shone through. He hated himself for it.

"No. It was what you chose to hear," he said, exhaling, smoke curling up towards the sky. "But I didn't correct you, I guess. I let you think we had sex because I used to have that teenage crush on you, and that it was the only reason I wanted... It wasn't. Isn't. I'm sorry for making you think that."

The silence that stretched between them felt like a thousand miles. Joshua had turned to look at Leo, the night draining him of colour, his posture betraying uncertainty for the first time since Leo had arrived. It gave Leo the courage to shuffle half a step closer, pure instinct as he reached out to touch Joshua's face—and froze with his hand suspended in the air.

What was he *doing*?

"You do want me," Joshua said slowly, so quiet it only just bridged the gap between them. He looked as though he'd been broken open, caught halfway between disbelief and hope.

Leo inhaled and dropped his hand. His intestines had rearranged themselves into a messy bow. "How could I not?"

"Then why?" Joshua asked, a hint louder than before.

The bitter taste of the gin and tonic coated the inside of Leo's mouth, and he turned away, tried to chase it off with another mouthful of smoke. He didn't succeed.

"Why?" Joshua repeated. He crossed his arms, tensing up again, voice rising. "Nothing you say makes any sense. Are you just—"

"A guy like me doesn't get to keep a guy like you. That's not how it works." The words were out before Leo could swallow them back down, escaping on a cloud of stale smoke.

Joshua shook his head, rapid and stubborn. He stepped closer, making it impossible for Leo to look anywhere else, and God, if Leo were to kiss him right now...

"I don't get you at all." Joshua sounded lost. "What do you mean? A guy like you, a guy like me—what does that *mean*? Is this about the stupid royal thing? Because, like, I know my life isn't normal, but we can figure something out if—"

"It just *is*," Leo told him.

"Explain."

"I can't."

"No, that's a lie." Abruptly, Joshua took a step back and looked away. His voice had regained its cool quality, as though he were addressing a stranger. "No," he repeated evenly. "It's not that you can't. It's that you won't."

Leo shivered. There was nothing he could say in his defence, nothing at all, so he took another drag of the cigarette. His hand was shaking the tiniest bit, but Joshua had already turned away and couldn't see it anymore.

When Joshua headed back inside without so much as another glance, Leo didn't try to stop him. Just finished his cigarette before he returned to join the others in time for the second half.

Fittingly, England lost. As soon as the final whistle sounded, Leo got to his feet and uttered a half-hearted goodbye which only Tristan and Ed echoed. Joshua was staring straight ahead while Mo shot Leo one of his deeply unimpressed looks.

Nate followed Leo out, standing in the corridor with a rather helpless expression as Leo crouched down to lace up his trainers. "Leo—"

"You can stay," Leo told him. He softened his voice and managed a smile that required conscious effort. "Seriously, you should. It's not like I had much hope, right?"

Nate's face dropped. "So he didn't... I thought, when he followed you out..."

Second shoe. Leo focused on the simple, menial task and kept his voice low. "Mostly just came to yell at me. Except politely, and no yelling because it's Joshua. So, you know."

"I can come with you," Nate offered. "Maybe grab a pint or something?"

After finishing with the laces, Leo rose to his feet and gave Nate a brief, impulsive hug. His chest hurt a little, but he refused to think about it. "Thank you," he whispered, nose pressed against Nate's throat. "Stay, though. I'll be fine, I promise. I'll just go home, catch up on sleep."

"If you're sure." Nate didn't sound convinced.

"I'm sure." Leo wasn't, but there was no way he'd rob Nate of the chance to set things right with Mo. Nate had already risked more than enough by taking Leo along when he shouldn't have. "Go back inside," Leo told him. "Talk to Mo. Don't let this come between you two, okay?"

Since Nate was still hesitating, Leo gave him a gentle shove.

Nate took a couple of steps, then stopped and glanced back. "I'll talk to you tomorrow?"

"Yes, you will." Leo's smile came just a tad easier. "Now *go*."

This time, Nate complied.

As soon as he was gone, Leo felt his smile drop, and he lingered for a moment to listen to the jumble of voices drifting out into the corridor. Then he rubbed a hand over his eyes, straightened his shoulders, and left.

A GUY like me doesn't get to keep a guy like you.

What did that mean? What the *fuck* did that mean?

Joshua felt like kicking something. Or like taking a swim, like diving deep, trying to hold his breath until his lungs were ready to burst with the need for air. Had it been a line, a variation of 'it's not you, it's me?' It hadn't seemed like a line. Not with the way Leo had reacted to Joshua's presence today.

You do want me.

How could I not?

Leo cared. He just didn't care enough to be honest.

And really, wasn't that just ironic when Leo had been so quick to

judge the first time they'd met. Wear it like a crown? Yeah, right. Leo
was a hypocrite.

Picking up a couple of empty glasses and a bag of crisps that
contained only remaining crumbs, Joshua slid off the sofa, leaving
the others to dissect all the things that had gone wrong with the
match. The kitchen was dark and silent, and he didn't bother flicking
on the light as he crossed over to the sink. When he'd gone out to
confront Leo, there'd been a mild, alcohol-induced glow around
everything. It had long since evaporated. Now he just felt tired and
confused, even more so than before.

"Joshua," Nate said from behind him, and Joshua startled, jolting
around. Outlined by the brightness falling in from the corridor, Nate
was reduced to a silhouette.

Joshua consciously loosened his posture and went for a light tone.
"Didn't hear you approach, sorry. Can I get you something?"

"Actually, I just wanted to have a brief word with you." Nate
sounded distinctly uncomfortable, but also determined. He took a
step into the kitchen so that they were both cast in shadows.

"A word about what?" Joshua asked, but really, he already knew.
Under the pretence of switching on the fairy lights above the work
surface, he averted his face.

"About Leo," Nate said, still in that decidedly firm tone. "Because I
think—just please don't be..." He broke off and sighed. When he
spoke again, it was softer. "You should give him a chance to explain.
He really cares about you, you know?"

He really cares about you.

Joshua shook his head to clear the fog in his brain. No, it wasn't
that easy. If Leo really did care, he didn't care *enough*. Not if tired
excuses were all he ever offered. He'd had about seven hundred
chances to explain, and he'd only ever pushed Joshua away.

Turning, Joshua leaned back against the work surface and met
Nate's eyes. "He's had that chance. He didn't take it."

The dim glow of the fairy lights was enough to reveal the flash of
unease that crossed Nate's face. He scrubbed a hand over the back of
his neck. "Look, it's complicated. I know he can be a bit of a dick, but

he's also—he's a good person, and he's loyal, and he's *trying*, okay? And he's opened up so much already, and you're a big part of that. Like, he took you to see his work with those kids, Joshua. Do you even realise how *personal* that is to him?"

Joshua took a moment to process the words, a tangled string of *personal* and *you're a big part of that* and *he's trying* reverberating in his head. He inhaled slowly. "Are you saying that... You're telling me that even you don't know the full story? Like, his past? Is that really —*Jesus*."

"It's complicated," Nate repeated, and really, was it? It didn't seem particularly complicated to Joshua.

"Remember when Leo told me that I was hiding behind a pretty lie to make my life easier?" Joshua's voice came out harsher than he'd intended, and he caught the way Nate flinched. He continued regardless. "Well, who's hiding now? And don't tell me he's protecting me, because I'm quite certain he's only protecting himself."

Nate's forehead creased into unhappy lines. "It's not that easy. He's been living like this for years—"

Joshua cut in with, "You say that like I don't know what it's like."

"I'm not sure you do," Nate said gently. "There's a difference between being closeted and being... Doing what we do. Those of us working for James, I mean. We're not just hiding one aspect of our lives, you know, but... much more. Generally speaking. Like, big things, from what I know or suspect about the others. So I don't think it's quite the same." His frown deepened, and Joshua exhaled in a rush, contrite. They were both quiet for a moment, Nate with his gaze fixed on the floor, clearly uncomfortable.

It was Joshua who ended the silence with a low, "I'm sorry, Nate. It's not you I'm angry with. I know you're just being a good friend, and I appreciate that."

Nate replied with a slight delay, worry still plain on his face. "Please just try not to... Don't judge him too harshly. Don't break his heart. Please?"

Don't break his heart.

Joshua blinked, blinked again, his heart in his throat because—

what. That was a lot more than *he cares about you*, far more than *you do want me*. Did that mean... But no. Surely not. Leo cared, yes. But if he'd been in love with Joshua, in actual *love*, he would have stayed.

Or not? Could he be in love with Joshua and still falter at the thought of what a relationship would entail? At the sheer amount of *baggage* that would come with being Joshua's partner? And, oh. Wasn't that just what Joshua had always feared? With a start, he remembered his own words from what seemed like years ago, from the first time Leo had been to this very flat and Joshua had dumped his own bitter fears and doubts on him without warning. *Show me the guy who'll stick around once the media calls on the hunt.*

But Leo was a fighter. He wouldn't give up that easily. Or would he?

Show me the guy who loves me enough.

"Nate," Joshua began, and then Mo ambled into the kitchen. Nate immediately turned to look at him, frown melting away to make room for a smile that seemed like an automatic reaction to Mo's presence. There was a strange tilt to it, though, something almost like guilt.

"Everything all right?" Mo asked, glancing back and forth between them.

It took Joshua a second to pull himself together. He nodded at Mo and waited for Nate to do the same. Instead, Nate lifted one shoulder by an inch and met Mo's gaze, appearing at a strange loss.

Mo narrowed his eyes. "Nate?"

Another second passed, then Nate swallowed. His gaze was fixed on Mo, and Joshua felt as though he was intruding on something private.

"Can we..." Nate wet his lips and started anew, looking straight at Mo. "Can we talk? I think, maybe, there's a few things you should know."

"Sure, yeah. Whenever you're ready, babe." Mo's voice was even, and if he was surprised, he didn't show it. Joshua remembered their conversation about this precise thing, Mo's remark that yes, he was aware that Nate was holding back some things about his past.

Well, at least Mo might be getting truths tonight. He deserved it; both Mo and Nate deserved it. Still Joshua couldn't fully suppress the bitterness that coloured the thought.

"Guest room is all yours," he told them. "And a bottle of red wine, if you want it. I'll be..." He made a vague gesture towards the living room and went to move past Mo, but was stopped by a light touch to his hip.

"Hey," Mo said softly. "Talk tomorrow?"

Joshua took a deep breath and relaxed, just slightly. He leaned in to kiss Mo's cheek, then shot Nate something that he hoped would pass for a smile. "Treat him well, will you?"

The surprise on Nate's face lingered for only a moment, then his expression shifted into one of hope. "I'll do my best," he said.

"I can hear you guys, you know," Mo put in.

Joshua pinched Mo's hip, nodded at Nate, and left the kitchen to give them some space. He rejoined Tristan and Ed, draping himself over both of them to demand cuddles, but even as he closed his eyes and sank into the familiarity of their closeness, his mind was churning, chasing questions from one side of his skull to the other.

A guy like me doesn't get to keep a guy like you.

KELSEY HAD ARRIVED some time after the game, drunk and giggly from a football night with her best friends. Joshua had told her and Tristan to kip in his bedroom—"Door stays open, no funny business in my bed."—and had agreed to share the sofa with Ed.

It was almost like old times. Joshua had caught Ed performing purely by chance in some London bar, one of those glorious nights when Joshua had been fortunate and no one had leaked his location, back before *PrinceWatch* had dug its claws into him. Ed had captivated every single person in the room with nothing but his voice and his guitar, with songs that felt like small revelations. When Joshua had approached him afterwards, Ed had taken one look at him, then given an incredulous laugh and asked, "Shit, am I expected to curtsy now? Think I might topple over if I try, mate. Not the most coordinated in general, and they pay me in drinks here."

They'd spent the rest of the night talking and drinking, and a few days later, Ed had shown up on Joshua's doorstep with a hopeful grin and a knapsack. Since Joshua's previous flat had come without a guest room, Ed had camped out on Joshua's sofa for a fortnight, and Joshua had learned a lot about life and dedication in those two weeks.

"You trust too easily," Ed had told him three days in. Joshua had shrugged and grinned.

"I wasn't wrong about you, was I?"

Unfortunately, nostalgia didn't make for comfortable sleep. It had looked too much like rain to use the bed outside, and while the sofa in the living room made a generous bed for one person, it was crowded for two. When Joshua woke for the third time from nearly tumbling to the floor, he gave up.

Leaving Ed to slumber in peace, he grabbed his tablet and padded outside. The morning sky was still overcast, grey light blanketing the city and everything quiet when Joshua sat down on the sofa bed and huddled under the afghan to ward off the chill. Unlocking the tablet, he told himself this was a bad idea. An invasion of Leo's privacy.

A guy like me.

Screw this. Really, just... God, Joshua was so bloody tired of Leo's cryptic clues. Why could Nate open up, but Leo couldn't? If Leo didn't trust Joshua at all—well, then what did Joshua have to lose? Nothing. There was absolutely nothing to lose.

Joshua navigated to Google, typed in Leo's name, and waited for the results to load.

HALF AN HOUR LATER, Joshua set the tablet aside and pulled the blanket tighter around his shoulders. So. Leo was a virtual ghost. No social media account, not even a picture linked to his name. Since

James worked without a website, there wasn't anything to be found there either. There was just... nothing.

How? In this day and age, how was that possible?

Joshua's stomach felt as though it was filled with lead. No one could be so paranoid as to erase all virtual tracks of their existence. What about school records, or the graduation list from a university? Odd jobs where Leo's name would be added to some 'our team' page? A random photograph taken at some event?

Picking the tablet up again, Joshua stared blankly at the screen for several moments, a little numb. Then he called up a new email to George. *'Who's that person at MI5 who sometimes helps you out? Can you send me the contact details? .x - J'*

Mo and Nate were the last to join them for breakfast, and one glance was enough to tell Joshua that something had changed between them —they sat just a little bit closer, hands bumping, knees pressed together under the table. With Tristan and Kelsey turned towards each other, speaking in some kind of shorthand code, Joshua was glad for Ed's presence.

Ed was the first to leave, shortly followed by Tristan and Kelsey, then Nate got to his feet as well, smiling as he thanked Joshua for the delicious breakfast as well as the hospitality. "I'll drive you home," Mo told him.

Nate's eyes were warm when they found Mo. "You don't have to."

"I want to," Mo said.

Joshua felt himself start to smile in spite of the unease that had taken up permanent residence in his belly, indecision weighing on him. More than once, he'd come close to changing his mind and contacting the MI5 bloke so as to call off the basic background check on Leo Graham, born twenty-seven years ago on the 24th of December.

"You're ridiculous," he said to Mo.

Mo's very mature response consisted of sticking out his tongue.

He seemed lighter than Joshua had seen him in a while, content, and it made Joshua's grin soften.

He walked both of them to the door, hugging Nate goodbye. While Nate brought his own arms up to return the embrace, he looked openly confused, and Joshua was prompted into a chuckle. "That's for making my best mate happy," Joshua told him. "I like people who make my friends happy."

Nate's features relaxed, and he gave Joshua's shoulder a quick squeeze, then hesitated briefly. "He'll—Leo. Don't give up on him, yeah? He really... I mean, not that I know anything for sure, but it's just—it's tricky."

Tricky, Joshua thought. Right, yes, tricky. Jesus, that even Nate had only pieces of the puzzle meant that it had to be bad, really bad, and —and Joshua had asked an MI5 officer to look into Leo's background. What the hell had he been thinking?

He couldn't do that. It was wrong, an abuse of power, and he needed to stop it. This was not him. This was not who he wanted to be.

As soon as Mo and Nate were gone, Joshua would put an end to it.

A little blankly, he echoed Nate's goodbyes and turned to Mo. "Hey," he remembered to ask, low with his mouth against Mo's ear. "So it's going well? He told you what's going on?"

"Starting to. Working on it." Mo pulled back, a genuine smile in his eyes. Joshua returned it.

He waited until the sound of their footsteps had faded down the stairs before he closed the door and leaned against it for a moment, letting the silence of his empty flat settle in his blood. All right. So he'd made a mistake. He should not have resorted to looking for virtual traces of Leo, should most definitely not have brought in MI5. He'd call it off. He'd call it off right now, and it would be as though it had never happened.

Pushing away from the door, he went to retrieve his tablet, was about to pull up George's email with the contact information when he noticed a new message in his inbox. The subject was a simple *'Your Request,'* sent by John Fallon. The MI5 guy.

Joshua held his breath.

He should delete it. He should.

Instead, he squeezed his eyes shut and clicked on the message.

It wasn't too late. He hadn't read it yet. He could still delete it, could still pretend he'd never, ever gone that far. Exhaling in a rush, he opened his eyes and focused on the single line of text.

'There is no record of such a person, Sir. Would you like me to explore alternate solutions?'

Joshua shoved the tablet away and struggled to control his breathing. Fought down the sour bile that rose to the back of his throat.

THE BLACK MERCEDES hadn't been parked in front of Leo's house when he'd left.

Drawing to a sharp halt, Leo startled when the football he'd been juggling bounced down next to him on the pavement, rolling a few feet before it came to rest against one tire of the car. With its tinted windows in the back, the Mercedes was blatantly too posh for the area. Could it be...? Under the excuse of picking up the ball, Leo peered into the front.

Zach. That was *Zach* behind the wheel.

Oh God. Joshua was here.

Had he changed his mind? Did he want Leo in his life after all? Even if it was just as friends—well, they couldn't be more, not if Joshua wanted to be open with the public. Leo needed to remember that. The one time he'd allowed himself to forget, he'd ended up in Joshua's bed, and Joshua had kicked him out in the morning.

Friends. It was better than nothing.

With a nod at Zach, Leo straightened and turned to enter his building. The front door hadn't locked in years, so Joshua had to be inside, waiting upstairs in front of Leo's flat. Why had he come? What had happened in between last night and this morning that would suddenly make him seek Leo out? Unease shivered in Leo's belly, and he was overly aware that he was sweaty and dishevelled from playing football in the park, an unsuccessful attempt to distract himself.

He climbed the stairs slowly, ball clutched to his chest. Last turn. A deep breath, and Leo made himself continue.

Fuck. Okay, yes. There Joshua was, sitting with his back against Leo's door.

At the sound of Leo's footsteps, Joshua looked up sharply. Shadows were braided into his hair, the green of his eyes reduced to a dull grey, and the moment he saw Leo, he clambered to his feet. Leo wanted to wrap himself all around him and cling until every last trace of tension had drained from Joshua's body.

Instead, he stopped a couple of paces away. "Hi," he said softly. His skin felt brittle, and he touched his knuckles against the wall to ground himself.

Joshua stared at him, motionless for several seconds that lurched like tidal waves. Then Joshua opened his mouth and drew a deep breath, dragging his gaze away. "Hi, Leo. If that's even your name."

What—oh God.

Fuck, no.

No, no, *no.*

"What do you—" Leo began, his voice echoing hollowly in the stairway.

"There is," Joshua's voice hitched, "no Leo Graham. At least there isn't one born on the 24th of December. Not in the UK."

How did he know, *how?*

Leo's veins had turned into barbed wire. Somehow, he managed to pull himself together, work up enough of a will to move past Joshua and unlock the door to his flat. Joshua knew; how *much* did he know?

There is no Leo Graham.

Stumbling into the flat, Leo left the door open. He was still clutching the ball to his chest. Static was buzzing in his ears, making it hard to focus.

"What did you *do?*" Joshua asked from behind him. "Whatever would make you change your name? Did you, like, kill someone?"

That last question punched through Leo's stupor. He shot around, found Joshua standing in the doorway and shook his head, a little desperately. "Jesus, no. Fuck's sake, how can you even think that?"

"I don't know what to think! I mean, hi, I just found out that the guy I..." Joshua waved a hand around, voice rising. "He doesn't even exist! I thought I knew you, but now it's like I don't even—"

"You do know me," Leo interrupted. "You *do*. Joshua..." He took a step forward and froze when Joshua shied away from him, bumping into the half-open door so it fell shut. It hurt. Fuck, it *hurt*. Joshua's eyes were wide in the grey brightness that flooded Leo's corridor, a hectic flush to his cheeks, and he was watching Leo with thick confusion.

He was here, though. That had to count for something.

When he finally spoke, it was with the air of someone wading through a nightmare. "I don't know what to believe anymore. I don't even know your name."

Leo's body pulled tight with the need to touch Joshua, to bridge that distance. "You know who I am," he squeezed out. "You know who I am *now*. This is who I am."

Joshua barely seemed to hear, his voice still that awful, bewildered rasp. "Did you do something illegal? Is that why you—Like, are you in trouble with the law?" He paused, reaching out one hand to steady himself against the wall. "I mean, a guy like you can't be with a guy like me? What the hell did you do that's so—"

Leo dropped the ball. It landed on the floor with a dull thud. "Please don't." He couldn't force enough air into his lungs. "I'm not, like, a criminal in hiding. I didn't kill anyone. Nothing like that, I swear. I just... I needed a fresh start. That's all. I needed to cut my ties." The words felt thin, translucent. Painfully inadequate. "This is who I've become. This *is* me." Breathe, *breathe*. They were too far apart, an abyss of space between them, and Leo couldn't swallow back the despair that weighed down his voice. "How did you even know? How did you find out?"

"Did a Google search." Joshua's exhalation hissed out through his teeth. "No results. So I asked MI5."

MI5.

Leo's ribs drew tight around his lungs, clenching down. So Joshua knew. He knew all of it. Why was he still asking what he already knew? Was this a test? Did he want to see Leo trip through the tale, punish him? Why was Joshua even *here*?

When Leo inhaled, he tasted metal. "You had fucking MI5 investigate me? That's so bloody... Jesus Christ, fuck you, Joshua. How dare you? I thought you were—"

"There'd be no need if you'd just been honest," Joshua cut in, and Leo took a step forward and raised his head, blood throbbing behind his forehead.

"That's no fucking excuse, and you know it. You make it sound like I forced you, which—no, *fuck* you. You had no bloody *right*." His hands were shaking so badly that he had to curl them into fists. "It's an abuse of privilege. Why the fuck are you here, why are you even asking me questions? Didn't your friends from MI5 already tell you everything there is to know?" His voice shook as badly as his hands did, but there was nothing to be done about it. "Hey, why not ask them to provide you with my DNA sample, while you're at it? Health records? Bank account statement? All yours for the taking, Your Highness."

"I wouldn't!" Joshua drew himself up, eyes clearing, narrowing. "I didn't even—I just asked for some basic confirmation, and all I know is that you're using a fake name. That's it. You don't *exist*, and I have no idea where you come from, no idea whether you even have sisters like you told me, or whether that was all—"

"I didn't lie to you," Leo grit out. His heart dropped. At least Joshua didn't know where Leo had been, the decisions he couldn't take back. "I never lied. It's my fucking story, and there are a lot of things I didn't tell you, but the things I did tell you? All true."

"And I'm supposed to believe you—why?" Joshua gave a hollow laugh that was a wretched, twisted variation of the sound. "You've been all about me coming clean, like, you told me to be honest and proud and out, but you're hiding behind all these walls. Wear it like armour, like a fucking crown? God, you're such a *hypocrite*."

All warmth drained from Leo's body. There was a blank moment when he couldn't do anything but stare at Joshua, completely out of words. Then he sucked in a breath. "It's not that easy."

Something shifted in Joshua's expression, everything about him sharpening. "Isn't it?" he asked, and the question cut to the very marrow of Leo's bones. Leo had never loved and hated him more, had never deserved him less.

Silence reigned for a moment, the ground swaying gently. The walls seemed to scuttle closer when Leo wasn't looking.

Joshua ended it, his voice dark and tight. "So you... what? You were raised rich, and then your parents threw you out and you washed up on the streets? Is that it?"

Leo's heart lurched in his chest. He didn't reply. *Couldn't.* All he could do was meet Joshua's eyes and struggle to stay upright.

Joshua made a sudden move, lips parting around a shocked noise. "Because you were gay," he said, no more than a whisper. "That's why they threw you out, isn't it? Because you didn't fit into their shiny construct. Oh my God. You... So you were born a noble, then."

Words. Leo needed to form words, sentences; he needed to... Needed to...

He stumbled back into the wall, felt it solid against his back. "How do you know? You just told me—"

"Finally fitting puzzle pieces together," Joshua said, still in that broken whisper. His gaze was glued to Leo's face. "I'm right, aren't I?"

"Yes." It was out before Leo could stop himself, before he could *think.* "You're right."

He was still disoriented from the aftershock when Joshua was suddenly there, right there, all up in Leo's space and pulling him into a rough embrace. Warm and real, and all Leo could do was sag into him, fighting to breathe. Something quivered in his stomach, a spark of brightness, and oh God, Joshua knew. Joshua knew, and he was still here. Leo should be scared, should be fucking *terrified* that Joshua would figure out the rest, but right now, there was nothing but deep relief thrumming in Leo's veins.

Turning his face into Joshua's neck, he inhaled deeply. He didn't dare bring up his own arms to pull Joshua closer, everything too fragile and uncertain, his sense of balance destroyed.

Again, it was Joshua who broke the silence. "You know what I also remembered? Like, just now. So you were a noble, and, like..." His words ghosted across Leo's temple, rumbling in Leo's stomach and making it difficult to focus on what Joshua was saying. "There was this teacher at Eton, like, the bloke who coached the football team? His name was Graham. And maybe it's a coincidence, but—I didn't really come to the games, but I just remembered that—I'm probably imagining this?"

Leo forced himself to hold still. Behind his lids, everything was dark and calm, and the room finally stopped spinning. His voice sounded frayed, though. "Imagining what?"

"One of the strikers..." Joshua hesitated, time suspended. "I think he was called Leo. And he looked a bit like you, I think. Like, mainly the eyes. There was an interview in *The Chronicle*. I must have been, like, fifteen because it was just after I'd realised I kind of liked guys. And I actually—I looked for the guy in the hallways, but—"

"I'd already left," Leo interrupted. Then Joshua's words caught up with him, the way he'd sounded a little embarrassed, and... Joshua had looked for him in the hallways?

"So you really did attend Eton?" Joshua pulled back, enough so that he could stare at Leo. He looked astonished, eyes big and so green, lips parted just slightly. Leo wanted to kiss him. Always, always.

Leo swallowed. "I was certain you wouldn't recognise me. I've changed a lot, and I was two years above you and Tristan. Also, we moved in different circles, and there were way more than a thousand boys at Eton, so..." It felt as though Leo's skin might peel off—just break open at the seams and come down, like old wallpaper. Still Joshua was staring at him, and after a moment, Leo continued. "When I arrived in London, I didn't have much use for a last name that was easy to connect to a noble title, you know? Not that I had much use for a last name in general, but—anyway. Coach Graham, he'd always been kind. I was a bit of a troublemaker in class, and

Graham was... There weren't that many adults who took me seriously. So whenever I needed a full name... It made sense to pick something positive."

It had felt strange at first, and Leo had practised his signature on scraps of paper until it hadn't looked quite so childish anymore, until it had come easily. He still remembered the first time he'd used it on an official form, how worried he'd been in spite of James' promise of a clean slate.

"That's so—Jesus." Slowly, Joshua shook his head. One of his hands was still resting on Leo's shoulder, and Leo abruptly remembered that he was sweaty and dirty. He probably looked a mess.

He took a step to the side and scrubbed a hand through his hair. "Sorry," he said. "I was playing football 'cause it's what I do when everything else sucks. Now I got you all..." He didn't finish, simply gestured at Joshua's silk shirt, unbuttoned over a blue T-shirt. Fuck, he looked good.

Joshua blinked, gaze tracking down Leo's body and lingering on Leo's thighs. Distant heat collected in Leo's stomach, and maybe they could—? Just once more, just *once*.

"Did you really have a crush on me?" Joshua asked into Leo's thoughts. "At Eton?"

Leo swallowed around what he hoped would pass for a self-deprecating grin. "It was abstract. I didn't know you back then, so it wasn't very... real. Mostly I just saw you in the hallways, and you were famous and really bloody cute, seemed nice enough. I suppose I projected things onto you." For a moment, Leo paused, considering. He'd revealed so much already, and there was one thing that he wouldn't—that he *couldn't* reveal, but... everything else was fair game. Joshua deserved whatever truth Leo could offer.

Leo's lungs felt too full, ready to burst, as though he'd been underwater for a while and was desperate to break the surface. *Joshua deserves this.*

"Back then," Leo said quietly, "I didn't know you. Now I do, and that's why I'm in love with you."

Joshua's head shot up, cheeks flushing. "You're in love with me?"

Surprise shone clear through his voice, and then his eyes brightened, so much hope. Oh shit, what had Leo done? He never should have said that.

"It doesn't matter," he croaked. Still he couldn't look away from Joshua.

"Of course it matters," Joshua said, so utterly convinced, a smile starting to spread across his face as he moved to reach for Leo.

Leo took a clean step back. He hated the way Joshua's smile dropped, hated himself for being the cause of it. If this was the price Leo paid for his past mistakes, why did Joshua have to pay along with him? Why, when they could have been so fucking *good* together?

Prince Joshua of Wales could never date a former rent boy. The public would rip them to shreds.

"It really, really doesn't make a difference," Leo told him, and his voice broke halfway through, ended up as no more than a harsh whisper.

For the longest time, Joshua simply stood there, staring at Leo as though he was trying to see past Leo's skin and unravel the mess of heart and lungs and veins underneath. Then his gaze dropped, lips pressing together briefly. His words came out slightly unfocused. "Because you're scared of what the public would say about us? You're the one who told me to wear my secrets like an armour, remember?"

Leo felt his throat constrict around the thick, wet pressure of tears. He forced them back down. "This is different. It wouldn't end well, trust me."

"You're still holding something back. You're always holding something back." Joshua exhaled, loud in the overwhelming stillness. "Do you want to know the difference between you and me? I'm scared, but I'm doing it anyway. You're just scared."

There was nothing Leo could say. He clenched his jaw and looked away, at the woollen light trickling out of the kitchen.

"And," Joshua added after five seconds, or ten, or a century, "you say you're in love with me. But why should I believe you when you don't act like it? When you don't even trust me?"

"You wouldn't like the truth." Leo's throat felt sandpaper-rough.

"All you need to know is that I couldn't possibly be with you. Not in the way you deserve."

Another stretch of silence twisted, poisonous like a snake. Then Joshua sighed, and there was no reproach in his voice, no anger. Just resignation.

"Well. I guess we'll never find out, will we?"

With that, he turned away and opened the door, stepped quietly out into the stairway. The door clicked shut behind him, and Leo stared at its blank surface for a shuddering moment before he squeezed his eyes shut. He wouldn't cry. He wouldn't.

Blinking, he moved towards the bathroom and didn't bother taking off his clothes before he stepped under the spray of the shower. Even though he turned the temperature so far up he could barely stand it, he felt frozen to the core.

He'd made the right decision. Hadn't he?

JOSHUA DIDN'T BOTHER CHECKING for people before he stepped out of the building. Without sparing his surroundings so much as a single glance, he crossed the short distance to the car, wrenched open the door and threw himself into the backseat.

In the rear-view mirror, he caught Zach's worried look. Joshua slid further down into his seat and bit his lip, nausea pressing down on his stomach. "Home, please," he said.

For just an instant, it seemed as though Zach would ask a question. Then he nodded and turned the key, the engine humming to life while the past few minutes rattled around Joshua's brain, spinning in circles, his own words getting tangled up with Leo's—*You're just scared* and *I couldn't possibly be with you* and *I'm in love with you. It doesn't matter.*

Closing his eyes, Joshua tried to make sense of it all. He couldn't. Whatever Leo had done, he'd said it hadn't been illegal. What could be so bad that he would refuse to explain, even when Joshua had asked him outright?

You wouldn't like the truth.

Something tugged on Joshua's consciousness, a statement Leo had made a while ago. It took him a moment to recall the small kitchen in James' office, the challenge in Leo's eyes. *Where I come from, the only currencies are money, sex, and power. More often than not, they're one and the same.* Nobility accounted for two of those three things, but sex? Why sex? How was sex connected to money? Or to power, or both?

And—God, there had been that other time on Joshua's terrace, talking about bottles and shot glasses, about friendship and sex. *Personally, I believe that shot glasses are overrated.* Or that time in the van, how adamant Leo had been about Shayna, insisting that selling her body didn't make her a victim. That Joshua shouldn't pity her. *I'm not saying they're good choices, but they're hers.*

And then... Oh shit. *Shit.* The way Leo had acted that night when they'd fallen into each other. That contradiction between his obvious experience and those sparks of innocence, those moments when he'd seemed almost surprised by his own reaction. As though his own wishes had never quite mattered before. As though he hadn't expected to enjoy himself.

Want to stay inside you forever.

Want you to.

The car swerved around a bend, and Joshua's stomach swerved with it. His heart was trying to beat a way out of his chest, and what if he was wrong? Jumping to conclusions?

But what if he was right?

A guy like me doesn't get to keep a guy like you.

10

————

Some minutes into the drive back from Leo's place, Joshua had tried to shove everything away and blank out completely. While the motions of the car had helped slow down his spinning thoughts, they'd still sparked and sizzled behind his closed lids. When the car pulled to a halt and the engine shut off, Joshua blinked his eyes open, the sudden sense of vertigo like a punch to his sternum.

"We're here," Zach told him, tone gentle.

Inhaling deeply, Joshua looked up at his flat. Through the car's tinted windowpane, the world took on a grey hue, sad and tired. God, he couldn't go up there. Right now, just the idea of facing his empty flat, littered with tiny traces of Leo's presence—no. This was too close, too personal for Joshua to see clearly. He couldn't do this alone.

Sinking back into the upholstery, Joshua fought to control the disorientation weighing him down. "Sorry, I should have..." Shaking his head, he slid down further. "Can you take me to Tristan's instead? Please."

"Of course," Zach said smoothly. A moment passed before he added, careful, "Are you all right, Joshua?"

Not even a little.

Joshua dragged up a smile and hoped it didn't look like quite as much of a grimace as it felt. "I'll be fine. Thank you."

With that, he closed his eyes again and waited for the rumble of the engine, thrumming in his blood and in his bones.

It wasn't a long drive, Tristan and Kelsey having moved into a flat near Hyde Park a couple of months ago, but it felt as though time was elastic. Ten minutes stretched to span twice their usual length. When Zach informed him they'd arrived, Joshua managed another smile.

He let a group of tourists pass before he scrambled out of the car and told Zach he'd call once he was ready to go back. Or maybe he'd just call a taxi. At some point, he'd have to stop hiding from the world —especially now that he, Mo and Tristan had booked flights to Brazil for next Saturday in time for the third English match. George was supposed to leak the news of Joshua's planned attendance tomorrow, giving them a chance to assess reactions.

It would be good to get out of London for a bit.

Joshua hunched into himself as he rang the bell, his back to the street, glancing up at the security camera above the door. It was Kelsey's voice that came through the intercom, a hint of laughter in her words. "Didn't we just leave your flat, J? Mo might be on to something with that co-dependency thing, you know."

For the first time, it occurred to Joshua that he should have called ahead; work had kept Kelsey out of the country a fair amount recently and she couldn't make it to Brazil either, so Joshua taking away from the time she and Tristan got to spend together... *Selfish*.

"I'm so sorry, Kels. I didn't mean—I need to talk to Tristan, but if this is a bad time..."

"Shut it," she told him. "You're always welcome here, you know that. Come on up."

The buzzer sounded a moment later, and Joshua stepped into the building, already breathing a little more easily. They were on the ground floor, Kelsey awaiting him in the doorway and pulling him into a tight hug as soon as she'd taken one look at him. She must have come straight from the shower, wearing a bathrobe with her hair hidden under a towel turban. Tristan appeared behind her a moment later, still drying off.

Shit. Joshua really shouldn't have barged in on them like this.

"I'm so sorry," he repeated, and Tristan gave him a light shove.

"Shut it," he said, just like Kelsey had. "You look like shit, mate. Do we need hard alcohol, or will beer do?"

"Vodka straight from the bottle?" Joshua asked, turning into Tristan's embrace while Kelsey patted him on the back and retreated with a warm, "Be good, boys."

Tristan tugged Joshua further into the flat, towards the spacious kitchen that faced their garden. He pushed Joshua to sit down on the bench that dominated one corner of the room, then slammed two glasses on the table, grabbed vodka and orange juice, and told Joshua to prepare their drinks while he went to pull on some clothes. Joshua did as he'd been told, adding just a dash of vodka to the juice. His fingers weren't entirely steady.

Sliding onto the bench beside Joshua, Tristan picked up one glass and clinked it against Joshua's before taking a small sip. "All right," he said quietly, studying Joshua's face. "So what's wrong? You're scaring me here."

What was wrong? What *wasn't* wrong?

Joshua gulped down some juice to buy himself a few moments. Distantly, he caught snatches of music from where Kelsey must have turned on the stereo, singing along in an exaggerated pitch that carried over the noise of her hair-dryer.

"Did you ever wonder..." Joshua set his glass down and rested both elbows on the table. Lead clung to the tips of his thoughts and made them sluggish, lethargic. His voice came out in a crawl. "Like, with Kels being who she is, doing what she does—that there are, like, other men staring at pictures of her body. Doesn't that ever bother you?"

Tristan was quiet for a moment before he raised his glass again. "They get pictures," he said around the rim. "Sure. But I get the real thing, and her body is only a small part of the package."

"But what if she took it a step further? What if... I mean, in the past, maybe." Shaking his head, Joshua tried to sort through the messy tangle in his brain. "What if there'd been guys touching her for money? How would you—"

He didn't get further than that, was cut off by Tristan clasping his shoulder in a harsh grip. "Joshua." Tristan's voice had gained a rare edge of steel. "I love you dearly. But right now, I need you to shut your stupid trap and understand that you just likened my girlfriend to a prostitute." He let go of Joshua's shoulder and leaned back, frowning. "If it had been anyone but you, I'd have punched them. Jury's still out."

Joshua stared at him, then swallowed. Shit, he hadn't meant—it had made sense in Joshua's head, the leap, but Tristan's reaction... Joshua wondered how often Tristan had dealt with similar comments made by people who didn't know Kelsey at all.

"I'm sorry," Joshua said softly. "I didn't mean it in a bad way, just... something about how her body is sort of... her capital? Not in a bad way. It just is."

Briefly, Tristan considered it. "But she's in full control, you know? They can look, yeah, but they can't touch. Touching belongs to me— and it's only because she gave me that right. Willingly, freely, and because she loves me." He raised his brows. "So it's the furthest bloody thing from a business transaction. Get it?"

"But if she had done that in the past..." Oh, for heaven's sake, what was Joshua even doing? He was probably digging himself into a ditch. At the same time, he had to know. He couldn't work this out by himself, needed to put his thoughts out there, bring them into a semblance of order. "Like, if there had been business transactions. At some point. Could you tolerate that? Could you still respect her? Love her?"

It took a moment, then Tristan's frown cleared, a newfound understanding in his eyes. His tone became gentle. "Is this about Leo?"

Joshua stilled, his thoughts tripping to a halt. This wasn't—he couldn't tell Tristan, could he? Only he had to tell someone, and Tristan wouldn't tell a soul, and... Jesus, Joshua needed him. With a sigh, Joshua picked up his glass and stared into the yellow concoction. "How did you know this is about Leo?"

"Because you're completely out of it." Tristan slid a little closer on the bench, enough for their knees to knock together. "And because you're asking me questions about love and respect and relationships. Of course it's about Leo."

He made it sound like an obvious truth, and that made something ugly twist through Joshua's stomach, something that felt a lot like desperation. Sucking in a sharp breath, Joshua ducked his head and kept his voice quiet. "This isn't, like... You can't tell him I told you, okay? It's not my secret to share, but it's also..." He broke off, words lodged sideways in his throat, and finished with a whispered, "Fuck."

Tristan slung an arm around Joshua's waist and pulled him in, almost making Joshua spill some of his drink. Joshua set the glass down and rested his head on Tristan's shoulder.

They sat like that for a moment before Tristan spoke up. "You need to talk to someone. And I'm the one who's in a scandalous relationship, so I come with relevant experience."

"I need to talk to a friend," Joshua corrected. "And you're in a loving relationship, so you come with relevant experience."

Tristan pressed a smile against Joshua's cheek. "All right. Let's have it, then."

Right, where to even start? Tucking himself further into Tristan's side, Joshua took a sip of his spiked juice before he began slowly, a little unsteadily. "So I just learned—I went to see Leo just before I came here. And he lived on the streets for a while. Born a noble, went to Eton with us."

"Shit, really?" Surprise plain in his tone, Tristan's arm tightened around Joshua's waist.

"Yes, really. Couple of years above us. He was on the football team, actually." Joshua took a measured breath. "Anyway, his parents... I guess they kicked him out, pretty much, when they learned he was gay. And then he lived on the streets."

"Holy fuck. Must have been tough." There was no judgment in Tristan's voice, just concern. Joshua closed his eyes and took a moment to weigh his next words, speaking quietly, only just loud enough to translate over the music in the background.

"Must have been, yes. So that's what he confirmed, but I also think... I think he might have, like—" His intake of air caught in his throat. "Sold his—I think he might have worked as a callboy. To get by."

Tristan hissed through his teeth. When Joshua lifted his head, blinking, and met Tristan's eyes, Tristan appeared speechless for once. He opened his mouth, then closed it again, frowning. Joshua could empathise.

Several seconds passed before Tristan settled on, "Did you ask him?"

"No." Dropping his head back down on Tristan's shoulder, Joshua wound his fingers into Tristan's T-shirt. His voice came out even lower than before, a small, helplessly rough whisper. "What if I'm wrong? I mean, this isn't my—I can't *force* him to tell me something like that."

"Jesus fucking Christ on a stick," Tristan said, heartfelt, and Joshua snorted.

"Basically." He paused. "Maybe I am wrong. But he keeps saying that someone like him can't be with someone like me. And some other things he said... It all fits. It's, like... It seems so unlikely, but if I look at all the clues together..." He raised a hand and dropped it again. "It somehow seems even less likely that they're not connected."

Again, Tristan was silent for a moment, then he said, "So that's why you asked me all this stuff. About Kels."

"I didn't mean to offend. Sorry. I *really* didn't mean—I just don't know what to think. Like, at all." Joshua cleared his throat, but his voice still came out in a thin rasp. He felt endlessly heavy. "But with the way you reacted, you do think it's a really bad thing. What Leo maybe did."

"Not bad in a way that makes *him* a bad person. Or, like, cheap or something." Tristan sounded as though he was trying to feel his path through a tunnel, one step after the other. "I think it's just... the sense of powerlessness. Selling your body like that, for sex, it seems like an act of desperation. It'd make me fucking *sick* if Kels ever had to resort to that. I mean, no one would want that for the person they love, or even just care about. Or for anyone ever, I reckon."

Joshua tried to recall what Leo had said in the van—something about choices, about not being a victim. "But it doesn't necessarily mean weakness, does it? It could still be a choice. What if it made sense at the time? What if he made decisions that he wouldn't make today, but he was young and dumb and needed the money? I think..." Joshua's lungs constricted. "I think he'd really hate it if I pitied him."

Tristan blew out a heavy breath. "Honestly? Unless he actually enjoyed what he did, it'd be hard not to pity him at least a little. Because those must have been some tough circumstances he faced."

"He didn't enjoy it," Joshua said immediately.

It was barely out when he wondered how he could possibly know that, but... somehow, he did. He had all the pieces, really. He had a collection of little moments which—God, which assembled into a mosaic that made *sense*. There was Leo's early claim that he'd believed sex to be overrated, and then... Oh, and also, how disinterested he'd seemed in relationships, like someone who'd lost all illusions. *Where I come from, the only currencies are money, sex, and power. More often than not, they're one and the same.*

No. Leo hadn't enjoyed it.

But then, there was also the way he'd reacted to Joshua's touch that night—how he'd opened up and strained into every kiss, shaking as he'd fought to stay still while Joshua had sucked him off in the shower. *Want to stay inside you forever. Want you to.*

Leo was in love with Joshua.

Oh God. Leo was in *love* with him.

He'd said so, and Joshua had been an arse about it. He'd told Leo it could hardly be true when Leo didn't act like it, when he wouldn't trust Joshua with the whole truth about himself. If Joshua was right in what he suspected, he couldn't possibly blame Leo for struggling to come clean. This was... massive.

Tristan squeezing his hip was what brought Joshua out of his thoughts. He startled and glanced at Tristan's profile. "Sorry, what?"

"I asked why you think that," Tristan said. "That he didn't enjoy it."

"Because of the way he acted when we had sex, like it was... like he was almost shocked sometimes, at how good it was? At how it could be... mutual? And trusting." Sitting up a little straighter, Joshua pulled one leg underneath him on the bench. His skin felt brittle. "Like, I'm not sure he'd ever laughed during sex before. He seemed so surprised by it. And he was all... uncertain, but also confident about technical things. Like, there's—he didn't expect me to prep him. He thought he'd have to do it himself, like it was—fuck. I should have realised. Why didn't I—?"

"Because you didn't know," Tristan cut into the sudden rush of words tripping out of Joshua's mouth.

But I should have.

Joshua choked on air. He coughed until his throat felt dry, his face pressed against Tristan's neck, Tristan hugging him close and patting his back. Joshua's eyes were burning, and he squeezed them shut, his breathing evening out.

"If he'd enjoyed himself back then," he managed, "he wouldn't be saying that a guy like him can't be with a guy like me. He wouldn't be hiding his past. He wouldn't be trying to help some street kids make their way out, to make better choices than he did."

"So essentially," Tristan's voice was low and serious, filled with awe, "he's a guy who went through hell and dragged himself out by his own bootstraps."

Joshua's heart performed a slow, sad twist in his chest. He needed a moment to raise his head, and his voice sounded as raw as his entire body felt. "Pretty much. I mean, I think he's had some help, like James giving him that chance, but... he took it."

"Gotta respect that."

Joshua forced some air into his chest. "He said he's in love with me."

There was no surprise on Tristan's face; he merely nodded. "Yeah. After last night, with the way he was looking at you—I figured. Why else would he put himself through an evening with people who hate him? What did you say?"

Joshua choked on an empty laugh. "That I don't believe him." Now that he had to put it out there, it sounded truly horrible, and he hurried to add, "Because I knew he was still holding back, so I thought he didn't trust me, and if he didn't trust me... I don't know what I thought. I only worked out the hooker thing after, and if I'd known—" Abruptly, he cut himself off.

For several moments, they were both silent. The music was still seeping in from somewhere in the flat, and Joshua was grateful for that tiny slice of normalcy.

"You know," Tristan said quietly, a cross between incredulous and dismal, "if this is true, if you're right... Fuck. You and him would be a huge scandal. The Prince with a rent boy."

"Former rent boy," Joshua corrected. Even as he said it, he knew it would be a minor distinction to many.

"Either way, it'll be sleazy. People won't care what he's done since then, how bloody well he's done for himself. They'll only focus on that one little thing."

"I don't give a shit about what strangers think," Joshua bit out. "They have no idea. They don't know me, they don't know him, and they sure as hell don't know us." Then he shook his head, shoulders sagging. "Except, I mean. There is no us. Obviously."

Tristan's tone was devoid of judgement. "So if it turns out you're right, about what he's done... You'd want him just the same. You wouldn't be bothered?"

The question pulled Joshua up short. Could he honestly claim it wouldn't make a difference? That it wouldn't change his view of Leo at all?

Stalling, Joshua reached for his glass and washed the bitter taste in his mouth down with some juice. Shit, this was... God. It was just... a little hard to digest. There'd been strangers with their hands all over Leo, strangers who weren't Joshua. Dozens of them, maybe hundreds. And it would have been different if Leo had wanted all of that, if he'd had a lot of one-night stands just for the hell of it, because it had felt good. Because it had been fun.

The little clues Joshua had caught suggested Leo hadn't had fun.

But the thing was... The thing was, even if Leo had offered sex for money, then that didn't change who he had become. Which—oh. Was that what he'd meant earlier, when he'd said that Joshua did know him, that Joshua knew who he was *now*? As though the past was a stepping stone.

Carefully, Joshua set his glass back down in precisely the same spot as before, a ring of condensation marking the place.

"I would hate," he began, nearly inaudible, "that all those people got to touch him without deserving it. When he probably didn't really want them to. I'd hate that he ever was at a point where he felt he had to do that, and I'd wish I could change it. But..." Turning his head, Joshua met Tristan's gaze and held it, felt his voice gain an edge of confidence. "But if that's part of what shaped him, then it's a part of *him*. So."

Tristan sent him a small, genuine smile. "You're in love with him." Oh.

The words bounced around Joshua's skull, stirred up dust and upset his sense of balance. Something in his stomach gave, like plummeting through a slow-motion fall. "I'm in love with him," he confirmed, toneless. Then, "Oh God. What do I do?"

The last part came out panicked. He gripped Tristan's shoulder, felt wide-eyed and disoriented, utterly shaken.

Tristan covered Joshua's hand with his own. "You know, if there's one thing I've come to learn? It's that honest communication saves you a whole damn lot of drama. It's not about pride, or having the upper hand or some crap like that. There's no tally. It's just..." He paused, then lifted his shoulders in a tiny shrug. "It's about what makes both of you happy. And if he already told you he's in love with you? Seems fair to return the favour."

"He told me he loved me right before he said it didn't matter." The memory cut through the haze in Joshua's brain like a sharp knife slicing through tulle. Leo had made his decision. Even if he was in love with Joshua, he didn't want the public exposure that would come with a relationship—and Joshua couldn't blame him.

The constant attention and judgment would have been a high price already, even for someone without Leo's baggage. It would mean sacrificing a slice of normalcy for Joshua, and he remembered his own words from what felt like years ago when really, it had been no more than a few short weeks. *Show me the guy who'll stick around once the media calls on the hunt.*

For Leo, the potential price was so much higher than normal.

"Of course it matters," Tristan said, an echo of Joshua's own response to Leo's words.

Leaning into Tristan's side, Joshua exhaled in a rush. He couldn't remember the last time he'd felt this drained. "No." He shook his head. "No, it doesn't. And it doesn't matter that I love him back. He doesn't want the publicity, and I have to respect that. If I told him... I'd only put him under pressure. That's not fair."

"Nothing about this is bloody fair." Tristan muttered a half-hearted curse, quiet for a moment before he asked, "Who's he protecting, though? Himself or you? And don't you think he has a right to know how you feel, maybe?"

Tired, God. So very, very tired. Joshua wanted to sleep for a century. "I don't know. I don't know anything anymore. All I know is that this... That Leo and I won't happen."

"You just said you don't care about the shitty opinions of strangers."

"I care if they rip him to shreds." Joshua turned further into Tristan. "I'm used to it, the scrutiny and all, but he isn't. I could never force him into that."

"I hate this so much," Tristan whispered. With a wet chuckle, Joshua rested his head on Tristan's chest and closed his eyes.

"You and me both."

Tristan didn't reply, but his arms came back around Joshua's shoulders, pulling him into a tight hug. Relaxing into it, Joshua waited for the second-hand warmth to sink in.

Leo had dragged himself out of the shower and climbed into bed still naked and damp, hadn't left it for the remainder of the day. He'd dreamt of shadows. Of pale skin and his hands tangled in dark curls.

On Monday, he was the first person to arrive at the office. When Carole got in half an hour later, she froze at the sight of him in the tea kitchen—the tea kitchen where Leo had argued with Joshua on that day he'd walked back into Leo's life. Had it really been less than a month? Three weeks, God. Was that all it had taken for Joshua to turn Leo's life upside down?

"Is it a ghost?" Carole asked, propping her hip against the door-frame. "You've never been here before me. Is it the apocalypse?"

"Zombies banging on the doors in T-minus five." Leo worked hard to send her a smile that he knew would turn out crooked, far from convincing. He was proven right when she shot him a worried look.

"Scary," was all she said, though. She nodded at the kettle. "Want me to make you a cuppa? You look like you need it."

"I do," Leo told her.

He didn't offer more, and Carole didn't ask. Because that how they did things around here. Part of the deal.

A month ago, Leo wouldn't have thought to question it.

With a steaming cup of tea, he retreated into his office and went to sort through his emails. Some of them were leftovers from last week, loose ends, contacting Leo about his involvement in Joshua's coming-out. He redirected all of them to George.

Nate came in a little after nine, and he didn't even pass by his own office before he dropped in on Leo. Planting himself in the seat in front of Leo's desk, he leaned forward, both elbows on the tabletop and a worried crease between his brows. "Mate, you all right? I tried to reach you yesterday, you know?"

Oh. Yes, right. Now that Nate mentioned it, Leo remembered that he hadn't charged his phone since Friday. He should probably do that. "Sorry," he said out loud. "My battery must have died. And yeah, I'm fine."

Nate's eyes narrowed as he studied Leo. "You're not."

After a few beats, Leo looked away, tried to focus on the blinking cursor of his mouse where it hovered over his desktop wallpaper—a shot of the English national squad huddled together before a match. Right now, their defeat by Italy seemed laughably insignificant.

"I will be fine," Leo amended, glancing back at Nate. "It'll just take me a little while to let it go, so if I'm a bit of a dick in the near future... Sorry, yeah?"

Nate lifted his shoulders, a half-smile tugging at the corners of his mouth. "Nothing new there. But you haven't actually told me what happened. When Josh came to find you on the balcony."

"I'd rather just... not. Not think about it, you know? It won't work, that's really all there is to it. I want Joshua to be happy, and I'm not— that's not me. I'm not the one who can make him happy." Leo swallowed around the open wound in his chest. "What about you and Mo? What did I miss?"

It was obvious that Nate considered pushing for more information, but in the end, he simply bumped their feet together under the desk. "He drove me home on Sunday, then stayed the day." While his tone was casual, there was a bright, happy gleam in his eyes that made Leo breathe a little easier than he had ever since he'd left Joshua's place on Saturday.

"I take it he also stayed the night?" he asked, and Nate grinned, soft and sweet.

"Maybe."

In response, Leo gave Nate's foot a light kick. Nate kicked back, then let his foot rest against Leo's, ankles pressed together. "Hey," he said, suddenly serious again. "You know that if there's anything I can do..."

"I know," Leo told him, and he did. He'd never been more certain of their friendship than in this very moment, and he supposed that was another thing he owed to Joshua—even if Leo couldn't have him, his temporary presence had prompted a change for the better in Leo's friendship with Nate.

"Okay," Nate said. "As long as you know."

"I do." This time, Leo's smile didn't feel quite so much like a parody of itself. "But I think there's nothing that can be done, really. I need time, that's all."

While Nate smiled back, he didn't look convinced. Leo was first to look away.

WORK WAS A BLESSING.

James accepted a new client on Tuesday, a politician claiming he'd been wrongly accused of corruption, and Leo threw himself into it. On Wednesday, he got home when Chile was already two goals ahead of Spain, watched the second half of the match in a blank haze before he headed off to bed and fell into an exhausted slumber.

He crawled out from under the covers on Thursday feeling as though he'd caught the flu, weak and disoriented. By eight, he was back at the office.

James sent him off on an errand late in the afternoon and expressly forbade him to return to work afterwards. That was fine, though; the England match was scheduled for eight that night, and Leo had already agreed to meet Nate at a no-frills pub near Nate's flat in time for kick-off.

As it turned out, Leo was some thirty minutes early. Claiming a seat at the bar, he ordered chips and a pint, then turned to face the large screen that had been put up on the wall, the usual pre-match commentary washing over the heads of the growing crowd. *Our lads need to win this one or they can start packing, pressure is on.* Leo listened with only half a mind.

He snapped to attention at the mention of Joshua's name.

Some of the lead-up remarks had escaped him, but it soon became clear the presenters were summarising the controversy around Joshua planning to attend the third match of the group stage.

Some conservatives—stupid arsehole *dicks*—argued that his sexuality no longer made him an appropriate representative of the English public. "Now, we could take a position here," Gary Lineker said, leaning towards the camera. "But why not let His Royal Highness speak for himself?"

And then Joshua's face filled the screen.

Leo felt his blood run cold. Fingers clenching around his glass, he soaked in the sight—that nervous hair flip Joshua did, his lips a little chapped, bitten red. A flickering smile. The screen offset all colours and tinged the green of Joshua's eyes with blue.

When Joshua spoke, his slow, deep voice resonated in Leo's stomach. "I think that many people conveniently forget that this country is diverse. I mean..." Joshua paused to tilt his head. "There are white atheists and black protestants, you know. There are some who are born to a title and money and others who are born to parents who just lost their job; there are some who are gay and some who are straight and some who are neither." Smile widening, he seemed to be gaining momentum with each word. "There are blue eyes and brown eyes and green eyes, and we're all a part of this country. You don't have to fit the norm to belong. Which is why" —his gaze found the camera, clear and direct— "I consider myself a perfectly adequate representative of this beautiful and diverse nation. Thank you."

The video ended, and Leo sucked in a sharp breath. He'd made to hold onto the countertop at some point, realised only now that his grip was white-knuckled and slowly eased it, set his glass down carefully.

"Gotta hand it to the kid," some bloke remarked. "He's got balls."

Leo glanced over his shoulder to identify the speaker as a balding guy in his late forties, unbuttoned plaid shirt over a dirty, white top. He'd addressed a bloke about his age, similar attire, and the second bloke scoffed. "Well. Certainly got practice handling balls, if you know what I mean."

"Can't say I give a fuck what the Prince does in his spare time. Or who." The original speaker raised his beer in a toast. "Only thing I care about is us sticking it to Uruguay. Sticking it *good*."

"Hear, hear," the second one said, and Leo turned away. His heart felt too full for his chest, ready to burst, so many words on the very tip of his tongue. He wanted to butt in and tell those blokes just how lovely Joshua was, how clever and genuine; *can't blame me for falling head over heels.* Instead, Leo tugged out his phone and called up a message, wrote, '*So in love with you*'.

His finger hovered over the send button.

Then he exhaled around all those words lodged in his throat and erased his text, letter by letter. He replaced it with, '*I'm so so proud of you .*'

He erased that, too, and switched off his phone. Taking a big gulp of his beer, he waited for Nate to join him.

∿

ENGLAND LOST TO URUGUAY. Their chances of making it past the group stage were close to none.

Leo hardly even cared.

∿

PEOPLE HAD SCATTERED QUICKLY after the match. When Leo and Nate stepped out onto the street, they found it dark and deserted, quiet once the pub door fell shut behind them. Leo shivered in the cool breeze, and Nate shifted closer. After a moment's consideration, Leo slung an arm around his waist and burrowed into his side.

"Hey," Nate said. Even though his voice was low, it carried in the silent night. "You wanna kip at mine? Saves you from having to share the tube with all the people getting back drunk from the game."

God, yes—a chance for Leo to avoid his flat that somehow, after four days, still carried traces of Joshua's cologne. He could go straight to work tomorrow, change into the set of fresh clothes he kept at the office.

"That'd be great," he told Nate. "Thanks."

"Sure thing."

Together, they set off for Nate's flat. For all that it wasn't particularly late, just past ten, the city was remarkably quiet around them, like in the aftermath of a catastrophe. Leo supposed that things looked different in the usual centres of activity, where tourists came and went at all hours and rowdy groups were likely drinking away the disappointment of the match. But here, now, it was easy to imagine that the world had slowed down for a little while, maybe just long enough that he could catch his breath.

They'd been walking in companionable silence for a couple of minutes when Nate spoke again. "Just so you know, mate... Joshua's leaving tomorrow with Mo and Tristan. Promised Mo I'd see him off at the airport, and I thought—the neighbour's lending me her car. I thought maybe you'd like another chance to talk to Joshua. You could drive us both?"

Leo's ridiculous heart skipped a beat. He kept his voice steady. "She's lending you her car? Do you even have a license?"

"I just don't like driving." Nate sounded uncomfortable. "It's nothing like... Not like a trauma or anything, but it kind of reminds me of stuff, so I avoid it if I can."

Stuff, it reminded Nate of *stuff*. Leo wanted to ask, only it would have meant giving up a few secrets of his own in turn. He thought that by now, he'd be fine with that. Probably. Just... not tonight. Not when Joshua's face on the screen was still too fresh in his memory.

You don't have to fit the norm to belong.

"I've noticed," Leo said eventually. "So that'd be tomorrow morning, then?"

"Yeah, flight leaves at eight. But you don't *have* to," Nate rushed to add. "You can stay over either way, but I thought—or you can stay in the car, if you prefer. Avoid Joshua."

It would be Leo's last chance to see Joshua in person for a whole two weeks. Or longer, much longer, depending on how soon there'd be a reason for them to meet once Joshua was back. At this point, their only connection was through Nate and Mo.

Leo should let it go.

"I can drive," he said. "I'm not sure yet whether I'll want to see

Joshua, but... Yeah, I can definitely drive. Seeing Mo off at the airport, though—bit cheesy, isn't it? In a teeth-rotting, sweet kind of way. Does that mean you're official now?"

"Sort of?" Nate put his arm around Leo's shoulder, tone hesitant. "It's not like—we haven't really talked about it. Part of why I want to see him, if I'm honest. Need to make sure I'm not making this into more than it is."

Giving Nate's waist a squeeze, Leo smiled at him. "No, I'm quite certain you're perfectly fine. Actually, you know, there's this thing that Joshua—" Leo swallowed. "Joshua mentioned that Mo doesn't do jealousy. Maybe you should put that theory to the test."

Nate was kind enough not to remark on the way Leo's voice had gone soft and wistful on Joshua's name. Instead, he shrugged one shoulder. "I don't want to play mind games, really."

"That's noble of you."

"I'm learning." Nate bumped their hips together. "It's a bit of an inspiration, isn't it, the way those three are so open with each other? Like there's nothing to be scared of, like it's okay to let someone else see everything. Makes you wonder, doesn't it?"

"Yeah, it does." Leo inhaled on a deep breath, felt the night swell around him. "Sorry I kept you away from him tonight. I'm sure he'd have liked you to watch the game with him."

"Don't be ridiculous," Nate said firmly. "Like I'd let you suffer through this alone. I'm not going to let some relationship come between me and my best mate, yeah?"

Leo loved him vigorously.

"You're a sap," he announced.

Nate snorted and tightened his hold. "Love you too, man."

"STOP FRETTING," Tristan ordered. "He said he'll be here, and he won't be here sooner if you wear out your watch."

"Can you wear out your watch by checking it excessively?" Joshua asked.

Mo rewarded both of them with an unimpressed look and absently fluffed a cashmere pillow into shape. Their private lounge in Heathrow's Windsor Suite was flooded with light, empty apart from the three of them, Zach standing guard outside the door and waiting for their passports to return stamped.

"What if he didn't get my directions?" Mo frowned.

"Fuck's sake, Mo. This is *Nate*." Tristan helped himself to a biscuit and continued while chewing. "He's probably mapped all emergency exits and alternate routes before you even sent him an access plan."

That served to relax Mo, and Joshua let himself relax along with him. They had about fifty minutes until take-off, at least thirty before they'd be taken through private security and straight to the aircraft. Two weeks away from London, away from this country, away from everything. Thank God.

A gentle knock on the door had Mo whip his head around. The lounge's manager entered a moment later, splendid in her red dress, a practiced smile on her face. "Excuse me, Sirs. A Mr Nate Biggs and a Mr Leo Graham are here to see you?"

Joshua felt himself stiffen, his stomach dropping.

Leo. What was he doing here? Why was he here? And how had he even—did he have a fake ID that withstood scrutiny? He probably did; if James was on Leo's side, these things weren't done halfway.

Why was he *here*?

He'd probably come with Nate. But then he could have waited outside, right?

"Show them in, please," Tristan said, before Joshua had a chance to process the idea of seeing Leo again. Before he had a chance to compose himself and school his features into something reasonably calm.

So THERE WAS an extra-special VIP lounge for the top of the crop, all marble floors and plush carpets and a number of private lounges, perfectly removed from the travelling public. Leo couldn't say he was surprised, but the exclusive surroundings didn't help in settling his pulse.

"You okay?" Nate whispered.

"Define 'okay,'" Leo replied, equally low, although he doubted it escaped the notice of the woman who'd introduced herself as the manager of this particular slice of subtle extravagance. He should have waited in the car. Fuck, it must have been a bout of temporary insanity that had prompted him to follow Nate for no reason other than a vague need to see Joshua again, just one more time before Leo would force himself to let it go.

Right. Because torturing himself with what he couldn't have was clearly how he rolled.

"Okay as in—" Nate cut himself off when they found themselves face to face with Zach. Subtly, Leo tried to shift behind Nate.

Leo could still turn around and run. Except for how Joshua must have been told that Leo was here, so it would be the act of a coward. Not that Leo was on the fast track to winning an award for bravery as it was, but—Jesus, fuck everything.

He entered behind Nate and kept his gaze on the floor, stopping just inside the room as he mumbled a greeting. With a squeeze of Leo's shoulder, Nate moved towards Mo. Only when he was gone did Leo glance up.

Joshua was staring at him, eyes wide. Leo stared back.

Dressed in comfortable clothes, light streaming in through the window behind him, Joshua was the loveliest thing Leo had ever seen. Curls licked at Joshua's temples, and even from across the room, Leo could make out the clear green of his eyes, no longer lost in digital translation. Vaguely, Leo was aware that Tristan was there as well, that Mo and Nate were talking, but his focus had narrowed to Joshua rising from his armchair, still staring at Leo.

Something had changed, Leo thought dimly. The resignation, maybe. Yes, that's what had changed—when Joshua had left Leo's flat, he'd looked resigned; now, he looked hopeful.

Leo's chest hurt. He didn't move from his position near the door as he watched Joshua draw closer. His fingers felt numb with how much he wanted to reach out and touch, body heavy with how he'd lost every right to do just that.

"What are you doing here?" Joshua asked, voice a soft rasp. Oh God, Leo wasn't ready for this. A hundred decades couldn't have prepared him.

He didn't know what to say. He didn't know anything anymore.

"I'm sorry," he managed. "I shouldn't have come."

Joshua swallowed. "So you're still scared," he said softly. The brightness in his eyes drained away, and it felt like watching a car crash in slow motion, like the sun winked out by a cover of clouds. And it was Leo's fault.

He shouldn't have fucking *come*.

"I'm sorry," he repeated. His throat was burning with all the words he couldn't say, *still scared, you're still scared*, and yes, fuck, he *was*. He'd never been more terrified. Joshua remained silent, looking at Leo with sadness tucked into the corners of his eyes, curled into himself, and Leo wanted him so much, so much.

"I wish—" Leo cut himself off abruptly.

"So do I," Joshua whispered. "I wish it could be easy."

I wish I could rewrite my history for you, Leo thought. Very lightly, he shook his head and made himself turn away, could barely force out a quiet, "Tell Nate I'll be waiting in the car, please."

Joshua let him go without a sound. Leo didn't know why he'd expected different.

THE MOMENT THE DOOR CLOSED, Joshua returned to his armchair, sat down with all the poise he could muster—and then spoiled the effect by sagging into himself, lids pressed shut as he fought not to cry. Almost instantly, Tristan squeezed in next to him, and then Mo was there as well with a warm touch to the back of Joshua's neck and his voice pitched to a soothing murmur.

"Shit," Nate said, lost and astonished, and oh, yes, Nate was still here and had to witness Joshua's breakdown. It didn't matter. Nothing mattered.

I wish, Joshua's mind replayed. *I wish. I wish. I wish.*

NORMALLY, Leo was good at forcing all his thoughts away until they became static noise in the back of his mind. It figured that Joshua would strip him of this very last resort, too.

Fuck. *Fuck.* Whatever Leo had hoped to accomplish by seeing Joshua just that one time more... What had he been *thinking*? Curling up in the driver's seat, Leo held his breath until his lungs felt swollen with blood, then exhaled. Repeated it.

By the time Nate wrenched open the passenger door, Leo's breathing had stabilised, and his heart was no longer trying to claw its way past his ribs. Slowly, he straightened in his seat and blinked his lids open to find Nate stooping low to stare at him.

After a silent beat that lurched in Leo's veins, Nate slid into the passenger seat. His voice was impassive. "You lied to me."

When had Leo—oh. Yeah. He'd played it so as to keep Nate from digging deeper, but by doing so, he'd implied that the distance between him and Joshua had been Joshua's call.

"I didn't lie," Leo said carefully. The dim light in the underground car park clouded his brain.

Nate scoffed, a sound edged with hurt. "You implied that he didn't want you, and that, like—you said you can't make him happy. Which is *such* bullshit, because the guy is—"

"I told him I'm in love with him," Leo interrupted. "He didn't say it back."

Nate's frown was dark and stubborn. "That makes no sense. The guy is completely gone for you."

Leo's heart gave a sharp throb, everything grinding to a halt. It took him a moment to catch up with Nate's next words.

"I mean," Nate sounded helpless, "the way you'd been acting, I thought he's the one who broke your heart. But this whole thing hit him just as bad. Leo, he *cried*. You did that."

No. No, no, no.

Leo couldn't *think*.

He squeezed out words past the choking sensation which had gripped his throat. The car felt claustrophobic. "He'll get over it."

Nate was quiet for several seconds, studying Leo with a heavy gaze. When he spoke, it was uncommonly solemn. "Yeah. He will. Eventually, he will. But do you realise what that means? He's the country's sweetheart, mate. If he gets over you—*when* he does, at some point..." He shook his head. "You won't be able to escape. It'll be all over the papers, him with someone else. Are you ready for that? Seeing him smile at someone else, kiss someone else—"

"Stop," Leo broke in. He couldn't fit enough air into his lungs. "*Stop*."

Nate made to grip Leo's shoulder, his hold tight enough to border on painful. "Explain it to me," he said. "Because I don't fucking get it. Why are you denying yourself the only thing I've ever seen you want for yourself?"

Because it's hopeless. Because I'd destroy him.

"Because I just... There's..." Falling silent, Leo sank lower in the seat, a sickening weight in his stomach.

Nate dropped his hand and leaned back, away. His voice carried disappointment. "Fuck, Leo. Will you ever stop running?"

A small, nasty part of Leo wanted to hit back, call Nate a bloody hypocrite who had no right to go casting stones. But... Jesus fucking Christ, it wasn't true. If Leo were to share a slice of his past, he knew that Nate would be ready, would match him step for step. The other way around... not necessarily so.

Leo's belly felt bloated with anxiety, as heavy and swollen as his lungs. "Tell you mine if you tell me yours," he got out.

It clearly took a couple of moments for Nate to understand, then he smiled. Somehow, Leo managed to smile back. His body expanded around it.

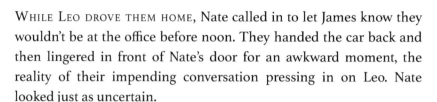

WHILE LEO DROVE THEM HOME, Nate called in to let James know they wouldn't be at the office before noon. They handed the car back and then lingered in front of Nate's door for an awkward moment, the reality of their impending conversation pressing in on Leo. Nate looked just as uncertain.

"How about," Leo suggested, "we grab tea and breakfast somewhere? And then maybe just... walk?"

"Sounds good," Nate said quickly. The idea of moving while they talked seemed to settle him just as much as it settled Leo.

They descended the stairs in silence, close together, and stopped at a café down the road. Steaming cardboard cups and pastries in hand, they emerged back outside. The worst of the morning rush was over, the sun warming their faces and promising a clear day.

"Left or right?" Leo asked quietly, and Nate twitched his shoulders.

"Doesn't matter, does it?"

"No. Not really." For no particular reason, Leo turned left and carefully sipped at his hot tea as he started walking, Nate falling into step. Another minute dragged by in silence, less awkward now that they weren't just standing there, the tension between them more thoughtful, hesitant.

It was Nate who broke it. He inhaled deeply, swallowing down a bite of his disgustingly healthy-looking oatmeal scone. "So. Shall I go first?"

Leo twisted a piece off his own caramel scone. "If I had to take a wild guess," he glanced at Nate's profile, "I'd say you worked for the government. Hacking into computer stuff, probably."

"Computer stuff?" Nate repeated, an amused tilt to his voice even though his expression tightened for a moment, a flash of discomfort in his eyes.

"Computer stuff." Leo nodded. Veering off to the right, he nudged Nate in the direction of the Thames. "However, that doesn't explain why you had, like, some kind of military training. Unless that's standard protocol, I don't know. And why you're so keen on taking the passenger seat."

"It's a control thing," Nate said. "Like, I'm not traumatised or anything, and I do know how to drive, but..." His words were slower than usual, almost as slow as Joshua's diligent way of building sentences like a child assembling bricks. "It's just that for a while, it reminded me too much of what I used to do, so I avoided it. And now it's been years since I was actually behind the wheel, so I feel a bit uncomfortable because of that. Still like to have a chance at interfering though, if something's about to go wrong."

"Go wrong how?"

"Just, um. Like, people shooting at the tires. Chasing our car."

"Right." Leo coughed. "The usual."

"I know it's not an actual concern anymore." Nate's face twisted in embarrassment, and Leo wanted to kick himself.

"Sorry," he rushed to say. "I didn't mean to... belittle that. Honest. I'm just struggling to grasp the concept. Doing something where that's a valid possibility, like, *how*?"

"I was the driver." Nate paused for a sip of tea, steam rising as he blew across the surface. His forehead furrowed as he appeared to search for a way to continue. "The one in the background, you know? Driver doubling as a bodyguard, entering gatherings in the wake of some diplomat or some such. So easy to miss the people in the background." There was no bitterness in his tone; he was merely stating a fact. "Allowed me to slip away and retrieve information, the kind of things that interest a government."

Holy shit. Yeah, so that wasn't too far from what Leo had suspected already, but hearing it confirmed still made a difference.

He let it settle for a minute while they approached Tate Modern, the brick building with its looming chimney an imposing presence against the blue sky. Leo had spent a few nights huddled underneath the footbridge that branched from the Gallery to the other side of the Thames, but he'd soon learned it was one of those spots frequently patrolled by the police. Some officers had been kinder than others.

Drinking from his tea, he sloshed warm liquid around his mouth and swallowed before he asked, "So how did you get pulled into that line of work? How does one become a hacker spy agent... thing?"

Nate snorted softly. "Wowed by your eloquence, mate."

"As you should be."

"Always. And as for your question..." Nate shrugged. "I grew up— I was one of those orphan boys in the system, you know, and if you're different, poor, no parents... Other kids can be cruel."

At a certain point in his life, Leo might have been one of those other kids. He inched a little closer, their elbows bumping, and waited.

"Got me into martial arts," Nate continued. "Had a bit of a knack for it, caught the eye of a scout. Seemed like the perfect opportunity to prove myself, you know? Show that I could be so much more."

It sounded familiar—that thirst to prove someone wrong, to be better, brighter than they could have ever expected. "So what changed?" Leo asked.

Nate dropped the rest of his scone into a rubbish bin. The birch trees that framed the grass in front of Tate Modern whispered above their heads, people sprawled out on the green—such a contrast to the hesitation in Nate's voice. "I obtained some information we'd been looking for for a while."

"Information?" Leo prompted, when Nate fell silent.

After a sip of tea, Nate gently shook his head, gaze fixed on the ground. "Location of a terrorist. Nasty piece, but when our guys got in there..." It was so quiet that Leo barely made out the words. "I didn't hear about this until a couple weeks later, but there'd been casualties. Two kids. A wife. A servant who probably didn't even know what the guy had done."

Jesus.

"And it was all because of intel I dug up." Bitter disgust shone through Nate's statement, and Leo couldn't tell whether it was directed at Nate's former employers or Nate himself.

Shifting closer, Leo linked their arms. "Not your fault," he said softly.

"It kind of is." Nate made an aborted gesture, then rubbed a hand over his hair. "I know I'm not, like, directly responsible, yeah? But I should have realised sooner that this would happen one day. Was bloody naive, didn't care much what they did with the information as long as I could brag about a job well done."

"We were all young and stupid once," was all Leo could think of, but it chased a tiny smile over Nate's face, tense features relaxing just slightly. Leo nudged their hips together, arms still linked. Together, they stepped onto the footbridge, and Leo tugged them both to a halt, leaning his elbows on the railing to watch murky water crawl by below.

"Does Mo know?" he inquired in an undertone.

Nate's shoulder was pressed against Leo's, an uncommon show of vulnerability. "Bits. I'm working on it."

"That's..." Leo took a deep breath. "Good. That's really good."

For a while, neither of them spoke, staring down into the water. Eventually, Nate straightened and watched Leo take a sip of tea before he asked, "Your turn, Grammy."

Fuck, okay. Leo could do this. He *could*. He couldn't keep running forever, could he?

Pushing away from the railing, he started walking again, Nate catching up easily. Leo swallowed, words weighing heavily on his tongue, rough and misshapen. "I slept under this bridge a few times." He cleared his throat. "Under other London bridges too. In tube stations, doorways, construction sites. Anywhere that's dry and somewhat sheltered."

A glance revealed that Nate didn't appear surprised. With a small nod, he said, "I guessed as much. Did your parents kick you out?"

"Being gay didn't fit into their view of a glossy world consisting of fancy titles and caviar-topped canapés." Leo snorted, the sound dry, rasping against his palate. "I suppose you've known this for a while, right? I mean, it took Joshua all but three weeks to figure it out, so..."

"Joshua knows?" Now Nate did look surprised, pleasantly so. The look he shot Leo was... proud, almost.

"That particular part, yes." Leo looked away, at the blinding reflection of the sun on the water. Half-hidden behind Southwark

Bridge, the two peaks of the Tower Bridge reached for the sky. They'd been visible from René's flat as well, from the bedroom which Leo had entered only twice, René preferring to stick to the bathtub routine.

For all that it was a warm morning, Leo zipped up his leather jacket. He didn't look at Nate when he continued. "But there's also..." He exhaled. "Look, it's not easy to land a job if you're seventeen and have no references to speak of, no real qualifications other than piano lessons since age four. Never held a real job, no permanent address."

Nate's chuckle was quietly fond. "You could talk your way into anything."

"Not back then. I was a little twat with absolutely no idea what reality was like." Leo blinked a couple of times, shaking his head. His smile must have turned out wobbly. "I ran from home thinking I was so clever. That I'd fucking *show* them. That I'd be just fine on my own and that the world would be at my feet in no time." God, it sounded bloody stupid out loud. He'd been painfully naive back then—innocent as well, brimming with hope and illusions. "I used to dabble in music, so I thought, you know, I'd do some open mic, play some piano and sing a little, and I'd be famous in no time."

Nate stepped aside to make room for a pushchair, then quickly caught up again. "Guess it wasn't that easy?" he asked.

"For some reason, London wasn't waiting with bated breath for me to show up."

"How revolting." In spite of the amusement in Nate's tone, his expression was serious, eyes kind. Leo countered it with a lopsided smirk.

"Truly was. Also my first taste of real life."

"Is that also part of why..." Nate's lips pressed together, and he paused to gulp down some tea. At Leo's questioning glance, he lifted one shoulder. "Just wondering whether you saw some of yourself in Joshua? Like, the slight naivety that comes with growing up sheltered. Is that part of why you reacted like that, all... derisive? I mean, I know it was more than that, with your teenage crush on him, but do you think—"

"Maybe a little," Leo cut in. "It's complicated."

Joshua. Joshua, Joshua, Joshua. Everything always came back to Joshua, didn't it? If it hadn't been for that one moment in the scrummage, for Leo's unexpected reaction to another boy's body as they'd been shoved close together, Joshua only fourteen at the time... It might have taken Leo longer to figure himself out. He might have finished school instead of dropping the news on his parents in the stubborn hope that just this once, they'd prove him wrong and would embrace their son, accept him as he was.

"Never doubted that it's complicated." Nate's voice was cautious, watching Leo as though expecting him to close off any moment. Leo felt abruptly exhausted.

Crumpling up his empty cardboard cup, he waited until they'd passed a group of teenagers who posed for dramatic selfies against the backdrop of St Paul's Cathedral, cracking up with laughter at the resulting pictures. It was sweet.

Leo kept his voice quiet and even. "Either way, as I said, I was a stupid little twat. I burned through my initial money pretty quickly, and then I was just—it was an accident." He avoided looking at Nate. The ground felt a little unsteady under his feet, as though the Millennium Bridge was swaying even though almost two years of construction had striven to prevent just that. "The first time someone paid me for sex, it was... a misunderstanding. But I needed the money, so I kept my mouth shut and took it."

Nate inhaled sharply. Leo didn't dare glance over, too afraid of what he might see.

A few moments passed in silence before he added, "And then, after that, I just thought, you know, why the hell not? The sex was okay. I didn't mind it, not initially, although it all got a bit... There's not much of an appeal if it's one-sided, not at all about what you yourself might want. It's different from sleeping with someone because you want to. Me, I had to deliver. So that wasn't very—I'd completely forgotten that sex could be fun. And then, with Joshua, that was—*fuck*. It was on a whole new level."

He'd pushed the words out, and as soon as he was done, it felt like his ribcage was collapsing in on itself. He kept walking, staring straight ahead, and didn't stop until Nate drew him to halt. His hand was warm on Leo's shoulder. "Leo," he said, so very gentle.

When he pulled Leo into an embrace, Leo stumbled before he sank into it. Nose tucked into Nate's T-shirt, he took what might have been his first real breath in hours.

They must have looked a right mess, clinging to each other in the middle of a stream of pedestrians, but Leo couldn't bring himself to care even a little. Oh God. *Oh God.* He'd—Nate *knew.* Leo had told him, and Nate hadn't cringed away. Lifting his head to gauge Nate's expression, Leo found mainly sadness in Nate's gaze, only the tiniest hint of pity.

Leo wiped a hand over his eyes and tried for a faint smile, stepping back. "So," he managed, his voice as unreliable as his sense of balance. "That's it, I guess. That's me."

"It's not you," Nate protested immediately. "It's just... one piece of you. It's not *you.*"

Nate's hand was a welcome, steadying pressure on Leo's shoulder. Leo glanced around, found no one paying them any attention, and while his heart was still thrumming against his ribs, it wasn't quite as urgent anymore. Like coming down after a mad dash from the police, or a breathless orgasm that had shaken him up from the inside, like breaking open. The kind he'd experienced only twice in his life.

Nate came to lean next to Leo, close enough that their arms brushed together. His question was low. "Does Joshua know?"

"No." Leo's breath stuttered in his throat, and he swallowed around empty air. "He'd think less of me. Even if he didn't... I can't be with him, so what's the point?"

"What's the point? What do you mean, 'what's the point?'" Nate sounded incredulous. When Leo glanced over, he found Nate watching him with a frown, starkly outlined by the bright sun. "The *point,*" Nate said, before Leo could think to interrupt, "is that you're in love with him. And I'm pretty sure it's mutual."

Leo's shrug turned out helpless, and he managed to hold Nate's gaze for only a short moment. "It doesn't matter."

"Look, mate." Nate sighed, nudging their shoulders together. "I love you to bits, all right? But remember when you called him a coward for, like, taking the easy way out, going with the status quo? For not being honest? Remember how you thought he should risk it? How it was worth it, taking a shot at something more?" He paused just long enough for Leo to catch up with the rapid-fire questions. "Practice what you preach, L. You're my best mate, but you're a bit of a hypocrite about this. You're hiding from him when he's been nothing but honest."

A hypocrite. Joshua had called Leo just that, open disappointment woven into each syllable, but it wasn't fucking *true*. It wasn't. Not when Leo was doing this for Joshua just as much as for himself.

He tensed up, shifting away. "I'm protecting him," he said sharply. "It's not just about... I mean, yeah, it's bloody scary to think that if I was his boyfriend, I'd have cameras following my every step. But it's also—more than that. If he wanted to try, with me? He could suffer for it. The media would—"

"That's not your call," Nate cut into Leo's words. "Jesus, mate. You can't just make the decision for him. You know he'd hate that, and it's not—I think you're not giving him enough credit here."

Something in Leo's chest stuttered to a sudden halt, then sped up again, a nauseating change of pace. His stomach felt hollowed out from the inside. *Not your call.*

"I'm," he began, then didn't know how to continue.

You can't just make the decision for him. He'd hate that.

"Leo." Nate straightened and stepped in front of Leo, studying him with a mix of concern and disapproval. "I'm serious, yeah? The guy is in love with you, and if you let him slip away..." He shook his head, voice much lower as he added, "You deserve to be happy."

Joshua makes me happy, Leo thought, and while he choked the words back down, he couldn't unthink them. They resounded in his mind, got tangled up in Joshua's, "Just happy," when Leo had asked why Joshua had been laughing that night. Fuck, Joshua had still looked happy the morning after, ambling into the kitchen naked and bright-eyed—until Leo had stamped out that happiness.

Had trampled all over it.

Maybe it had been about himself once, but this wasn't just about him anymore. It was about Joshua. God, how had Leo believed that he was protecting Joshua when all he'd ever done was hurt him? If Joshua didn't want Leo after learning the truth—then at least Leo had given him a *choice*.

Nate was still talking, something about how things could absolutely work out, *hey, remember we handle potential scandals for a living*, but it didn't really make it through the rush in Leo's ears. With his heart giving a violent lurch, Leo gripped Nate's shoulder to steady himself. "Fuck," he whispered. "*Fuck*. Nate, I..."

Nate pulled him into another hug before Leo could finish the thought.

11

"You need to fly to Brazil." It wasn't quite a question, but it wasn't quite a statement either. James' expression didn't give away much.

"Yes," Leo said. He laced his hands in his lap.

"And you have to leave right now."

"I—yes. Because I did something really stupid." Leo unlaced his hands and crossed his legs at the ankle, then forced himself to sit still. Honestly, he was better than this; he wasn't a pre-schooler who couldn't keep his nerves in check. "I need to set it right. I need to... I just..." Breaking off, he gave a helpless shrug while his intestines performed a sad pirouette. The team's current case wasn't fully closed, so if James needed Leo here—Leo owed him that much.

A sudden smirk sparked in James' eyes. "You need to see the Prince."

"I need to see Joshua," Leo corrected.

James nodded, his smirk softening. "Point taken." He paused, leaning back in his desk chair. "All right. I'll give you your big, romantic gesture. On one condition."

Your big, romantic gesture.

It wasn't like that; it really wasn't. This wasn't a big gesture, just a necessity—Joshua wasn't here, and Leo needed to talk to him. Desperately so. He'd been stupid, and he'd hurt Joshua, and he needed to set it right, needed to know if there was a chance, any chance at all. He couldn't wait two weeks for Joshua to get back, even if it meant spending a thousand pounds on a one-way flight with no idea where he'd turn if Joshua didn't want him.

Oh. So maybe this did qualify as a big gesture.

Leo exhaled slowly, measured. "What's the condition?"

"Take a couple weeks off." James raised a brow. "That's how long he's staying, isn't it?"

Leo sagged into himself, felt like a puppet with its strings cut. He was flying to Brazil. Wow. "Thank you," he whispered.

With a little sigh, James shook his head. "I've been telling you to take a real holiday for years."

He had. There just hadn't been a particularly pressing need, not when Leo loved his work, not when his place was here in London. There was his Saturday gig with the kids—which, he'd need to let Kylie know he wouldn't be able to make it tomorrow. Maybe Nate could fill in for him?

Also... Fuck, he'd need more than a fake ID to travel to Brazil. His was enough to withstand a cursory inspection, but certainly not enough to get him halfway across the globe.

"Hey, James?" Leo got up from his chair and crossed over to the window. Restlessness itched in his bones and buzzed in his fingertips, had him watching the sky with a mix of hope and apprehension. In just a few hours, he'd be up there. Christ, it had been over a decade since he'd last been on a plane. Turning, he found James studying him with fond amusement, and Leo cleared his throat. "Do you know someone who might—my old passport is way expired."

"Surprised you even have one," James said. "Thought you might have left it behind so your parents wouldn't find you."

Leo gave a hollow laugh. "I really don't think they even tried. But, yeah, that's why I always used my fake ID. I was not so stupid as to run away without my passport, though. Plenty stupid, yes, but that one I had covered."

"Good thinking." While James had never learned the specifics of Leo's background, he merely smiled. "I can pull some strings."

"Of course you can," Leo said. Smiling back, he shifted his weight and tried to control the hectic pace of his pulse. Unsurprisingly, his success was limited. He probably wouldn't get so much as a wink of sleep on the twelve-hour flight, would instead get high on complimentary snacks and sugary drinks instead.

God, please let there still be a free seat for him when he got out of here. He didn't want to wait another twenty-four hours for the next flight out.

About to excuse himself, he was stopped when James spoke up again. "So, with what I know of your backstory, I'm aware we're looking at a potential scandal. Shall I ready the troops?"

Leo stilled. The question sat strangely in his stomach, like a weight that had dropped quite suddenly. What had seemed like an abstract possibility had just become a lot more concrete because— fuck. If Joshua was willing to take that chance, it could cost them. And if they failed in spinning this *just* right...

Buckingham Palace would be under siege. Again.

Jesus fucking Christ, Joshua would have to be *mad* to risk it. But Leo would give him a choice all the same. And if Joshua wanted him... Well. Leo's life would change. Enormously so.

It would be worth it.

"Not quite yet." Leo fought for an even tone. "And you know I can't afford—"

James didn't let him finish. "You're not a paying client, Leo. Don't insult me." He sounded genuinely offended, and Leo had no idea how he'd got so lucky. If he hadn't been at that bar while James had been waiting for a contact that never showed, if James hadn't seen *something* in Leo that evening, hadn't been willing to take a chance on a boy who didn't possess much beyond a cheeky smile and a worn leather jacket...

"You might be the best thing that's ever happened to me, you know?" Leo told him. On impulse, he closed the gap between them to lean down for a sideways hug. James grinned into it.

"Or maybe Joshua is."

Pulling back, Leo managed a grin that was bound to turn out a little watery. Ever since this morning, everything about him felt broken open, unsteady. A few short hours ago, he'd believed that he should let Joshua go without a fight. How could he have been so stupid?

"Maybe," Leo agreed softly. "Maybe he is, yes."

James' grin widened in response. Steepling his fingers together on his desk, he kicked his chair back a little, shooting Leo a shrewd look. "Nate's coming with you, by the way," he said, matter-of-fact.

"He *what*?" Then the implication caught up with Leo, and he crossed his arms, narrowing his eyes. "Wait a minute. Are you telling me that you knew the whole time why I was here, and yet you let me squirm through this? Not cool."

If anything, James' amusement seemed to increase. "It's my job to know things, and I so rarely get to see you squirm." He tilted his head, gaze warm and direct. "Really, though. I felt it would do you good, having to ask. Some things shouldn't be easy."

"You're a closeted sadist." Leo inhaled and swallowed, dropping his arms back to his side. "Also a better father figure than mine ever was."

"Don't think that's saying much, from what little I gleaned. But," James' tone grew serious, "I'm honoured, Leo. Don't mean to brag, but I think I did a pretty good job with you, all things considered."

"All things considered," Leo echoed flatly. "Such praise, oh, you flatter me." It took a moment, then a grin tugged at the corners of his mouth.

"Well. You go through with this, put yourself out there..." James' eyes held a challenge, bright and fond. He inserted a significant pause. "Then I'd say I did an all-around spectacular job. Now *go*. Collect Nate, book your flights, and I'll let you know what to do about your passport."

"Thank you," Leo told him. His chest swelled on a deep breath.

"Go," James repeated.

Leo did.

∾

£1,290.

£1,290 per person, just for the flight to Rio de Janeiro. One-way, and then it'd be a similar sum for the way back. The financial cushion Leo had managed to squirrel away would be a little less comfortable after this trip.

It was worth it.

After a quick thank you, Leo angled himself away from the sales clerk to face Nate properly. The airport was bustling around them, travellers rushing to and fro, announcements from the speakers reminding them not to leave their baggage unattended. Leo rather doubted anyone wanted to mess with his hastily packed suitcase— but anyway. £1,290.

He cleared his throat. "Can I just reiterate that you do not have to come along? This isn't a bargain, right, and I can do it on my own because I'm a strong, independent man and all that shit. You know, maybe it's the kind of thing I *should* be doing on my own."

"You've been doing things on your own your whole life." The corners of Nate's mouth curved up. "Also, who said I'm going for you, mate? Mo actually asked me to come along, like, this morning."

That was news to Leo. Unsurprising news, but news all the same.

He pressed the side of his foot against Nate's. "You're boyfriends, then? All proper and official, making an honest man out of you? Do I need to give him the you-hurt-him-I-kill-you best friend talk?"

Nate scoffed. "Hate to break it to you, but you're not that scary."

"Excuse you, I am bloody terrifying. You're probably just jaded, been up against super spies or something, so I don't think you're a good judge here." After another second's pause, Leo nodded and turned back to the clerk, sliding his provisional passport across the counter. "We'll take them. Thank you." Then he turned back to Nate and added a slightly belated, "Hey. Happy for you, man."

"Kind of happy for myself." Nate didn't sound smug, just honest.

"At your next class reunion, you can totally brag about dating a supermodel. Stick it to the arseholes who bullied you."

"Not what it's about at all." With a snort, Nate shook his head. His attention was on Leo's passport when the clerk opened it, a beat of silence spiralling out as he appeared to study the information upside down. Birth date and place of birth, family name—not the one Leo had made his own and which had come to fit like a well-worn glove, but the one he'd grown up with.

Austin, Leo Troy.

Nate seemed to roll the name around his mouth, test it out in his head, before he nudged their hips together, voice low. "Leo Troy Austin, huh. Sounds weird, mate. Is it the kind of fancy name that could get us into that extra special lounge here? Like, the one where we met the others this morning?"

That extra special lounge where Joshua had looked at Leo with disappointment in his eyes and heaviness in his voice. *I wish it could be easy.*

Leo shook himself free of a memory that felt like an open cut. "Most certainly not. As much as my parents liked to pretend otherwise, we weren't that important. Definitely not important enough to be on the shortlist for the Windsor Lounge back when it was invitation only. Barely even important enough to have heard the rumours about it." Sending Nate a lopsided grin, he assumed a posh air. "And anyway, things have gone downhill now that they let in just anyone who'll pay the price. Riff raff, really. Actors, nouveau-riche, *those* sorts of people. Anyone who wants to avoid contact with the travelling public, basically."

"Really?" Nate processed the information, then twitched one shoulder, suddenly serious. "As the guy by Joshua's side, you just might become that kind of person."

Hope flared bright in Leo's chest, untampered *want* at the mere idea of getting to do that, be that—the guy by Joshua's side. It was tainted by a burst of unease at the truth of what Nate had said. If Joshua wanted him, Leo would become a public figure.

If.

Leo focused his gaze on the countertop. "But I'm not that guy," he said softly.

"Yet," Nate told him.

The flare refused to die. Leo took a deep breath while the clerk was clacking away. "Yet," he confirmed, and it felt as though his entire body expanded with that one word.

JOSHUA HAD SPENT part of the flight curled into Mo or Tristan's side, pretending to doze. The rest of the time he'd watched episodes of *Game of Thrones*, mostly because they reminded him of Leo. He was pathetic.

It was early evening when they touched down in Rio de Janeiro and were shuffled out of the airport, through a private exit straight into a waiting car. The time difference to London was only a few hours, but each one weighed like a brick on Joshua's shoulders.

"Hotel?" he asked. "Or if the two of you already want to go exploring tonight... Don't stay in on my account."

"A swim in the pool sounds nice," Mo said.

Nodding, Tristan reached over to twine his fingers with Joshua's. "Then order in some food and enjoy it in one of our rooms. Whoever has the terrace with the nicest view wins. We can watch the sun set over the ocean. It'll be romantic and shit."

All Joshua wanted was to fall into a deep, dreamless sleep and wake up tomorrow having forgotten all about Leo. Since that wasn't an option, a platonic date with his two best friends was the next best thing.

"Will there be wine?" he asked.

"There'll be Caipirinhas," Tristan said firmly.

Joshua squeezed Tristan's hand and worked up a smile. Outside the car, palm trees bent in the wind. The clear blue of the sky was dotted with white, fluffy clouds, the evening sun casting everything in warm hues. From a distance, Rio de Janeiro gleamed like a promise. The difference to London couldn't have been more striking.

Two weeks. Surely it would be enough time for Joshua to start getting over Leo, to stop hoping that somehow, in some miraculous way, things would work themselves out.

Surely.

AT HALF PAST five in the morning, Rio de Janeiro's international airport was a surreal experience—maybe it was the heavy cover of night blanketing the landscape, or the colourful traces of the World Cup that were everywhere. It could also be that Leo didn't understand a word of Portuguese. Or maybe it was because he hadn't slept more than a couple of short, fitful hours, and his inner clock informed him it was well into the morning.

They collected their bags and stepped out of the building into a velvety night, the sky only just beginning to brighten. "Texted Mo yet?" Leo asked around a yawn. In spite of the tiredness weighing him down, there was a low-level buzz of adrenaline coursing through his blood.

He was in Brazil. He was about to see Joshua, and this time, he wouldn't hold back. Was this what Johnson had felt like when he'd put everything on a number, on a horse? This rush? All or nothing; *rien ne va plus.*

"I did, yeah." Exhaustion blurred the contours of Nate's words. "Bit earlier, while we were waiting in Immigration. Hasn't replied yet."

"Probably still asleep," Leo said. Joshua would be asleep too. Were he and Mo—but no. Mo was Nate's boyfriend now, and Joshua wouldn't get over Leo quite so quickly, would he? Or bring a random guy back to his room to make himself forget?

Oh God. What if Leo showed up, and Joshua wasn't alone?

"Hey," Nate said, quiet concern, and Leo glanced up sharply.

"Let's grab a taxi." It came out a little off-kilter, betrayed the sudden, nauseating pressure that squeezed down on his chest. "The *Copacabana Palace*, right?"

"Right. Top of the hotel crop." Nate was frowning, studying Leo for a beat too long. Leo shifted under the scrutiny. In the end, Nate settled for a comforting touch to Leo's shoulder before he turned to lead the way to the taxi rank. With a deep breath that rattled his bones, Leo followed.

It was a drive of nearly an hour.

They spent it mostly in silence, watching the world streak by outside—the silhouettes of palm trees against the inky sky, little boats out on the water, their position lights winking in the approaching dawn. There were also run-down houses that rose high, air-conditioning units protruding from the walls; there were hotels that had been constructed in an obvious hurry and without a single consideration for individuality.

As they neared the *Copacabana Palace*, the ocean, previously confined by a large bay, opened. The water was a slim, blue band that faded into the horizon. When the taxi pulled up in front of a white-washed hotel complex that glowed against the brightening sky, Leo felt his heart constrict in his chest.

He wasn't ready.

A little numbly, he paid the driver and had no idea how much the sum would be in British pounds. Nate had told him the exchange rate, but Leo couldn't recall it right now. He could barely recall his own name.

Leo Graham. Leo Troy Austin. Jason. Zack. Mo. Whatever you want it to be.

Hotel employees jumped to help them with their baggage, the black buttons on their uniforms contrasting with the white of their jackets. Leo followed mutely behind Nate, and while this wasn't his first brush with luxury, it had been years and only added to the sense of disorientation that had gripped him. Everything was tempered air and polished gold coating and lavish flower bouquets, and he really just wanted to see Joshua.

Joshua. Who was probably still asleep. Hopefully alone.

Nate exchanged a few words with the receptionist while Leo stood staring up at a chandelier that hung suspended above their heads. He jolted out of his haze when Nate nudged him. "They can't tell us the room numbers, won't even confirm Mo, Joshua and Tristan are staying here," Nate said, and... what? Oh. Right, of course.

"Hotel policy." Leo shrugged. "They wouldn't confirm they're here even if we saw them hanging out in the lobby. Places like this, they pride themselves on their discretion. Can you—if you try calling Mo?"

Nodding, Nate retrieved his phone and took a few steps off to the side before he made the call. A frown settled on his face, and he returned with a, "Straight to voicemail. Must have switched it off."

"Tristan?" Leo asked. Then he pushed out a heavy breath. "No, never mind. I might as well call Joshua now, give him a fair warning. If he doesn't want to see me—"

"*Hey*," Nate said firmly.

"If he doesn't want to see me," Leo repeated, and even though he tried to make it sound composed, his voice caught halfway through the sentence, "then at least I won't stand there like an idiot while he slams the door in my face."

Without waiting for a response, he turned away and unlocked his phone, briefly closed his eyes and saw sparks dance behind his lids. When Nate rested a warm palm on his back, Leo swallowed and leaned into the touch. Blindly, he brought the phone to his ear and waited for his call to connect.

JOSHUA HAD BEEN UP since five. He'd fought his own body, willing himself back to sleep, but he'd given up after half an hour, had turned on a reading light and struggled to focus on a book even though the words kept swimming in front of his eyes. *Fever Pitch*. Leo had recommended it, and Joshua had been meaning to read it for a while.

He shoved all thoughts of Leo to the back of his mind.

Once the sky started to brighten, he rolled out of bed, pulled on a pair of swim shorts and padded out onto the private terrace to watch the sun rise. So. Saturday. In London, Leo was probably picking up the van, determined to help out a bunch of street kids because he knew what it was like.

Jesus. Of course he'd lashed out at some of Joshua's comments. He must have seen himself in them, felt under attack each time Joshua didn't quite know how to voice his thoughts, and if Leo really was in love with Joshua... It must have hurt.

Joshua had never intended to hurt Leo, but that didn't mean he hadn't. At some point—when things weren't quite this fresh, weren't quite this painful—he'd apologise. And then he'd let it go.

In the quiet of the new day, the ringing of Joshua's phone seemed shrill, out of place. He considered ignoring it where it lay on his bedside table, the screen glowing bright in the still-shadowed room, easy to make out through the windowpane.

What if it was important, though? He sighed and pushed away from the railing.

Ever since his interview had aired, he'd made certain to keep his phone nearby and charged at all times. Just in case. So far, there'd been no emergency, and the big fallout he'd feared hadn't come. Some nasty comments, yes, but—well. While he could do without them, they didn't cause tangible damage. There had been no economic impact, not one threat of secession by a Commonwealth Member. Those driving Scotland's independence referendum had even made it a point to reaffirm that an independent Scotland would seek membership of the Commonwealth.

He snatched the phone, checked the display—and froze.

Leo.

That was Leo.

Why was Leo calling him?

Sitting down on the bed, Joshua felt his blood crawl through his veins at a hypnotic pace, slowing everything down. The room was as paralyzed as Joshua himself, his thoughts like building blocks, angular and monotone. *Why was—with the way they'd parted—why would Leo... Why. How, why. Leo. Why now. Leo.*

Only when the ringing stopped did Joshua abruptly snap back to himself. He gave it a few seconds, long enough for Leo to end the call, before he called back.

Leo picked up on the first ring, with a low, oddly breathless, "Josh."

"Hi." It was one word, just one word, but it took a conscious effort for Joshua to push it out. His lungs squeezed down on his heart and made thinking difficult. The morning felt cool on his bare skin.

A gap followed, and Joshua could hear Leo inhale on a hissed intake of air. When he spoke, it was just as low as before, shaky. "You picked up. I, um." Another gap. "I was wondering if you'd see me."

Nothing made sense. Joshua's head was a minefield.

"What do you mean?" he asked—too soft and affected, bordering on helpless. Twisting his fingers into the duvet, he tried to ground himself and stared out of the window at the endless expanse of the sky.

"Like..." Leo cleared his throat. "I'd like to talk to you. Right now?"

Nothing made sense. Shaking his head, Joshua squeezed his eyes shut. "Leo, I'm in Brazil."

"I know." Leo gave a wet laugh. "So am I."

What?

"What?" Joshua whispered.

"I'm downstairs." Again, Leo cleared his throat, gaining just a hint more confidence. "*Copacabana Palace*, right? I'm in the lobby. Nate as well. They won't let us up unless you tell them it's okay."

Joshua clambered to his feet, pressed the phone to his ear and tried to still the rush of blood to his feet. Leo was... here? Why would... Leo was in Brazil? In *Brazil*? Half a day after Joshua had arrived?

Flattening one hand against the windowpane, Joshua tested out the words. "You're here."

"That's what I just said." Sudden humour glinted in Leo's voice. He still sounded small and uncertain, but there was a newfound brightness to it, a teasing edge that was so familiar it made Joshua feel vaguely sick to the stomach. "Do try to keep up, little prince.

Now, if you could convince these nice people here that I am no danger to your virtue..." Leo paused. "Well. *Then again.*"

Joshua barely heard him. "You flew to *Brazil*?"

"I..." For just a moment, Leo's composure failed. "Yeah. I did."

"To see me," Joshua said, not really a question. *Leo was here.* That had to mean—he'd changed his mind. He wouldn't have flown twelve hours just to break Joshua's heart all over again. Would he?

"Actually, I've always wanted to piss on the foundation of that oversized Jesus statue." Then Leo sighed, all humour draining away to make room for quiet sincerity. "Sorry, stupid defence mechanism right there. It's—I am here for you. Yeah. If you'll see me. If you..." The shortest of breaks. "If you'll have me."

If you'll have me.

Joshua's lungs felt swollen, like a tick gorged on blood. He needed a moment to make his voice work. "I'll ask them to take you up. And Nate is here as well?"

"For emotional support, mainly," Leo said, still in that quietly sincere tone. It was the most open, the most *vulnerable* Joshua had ever heard him. "Also a tad bit for Mo, of course."

"I'll wake him." Dropping his hand, Joshua stared at its imprint on the windowpane for a stunned second, then tried to focus. He needed to call the reception, and he needed to put on some clothes. God, he probably looked a dishevelled mess. "Yes. I'll wake him, and I... We're all on the top floor."

"Of course you are." Leo sounded immeasurably fond, and something in Joshua's stomach gave, like a knot had been tugged loose. "I'll see you in a minute, all right?"

"All right," Joshua echoed softly.

Once the call had ended, he stared at his own reflection, blurred and translucent on the windowpane. Then he straightened his spine and raised his head, felt the ghost of a disbelieving smile tug at his mouth.

Leo was here.

～

WITH EACH FLOOR number that flashed by, Leo's stomach sagged just a little lower. He'd never been more grateful for Nate's steady presence by his side.

On the phone, Joshua had sounded... surprised, yes. Disbelieving. A little shaken, but not in a bad way. And maybe he was simply too kind to turn Leo away right now, when the sun was barely out and Leo had flown all night, but if Joshua listened just long enough for Leo to explain himself...

The lift glided to a smooth halt. Its doors opened before Leo was ready.

Mo was waiting in the hallway, sleep-ruffled and dressed in only a pair of pyjama bottoms. He was undeniably hot. Leo noticed it rather absently as his gaze slid past Mo to settle on Joshua. Half-hidden behind Mo's figure, Joshua looked alert, his hair a wild mess, eyes a clear green when they met Leo's. Good God, Leo was in love with him. So in love with him.

He thought about putting it out there, again—*I'm in love with you. And I was wrong because it matters, it does.*

Mo's voice cut through the haze. "Babe." He sent Nate a sudden smile. "This is unexpected."

"Good unexpected?" Nate asked. He was grinning already, even though his hand remained clasped around Leo's elbow.

"Very good," Mo confirmed. Then he glanced over at Leo, down at the bags they'd brought, and oh, fuck. Both the lift boy and the bellboy had been present for the entire exchange. What did this look like to them? What if the security cameras saw Leo disappear into Joshua's room, bag in hand? What if the story would spread before they'd got a chance to even *talk*?

Leo's discomfort must have been obvious, because Joshua shook his head, very lightly. But he didn't know, *couldn't* know just how bad it would be if word got out. Panic was a perfectly appropriate reaction, the *Hitchhiker's Guide* be damned.

Holy hell, Leo really hadn't thought this through.

Again, Joshua shook his head, more emphatically. 'Discretion,' he mouthed, and Leo was still processing it when Joshua addressed the hotel staff. "Thank you both. I think we can handle it from here." With that, he drew forward to hand over a tip and pick up one of the bags. Nudged into motion by Nate, Leo stepped out of the lift. He was vaguely aware of Mo grabbing the last bag.

Fuck, maybe Leo should have caught some sleep before doing this.

Only when the lift was back on the descent did Joshua speak again. Turning in the hallway, Leo's bag slung over his shoulder, he told them, "Places like this rely on discretion. It's one of their biggest selling points, and if they lose that, they're done for. No one will know you're here."

"That's what Leo just said a few minutes ago," Nate put in. With a squeeze to Leo's elbow, he let go and walked right into Mo's space, tugged him in for a kiss. And... okay. So they really were official.

Blinking, Leo averted his gaze and tried to douse any spark of envy.

He looked up to find Joshua watching him with an expression that was hard to read, something between confused and hopeful, wary and guarded, but still so painfully open. Leo wanted to touch him so much that he felt completely frozen with it.

"You're here to talk to me?" Joshua asked, and Leo exhaled around the crushing weight of what he was about to do.

His voice came out in a croak. "Yes. Talk to you."

Joshua bit down on his bottom lip, little indents of his teeth, and nodded. "Talk, okay." After a sideways glance at Mo and Nate, Joshua took a hesitant step towards an open door. His room, probably.

Just as Leo made to follow, Nate held him back with a hand on the shoulder. "Good luck," he whispered, and behind him, Mo looked on in what might have passed for a bored expression, had it not been for the worried glint in his eyes. Leo wondered just how much Mo knew. As much as Joshua, probably.

But Joshua didn't know nearly enough.

"Thank you," Leo replied, just as quietly. Shoving a hand through his hair, he adjusted his carry-on and moved towards the door Joshua had left open for him.

When he entered, Joshua had already dropped the bag in the middle of the room—suite, really—that was flooded with sunlight, still pale with the early hour. Open glass doors led out onto a terrace, and beyond it, the ocean extended, gleaming like a silken scarf and melting into the sky. Leo's tired mind needed a moment to process it as more than a lucid dream.

An enormous bed was set against one wall, and Leo's attention lingered there. He took in the pristine, white sheets. Only one pillow was slept on, one open water bottle on the left of two bedside tables. Irrational relief settled in his bones. In theory, he'd known Joshua wouldn't go out and fuck the first random bloke, but it had still been a distant possibility. And Leo couldn't have blamed Joshua. Not when things between them were... *this*.

Leo lifted his head and worked up the courage to meet Joshua's gaze. For a long beat, they stared at each other across the expanse of carpeted floor. With the way Joshua was standing near the open terrace doors, light streamed in behind him and smoothed out the details of his features, caught halfway between a cut-out and a real person.

Jesus, okay. Leo needed to get a grip.

"I should warn you," he said, a little unfocused, "that I've barely slept since... before the last time we saw each other. So if I maybe don't make perfect sense... Sorry."

"Do you want coffee?" Joshua asked. "Or English breakfast?"

"I just want you," Leo told him, completely honest. It was out before he could think better of it, but he didn't want to take it back. For fuck's sake, he had not flown twelve bloody hours to chicken out. "I want you, and also maybe some sleep in the near future. But mostly you."

Something unbearably bright skittered over Joshua's face, and Leo had to look away. No. He didn't get to keep that, not yet. Not until he'd put himself out there.

After a dragging second, Joshua moved away from the terrace doors, turned his back to Leo as he fiddled with the kettle that sat in a corner of the suite, next to a coffee maker and a selection of tea. Leo didn't think he could stomach even water right now.

"You said..." Joshua glanced over his shoulder, voice careful. "In your flat, you said it didn't matter what you want. Or what I want. Because it couldn't be."

"I was—fuck." Leo wiped a hand over his eyes. Everything felt hazy, and the only thing he could focus on was the dip between Joshua's shoulder blades, the curls at the nape of his neck, and how much Leo wanted to kiss the exposed skin above the collar of his shirt. "I wasn't wrong," Leo said slowly. "Except I was. But... Just, before we can be—if you still even maybe want to, there are things you should know. About me."

"Things?" Joshua repeated. Flicking the kettle on, he kept his hands busy by readying two cups, selecting tea bags. He'd have seemed thoroughly distracted, unresponsive, if it weren't for the tiny glances he kept shooting at Leo.

"Things." Leo fought against the bile rising to the back of his throat. He could do this. "Things that I should have told you sooner. But I was..."

"Scared?" Now Joshua had turned around, studying Leo. It wasn't with anger or reproach, rather with something cautious, the way one would hold perfectly still to watch a flock of wild birds just a little longer before they took flight. Leo was momentarily unsettled, confusion tangling with the bright sunshine that slanted into the room.

"Scared," he confirmed, slightly delayed. "Because I thought you wouldn't like it, and you *won't*. But I also thought... I told myself I was protecting you. Took Nate to make me realise that maybe you don't even want that. That I had no right to take the decision from you."

"So you're ready to tell me now?" Joshua asked, so quiet it nearly got lost in the distance between them.

"I'm... Yes." Leo sucked in a breath. "I'm ready to tell you..." *Everything.* "Everything. Starting with—" No. He couldn't just drop that bomb without preparing the ground first, giving Joshua a chance to adjust. "Starting with how you already know I had a crush on you, at Eton. But I didn't tell you that you made me realise I was gay."

Surprise widened Joshua's eyes. God, they were lovely; *he* was lovely. "I did?"

"Bit creepy, maybe." Leo pursed his lips and gave a little shrug, not quite able to hold Joshua's gaze. His cheeks felt hot. "I mean, you were fourteen, and we were, like—in the Wall Game. We ended up shoved close, and that rather... I liked that rather more than I should. Which was how I realised that yeah, definitely more interested in that cherubic little thing with the curls and the 'look at me, I'm a prince' swagger than I'd ever been interested in a girl."

Joshua made a soft noise, a half-formed chuckle. He messed up his curls with one hand and seemed to search for an appropriate response, but was saved by the kettle announcing it was done.

Leo waited until Joshua had turned away to pour water into the cups before he continued. "Sometimes I wondered whether perhaps, if it hadn't been for you, it would have taken me longer to figure things out."

Some water spilled when Joshua's hand jerked. He stilled for a moment, then resumed preparing the tea, his voice heavy. "Long enough that things could have been—with your parents..." He trailed off, and Leo finished for him.

"Long enough that things might have gone differently, yes. If I'd been a little older, a bit more mature, already at uni or something..."

"Oh." Setting the kettle down, Joshua leaned against the cabinet, his head bent as he exhaled. "I'm sorry?"

Distant amusement tugged at Leo's mouth, made the corners curve up. "Did you really just apologise for being too cute for your own good at age fourteen? That's ridiculous."

"No, I just..." Joshua glanced up before Leo had a chance to control his expression, and there was a beat when they simply looked at each other, miles of space between them. Leo steadied himself with one hand on the back of an armchair, but he still felt completely out of his depth. He didn't look away, though, and neither did Joshua.

"You just?" Leo prompted.

"I just wish things had gone differently for you." Joshua swallowed. "I wish your parents had been understanding, wish that you hadn't gone through living on the street and... You know, the things that entailed." With a helpless shrug, he focused on the steeping tea, set one of the cups on a saucer and carefully placed a teaspoon on it. His hands shook just enough for Leo to notice.

Joshua's voice hadn't carried pity. Sadness, yes, but no pity.

Leo felt his breathing ease. "No use in crying over spilt milk, is there? *C'est la vie.*"

He fell silent as Joshua drew near to hand over the saucer, and he still didn't think he could stomach anything, but—the simple act of Joshua offering Leo tea, even after everything... Their fingers brushed over the porcelain, and Leo fought the impulse to wrap his fingers around Joshua's wrist and hold on.

Perhaps Joshua would let him. But until Leo had come clean, it wouldn't feel right, wouldn't feel like something he deserved.

Accepting the tea, Leo withdrew by half a step and stared into the steaming water, clouded with murky brown that seeped from the tea bag. The sharp, bitter scent distracted him from a whiff of Joshua's cologne, mixed with soap and a hint of sleep-sweat. So close, so close. Leo wanted to tumble him onto the bed and learn every inch of Joshua's body with his fingertips and his mouth, to the point where he'd never be able to forget. To the point where Joshua wouldn't ever forget either.

When Leo looked up through his lashes, Joshua was entirely focused on him, eyes dark. Leo lowered his gaze.

It took him a second to remember what they'd been talking about. "I guess," he picked the thread back up, a slight rasp to his voice, "there are some life lessons in there as well. Things I learned out there. Of course there are things I'd change if I could, if I'd known better..." He paused, then made himself continue. "But in the end, it's made me grow, I suppose. I was a self-centred little twat at Eton. More than just a tad obnoxious, convinced that the world was my playground. I had no idea what real life was like." With a snort, he shook his head. "You probably wouldn't have liked me very much back then. Honestly, I don't think I'd have liked myself."

A light touch to his waist made Leo still entirely. He hadn't realised Joshua was still close enough to reach for him, and he didn't dare glance up, didn't dare move.

After a quiet second, Joshua's hand fell away. "I think you're too harsh on yourself."

Leo's mind was a mess of tangled thoughts and hopes, of *touch* and *hold* and *keep* and *Joshua*. "Maybe," he managed.

The silence that followed was loaded, heavy with all the words Leo should say. He didn't know how to begin, tried to ground himself in the act of fishing the tea bag out of the water, squeezing out the last dregs of taste by winding the thread tightly around the bag and tugging on the end. Jesus fucking Christ, why was this so bloody *hard*?

It was Joshua who broke the silence. "Is there more? You said you had things to tell me."

Okay. So this was it. This was *it*, and if Leo didn't do this now— then he might as well give up, because he'd never be what Joshua deserved.

He made himself look up and hold Joshua's gaze. "There is more, yes. There is a very good, very concrete reason why I think—why I thought that as much as I wanted it, as much as I wanted *you*, it couldn't work. Even though I was in love with you." He paused. "Am in love with you."

The bright, gentle warmth in Joshua's eyes sent a shiver down Leo's spine. While Joshua stayed quiet, he was smiling, so faintly it seemed like a distant idea.

To distract himself, Leo took a quick sip of his tea, coughing as he inhaled some steam. He set the cup aside and used it as an excuse to turn away so he wouldn't have to say this and see the warmth fade from Joshua's face. "So the thing is that I—I was young and naive, had no idea where to turn, you know? So I slept with guys. For money." Oh God. *Oh God.* Intestines twisting, Leo pushed on. "It wasn't a big plan, nothing like that, but the first time just somehow happened, like... I'd only wanted a place to sleep for the night, and instead I was handed some money and kicked back outside, and—it made sense, after that. It wasn't too bad. It was money, straight-up cash that could buy me food, or a new pair of winter boots or a sleeping bag. I didn't need references I didn't have, and I wasn't begging on some sidewalk or something like that, because I've always been a proud fucker, and..."

Abruptly, he felt like choking on the rush of words, his throat too tight to continue, lungs compressed to a tiny ball of fear. The sheer amount of *nothing* that followed pressed down on him. Just silence.

Then Joshua stepped in front of him, walked right into Leo's space, so close that Leo couldn't help but look at him. Very slowly, carefully, Joshua reached out to lace their fingers. Leo inhaled on a gasp.

"I wish," Joshua whispered, rough and thick, "that someone had told your younger self it's okay to accept help."

There was no surprise on Joshua's face. No disgust, no shock. Just deep sorrow. It was like being submerged in ice-cold water, then resurfacing to a world that was spinning too fast.

"You knew." Leo's voice almost gave out. "How?"

"I suspected." Joshua's lips pressed together, and he squeezed Leo's hand, but didn't let go. "After I left your place, that's when the pieces fell into place, and I thought... It was your secret to share. Not mine to force out of you."

How was he so composed? Why wasn't he running? Why had he let Leo into his room and made him tea; why was he still *listening*?

"Talk to me?" Joshua asked, uncertainty woven into the question. It helped, somehow. Leo tightened his grip on Joshua's hand, focused on the warmth of that touch.

"You're not shocked? Upset?"

"I was, a little. At first. But I realised it doesn't matter. It doesn't define you."

"I was a rent boy, Joshua." Drawing a painful breath, Leo forced himself to meet Joshua's eyes. "I got on my knees for money. In toilet stalls, in dirty alleys that smelled like piss. I pretended to like it when someone fucked me without prep, something that would have hurt like a bitch if I hadn't learned to do it myself. I mean, it wasn't—it wasn't always bad, it was mostly okay, most of the time, but... Fuck."

Unease flashed over Joshua's face, and now, *now* he'd understand. He'd drop Leo's hand and take a step back.

"I'm in love with you," Joshua said.

He—what? Now? *Now?*

Leo's heart thudded against his ribs. "You are?"

"I'm completely in love with you." Joshua didn't look away. While his voice was even, his palm was a little sweaty against Leo's, betraying his nerves. "And yes, it does bother me that those guys got to touch you. But mostly because they didn't deserve it."

Everything was blurry, swimming in front of Leo's eyes. "Well, they did pay."

"They didn't care for you," Joshua said roughly. "So no, they did not deserve it. *Leo.*" He reached out with his free hand, thumb brushing the skin under Leo's left eye, and only then did Leo realise he was fighting tears.

Joshua knew.

Joshua knew, and he was still here, was watching Leo with the same warmth as before.

Without thought, Leo stumbled into him, brought both arms up around Joshua's back to pull him as close as possible and hold on. *I'm completely in love with you.* The words threaded themselves through every thought that spun through Leo's brain, and he shut his eyes and struggled to breathe. Joshua was clinging back just as tightly.

"It's such a tiny part of you," he murmured, lips brushing Leo's cheek. "I hate that you went through it, but it's not—you can't let it hold you back. Don't let it define you. Don't let it... I want to be with you. So if you want—"

"How are you so bloody wonderful?" Leo interrupted. Blindly, he turned his head to find Joshua's mouth and draw him into a kiss that tasted like tea and salt, tinged with exhaustion. Another. Leo's body went weak with it, and it felt as though Joshua was the one thing holding him up.

Fuck, Leo needed to pull himself together. If this was supposed to work... If this was supposed to work, then Leo couldn't be a blubbering mess. They'd need to hold each other up, and he couldn't do that if he could barely walk straight.

I want to be with you.

He slowed the pace of their kisses, eased them up until it was just gentle, light brushes of their mouths. It was still enough to send heat spiralling down his spine, one of his hands fisted into the back of Joshua's shirt, fabric bunched up in his grip. Jesus. He'd thought he'd lost this. How had he convinced himself to let Joshua go without so much as a fight?

Bringing just enough space between them to focus on Joshua's face, Leo watched the way Joshua's lashes trembled, lids fluttering open. So beautiful. God, he was so fucking *beautiful.*

"You're so beautiful," Leo blurted, then shook his head to clear it. "But you get why this is—why my past is complicated. If the media finds out, it would be chaos."

Joshua blinked, then his eyes cleared. "I want you in my life. And if you're not ready to be with me in public—"

"I'm ready," Leo cut in. "You're the one whose reputation is at stake, Joshua. This is your risk, not mine. Me, I'm just a nobody."

"You're not a nobody to me. And" —Joshua's jaw clenched— "I don't fucking care. Let them talk."

Leo kept his fingers twisted into Joshua's shirt, knuckles digging in. He met the petulant defiance that had crept into Joshua's expression with what he hoped passed for a smile, his stomach too heavy. "You don't mean that."

"Well." Joshua sounded reluctant. "I do care a little, yes, but not about opinions. If strangers want to hate me, that doesn't hurt me. I just don't want it to harm my family, or the country. But maybe..." He hesitated. "Maybe it wouldn't be so bad? We don't have to tell the whole truth, right? It's not like you owe the public anything, certainly not your past."

"You don't owe them either."

"But I have a certain kind of duty to set an example."

Leo wanted to kiss him and never stop. "Which might be a problem if you date me. It's a risk."

For a moment, it looked as though Joshua would protest out of principle. Then he sighed, shoulders slumping. He hooked one hand in a belt loop of Leo's jeans, tugging him close again, close enough for all features to blur. His voice was low, yet firm. "I know it's a risk. For both of us. But I think we're worth it. Right?"

"Right," Leo whispered. There was so much more he needed to tell Joshua, a rush of words that clamoured for attention in his mind —that Joshua was lovely; that he made Leo want to be better and braver; that up until Joshua, Leo hadn't ever seen himself with anyone by his side. That he'd never wanted anyone like this, never *loved* anyone like this.

He settled for winding his fingers into Joshua's hair and dragging him in for another kiss. Joshua's mouth was already open, and Leo let his lids drift shut, let himself believe.

"We need to plan this," he squeezed into the gap between one kiss and the next. A moment later, he tugged on the buttons of Joshua's shirt, tried to fumble them open and made a disgruntled noise when they wouldn't cooperate.

"I want you inside," was Joshua's mumbled response. Then he stilled, suddenly tense. "I mean, if that's—"

"*Yes*," Leo interrupted, "yes, come on," and gave a sharp pull that had both of them stumble towards the bed. He felt almost disoriented with the brightness that filled the room, with Joshua's body pressed close, with all the things he wanted to do to him.

Joshua went down first. He landed on his back, bouncing on the mattress, and Leo crawled after him, straddling his hips so he could attack the buttons of Joshua's shirt again. Their fingers tangled over the material, held for a moment before Joshua let go, melting into the sheets as he shot Leo a brilliant smile.

"Love you. Now hurry up and get me naked."

"So demanding," Leo countered, but he couldn't bite down on his answering smile. Didn't want to. "What a royally spoilt brat."

"*Your* royally spoilt brat."

Yours, Leo thought, mind stuttering over it. Joshua was *his*.

Something in his expression must have shifted, betrayed his

instant of disorientation, because Joshua reached for him, drawing him down until they were looking at each other from up close. "Hey," Joshua murmured. "This isn't... I didn't misread you, the last time. Did I? You do enjoy sex with me."

It seemed so absurd that Leo needed a second to even process Joshua's meaning. Then he gripped Joshua's shoulder and frowned, leaning down further so he could nudge their noses together. "Don't ever doubt that, okay? Nothing has ever felt like you. My past is... tricky, yeah, and I had a lot of sex and didn't always like it very much, was often just going through the motions." He inhaled on a slow breath, so close that all he could see was the clear green of Joshua's eyes. "With you, it's nothing like that. *Nothing* like that."

Joshua's smile started in his eyes. "Yeah?"

"Yeah," Leo said. A strange lightness spread in his bones, and it might have been prompted by the tiredness that fogged up the edges of his vision—but maybe it wasn't. He drew another breath. "You make me happy. I don't quite know how I got so lucky, but—"

"Because," Joshua broke in, "you act all tough, but you're really not, and it's the most stunning thing when your face softens. And you don't let me get away with crap. You don't indulge me, but when I needed you—like, all that time, with my coming out, when I didn't feel good... You were right there."

There was nothing Leo could say that wouldn't sound like a line from a cheesy love ballad. He settled for dragging Joshua into a harsh kiss and hoped it would convey the idea.

Joshua turned into it like it was instinct, tilting his hips up— responsive, so beautifully responsive as Leo pressed down, *Jesus.* Joshua's fingers grappled at Leo's T-shirt, then moved to the front of Leo's jeans, tugging with both hands, a little aimlessly as though he was already stupid just from this, from their kiss and the slow grind of their hips. Leo caught both of Joshua's hands and trapped them against the sheets.

"What do you like?" he managed, words only just within his grasp.

For a beat, everything came to a halt, then Joshua's body relaxed under Leo's weight. His voice was like rough-spun silk. "What do *you* like?"

You. I like you.

Leo opened his eyes and found Joshua watching him with a gentle smile. Leo smiled back. "Why don't you guide me?"

"Why don't *you* guide *me*?" Joshua shot back. He was still smiling, but there was something slow and careful behind it, something Leo didn't quite understand. It didn't feel as though Joshua was trying to mock him, but—what was this?

"You can't just keep answering a question with a question," Leo told him.

Joshua shook his head, curls dragging over the sheets. He was dark hair and green eyes and red lips, and Leo lost himself in it for a moment, almost missed it when Joshua said, "That's not what this is about. This is about..." He twisted one hand in Leo's hold so that they were palm to palm. "I already know what I like, and I'll let you know if something doesn't work for me. But the thing is, I'm not so certain that you know what it is that *you* like?"

His voice had tilted up towards the end, turning it into a question, and... Oh.

"No one's ever asked," Leo whispered. Joshua's expression flooded with so much tenderness that Leo struggled to keep looking at him. He couldn't look away either.

Joshua twisted one hand free to touch Leo's jaw, fingertips gentle, reverent. "Not even your first time? He didn't stop to ask what worked for you and what didn't? Whether you wanted it slow or fast?"

Leo couldn't remember the last time he'd felt like this—ribcage split open to expose him completely, yet trusting Joshua to keep him safe. "My first time," he made himself hold Joshua's gaze, "was in Rose Garden. So, you know."

"Rose Garden?"

Right. Of course Joshua wouldn't know London's favourite destinations for gay cruising. For some reason, it lightened Leo's mood. "Rose Garden," he said grandly, "is Hyde Park's number one spot to get your dick sucked. Lots of bushes, not a lot of romance, but it seemed as good a place as any for a first fuck. That was shortly after I'd arrived in London, when I'd decided that losing my virginity was overdue. Not exactly the place for candlelight and sweet nothings, mind."

Joshua looked sad for just a moment, then it made room for a hint of teasing. "So, hey. Is that what you want—candlelight and sweet nothings?"

For all that there'd been humour in Joshua's tone, the underlying question had been a genuine one, and Leo considered it. "I want," he said slowly, slightly transfixed by the sunlight slanting over Joshua's face, "to fuck you on that sofa bed, the one that's on your terrace at home. In full daylight, and there's the tree hiding us, sure, but with the noise we're making, anyone who passes by below will hear."

Joshua's throat clicked as he swallowed, and he blinked once, drugged-slow. "We can do that," he mumbled. "Once we're back home."

"Until then..." Leo leaned down until their noses were almost touching, and oh, *oh*, the way Joshua's pupils dilated was brilliant. He felt on top of the world. "Until then, I want to spend hours mapping your body. And then fuck you. Then sleep a little and wake up with your fingers inside me."

"Jesus," Joshua breathed.

"Leo will do."

Some focus returned to Joshua's eyes, and he giggled quietly. "I can't believe you made that pun. Also, I thought you were tired."

"Hit a second high," Leo declared. It was mostly true, although there was this mild haze floating through his brain that slowed the spinning world down to a crawl. He rocked his hips down. Joshua's lips parted, lids drifting shut, and Leo was so in love with him it was hard to breathe.

He rolled off. "Get naked," he ordered, almost too soft for a command, but Joshua complied instantly. With a bright look at Leo, he shucked his shirt and shuffled out of his trousers, then lay back on the duvet in tiny shorts.

"*Naked*," Leo repeated, more confident.

Grinning, Joshua shoved the shorts down his legs and let Leo study him in the full brightness of the morning. His skin, still pale, was bound to bronze over the course of the two weeks ahead—two weeks that Leo would get to spend with him, right by his side. Already, he longed to trace tan lines that were yet to take shape.

"So beautiful," Leo repeated, and fuck, it was sappy, but he didn't care. Not when it made Joshua smile softly, cheeks red.

"But will you still love me when I'm no longer young and beautiful?"

It took Leo a moment to work it out, then he snorted. "Did you just quote Lana del Rey while lying naked on a huge hotel bed on the top floor with a view of the ocean?"

"Sure did." Joshua sounded perfectly smug, and Leo couldn't, just *couldn't* help leaning over him for a quick kiss.

"Well," he said, sitting back on his haunches. "When you're no longer young and beautiful, you'll still be rich. So there's that."

"Hey," Joshua drawled, eyes laughing.

Leo dipped down for another kiss and told him, close enough for his breath to tickle Joshua's skin, "Of course I'll still want you, Princey. Happily ever after, isn't that how it's supposed to be?"

"So we're a fairy tale after all," Joshua murmured, and Leo released a chuckle, then let his fingernails catch on the bump of Joshua's collarbones. Joshua went still before he exhaled in a rush. Ah.

Leo did it again, more purpose behind it. This time, Joshua shivered, gaze glued to Leo's face. Shit, if Joshua continued to be this open and responsive, there was no way Leo's resolve would last, no way he'd be able to take his time when all he wanted was to be closer.

Well. He'd just have to practice, then. Build up his immunity.

"Why are you smirking?" Joshua asked, noticeably breathless.

Leo shook his head and slid his hand lower, kissed the resulting gasp right out of Joshua's mouth.

As it turned out, Joshua truly did prove a challenge for Leo's willpower—moving into each touch, sighing at each mark Leo left in his path, hissing when Leo bit down on a nipple, then soothed the skin with his tongue. Fully untouched, Joshua's cock was leaking precome already, and Leo was no better off; once he'd rid himself of his clothes, the friction on his dick, sheets sliding against his skin as he moved around Joshua, had his breathing come in quick, sharp bursts.

Never like this.

At Leo's command, Joshua rolled onto his stomach and spread his legs. He was tightly coiled energy, yet pliant under Leo's hands. Leo draped himself over his back, his cock slotting into the gap between Joshua's thighs, and pressed his hips down. Christ, he could come like this. Make a mess of Joshua's body.

"Can't wait to be inside you," he said, his voice rough even to his own ears. "Can't wait to fuck you, make you mine. No one else gets to see you like this, yeah?"

"Yours already." Joshua twisted his head to look over his shoulder, eyes glassy and lips plump and red, bitten. "No one else, Leo."

Leo's heart gave a dizzying lurch. He lifted himself up, rolled off Joshua to lie down next to him and study his face from up close. "It's mutual. You know that, right?"

Joshua watched Leo for a heavy moment before he smiled. "I know." He paused briefly before he added, all politeness if it weren't for the spark of mischief in his eyes, "Now fuck me, please."

Please, Leo's brain echoed, and Jesus, Joshua was just too fucking much, too good to be true—and yet here they were. Leo reached out to twine a corkscrew curl around his finger, tugging, and watched Joshua's lashes tremble and his eyes lose focus.

It took Leo several moments to find his ability for coherent speech. He needed to say this, though, needed Joshua to know everything. No holding back, not anymore. Leo's throat felt tight, his voice a rough whisper. "Just so we're—I mean, full disclosure. I've had sex with exactly one person in the last six years, and that's you."

Joshua's smile widened. "I love you," he mumbled, the contours of the syllables slightly blurred.

"Same." Leo remembered to get some air into his lungs. His head was as empty and light as a hot air balloon. Draping himself over

Joshua's back once more, Leo pressed him into the bed with the weight of his own body. He considered dragging it out just for the hell of it, but his resolve crumbled when he nudged the dry tip of his thumb against Joshua's rim, and Joshua *shuddered* into it. He turned his head for a glimpse at Leo's face, and Leo felt his skin crawl with molten heat, was probably flushed down to his collarbones.

Fumbling for lube and a condom, he settled between Joshua's legs to work him open with his fingers. With sunlight streaming all around them, tangling in Joshua's hair, everything felt slow and warm and golden, far removed from the distant noise of traffic. Leo shaped soundless words against Joshua's skin, combined it with sharp nips at the sensitive skin between Joshua's thighs, and Joshua responded with gasps and sighs, twitching against the sheets.

By the time Leo coaxed Joshua up on his hands and knees, Joshua seemed barely able to support his own weight.

"You ready, love?" Leo asked softly, a palm between Joshua's shoulder blades, steadying him with the other hand gripping his hip.

Joshua gave a choked laugh. His voice sounded wrecked. "Been ready for hours."

"Should have said so."

"I did."

"Truly sorry." Dipping down to kiss Joshua's back, Leo rolled on the condom, then shuffled closer and reached for the lube. "Must have missed it over the racket you made."

"God, you're a bloody tease," Joshua muttered. When Leo leaned slightly to the side to glance at Joshua's face, Joshua was biting down on a grin, eyes closed, his lashes feathery against his cheek. Leo felt warm all over.

Coating himself up, he moved in close, his front to Joshua's back. With a little bite to Joshua's shoulder, he ordered, "Be a good boy and grip the headboard."

Joshua exhaled and complied.

Sliding in slowly, Leo stilled once he was all the way inside. Jesus, this was—tight pressure around his cock, Joshua shifting in tiny increments, and Leo squeezed his eyes shut against the overwhelming need to make this quick and dirty, finish in just a few sloppy strokes. No, *no*, he wanted to savour this. He wanted to cherish every second, wanted to make this every bit as good for Joshua as it already was for him.

He pulled back by a mere inch, hissing at the slow drag. When he twisted back into the dark heat of Joshua's body, Joshua hitched in a shaky breath. Joshua's hands were white-knuckled around the headboard, and Leo loved him so much, so much.

Repeating the motion, he listened for the telltale catch of Joshua's breath. Yes, *there*. Another torturously slow thrust, exhaustion clouding Leo's vision. He bit his lip against it.

"Leo," Joshua got out, nearly inarticulate.

It made Leo snap his hips, eyes drifting shut and sparks flitting behind his lids. He forced them back open to watch Joshua stutter out a groan at another thrust, Joshua's forehead pressed against a raised arm. His back was arched, a lovely dip at the waist. Leo fitted his fingers around the curve of one hip and pulled Joshua into him at the same time as he nudged forward again. Repeat. Fuck, Joshua was beautiful like this—helplessly moving into each roll of Leo's hips, instinctual as they found a rhythm, and Leo thought of the ocean, of waves washing up on the shore. *Never like this. Never, never.*

He dipped his head to kiss Joshua's shoulder blade, give it a little nip with his teeth, a distant memory tugging on his conscience. "Want to stay inside you forever," he uttered, almost too low to carry, but Joshua's shaky sigh proved he'd heard it.

"Want you to," was Joshua's blurred response, and Leo kept his mouth open against Joshua's skin, twisted deep, *deep*, before he pulled back. Lifting his head, he watched himself slide in and out of Joshua's body as he ran his palm down Joshua's back, kneaded his arse and fought against the pull of gravity.

No, not quite yet. Not until Joshua had come.

Leo tightened his grip on Joshua's waist, fingers digging into the soft skin, and brought the other hand around to circle Joshua's cock. "Let go," he told Joshua.

"Let go?" Joshua sounded utterly lost, panting with each thrust.

"Of the headboard."

The moment Joshua did, Leo draped himself over his back and tumbled both of them down. He didn't know what it was that did it— the shift in gravity, the loss of control or Leo's fingers on Joshua's cock —but Joshua came in that instant, body clenching around Leo, and oh Jesus, holy fucking Christ, okay, *okay*. Almost there, yes, *God*, and Leo needed just a little more, just one more thrust, another one, and then everything whited out. He came with his mouth pressed against Joshua's shoulder.

By the time he worked up the will to move, Joshua had melted into the sheets, still gasping a little. Leo pulled out slowly, the friction on his softening cock just this side of too much. Quickly, he rid himself of the condom and knotted it before dropping it over the side of the bed. They'd need to dispose of it later so the hotel employees wouldn't trip over it. "Hey," Leo whispered, sinking back down. The word hardly translated over the sound of a car alarm, and, ah. So there was a world outside.

"Hey," Joshua whispered back. With a small groan, he rolled onto his back and pulled Leo to lie halfway across his chest, their legs slotting together. Joshua's cheeks were heavily flushed, eyes bright.

Leo grinned down at him, then sneaked a hand between Joshua's thighs to nudge a finger into Joshua's body, everything slick with lube. While Joshua sucked in a sharp breath, he didn't move away. A beat later, Leo realised just how possessive of a move that was, and he froze, lungs tight, until Joshua puffed out a quiet laugh.

"You look quite pleased with yourself," Joshua said.

"I did just fuck you through the mattress, Princeling." After a deep breath, Leo slid his sticky hand up Joshua's torso and let it rest over his heart. His grin widened without thought. "That was the royal treatment, you see? Exclusive service, that."

It was barely out when Leo wanted to swallow it back down. He didn't think they were at the point where they could joke about this kind of thing. Or were they?

Then Joshua giggled. He *giggled*, and Leo was probably, most definitely, staring like a lovesick fool. That was all right, though. It was true, after all.

"Too bad that exclusivity always comes at a price," Joshua said. "Whatever shall it be? Breakfast in bed? A walk on the beach? A title to your name?"

"Got that last one covered. At least in theory." Leo inhaled, and now it wasn't just his head that felt as though it had been filled with helium; it was his entire body. He tangled his dirty fingers in Joshua's hair so he wouldn't float away. "No, really, I'm a bargain. Your heart will do."

"Done," Joshua told him.

There were so many things they still needed to talk about. So many, many things they needed to discuss, plans they'd have to make, and Leo needed to call James and catch up on sleep. But when Joshua drew him in for a kiss, Leo shoved every single one of his worries away.

Right now, he had Joshua in his arms, warm and pliant and all his. The world outside could wait a little longer.

12

They slept well into the afternoon, or at least Leo did. Joshua woke around noon and needed several seconds to orient himself—the bright sunshine, the warm weight plastered to his back, the memory of a conversation that felt like the hazy remnants of a dream. The lingering impression of Leo's hands all over him. *Of course I'll still want you, little prince.*

Moving a little, Joshua's muscles gave a faint twinge. With a smile, he shifted in the circle of Leo's arms to study him from up close.

In sleep, Leo's features were lax, lips parted slightly to release long, regular breaths. Joshua was briefly caught in wanting to trace Leo's long lashes with his fingertips, their ends brighter, paled by the sun. Then Joshua noticed the dark smudges under Leo's eyes, hinting that Leo's lack of sleep went beyond just that one night.

Slowly, careful not to wake him, Joshua slid out of the embrace and went to take a shower. A glance into the mirror revealed several fresh bruises that Leo's mouth and hands had left, littering Joshua's torso and the insides of his thighs. Finger-shaped marks decorated the spot where Leo had held on tightly, shadows pressed into the pale skin right next to the jut of Joshua's left hip bone. Joshua fought the shiver of arousal and thought about it—waking Leo with his mouth and his hands, fingers nudging into him.

No, there was plenty of time for that later. Let Leo catch up on sleep first.

After a quick message to Tristan and Mo (*'Happy like a room without a roof!'*), Joshua retreated onto the balcony. He ordered a late breakfast, then settled in to wait with his book in his lap, the sun pouring down on him.

The knock at the door came some fifteen minutes later. While Joshua sprinted inside to answer it quickly, before it would disturb Leo's sleep, he wasn't fast enough; Leo gave a little jolt and came awake with a start. He sat up, the thin sheet pooling at his waist, and dear God, he was breath-taking. No one could blame Joshua for stopping to tug him into a close-mouthed kiss, smiling when Leo responded immediately, seemingly on instinct, skin warm with sleep. "Breakfast," Joshua told him in an undertone, straightening. "If you want. You can sleep some more after."

Leo's eyes were slightly unfocused, staring up at Joshua. "Breakfast," he repeated blankly. "Yeah, sounds good."

Shooting him a bright look, Joshua went to open the door and made certain that Leo couldn't be spotted. He rolled the food cart into the room himself, and Leo climbed out of bed a moment later, fully naked. After looking down at himself, he grabbed the sheet off the bed and wrapped it around his waist.

"What did you do that for?" Joshua asked.

"You're dressed," Leo pointed out. "So you don't get to complain."

"Just my pants. I didn't want to flash a passing plane or something."

Leo's gaze dragged down Joshua's torso, lingered on the bruise at Joshua's hip, then moved lower to assess the flimsy boxer briefs Joshua had shuffled into after his shower. "All right," Leo allowed, slow and sweet. "The pants can stay. Not like they hide much."

"Which is why it's still unfair that you're donning a toga," Joshua told him.

Leo's only answer consisted of a smirk. He followed leisurely when Joshua moved the cart over to the balcony doors and watched, head tilted at a curious angle, when Joshua laid everything out on the table outside. "Some help?" Joshua asked.

"Certainly." With that, Leo draped himself along Joshua's back and clung to him, mirroring his every step and slowing Joshua down with the effort of coordinating them both.

"You're such a little shit," Joshua said, but it came out soft and fond.

"Sorry about that." Leo didn't sound sorry at all. "Afraid I can't help it, love. And since this is happily ever after, you're stuck."

"Well, I suppose it's my cross to bear." Reaching one arm around, Joshua brought Leo closer. Leo moulded himself to Joshua's back and dropped light, fluttering kisses to the nape of his neck while Joshua continued laying out scones and jam, scrambled eggs, bread rolls and pastries.

"Fancy," Leo murmured. "You trying to seduce me with food?"

Joshua snorted. "I think you're a sure thing."

"Smuttily ever after," Leo said brightly, and Joshua laughed and twisted his head for a gentle brush of their lips.

Throughout breakfast, Leo was mostly quiet, looking out at the ocean with sunlight reflected in his eyes, loose and relaxed in a way Joshua had hardly ever seen him. Like a weight had been lifted off his shoulders. It was stunning. Even more stunning to think that Joshua had played a role in it, however small; that he'd contributed to Leo facing his past and opening up rather than hiding behind a veil of evasive half-truths.

Still he didn't think Leo had fully grasped the concept of not letting himself be defined by what he'd been through. That was all right, though—Joshua would be there to remind him.

After breakfast, Leo pulled Joshua back to bed for another few hours of sleep. Joshua waited until Leo had drifted off, then he picked his book up from the bedside table and settled in to read with Leo a warm, steady weight on his chest.

～

Tristan barged in at around four, Mo and Nate in tow, dramatically covering his eyes as he shoved past Joshua into the room. "Honeymoon's over, bitches," he declared. "Wipe yourselves clean, get dressed and let's go do some exploring. We only have a couple of days here. I don't want to waste them twiddling my thumbs because you arseholes finally figured out how to work this thing."

"Was that a pun?" Leo asked from the bed, bright-eyed and wild-haired. Jesus, Joshua wouldn't mind spending the rest of eternity in this room.

"You be quiet," Tristan told him. "I'm still mad at you for making our Joshy-boy cry." Belying his own words, he jumped onto the bed to hug Leo, then pulled back with a grimace and bemoaned the disgusting state of the sheets.

They agreed to leave in thirty minutes, and as soon as the others were gone, Joshua sat down on the edge of the bed. "You'll stay with us, right? For the whole trip? When's your flight back?"

"Haven't booked it yet," Leo admitted, almost sheepish. He glanced away with a little shrug. "Didn't know whether you'd want me to stay, and traipsing around the country all by myself would have been stupid."

There was really no better option than to kiss the spark of remembered uncertainty right off Leo's face, so that's what Joshua did —littered Leo's cheeks and chin with butterfly kisses until Leo was laughing and pushing at his shoulders, then tangled both hands in Joshua's hair to drag him into a deep kiss that ended with Joshua sprawled on top of Leo, pressing him into the mattress.

"We still need to talk," Leo squeezed out. "And I need to call James."

"We have half an hour," Joshua told him. "That's totally enough time to talk, call James, and get off in the shower. *Not* in that order."

In spite of that, Joshua went easily when Leo shoved him off, stretching out next to Leo on the bed. He did pout, though, which made Leo lean in to nibble on his bottom lip, all sharp teeth and laughing eyes. "Civil disobedience," Joshua exclaimed, wriggling away, and Leo smirked at him.

"Darling, I don't think you quite understand the definition of that."

"Call James," Joshua told him. His put-upon frown fell short of its mark, and his smile broke through as soon as Leo bopped him on the nose.

He shifted closer when Leo reached for his phone. Putting his head on Leo's shoulder, he listened in when Leo did indeed call James. They received instructions that basically told them not to get photographed together until a strategy had been worked out. "We need to look at all options," James said. "Is there anything you wouldn't do? Any no-goes? Say, if we consider spinning this in a way that relies heavily on the fairy tale aspect of this? Noble heritage, prejudiced parents that led to rough times, picking yourself off the ground and finding true love in the process. It's a beautiful story. Would sell like hot cakes. But," a significant pause, "it would affect your parents."

Leo was quiet for a short while, staring out at the blinding brightness of the sky. Tucked into his side, Joshua stayed silent. "Let it," Leo said eventually, voice firm. "They don't deserve my protection. Just keep my sisters out of it."

As soon as Leo had ended the call, Joshua wrapped a hand around his wrist. He felt the flutter of Leo's pulse under the pad of his thumb. "Hey," Joshua said lowly, yet it seemed loud in the still room. "Are you quite sure you want to do that?"

"I don't *want* to do that, no." Leo's tone was calm. "Which is new, because before I met you, I might have enjoyed hurting them out of spite. Now, it's simply a question of... If this is our best chance to make things work, make *us* work, then that's what we'll do." He twisted his wrist out of Joshua's hold, but only to lace their fingers. His eyes were warm. "I'm choosing you, see? Simple."

It didn't feel simple at all to Joshua; it felt massive, felt like Leo had casually handed him his heart with an off-handed, 'Oh, hey, thought you might have some use for this.'

Breathing through the ache in his throat, Joshua tightened his grip on Leo's fingers. "What about your sisters, though?" he asked, and Leo's gaze lowered, exhaling on a sigh.

"They're old enough to handle it now. It's been a decade, you know? Charlie is... twenty-two now? Twenty-three?" Leo paused, frowning. "Holy shit. Yeah, she should be. And Rosie must be eighteen, almost nineteen. If I talk to them before, make them understand..."

Oh. So there were two of them, around five and ten years younger. From what little Leo had let slip before, Joshua hadn't been able to tell much, but now that Leo's walls had crumbled to dust and ashes... Well, there was plenty of time to learn. Joshua wanted to learn *everything*.

Tugging Leo closer, Joshua draped his legs over Leo's lap and kept all urging out of his voice. "How come you haven't contacted them before? You never thought about it?"

Leo turned into the contact and didn't answer immediately, swallowing a few times in rapid succession. "Of course I thought about it. Often, at least in the beginning, but eventually, it just... faded." He wrapped an arm around Joshua's waist and hid his face against Joshua's neck, words fanning out in a warm rush. "At first, I just wanted to get away, leave everything behind. Fresh start. And I suffered from the delusion that I'd show them all, that I'd make it big on a little starting cash and some song writing and piano skills. So when that didn't work out, you know... I felt like a failure. Not the big brother the girls would look up to." Leo gave a thin laugh.

Hugging him close, Joshua's ribcage might have been the only thing holding him together. He wanted to punch anyone who'd ever contributed to the self-deprecating humour in Leo's tone, a hot flare in his stomach that took him by surprise. He inhaled through it, forced it back down and settled for holding on tightly.

Once he felt Leo relax, he eased his hold and said softly, "You're not a failure."

Leo stirred, then raised his head. His eyes were unnaturally bright. "No, I guess things worked out for me in the end. I mean, hey, I've got a job I love, and I get to help people and be useful. Even make enough money to pay off a small flat and put a little aside to help out some kids in trouble. Oh, and last but not least..." His expression softened, and Joshua's stomach gave a gentle tug in response. "I fell in love with a beautiful prince. Which is about to flip my life upside down, but hey. Worth it."

"You're a bit of a sap," Joshua told him. It came out like an endearment.

"How very dare you," Leo said, tipping up his chin and narrowing his eyes. A grin lurked around their corners. "I am tough and hardened by my years on the street, by hunting for a warm meal and a safe place to sleep. Brave men cower at the whisper of my name."

Snorting, Joshua traced the curve of Leo's cheekbone, moving down, then letting his fingertips rest against Leo's jaw. "You're a marshmallow on the inside. Those songs you wrote, I bet they were cheesy ballads about finding true love and making it through the hardest times."

"Lies," Leo declared, grin coming fully alive. "Lies and guesswork. You cannot prove a single thing. Also," the curve of his mouth tilted into something a little thoughtful, "I haven't written anything in years. Maybe I'll give it another try at some point."

"I could buy you a piano," Joshua offered without thought, and Leo stiffened. Sudden sharpness defined his tone.

"No, you won't. You will not buy me anything."

Joshua dropped his hand, flinching back as though he'd been slapped. His instinctive response was to curl away and question everything—why had Leo reacted like that, quick as a whip? Why didn't Leo want him involved?

Joshua opened his mouth to ask, Leo watching him with a steely expression. Then Joshua remembered something Mo had said not that long ago, something that—oh. Shit. *I didn't ever want you to feel like you were paying for my company.*

Joshua snapped his mouth shut and grappled for a way to respond. After a long moment of silence, Leo's features relaxed, suddenly contrite. "Sorry. I didn't mean to be so... harsh. But you really can't."

"It would be my pleasure," Joshua said carefully. "Not anything I feel I'd have to do, just something I'd like to do. And if you think it would make me question your intentions, you're wrong. I wouldn't, and I also won't hold your past against you like that."

Leo looked away, presenting Joshua with the clear line of his profile. His answer was barely audible. "Not now, you wouldn't. But maybe in a fight. Maybe you would one day, if we don't handle the public stuff right and it all blows up and you hear all those insinuations about me, about how I'm using you..."

"I wouldn't believe some nasty strangers over what I see with my own eyes," Joshua told him, already reaching out again. "Ever."

Leo sagged like a balloon that had been pierced. All the fight went out of him, and he fisted his hands into the sheets, bunching them up. He didn't shy away from the hand Joshua wrapped around his elbow, instead lifted his head to meet Joshua's gaze, his tone serious and heavy. "Still. You can't buy me expensive gifts. It wouldn't be right."

After a quiet moment, Joshua nodded. "Okay." He paused to gather his thoughts, continuing slowly, like taking steps on thin ice. "But there will be expenses that you'll have *because* of me, expenses you wouldn't have otherwise. Like, when you accompany me to an event, for example, and you'd be expected to wear expensive bespoke clothing. Or travelling on official Crown business. I don't do that often because it's mostly Ems, but still, it will happen. And it would be unfair if you had to cover things like that."

"Oh, I thought I'd just show up in a ratty old T-shirt and a cap," Leo put in lightly.

Joshua shot him a tiny smile and stayed silent, waiting. He kept his fingers loosely clasped around Leo's elbow, and after a long, lurching beat, Leo sighed. His eyes narrowed in consideration, and when he spoke again, all humour had drained from his voice. "I see your point. And I guess I could—things like that. I could accept them from you. But you will *not* just go out and buy me stuff, got it? You will run everything past me first, and then we'll decide together."

"Together," Joshua echoed. Weirdly, it felt as though he had just swam ten miles, his muscles a little shaky. He hesitated before he squeezed Leo's elbow, leaning in a little. "Hey. Do I please, please get permission to spoil you once in a while?" He continued quickly to head off Leo's protest. "No expensive gifts, I promise. Just things like cooking you dinner, or a trip to one of our country homes, which doesn't cost me anything but fuel. A generous stock of your favourite cereal and tea at my flat. Scented toilet paper."

When Leo gave a soft snort, Joshua knew it was half the victory already. They'd be all right; they'd figure this out.

Still Leo took his time examining the idea from several angles before he gave a slow nod. "That works for me. But as for other things, such as... luxury resorts in exotic locations, that sort of thing. I'm not poor, for the record. James pays me well enough. Just maybe not quite enough to afford your jet-set lifestyle."

Joshua bit back his first, thoughtless impulse to extend his offer to paying for whatever holiday they spent together. "Then I'll adapt," he said instead. "Within the constraints of security requirements, that is."

"Fair enough." A smile flitted over Leo's face. "Seriously, you'd be willing to go camping? Not saying I'd even want that, but if I asked, you'd go, right? Christ, you really are completely gone for me."

"Save the smug," Joshua told him, smiling back. It quickly grew into a smirk. "Hey. This reminds me that I've always wanted to own an island. Maybe something in the Caribbean Sea? I should talk to my mum about investment in property. And, I mean, camping on a deserted island sounds plenty romantic to me."

Leo's expression was a cross between disbelief and amused indulgence. The latter won out after only a second. "Romantic? Yeah, I'll remind you when you're whining about insects in the tent and your back not being used to sleeping on a camping mat."

For a moment, Joshua considered pursuing that further—Leo must have slept outside on a camping mat numerous times, sheltered only by a bridge or some doorway. Joshua wanted to whisk Leo's younger version away to a safe place that provided him with a hot meal and a soft bed whenever he needed it, a place that would ask for nothing in return.

Joshua's questions could wait, though. Right now, he wanted nothing more than to preserve the gentle glow of happiness in Leo's eyes.

He poked Leo in the chest and raised a challenging brow. "Guess you'll just have to make it worth my while, then."

"I shall consider it my duty to the country," Leo said primly. He broke character when he laughed once, loudly, and tackled Joshua into the sheets.

In theory, they should get ready. In reality, the others could wait a bit longer. Joshua figured they'd earned every minute they could steal for themselves. He shoved away all thoughts of this being the calm before the impending storm, caught Leo's mouth in a deep kiss and yielded when Leo pressed him into the mattress.

RIGHT AS THEY left the hotel, Leo was hit with a bout of unease at the realisation that whatever Joshua had suspected about Leo's past, he'd certainly shared it with Tristan and Mo. Trying to hide his uncertainty, he remarked on how the Pão de Açúcar indeed looked like a sugarloaf, how it reminded him of winter in a Swiss ski cottage with his family, of soaking a sugarloaf in rum and setting it on fire so that it dripped into mulled wine. Tristan jumped on that and demanded details, then set about planning a *Feuerzangenbowle* theme night in November. The way he casually included Leo into his scheming— into an event that would take place months from now—eased the tight clench of Leo's stomach.

Skipping a few steps ahead, he teased Joshua about not keeping up, which ended with both of them beaming at each other. Shortly after that, Mo sent Leo a crinkly-eyed smile which finally allowed Leo to relax. If Mo's approval was in part due to Nate's hand entwined with Mo's... Well, Leo wasn't going to look a gift horse in the mouth. He also wasn't going to think about how he and Joshua would need to cross about half a million bridges before they could do the same in public. Nope.

As it turned out, Rio de Janeiro was board shorts and flip flops, was a mosaic of colourful tiles that lined the Escadaria Selarón. It was rhythmic music pouring from open windows and youths kicking a football over a net. It was the smell of freshly grilled meat, of traffic exhaust and piss, of concrete.

Late into the evening, they were snuck in through the backdoor of a club that played live music, something called *Chorinho* that sounded like a Brazilian kind of New Orleans jazz. Their table was set above the main section of the club, granting them with the kind of privacy that allowed Leo to lean into Joshua, alcohol bubbling in his blood and his hand high up on Joshua's thigh, playing with the inseam of Joshua's trousers until Joshua was watching him with dark, hooded eyes.

By the time they returned to the hotel, the sky was already starting to brighten. All they managed were quick, sleepy hand jobs in the shower before falling into bed, naked and loose, curled into each other.

LEO WOKE to Joshua's fingers pressing into him, slick with lube, and it took his foggy mind a second to make sense of the sensation. He remembered his own words with a start—*I want to wake up with your fingers inside of me*—and gasped, still partially tangled in dreams. His hips twitched up when Joshua's mouth wrapped around the tip of his cock.

Joshua lifted off a moment later, slithering up Leo's body to smile at him with wild hair and bright eyes, a pillow crease imprinted on one cheek. He was so incredibly lovely, and his happiness was all for Leo. *Joshua* was all for Leo.

"Can I?" Joshua asked in a hushed whisper, smile widening at whatever it was he must have seen on Leo's face. "Are you ready?"

"Yeah," Leo mumbled, barely coherent.

Joshua brushed a kiss against his mouth, and Leo was slow to move into it, mind still hazy with sleep and the radiance of a new day that streamed in through the open windows. He parted his thighs for Joshua, shifted to let Joshua slide a pillow under his back and then melted into the mattress, accommodating the weight of Joshua's body. After that, it was all languid, drowsy movements of Joshua's hips, nudging deep and staying like that, shifting back by only an inch before driving back in. At some point, the heat collecting under Leo's skin became too much. Wrapping his legs around Joshua's waist, he sought to control the pace, and Joshua let him.

Later, cooling down, Joshua raised his head off the pillow and smoothed his palm from Leo's stomach over his ribs, up to the letters inked across his collarbones. Gently, Joshua traced the contours with the tip of his index finger. "You told me it was a sad story," he whispered. "Are you willing to talk about it?"

Leo rolled onto his side to face him. "It's somewhat sad, yes," he started, briefly distracted by the heavy flush to Joshua's cheeks. Holy shit, how had Leo spent twenty-seven years on this earth without knowing just how fucking *brilliant* sex could be? Since Joshua was watching him with calm patience, Leo made himself continue. "But it's sad mostly because I was just emerging from a sad place, and this signifies... trying to make my peace with it, I guess. I got it a day after James offered me the job."

Joshua nodded slightly, gaze flicking back down to take in the cursive 'Sometimes things just happen, other times you make them happen' as though seeing it in a new light. Then he looked back up to meet Leo's eyes. "How did that come about? James, I mean?"

"Stroke of luck." Leo shifted a little, felt a pleasant twinge in his muscles. Sleepiness had dissolved into a lazy, content kind of looseness. "He was supposed to meet a client in the bar I happened to browse that night. James' client never showed, but something about me caught his eye. And, see, I noticed this guy staring at me while I was making the rounds and trying to charm the right person into buying me a beer, and then buying me, period."

To Joshua's credit, he didn't flinch—simply pressed his lips together, a downwards tilt to his mouth. He didn't interrupt.

"So anyway." Leo's shrug turned out awkward with the way he was lying down. "This guy comes up to me, all easy smile, and tells me he's been watching me and likes what he sees. Bit creepy, mind, and I knew better than to go with the creepy ones. Which is exactly what I told him." He shook his head, very slightly, and when he closed his eyes, he could still picture it perfectly behind his lids: the smoky interior of the bar, James' face caught in shadows, his gaze heavy and knowing. "Can't say I felt particularly reassured when he laughed and was all, 'Glad to see you've got a sense of self-preservation, kid. That'll serve you well. But I'm not a punter.' And then he, like, told me he was interested in my *other* skill set. As in, uh... 'The one that had that bloke over there go from frowning to buying you a drink even though he's got a wife and no interest in your services.'"

Flexibility and charm, that was how James had described it later. The skill to adapt to different situations and people, and then play them with ease. If it weren't for that lucky coincidence of Leo being in the right place at the right time... If James' client had shown up that night, if Leo had settled on a different bar or decided to take the night off...

He wouldn't be here today.

The notion had Leo reach out and twine a hand into the corkscrew curls at Joshua's temple. Joshua leaned into the touch. "Good judge of character, that James," he said.

"The very best. And we made it a rule not to talk about his saviour complex." Leo paused to organise his scrambled thoughts. "So, he asked me how I'd feel about a steady job, one where I could keep my clothes on, and I told him I wouldn't sell his drugs. To which he said..." With a little grin, he shrugged again. "'I don't sell drugs. I sell stories.'"

Joshua pondered this for a moment before he smiled, sudden and glowing. "Would it be outrageous if I gifted him with a title?"

Leo was startled into laughter, warmth seeping from the sunlit room into his bones. "Only you would say something that ridiculous, Princey."

"That's not a no," Joshua decided. "Also, when did we go from Princeling and little prince to Princey?"

"Not sure, but I like it. There's something very Disney about it, you know? *Cinderella*, I think. It suits you, what with your big, green Bambi eyes and long, gangly limbs and all."

"So you'd be, what? Aladdin?" Joshua asked. "Because if so, I'd be Jasmine, and I want a pet tiger. I would rock a tiger."

Since it was a moral obligation to stop him from spouting bull-shit, Leo covered Joshua's mouth with his own. It was a sacrifice, of course, but Leo had always believed in doing right by the people—and now that he'd begun to reclaim his birth name, he had better live up to the noble responsibility that came with it.

DUE TO ROAD conditions and everyone advising against travelling the distance by car, the group took Joshua's private jet from Rio to Belo Horizonte. Leo spent the drive to the airport in the backseat of a steel-plated Mercedes, its tinted windows veiling the morning in grey. With his head in Leo's lap, Joshua had fallen back asleep almost as soon as they'd climbed in, and Leo was carding his fingers through the tangled mess of Joshua's curls while casually feeling out the body-guard who'd come to replace Johnson.

True to Nate's background check from a few weeks ago, this Zach bloke seemed perfectly all right. When he talked about Joshua, there was true affection in his tone, and at the mention of Johnson, his eyes narrowed in disapproval—he hadn't been told the full story behind Johnson's sudden replacement, but it was obvious he'd formed a suspicion.

Yes, Leo decided. Zach could stay.

The flight to Belo Horizonte took them about an hour, and then they were whisked to their hotel with smooth efficiency. Joshua refused Leo's offer of contributing to the flight and the cost of their shared suite on the grounds that Joshua would have had to pay for it regardless, and Leo decided to let it rest. He needed to pick his battles, and this wasn't an important one.

On the other hand, he did forbid Joshua from pulling some strings to get Leo and Nate some last-minute tickets to tomorrow's match of the English team. They could have tried buying some for themselves, but since the black market was more likely to supply them with forgeries than the real thing, they would be watching it on the telly, and that was that. After considering Leo for several moments, Nate agreed with an easy shrug.

Neither Mo nor Joshua fought them on it.

The five of them got up early on Tuesday, the overcast sky only just beginning to brighten, and visited what was considered the closest thing to a central square the megacity had to offer. At this hour, the Praça da Liberdade was largely empty. They took a stroll around the perimeter to get an impression of the different architectural styles, although Mo was the only one with actual knowledge— in all honesty, his rambling monologue about modernism and French neoclassicism was a strain for Leo's sleepy brain. Nate, on the other hand, was gazing at Mo as though his mere existence was the best thing since the invention of superheroes. It made Leo hide a grin against Joshua's shoulder.

"Please tell me we're not on their level of ridiculous," he whispered.

"We're not on their level of ridiculous," Joshua parroted obediently, following it up with a cheeky squeeze of Leo's bum.

Leo twisted away with an outraged exclamation of, "Not in *public*. Have you no shame?"

"He doesn't," Tristan supplied, and Joshua pointed at him.

"Be quiet, you. I have *seen* things, and you have no room to talk."

Shoving his hands into his pockets, Leo tipped his face back to study a tall building shaped like a colossal wave, and found himself grinning at nothing in particular. *Just happy.*

Afterwards, they took a trip up winding mountain roads to visit Ouro Preto, a former colonial mining town, and ate breakfast while following cobblestone streets through a maze of well-preserved Baroque buildings. They returned to Belo Horizonte just past noon, and then Joshua, Mo and Tristan had to rush to get to the stadium in time for the match.

Leo and Nate ended up in a bar around the corner from the hotel, sipping on Caipirinhas, ice-cooled glasses sweating in their hands. The match ended in a tie with Costa Rica, which meant that the English squad dropped out of the tournament with one sad, lonely point to their name. To dull the pain, Leo ordered another Caipirinha, tucked himself closer to Nate's side and ranted about the English team employing a guy solely to spray overheated players with water, yet the whole football thing appeared beyond their comprehension. Nate made sympathetic noises in all the right places and patted Leo's back.

The moment Joshua's face appeared on the screen, Leo's head snapped up.

"Well, of course we did hope for more," Joshua told the camera, and the state of his hair hinted he'd been running his hands through it repeatedly. *Leo* wanted to run his hands through it repeatedly.

"In fact," Joshua continued slowly, with a little smile, "I actually have a bit of a tipping game going on with some friends, and it just so happens that my chances of winning it are significantly diminished now that it's clear I got the champion wrong. There are two of us who bet on the English squad. Guess our loyalty didn't pay off in this case." His smile broadened, and he gave a small shrug, all bashful charm, and—and had he just indirectly mentioned Leo on international telly? Holy shit.

"That was me," Leo mumbled quietly, meant for Nate's ears only. "The other loyal—I'm the one who also picked England. That's me."

"Stupid of you," Nate said. "Kind of sweet, but stupid. I keep telling you, it'll be Argentina taking the title."

Leo shook his head. "You're missing the point."

"Which is?" Nate was grinning, and Leo shot him a glare.

"You know what the point is. The *point* is that Joshua just talked about me on TV. I mean, no one knows it's me, and it was subtle enough that it won't raise any eyebrows, but—*Nate*." On its own accord, Leo's mouth curved up.

Nate had the audacity to laugh at him. "You're hopeless, mate. I bet the glow on your face could power this entire city."

There was no use denying it. Leo didn't even want to, but he also wouldn't stand for Nate making fun of him. It would set a bad precedent. "Careful there, mate," he said. "I can always bring the topic of Armani underwear campaigns to Mo's attention."

While Nate's amusement was still blatantly obvious, he chose not to make a further remark. Clever bloke. As a reward, Leo ordered more drinks for both of them even though they were barely halfway through their current ones. Hey, they were on holiday. And Leo was very much in love, and Joshua had just acknowledged him in front of the world. Also, the two of them would have to sit through a Skype conference about the public conduct of their relationship tomorrow.

Another drink sounded like a splendid idea.

"HONESTLY. I think you should have skipped the last two rounds." Joshua was trying not to smile. For the most part, he failed. "Not that you weren't very cute yesterday, clinging to me while drunkenly rambling about green eyes and red lips, but... You know. I bet your hangover is very real right now."

If anything, Joshua's cheerful attitude served to deepen Leo's frown. "One," he said, shooting Joshua a grumpy look through bleary eyes, "I am not cute. Ever."

"Beg to differ," Joshua interjected.

Leo acted as though he hadn't heard. In only a towel, still damp from his shower, he crouched down in front of his bag and began rifling through it. He continued speaking, all the while presenting Joshua with a highly distracting view of his profile and bare chest, his calves and naked ankles. "Two, I'm glad this is amusing to you. But my head is killing me right now, and we have a Skype date in less than thirty minutes. So if you could get me some painkillers, that would be highly appreciated."

"Already done," Joshua said, and Leo's head shot up, then he grimaced.

"Well, then fucking hand them over, Princeling."

Joshua rocked back on his heels, smiling openly now. "Say please."

"Please, for the love of *God*," Leo grit out. "Gimme. Or I will never suck your dick again."

"Now, that's not very nice," Joshua told him.

"Neither is withholding a man's medicine."

"Well, hey, if that particular man hadn't decided to get roaringly drunk in the middle of the day..."

"But that's your fault, isn't it?" Leo waved a vague hand about the air, towel slipping to reveal the strong curve of one thigh, and Joshua needed a moment to focus back on Leo's voice. "I mean, if you hadn't casually mentioned me in that interview, I would not have been in the kind of emotionally fragile state that made another Caipirinha seem like a wise choice. Therefore, your fault."

Ah, so Leo had caught the reference.

Joshua felt his smile soften into something more private, less amused. Sitting down on the edge of the bed, he watched Leo's face closely. "Did you like it? Me talking about you in public?"

For the first time since Joshua had roused him this morning, Leo's face relaxed out of its frown. "I did," he said quietly, sincerely. "Quite a lot. Can't wait until you won't have to lob me into the general friends category anymore."

"Same." Getting back up, Joshua went to pour Leo a glass of water, restless energy humming in his belly. If *he* was already nervous about the upcoming discussion with James' team, he could only imagine what it must be like for Leo—Leo was the one who'd have to divulge his entire past to people he'd known for years. That he was willing to do this, to pay that price just so he could be with Joshua...

It meant a lot. It meant the fucking world.

That Leo had insisted on also involving Tristan and Mo meant nearly as much. They should arrive alongside Nate in a quarter of an hour, allowing for about ten minutes to get everything ready and distract Leo with aimless banter before the serious talks were to begin. By then, Leo had better be dressed, or Joshua couldn't guarantee he'd be able to concentrate.

With a glass of water in one hand, a couple of painkillers in the other, Joshua dropped to the floor next to Leo. Leo eyed Joshua's offerings, then opted for tugging Joshua into a gentle kiss before prying the pills out of his fingers.

"My hero," he said.

"You can call me Prince Charming," Joshua told him, grinning, and Leo flicked him on the nose.

"You're not half as charming as you think you are."

"Then I guess you're just easy."

"Fuck off," Leo muttered, but he was smiling around the rim of the glass. He'd been smiling a lot since Rio, and Joshua hoped it would stay that way even after they'd be back in the UK.

Blessedly, the painkillers set in a few minutes before the Skype conference was due to start. Leo still felt a little queasy, but he wasn't certain he could blame the remnants of alcohol in his blood.

With Joshua on one side, Nate on the other, Tristan and Mo sprawled on the floor in front of the sofa, he waited for the livestream to connect. It did so with a noticeable lag, the image stuttering before it finally displayed James' conference room, along with slightly blurry versions of Carole, Ben, James and George spread around the table.

Throughout the introductory small talk, Leo was mostly quiet and focused on keeping his breathing steady and easy. Joshua's hand was a warm weight on his thigh.

"So," James said eventually, clapping his hands. On the screen of Nate's notebook, James' mouth moved out of sync with his words. "Are we ready to do this? Leo?"

Sucking in a deep, harsh breath, Leo glanced at Joshua and found

Joshua looking at him already. The nauseating pressure in Leo's stomach eased just slightly.

All right. Okay. If this didn't break them, nothing else would.

"I'm ready," Leo announced, turning to face the camera lens. It was partially true. "First things first, though: I want there to be a backdoor for Joshua. Plausible deniability. If this turns sour, I want to give Joshua the option to deny that he knew the details of my past so he can walk away mostly unharmed."

"No," Joshua said briskly. His fingers tightened around Leo's thigh, digging into the muscle. "Absolutely not. We're in this together."

"I'm James' client," Leo told him, as calmly as he could. "Means that I'm calling the shots, love."

Leo found it difficult to maintain his resolve when Joshua's eyes narrowed, disappointment written into his frown. "I'm your *boyfriend*." Joshua's voice was firm, yet quiet. "This is a relationship of equals, and you can't just go ahead and decide things without me."

Oh, fuck. *Boyfriend.*

In theory, Leo shouldn't be caught off-guard by a word as simple as that, but there was something disarming about hearing it out loud, stated so casually. It made him hitch in a breath, his chest too wide and too narrow at once. He turned to face Joshua fully, deliberately angling himself away from the webcam.

"Joshua." The name felt loaded, like a declaration in itself. "I'm not trying to make a decision for both of us. I won't push you out that backdoor. Never. But I do want to give you the option."

"I won't use it," Joshua told him, a stubborn tilt to his chin. "So you might as well scrap the thought."

"You're absolutely impossible, you know that?" With a sigh, Leo leaned in to press their foreheads together, closing his eyes for a second before he added, so low only Joshua would hear, "But please give me that. Okay? It'll make me feel better."

A palpable moment of hesitation passed, and Leo was keenly aware of the others around them, watching and waiting. He didn't know how much James had told Carole and Ben in advance, but since no one uttered a single word, he assumed that they'd had a vague notion, at least.

Just as the silence became heavy, Joshua shifted to drop a kiss to the corner of Leo's mouth. "All right," he agreed.

"Good," Leo told him. *I love you*, he thought, and maybe Joshua could read it in Leo's eyes, because the tension in Joshua's features drained away and made room for a beaming smile. Without thought, Leo returned it.

After that, the questions set in.

James fired them off in rapid succession, and Leo fought to keep his voice even and his posture relaxed as he answered as honestly as he could. Joshua's hand on his thigh was grounding, as was the press of Nate's shoulder against his. A few minutes in, Mo sat up from the floor to lean against Leo's thighs, and Tristan's fingers snaked around Leo's ankle, clasping it in a light grip. Leo loved all of them wildly, aggressively, with every single molecule of his body.

"What are the chances of someone recognising you?" James asked. "Past clients, I mean."

"Generally slim." Leo cleared his throat. "For one, I used all sorts of fake names when I worked. I also had really short hair, which—maybe you guys remember that from early on. Because easier to keep clean, you know, and more hygienic when regular showers are a bit tricky. Made me look like quite a different person, and I was younger, thinner, much more of a twink." He paused for a chuckle that didn't come out entirely convincing. "I mean, hey, I had hair a bit like now at Eton, tousled fringe and all, and Joshua and Tristan still didn't recognise me."

"But I sort of did," Joshua protested, and Leo sent him an indulgent look.

"You really didn't, darling." Directing his attention back at the screen, Leo steeled himself. The low quality of the stream made it difficult to assess the reactions of Carole, Ben and George. "Anyway, back to your question. There are two regulars who are likely to recognise me. Other than that, it was one-time things, usually with bad lighting, often with alcohol involved, and a minimum of six years ago.

I think the risk is..." Again, he cleared his throat even though his mouth was dry. "Manageable."

"We'll need names and addresses of your regulars," Ben inserted, business-like. "See what kind of dirt we can find on them."

"Nate will handle that part," James said.

Leaning further into Joshua's side, Leo slotted his fingers into the gaps between Joshua's, his knee pressed against Nate's. "I was seventeen." The words were reluctant to leave his mouth, but he pushed them out all the same. "My first time with one of them, I was only seventeen, so that's definitely illegal. The commercial aspect, that is. More so for him than for me."

"Jesus fuck, Leo." Ben sounded a cross between shocked and disbelieving, and Leo shook his head, staring directly at the screen.

"Don't, okay? I'm not proud of the whole thing, but I certainly don't want your pity. Or your disapproval. It is what it is."

At that, Joshua's fingers clenched around Leo's. A quick sideways glance revealed that Joshua looked guilty and miserable. Did he believe it was *his* fault that Leo had to go through this whole messy ordeal, come clean with the team? Leo squeezed back.

The small gap in the discussion was broken by Carole. Her voice was gentle and slightly careful, but devoid of judgment. Not for the first time, Leo wondered just how much of her story resembled his own. "What about the street kids?" she asked. "The ones you see on Saturdays. Do they know?"

"I'm sure they suspect I was one of them," Leo told her. "But not the sex work bit, no. And as for when I was actually doing that, I was... discreet, mostly. It's not like I worked the kerb, you know. I picked clients up in bars, chatted with them for a while, so it probably looked like regular fun."

"Which bars?" James asked.

"Switched it up." Leo paused and let himself remember some of the places—dim lights, crowded, the air tasting of sweat and beer, his leather jacket the only armour that protected him. "I didn't work any of those places enough for anyone to notice and throw me out. With the exception of one that belongs to my friend Kylie now. It belonged to her parents at the time, and she's... a good person. Helped me out a fair bit."

"I like her," Carole contributed, and right; they'd met when she'd filled in for Leo last Saturday. "I don't think she's the kind to blab."

"She's not," Leo said.

"Still, let's assume that one of your old contacts goes to the press. Maybe with just a suspicion." James set down his pen and leaned back in his chair, lacing his hands on the table. "What do we do?"

"Sue them into oblivion," Ben said. "Unless there is proof."

Of course that would be his choice course of action, Leo thought with distant amusement. Bloody lawyers. "They won't have proof," he said out loud. "There *is* no proof. I was careful. Always thought that if I make it out, in a later life, that I didn't want to become susceptible to blackmail." He snorted. "Didn't realise it'd have to withstand this scale of public attention, though."

"I'm sorry," Joshua whispered, and Leo bumped him with his elbow.

"Shut it," he whispered back. "It's about time I stop hiding. Go big or go home, right?"

The moment it was out, he realised that he meant every word; while the low-level buzz of unease still quivered in his stomach, his ribcage had widened, and he felt lighter somehow, like a knot had come loose.

George spoke up for the first time. "In addition, between James and myself, we have the network to hear about any such story before it runs. There's a good chance we could stop it."

"And," James added, "Nate can figure out the source so we can make sure they will think twice about talking to the press in the future."

Shifting against Leo's side, Nate gave a humourless smile. "It'd be my pleasure. I mean, everyone has some dirt they'd rather not see exposed to their friends and family, so... Yeah."

"Whoa," Tristan breathed out, more admiration than disapproval. "Mate, remind me not to get on your bad side, like, ever."

While Mo stayed quiet, he'd tipped his head back to study Nate with quiet, fond understanding. Nate met his gaze, and his smile twisted into something more genuine as he added, "As for what happens online, that doesn't really matter without proof. It's just chatter. Which, by the way—I already set up a few sock puppets for Joshua's coming out. Guess we could use those."

"Leo," James said, low and serious. "It's your call. Are you ready to do this?"

Swallowing around what felt like a rough-edged lump in his throat, Leo turned his head to look at Joshua. For a moment, their gazes held, Joshua's eyes clear and his expression calm, fingers sure around Leo's own.

"I'm ready," Leo said out loud, repeated it. "I'm ready."

He didn't avert his eyes, and Joshua didn't look away either.

IT WAS STRANGELY quiet once everyone had left the suite.

Leo threw open the curtains and leaned his forehead against the cool glass of the windowpane, staring out over the cityscape—highrise buildings crowded together, smog clouding up the view of distant mountains. He closed his eyes and focused on the faint noises that filtered into the room.

He heard Joshua draw close, the thick carpet reducing his footsteps to a vague whisper. Then Joshua hugged him from behind, moulding himself to Leo's back, and Leo leaned into him with a little gasp. His throat felt raw.

"You okay?" Joshua asked, sticky-slow like a dream.

Leo considered it carefully, tipping his head back onto Joshua's shoulder and covering Joshua's hands on his stomach with his own. Holding him in place. "I'm okay," he replied eventually.

"I'm so sorry," Joshua told him. "So, so sorry you have to go through this because of me."

Leo turned in the circle of his arms, leaning back against the window as he looked at Joshua. "I'm not sorry. I guess it's kind of... liberating, even. Coming clean to my closest friends, and reclaiming a good part of my past in general. Or it will feel liberating very soon, I'm sure."

The brightness that filled the room made Joshua's eyes seem luminescent. His embrace had loosened so Leo could turn, but he tightened his arms again as he shuffled closer to cage Leo's feet with his own, voice low. "Have you thought about... When we go public, you'll be famous. There'll be things you won't be able to do anymore. Like, of course you can still do investigations for James, but undercover work when everyone knows your face—just, that doesn't make much sense. And regularly trespassing on private property is also... not good. Your work with those kids, it would need to be turned into something more..." He bit his lip and shrugged, appearing helpless and a little sad. "Something more official, I guess."

Leo exhaled around the tight pressure that radiated out from behind his sternum. Joshua was right: Leo's life would change—but it would be *his* life, more so than the half-arsed game of hide-and-seek he'd played before. While there would still be aspects of his past that he'd keep away from the public eye, he'd reclaim his name, his heritage, would own up to the years he'd spent scrounging for food and a safe place to stay, never knowing whether he'd wake up to a torchlight shining into his eyes or where he'd end up the next day. Those experiences had shaped him just as much as the times he'd negotiated the price of a blowjob or a fuck. Probably more.

And whatever the future held, Leo would face it with Joshua right by his side.

"I know things will change," Leo said, only just a whisper. "It's not like I haven't thought about it before I came to Brazil, you know?"

"You have?" Joshua asked, a glint of relief shining through the question.

"I'm not stupid, Princeling. Of course I realise that things will change. Massively and in ways I probably can't even imagine." Leo lifted a brow and shot him a smile that felt foreign on his face, not fully at home in the serenity of the moment. "But I picked you anyway, which should tell you something. Remember what you told me, that day in my flat?"

I'm scared, but I'm doing it anyway. You're just scared.

While Joshua didn't repeat the words out loud, Leo could tell that he understood. His nod was faint, and they were quiet for a short while, simply watching each other, pressed together and so close that details were beginning to swim in front of Leo's eyes. He was the one who picked the thread of conversation back up.

"James already mentioned redefining my role, making me the public face of the team or something. And..." He pressed his lips together before he continued. "Well, yeah, I suppose I couldn't be as directly involved with the kids anymore. It would have to be Kylie running the show, maybe with Carole's help. Or we would need to find a place that tolerates us."

Joshua dipped his head to nose at Leo's cheek, his breath fanning out in a warm gust of air. "I could help," he offered. "Not, like, buy you a place because I know you wouldn't let me, but... I know people. And obviously, I can do something with my name, so if I declare myself a patron, there's a good chance some businesses would offer up their premises for the great promo. Win-win." A second of silence followed, then Joshua chuckled, the sound so quiet it hardly registered. "Actually, as my boyfriend, you'll probably have the kind of impact that means you can be the patron yourself. You don't need my name."

That was...

Kind of true. Huh.

The sudden onslaught of possibilities made Leo's head spin. He could use this, take advantage of the connections that came with his new role—not only to procure a place for his kids, but also to provide James' team with direct insight into opinions and rumours circulating within the high society. It would be a different kind of undercover work, something like recon in plain view. Leo would have to discuss it with James, but even more importantly, he'd have to discuss it with Joshua.

Later, though. They didn't need to have all the answers just yet.

Angling himself so his lips caught the corner of Joshua's mouth, Leo brought one arm up around Joshua's back and pulled him in. He kept his voice low. "That's a good point, but how about we postpone this? Right now, I need you close and with me all the way."

"I am," Joshua murmured, turning further into Leo's touch. His mouth curved up, and Christ, Leo hoped he'd never get over the raw punch of *want* just at the sight of him.

"Thank you," Leo said quietly, and Joshua's heavy gaze fixed on Leo's face. His words were slow, but firm.

"No, thank *you*." He paused, expression smoothing out into something calmly hopeful. "Hey, we can do this, right? We'll get through this. Together."

"We will," Leo whispered. Most of him believed it.

THEIR REMAINING time in Brazil rushed by in a blur. The five of them visited subterranean lakes of an iridescent blue and stared at the astonishing natural spectacle that were the Iguazu Falls; they hiked through a tropical rainforest and bathed in a plunge pool, water the colour of Pepsi rushing around them; they canoed through blackwater-flooded Amazonian forests and jumped into one of the lagoons hidden between the sand dunes of the Lençóis Maranhenses National Park.

"This is our intermission," Joshua had murmured one night, low like a secret and brushed against Leo's skin. While Leo had teased him about his posh choice of wording, he couldn't help but agree. This was their time to learn each other by heart and touch, before the world would come crashing in.

Fourteen days. It would have to do.

Leo spent most of the flight back with Joshua curled into his side and dread a bleak weight in his bones. Fortunately, the others were in a bantering mood, and Leo was jolted out of his anxiety by Tristan bragging about having taken the lead in their tipping game a couple of matches ago.

"Brazil will kick Germany out in the semis," Leo told him, "and you'll be done. No wine for you."

"It's going to be Brazil against Argentina in the final," Mo said, not even bothering to open his eyes. "Political reasons. Just wait for it. And then Brazil will take the Cup."

"Argentina," Nate argued.

"Brazil," Mo repeated.

Tristan shook his head, perfectly content. "Nope. Germany. Adidas already printed the jerseys."

"Who even cares?" Leo asked. "And anyway, if it's like that, I'm going to go with the Netherlands."

Nate scoffed. "That'd be a first."

"Not sure you have room to judge when your country is already out," Tristan said, grin wide.

"Not sure you have room to judge when your team didn't qualify," Leo shot back. He was rewarded with Joshua giggling into his T-shirt, a warm puff of air, and immediately found himself distracted from the conversation. Grinning at Joshua, Leo tugged on a curl and watched it spring back into place.

By the time he tuned back into the conversation, the topic had moved on to sea serpents, of all things. Resting his cheek on Joshua's head, Leo took a deep breath, inhaling the familiar mix of cologne, shampoo and *Joshua, Joshua, Joshua.*

"Hey," he whispered, so quiet it wouldn't travel over the roar of the plane's engines. His stomach quivered through a turbulence. "We can do this, right? We'll get through the shitshow that's about to happen? You won't regret it?"

Joshua lifted his head. "I won't," he said. "I won't regret you, okay? Never." There was no trace of doubt in his features, just calm certainty. Leo took another deep breath and nodded.

"Me either," he replied. "No way could I ever regret you."

Joshua remained silent, but his smile bloomed true and bright. He dropped his head back down onto Leo's shoulder, and Leo wrapped an arm around his waist to pull him closer. Always closer.

~

IN THE REAR-VIEW MIRROR, Carole's eyes were worried. "Are you sure you want to do this?" she asked.

"Actually, I'm quite sure I don't want to do this at all." Leo adjusted the cuffs of his leather jacket, then looked up and set his jaw. "However, this very thing is my specialty. So."

"I could do it alone," Nate offered from the passenger seat. He sounded unconvinced, and Leo sent him a smile, shaking his head.

"You really couldn't, mate. You're not ruthless enough." With that, Leo threw open the door and squinted up at the unfamiliar building.

Six years. It figured that both René and Jake would have moved in that time. The latter was now married to a woman who was blissfully unaware that her husband's weekly outings with some mates for a round of bowling were, in fact, Jake meeting another boy just like Leo in a hotel which rented out rooms by the hour—Carole had procured the pictures to prove it. Just in case Jake happened to be obstinate.

But first off: René. Funny how Leo wasn't the only underage prostitute the guy had picked up. Funny how it wasn't funny at all.

Oh God.

They didn't deserve you.

Joshua's voice a soft echo in his head, Leo sucked some air into his lungs. They still felt punctured, like a flat tire that had collapsed into itself, but when Nate stepped up next to him, Leo squared his shoulders. Without a backwards glance, he set off for the front door.

He let Nate do the honours of fiddling with the lock until it sprang open, then he took the lead up to a door on the second floor. *Karl Nible.* His finger on the doorbell, Leo paused to collect himself. Nate's hand came to rest on his shoulder, heavy and *right there*.

Leo pressed the button.

His heart rate cut each second that they waited into three hectic slices. Then there were footsteps, and Leo moved slightly to the side so he wouldn't show through the spyhole. He rapped his knuckles against the wood, just once.

It took a moment, then the door opened by a cautious crack. Nate shoved it open the rest of the way.

Leo's first thought was that René had grown old. His hair, already thinning the last time they'd met, had receded further and showed traces of grey, and his face looked weary, drained. What a sad, sad man.

Dragging up a smirk from the bottom of his stomach, Leo tipped up his chin and kept his tone perfectly pleasant. "Hello there, René. Or would you prefer Karl?"

A short second passed, then René's eyes widened. His gaze flicked from Leo to Nate, then back. He hurried to shut the door.

Leo stopped the attempt with his shoulder, pushing into the flat past René, and felt Nate right behind him. "Now, now," Leo chided. He kept his voice light and sweet, fit for afternoon tea with the in-laws. "I know it's been a while, but surely that's no way to treat a guest?"

"What do you want?" René asked, thin and reedy. Maybe it was the time gap or maybe it was that Leo had grown into a different person—either way, he didn't remember René ever sounding this... weak. Leo glanced at the man's hands and fought the sick lurch of his stomach.

"What do I want?" he repeated slowly, pursing his lips in demonstrative thoughtfulness. Next to him, Nate crossed his arms in a way that brought out the bulging muscles of his biceps. "Hmm. That's a good question, actually. A *very* good question. How about we sit down for a little chat while we discuss the answer?"

René swallowed. Leo felt his smirk twist into something that tasted like triumph.

～

'*Need you home right now*'

That had been the extent of Leo's message. Joshua had received it just as he'd paid for his purchases—crisps and salt sticks, beer, tequila, ice cream, frozen pizza. Everything that was needed for watching tonight's semi-final, Brazil facing Germany. If Germany made it through, Tristan would prematurely take the betting crown and be unbearably smug about it.

When Joshua read Leo's text, he nearly dropped his purchases and ran. It could mean anything, and knowing that Leo had led the charge on his two ex-clients today... Well, shit.

Joshua grabbed the bags in a hurry, hopped into the car he'd parked outside the shop, and pushed the speed limit in a way he usually wouldn't. Leaving everything in the car, he barged up the stairs to find Leo sitting cross-legged on his doorstep. As soon as their eyes met, Joshua breathed a sigh of relief at the wide, near-manic grin on Leo's face.

Leo jumped to his feet, fisted one hand in the front of Joshua's shirt and dragged him into a bruising kiss, already reaching for the zip of Joshua's jeans. "Hi," Joshua got out, and Leo swallowed the word, exchanged it for a wild laugh. Turning them around, he crowded Joshua back against the surface of the door, trapping him against the wood with his hips.

Fuck, they were still in the stairway, and it was sort of private with Joshua's flat the only one on the top floor, but not a good idea. Probably.

Oh God, also, wait. *Wait.* Joshua needed to—Leo had just—he'd just come from confronting his past, and was he all right, was he really and truly all right? Was he?

With some difficulty, Joshua worked up enough of a will to turn his face away and breathe, hands gripping Leo's shoulders to still him. "Leo," he uttered. "Hey, are you okay? Is everything okay? Are you all right?"

It took a second, then Leo relaxed a little, tight-strung energy uncoiling under Joshua's touch. "I'm all right, babe." His voice was bright and airy, his earlier grin resonating in it. "I am so *very* all right. Like, no one's been this all right in the history of forever. I'm brilliant, and you're brilliant, and everything is brilliant. Also, I love you a stupid amount, and I want you *now.* Get us in there."

Jesus Christ, okay. Joshua fumbled the key out of his pocket as one of Leo's hands slipped under his shirt, fingertips pressing into Joshua's stomach. "Need to make you a copy," Joshua mumbled, not really thinking. "So you can let yourself in next time, wait for me inside, like, naked in my bed."

Leo froze for an instant, then pushed himself even closer. "Outside," he hissed. "Want you to ride me on your balcony." Standing on his tiptoes, he rolled his hips against Joshua's, and holy shit, Joshua needed a moment to recover. The backs of his lids were drenched in velvety black.

"Okay," he said. "Okay, yes." Blindly, he shoved the key into the lock and twisted, almost tripped when the door gave behind him. Together, they stumbled into the flat, still intertwined. Leo kicked the door shut behind them, walking Joshua towards the balcony, hands frantic as they tugged at the buttons of Joshua's shirt.

"Are you really good?" Joshua remembered to ask. He forced his lids open to study Leo's face. "This isn't just, like, a displacement activity?"

Leo pulled back enough for a radiant grin. "A displacement activity? The fuck you're talking about, love?"

"You know, when an animal is cornered, and then it kind of..." Joshua faltered at Leo's raised eyebrows, at the plain amusement in his eyes. After a pause, Joshua finished with an uncertain, "Because you went to see—you know?"

"A displacement activity," Leo repeated. His laugh was true. "No, Princey, I'm not a cornered animal, thanks. But..." While his laugh petered out, his eyes remained bright even as he continued. "About René and Jake. Yeah. Just, holy fuck, you should have seen their *faces*. I'd built them up to these larger-than-life shadows in my head, and they were just so weak. Pitiful, really. Such sad, sad humans. Fuck, they don't even—they're *weak*, babe. They can't hold me. They have no fucking power over me."

Free, Joshua thought—and yes, Leo did look free, like a weight had slipped off his shoulders. *They can't hold me.*

"Love you," he told Leo, and there was a short, pulsing moment while they simply grinned at each other.

With a violent tug, Leo got Joshua's shirt open and dug his knuckles into the tattoo on Joshua's hip. He leaned in, mouth against the shell of Joshua's ear, words escaping in a warm rush. "Love *you*. Only ever want you to touch me, yeah? Be the only one who gets to touch you like this."

"Yes," Joshua managed. "*Yes.*"

Leo continued without missing a beat, his voice low and firm. "Because you're nothing like them, *we're* nothing like them, and this is—fuck, everything. You're everything."

In response, Joshua tangled both hands in Leo's hair and roped him back in for another deep kiss. He went easily when Leo nudged him further back towards the balcony.

"DID YOU MEAN IT?" Leo asked later. They were sprawled naked on Joshua's outdoor bed, the afghan thrown haphazardly over their cooling bodies to protect them from the breeze, skin tacky with sweat and lube and come.

"Probably," Joshua replied. "Which part in particular?"

"The thing with the key."

Oh.

Leo's voice had been hard to read, fairly neutral and too quiet to give away much. Lifting his head from Leo's shoulder, Joshua stared at Leo's face, tinged in gold by the low-hanging evening sun. Leo met his gaze and held it.

"I know it's, like, weird," Joshua began carefully. "I mean, we haven't been together very long, and it's kind of soon, but..."

"But we've already gone through more than most other couples do in years," Leo finished for him. "Affected each other's lives more, too." His eyes were warm.

Joshua exhaled around the radiant glow in his veins. "Yeah. That."

"Eloquent, little prince." Leo combined it with a squeeze of Joshua's hip, thumb fitting into the dip next to the bony jut. He smiled, and while it started out bright, it quickly faded into something slower and more thoughtful. "I'd love a key," he said lowly. "I'd also love for you to be right here with me when I call my parents."

Joshua shifted further into Leo's side, throwing a leg over Leo's thighs. "You want to do it now?"

In lieu of an answer, Leo twisted his torso to grapple for his jeans that lay discarded on the floor, tugging them closer to retrieve his phone. "Slay all the dragons in one day," he told Joshua. The faint apprehension laced into the statement made Joshua snake an arm around his waist and hold on.

"You know it could wait another day."

"I know. But I'd rather do it now, get it over with." Leo breathed out a half-formed sigh, and for all that his fingers tightened on Joshua's hip, his body was still fairly relaxed.

"What if they're sorry?" Joshua asked, breaking the silence which had enveloped them for a few moments. "What if they apologise, say they'd like you back in their life? Do you think you could...?"

He didn't complete the thought, but he didn't have to; Leo's eyes were pensive when they met Joshua's. "I don't know," Leo said softly. "For one, that's a big if, and unless the last ten years have changed them... I don't know." Then he scoffed, the corners of his mouth turning down. "They'd probably love to take me back once they learn I'm with you. Get them a direct in to the Crown. No, thanks."

Anything Joshua could think of were harsh words about people who didn't deserve to be parents. He choked them back down and settled for kissing the corner of Leo's mouth, then rested his head back on Leo's shoulder.

Chest rising with a deep intake of air, Leo brought the phone up to scroll through his emails. He selected one from Nate which contained some contact information. After another deep breath, Leo dialed the number, and they both tensed as soon as it started to ring. Leo had the phone tilted at an angle which allowed Joshua to listen to each ring, count them out—one, two, three, four.

"Austin Residence," a female voice said, smoothly professional.

Leo was silent for a beat, going still against Joshua. Then he cleared his throat, the certainty he usually possessed stripped from him. "Hi, excuse me. I'd like to speak to either Marianne or Troy, please?"

"Whom may I announce?" the woman asked.

Leo turned his head to bury his nose in Joshua's hair, his answer slightly muffled. "Their son."

A noticeable pause followed. Then the woman had apparently regained her composure and told him to wait a moment, please; she'd be right back. In the ensuing silence, Joshua lifted his head to kiss Leo's mouth, the tip of his nose, his cheek, peppering the line of his jaw with little pecks until Leo's tension eased slightly and he turned his head to catch Joshua's lips with his own.

The woman's voice startled them apart. "I am deeply sorry," she said, and while her tone was still professional, Joshua was close enough that he caught a hint of discomfort she couldn't quite hide. "I'm afraid your parents are unavailable, Sir."

Jesus fucking *Christ*. Biting down on the sharp exclamation, Joshua tried to wrap himself all around Leo, breathe him in and shield him from the cool evening air, from an unaccountably cruel world. His lungs were burning.

"Are they unavailable on a permanent basis?" Leo asked, a tiny hitch in his voice.

"Unfortunately so. Should there be a problem, their lawyer will be at your service." The woman hesitated, then added quietly, "However, if it's of any relevance, I just thought—I heard the young misses mention their lost brother on occasion. I'm sure they would be more... receptive."

Leo shifted to fit perfectly into the circle of Joshua's embrace, their legs slotting together, bodies aligned from head to hip to toe. For a second, everything was quiet, the rustle of leaves and the distant statics of a London evening fading away. Leo's chest expanded on a slow, measured intake of air.

"Would you happen to have a current phone number for Charlotte?"

"Certainly," the woman said, and Joshua tried to memorise the number she dictated. Once the call had disconnected, Leo dropped the phone and rolled them over, draped himself on top of Joshua and sagged into him, shaking a little. All Joshua could do was hold on and whisper low, soothing reassurances into his hair.

Slowly, the strain in Leo's body subsided, making room for what appeared to be deep-seated exhaustion. His lips parted against Joshua's jaw.

"Hey," Joshua murmured, voice so low it blended in with the golden evening light. "D'you want me to cancel the match later? Tell the others to raid someone else's fridge. Which—shit, that reminds me. The ice cream is probably sludge by now. I left it in the car."

Leo puffed out a watery laugh and raised his head to study Joshua. There was a wet sheen to his eyes. "What a waste of good ice cream. What did you do that for?"

"I was trying to get to you right away," Joshua told him. He lifted a hand to thumb at the corner of Leo's mouth, smiling a little. "With that message you sent, I didn't know if it was good or bad. Turned out to be pretty good, I guess. At least that particular bit."

"Just so you know..." Leo's expression was gentle, painfully open. "You're doing kind of all right with that whole supportive boyfriend thing, Princey. Not complaining."

Joshua chuckled and pretended that his heart hadn't performed a dizzying twist in his chest. "The highest form of flattery, I assume."

"Sure is." Framed by the fading daylight behind him, Leo didn't move for a short while, propped up on his elbows above Joshua, his gaze tracking slowly from Joshua's mouth up to his eyes. He seemed at a loss for a moment, then shook himself out of it. "Anyway, no. Don't cancel tonight. Think it'll be good, you know, having a laugh with the others. It's not like I expected much, so... Fuck. If my parents don't want a fair warning, they won't get one."

"They're your *parents*, though," Joshua said faintly, and God, how could two people do that to their child? How could they be this indifferent to his brilliance, his sharp angles and soft contours, his wit?

Leo's response came with a delay, but when he spoke, his voice was firm. "Only on paper. My sisters, though—that's different. And that woman on the phone did say that they mention me sometimes.

So I guess... I guess my hopes are better placed with them than with two people who happened to provide my biological material."

Hate was such an ugly emotion, and usually, Joshua tried to be above it. Right now, he found it hard to ignore the nasty ball of acid sitting somewhere below his ribs. Something must have shown on his face, because Leo dipped down to rest their foreheads together.

"Don't waste your energy on them, love," he murmured. "They're simply not worth it."

"I guess they're not."

"I know they're not."

"Okay." With some difficulty, Joshua pulled his thoughts away from that dark corner and tilted his head to press his nose to Leo's. "Help me get the supplies upstairs, then?"

A glint of tentative humour lurked in the corners of Leo's eyes, so close that his lashes were out-of-focus. "Do you have to get dressed for that?"

"Sadly, yes."

"In that case..." Leo exhaled in a rush, then rolled off Joshua. His grin came with a stubborn edge. "How about you stay right here, love? I'll get the stuff up, and you wait for me just like this, entertain yourself until I'm back. We're not done yet."

Joshua needed a second to relocate his ability for coherent speech. Jesus, if this was how Leo dealt with tackling his past, Joshua certainly wasn't complaining—and if there was a hint of sadness still lingering in the set of Leo's shoulders, then Joshua hoped he'd be able to change that. They had nearly two hours until the others would be over, two hours to lose themselves in each other.

"Is that an order?" Joshua asked out loud.

"It's an invitation," Leo corrected. "RSVP."

"Confirmed." Melting into the mattress, Joshua shoved the afghan off himself, smiled at Leo and circled his half-hard cock in a loose grip. Leo froze where he'd been about to fish the car key out of Joshua's jeans. His throat moved as he gulped in a little air.

Then he crawled right back into the space beside Joshua, slapped

Joshua's hand away and hovered above him, a mere inch between their mouths. "Fuck the ice cream," he announced.

"Fuck *me*," Joshua told him, wrapping both arms around Leo's waist and pulling him close. Leo came easily.

THEY'D MADE the mistake of agreeing on a one-shot-per-goal rule. With Germany flattening Brazil seven goals to one, the process became... painful. At least it did so the next morning, even though Leo had switched to taking watered-down shots after number four. When he woke up, his head throbbed, mouth stuffed with cotton, and his vision felt blurry with sleep. A glance at the clock revealed that it was just past eight.

In theory, it was a perfectly average Wednesday with normal office hours. But office hours with James had never been normal, and they'd grown more erratic ever since Leo had become his own client.

His own client. *Fuck*. In three days, he and Joshua would stage the picture that would set the wheels turning, and then there was no way back. Only forward. Whatever that meant.

With no small amount of effort, Leo managed to sit up. The room lurched around him in a drunken swagger, Joshua's arm around his middle reluctant to release him. Since Leo needed to piss and maybe throw up, he freed himself all the same, and Joshua made a sad noise in his sleep. Which—okay, no. Right now, Leo had no patience for Joshua being adorable. Not when his bladder had swollen to three times its usual size.

Stumbling out of bed, Leo almost tripped over Tristan's feet, sticking out from where Tristan had sprawled in an armchair near the door, dirty clothes serving as his blanket. He looked blissfully dead to the world. Maybe Leo would draw a penis on his forehead later, fair punishment for winning their betting pool.

Anyway. Pissing.

Leo felt marginally more awake once he had relieved himself, swallowed a couple of painkillers dry and then brushed his teeth—

although he was just dizzy enough to take a mental nosedive at how he had his very own toothbrush at Joshua's place now. It sat right there in the same glass as Joshua's, privileged compared to the other glass which hosted toothbrushes for Tristan and Mo and, ever since last night, also one for Nate.

A key and a toothbrush. Some of Leo's clothes had transferred to this flat as well, and he had been home only once in the last three days. Wow. The mild queasiness in his stomach didn't feel too unpleasant anymore.

Traipsing past the closed door of the guest room and back into the master bedroom, Leo stood at the foot of the mattress for a long moment to study Joshua's sleeping form, bathed in sunlight that streamed in through the alcove's window. Despite the pounding in his head, Leo felt calm and certain. Somehow, the restlessness that had been his constant companion for years had subsided, was maybe even gone.

He owed Johnson a fruit basket. Or a voucher for some A+ therapy sessions.

Stepping around Tristan's prone form, Leo crouched down to grab his phone, then retreated to the balcony. Both elbows on the banister, he stared out at the old acorn tree and tried to cling to his state of zen. One phone call, that's all it was. Easy. *Easy.*

Christ, Charlotte was studying in London. She was twenty-three now. Rosalind was nineteen. *Nineteen.* She'd been nine when Leo had ran, and did she even remember she'd had a brother once? Did she care? What was it their parents had told her?

This wasn't helping.

Leo unlocked his phone, selected Charlotte's number from the list, and waited for the dial tone. Only then did he realise that it was early still, and as a student, she might not even be—

"Yes?" a confident, female voice asked. Young, yes. Early twenties could have fit. Was this...? Maybe. That one word wasn't nearly enough to tell anything for certain, and Leo felt abruptly out of words.

What had he even wanted to tell her? He hadn't thought that far.

"I can hear you breathing, you know. Is this a joke?" the girl asked, tone sharpening. "I'll have you know that if you're prank calling me, or if you want to sell something—"

"It's Leo," he interrupted.

Vast silence.

"Your brother?" he tried.

"You bloody *bastard*," Charlotte hissed. Then she started crying.

Leo's first thought was that his sister looked like Daenerys in *Game of Thrones*—the same sweet face, the same white blonde hair and pale skin, a similar style of dress that left her shoulders bare.

"You look lovely," were his first words.

Charlotte was silent for a beat, studying him carefully, her eyes narrowed. Around them, life in Hyde Park was moving at a normal pace, tourists and locals strolling through the afternoon sunshine, a squirrel darting across the path. "So do you," she said eventually, almost reluctantly so. "All grown-up, and, like." She made a helpless gesture. "Relaxed?"

"Thank you." Very slowly, Leo reached out, watching her expression and giving her plenty of time to pull away. He felt like someone testing out a weathered wooden footbridge, uncertain whether it would support the weight of a body. While her gaze flickered, she didn't move back. Then he was drawing her into a hug, holding on until she sagged into it and went weak against him.

"I thought you might be dead," she whispered, broken, and Leo's felt as though the inside of his ribcage had been plated with lead. He'd never imagined—oh God.

"I'm so sorry." He choked on it. "I thought—didn't they ever tell you what happened? Mum and Dad? They never..."

"When do they ever tell us anything that matters?" Straightening out of his embrace, she rubbed at her eyes, smudging mascara. Gently, Leo lifted a hand to wipe it away.

"Point," he said softly. "So you thought..."

"I didn't *know* what to think. All they told us what that you were, like, a failure and had brought shame to our family or some crap like that. That we should be glad you were gone." Charlotte's chest rose on a breath. "I wasn't glad. But I also—how could you just *leave*? Without a word, and then you never even tried—"

"Because I *did* feel like a failure," he cut in. "For a while there... I didn't think I was the big brother you deserved, and I couldn't... I was hardly an example."

"Like I'd have bloody cared." Her voice cracked, and she wiped at her eyes again, angrily, turning her back on him. Leo inhaled around a raw ache.

"I'm so sorry," he repeated, perfectly inadequate.

"It's been a decade, and you never once bothered to let us know you were alive. Or how you were doing."

"I thought about it so often," he told her, moving close enough to touch her shoulder. "I thought of you girls all the time, but for the first four years, I was just..." Trailing off, he didn't know how to finish that. Did he really want her to know just how low he'd sunk?

Very soon, the whole world would know his past. Not all of it, but a good portion. He didn't want her to learn it from the papers.

Gritting his teeth, he counted out a few beats, regular and steady. It took effort to keep his voice even. "I ended up on the streets. I didn't feel that was the big brother you'd have wanted."

"Just having a big brother would have been a start," she snapped back, and then she twisted around to stare at him, eyes wide. "I mean —shit. *Leo.*"

This time, she was the one who reached out.

THEY RETREATED to a corner table in a café shortly after that, Leo assuring her she was invited upon noticing her slightly worried glance at the price list. So it seemed their parents kept her on a financially short leash; it had always been their preferred method of punishment. His suspicions solidified once he'd noticed that her phone background was set to a picture of her kissing a girl.

"Do they know?" he asked, pointing, and she squinted at him before shaking her head.

"I'm not stupid enough to tell them. Doesn't mean we don't clash over a lot of other things."

"Well. Personally, I *was* stupid enough to tell them," he said.

A few seconds passed, then she took in a sharp breath and bit her lip, a new kind of understanding clear in her eyes.

From there on, it was easy. Well, *easier*; a couple of hours couldn't bridge ten years spent apart. But by the time they left the café, the gap had shrunk to something that Leo hoped would disappear entirely if they had the will and the patience to work on it. He certainly intended to try.

They were walking close enough for their hands to brush on occasion when Charlotte said, "I'll talk to Rosie, okay? She'll probably want to see you."

"I'd really like that." He glanced down to fumble his sunglasses out of his pocket, and when he looked back up, he found her smiling at something over his shoulder.

"What is it?" He turned around.

Balloons. A multitude of vibrant balloons was floating above a vendor's head—the British flag and Mickey Mouse, stars and a character from Toy Story. Amongst all that: a fish that gleamed in the colours of the rainbow.

"Do you remember?" Charlotte asked, a little wistful, and Leo hooked their pinkies together.

"How could I ever forget? I probably still know most of the story by heart." He pinched his voice low. "'The Rainbow Fish shared his scales left and right. And the more he gave away, the more delighted he became.' Classic, if somewhat finger-wagging. Possibly a better influence than our parents ever were, mind."

She snorted and leaned into his side. "I really did miss you." The words came out soft and genuine. In reply, he wrapped an arm around her shoulders and squeezed her to him.

"Want me to buy you a rainbow fish balloon?" he asked.

With a small giggle, she shook her head. "I'm not five, you know."

"You'll always be my little sister, though. Jesus, next thing you'll tell me is that you're old enough to have sex, which, *no*. Not now, and not when you're thirty, or fifty."

Her laugh was throaty, true. Then it faded, her gaze finding his, scanning his face. When she spoke, there was a clear note of hesitance to it. "Hey, is he... He's good to you? The Prince?"

"He's just Joshua, really." Leo felt his smile brighten just at the mention. "And he's—God, Charlie. He's the best."

She gave a nod, and the initial, shocked disbelief at learning about Joshua had melted into something that was still a little incredulous, yet tinged with amusement because *only you, Leo, seriously*. "He does seem quite lovely." She shrugged. "I mean, like, from the telly and all."

"He's lovelier in person," Leo told her. "Just wait until you meet him."

Her smile was sudden, and wait—had she wondered whether this was a one-time thing? No. Hell no. If Leo had any say in this, they'd have regular brother-sister time from now on. He could ramble about his boyfriend, she could ramble about her girlfriend, and it would be brilliant all-around.

"I'd love to meet him," she said.

"You will." Tightening the arm around her shoulders, he kissed her cheek, then pulled back with a grin. "But it'll cost you at least three coffee dates with your big brother first, and a lecture on how you always need to stay true to yourself and follow your heart and some such. I feel like imparting some hard-won wisdom."

"Wisdom," she repeated, deadpan. "*You.*"

"Careful, Munchkin. I still know where all your ticklish spots are."

"Careful, Fun Size. I've learned all the spots that make a bloke cry with pain."

He chose not to ask why and how she'd learned that. Instead, he widened his grin. "Challenge accepted. What do you say, same place and time next week? Although I guess we might speak before. Depending on how soon the story breaks."

"Oh, that should be fun," she said. "Can't wait."

To his surprise, it sounded genuine. Well, she didn't know that the media wouldn't tell the entire story and a risk of exposure loomed beyond what they intended to reveal.

"Fun? Says you," he told her. "You know this could affect you girls as well, right?"

"We're old enough. Also, I think we might all benefit if our parents are taken down a peg. Maybe," she cocked an ironic brow, but there was a hint of hope to her tone, "it'll open their eyes. You never know."

Leo had wished for understanding parents once; he wasn't going to repeat that mistake. He also wasn't going to infect Charlotte with his cynicism, so he settled for a smile and kept his arm around her shoulders, his steps in time with hers.

IT STARTED with a snapshot of Prince Joshua with an unknown guy about his age. The two of them were surrounded by construction tools and unloading boxes with food onto a blanket, the ground dirty. A couple of youths were nearby, facing away from the camera, appearing toughened in their hoodies and snapbacks.

The picture went viral within minutes of being picked up by *PrinceWatch*.

An hour later, the construction site had been identified, and three hours later, Buckingham Palace released an official statement to address the allegations of Prince Joshua trespassing on private property: the Prince was sorry, truly sorry, for breaking the law and would gladly suffer the consequences. In his defence, he'd only intended to help out. He'd aimed to do something practical and tangible for a bunch of kids who were in a bad situation because he'd learned what it was like from a friend who'd lived on the streets for a while.

"What friend? The one who was in the picture?"

Buckingham Palace declined all comment and asked the media to respect the privacy of those involved.

The name 'Leo Troy Austin' hit the online news the same evening, and his entire tragic story made the morning headlines—the fallen noble who'd been treated unfairly by ignorant parents. He had picked himself up, shaken off the dust and become stronger and better for it, had befriended the Prince without divulging the secret of his noble heritage.

Beautiful. A real-life fairy tale. An *inspiration*.

The next few days brought interviews with people from Leo's past and current life—one with his old friend Kylie, who'd given Leo odd little jobs at her parents' bar so Leo could keep above water; one with the Leader of the Opposition, who highlighted Leo's role in resolving a kidnapping of his only child; one with an anonymous girl who lived on the streets and called Leo a mentor for kids like her. Eventually, there was an interview with Leo himself, in which he talked freely about how even a warm meal or a dry place to sleep could feel like luxury. He also countered his parents' public claim that he'd brought it on himself with a little shrug and a sad smile. "If you believe that homosexuality is something like a disease that I caught, or that a child should lie to their parents rather than risk challenging their preconceived notions... Well. I strongly disagree with that."

Some guy on Facebook made a post which said, *'Leo eh? pretty sure we met when u were called kev and sucked my dick for money.'* The bloke was quickly forced to admit that he had no proof, and yeah, maybe that Kev person had looked a bit different, true. It was dismissed as an attention-seeking twat trying to stir up shit.

There were also pictures, a whole flood of them. They showed Leo slotting in with Joshua's circle of friends—buying supplies for the World Cup final, or a trip to the zoo, a picnic on Primrose Hill that looked like a triple date in unclear constellations (with the exception of Tristan and his Victoria's Secret model). Then again, things turned rather less ambiguous when supermodel Mo attended a gallery opening with the as-of-yet unidentified sixth member of the picnic group.

In all honesty, that particular mystery was rather less fascinating than the speculation about Prince Joshua's love life because *could it be*? Prince Joshua and Leo Austin? A boy who'd fallen from grace and gone through hell, only to fall in love with a prince. Wouldn't it just complete the fairy tale?

Neither Buckingham Palace nor Leo himself deigned to comment.

IT WAS EARLY, but not so early that Millennium Bridge was devoid of tourists and their cameras. Leo and Joshua had been up for hours already, first to go through the final stage of the plan, then to stroll through London on a tiny tour of what Leo had cleverly titled 'The City as I See It' with Zach trailing behind at a polite distance.

Now, they were pressed close together on the bridge, and Leo was the one to link their arms. He turned his head to take in Joshua's face —the cut of his nose and the generous bow of his lips, a hint of stubble dusting his chin, grey daylight tangling in his irises. When Joshua caught Leo looking, he began to smile and angled closer, just enough for Leo to notice. The sides of their feet were touching.

"Have you ever wondered" —Joshua's voice was as slow as the water crawling by below— "about all those times we must have missed each other? First Eton, then those years we were both here in London."

Over Joshua's shoulder, Leo caught a camera pointed at them. He deliberately ignored it and trusted Zach to ensure that no one approached them without permission. "We didn't miss each other," Leo said, grinning back. "That was all you, not me. First boy boner, remember?"

"I'm serious, though." Joshua possessed the astonishing ability to smile through a pout. He was possibly magic; Leo hadn't ruled it out yet.

Chuckling, he bumped their hips together. "I know, babe. But if I think about it too much, I'll probably start spouting nonsense about fate and destiny. And no one wants that."

Joshua laughed softly. He shoved his hair back with one hand, an insistent breeze blowing curls into his eyes, and Leo reached up to tuck a strand behind Joshua's left ear. He let the touch linger while Joshua watched him with warm eyes that turned thoughtful.

"Listen," Joshua said, after a second of them just studying each other. "I've been thinking."

Leo smirked at him. "You realise you have people who are paid to do that for you, Princeling?"

"Fuck off," Joshua told him, and continued without missing a beat. "I want to make a deal."

"A deal?"

"I understand that you don't want to feel like..." A pause followed while Joshua appeared to ponder his next words. In all honesty, Leo loved that—the way Joshua took the time to consider things carefully, didn't rush into them head first. Although Leo himself and the way they'd fallen into each other might have been the exception to that rule.

When it looked as though Joshua might have lost his courage, Leo bumped their feet together. "I'm waiting."

"Right." Joshua nodded. "So, I understand that you don't want to feel like you're taking advantage. Like, by accepting things from me, or letting me treat you. I get that. But." He inhaled. "I don't actually need you to prove anything because I already know. And you do, too."

Leo's initial impulse was to react with a flat-out 'no' to cut the discussion off before it started. Seriously, did Joshua believe that *this* was the time and the place? On the other hand, they were about to take the final step, jump off the cliff together. After this, so much would change, for both of them. Maybe this was indeed the time and the place.

"I can't just take your money," Leo said. "It wouldn't feel right."

"I'm not saying now," Joshua assured him, his gaze clear and steady. "But a year from now. Let's make a deal that in exactly a year, when we're still together—"

"*If* we're still together," Leo suggested, not quite a question and not quite a statement.

Joshua shook his head. "*When* we're still together," he repeated.

"Okay, when." Something about the word settled like molten gold in Leo's stomach, radiated certainty. *When.*

"Yes. So..." For once, Joshua appeared determined when he was usually easy to distract with both kisses and banter. "Starting a year from now, you'll let me toe the line between what's yours and what's mine a bit more."

A year from now.

It sounded massive. At the same time, Leo was planning to stay with Joshua for—for something as thoroughly cheesy as forever, and a year was only just the beginning.

Joshua must have mistaken Leo's silence for refusal, because he widened his eyes, voice intent. "Just think about it, please? Like, if this is supposed to be an equal relationship... I do have so much more money than you do, Leo. It's just a fact, and if we make it fifty-fifty, it's actually *unfair* because the relative impact on me is way smaller." He made a sweeping gesture, then dropped his hand and continued with quiet sincerity. "There are different ways of fairness, you know? And in that sense, it would be fair if I contributed more because I can afford more. Like, it should mean the same, yes, but in the respective context."

It made sense. It did, but Leo couldn't quite bring himself to admit it, not just yet. Not when the following days would determine the public reaction to their relationship and carried the risk of a violent backlash.

The glimmer of hope in Joshua's eyes dimmed. He hesitated, studying Leo, and eventually added, "It doesn't make you dependent on me. Or, like, a kept man or something. You'd still have your job, your financial independence. But we're also in this together. And I *want* to share the good parts of my life with you. You know?"

It made sense.

"I'll think about it," Leo said. "I... Maybe. Just give me a little time, okay? Might not even require a year."

Joshua's eyes shone with startled delight. "Really?" he echoed, his whole face brightening. Clearly, Leo had made the right decision.

He nodded. "Really. I'll think about it, I promise. But definitely no jumping right into it by paying off my flat or some such, are we clear?"

"Perfectly clear, yes." Joshua still seemed a little disbelieving, watching Leo as though expecting him to retract the easy agreement.

"Don't look at me like that," Leo grumbled. "I know how to compromise."

"Only when it suits you," Joshua told him, mouth curving up.

"It suits me when it makes you happy."

"For the record..." Joshua's voice dipped low, and he leaned in, disregarding the attention focused on them. "You're doing kind of okay with the making me happy thing."

Leo arched an eyebrow. "Only kind of?"

"Kind of very, perhaps."

"Your eloquence continues to astound me."

"You're being a little shit." Joshua grinned, wide and true. "How about you put your mouth to better use, huh?"

"Such as?" Leo asked, shuffling closer, *closer*, anticipation humming in his bones. He rested one hand on Joshua's hip. Even through the layer of Joshua's shirt, Leo's thumb fit perfectly into the hollow dip next to the jut of Joshua's hipbone, a spot Leo had come to consider a personal favourite, right along with all other spots of Joshua's body.

"Shut up," Joshua said, barely more than a whisper, "and kiss me."

So Leo did.

THE PICTURES HIT the news before they even made it home.

"We look gorgeous," Leo decided, and while Joshua laughed at that, he couldn't disagree. They did look good together—their bodies aligning naturally, turned into each other with Leo's fingers tangled in Joshua's hair and Joshua's hand clasped around Leo's bicep. It spoke of warmth and intimacy, and there was another angle that showed their faces after they'd separated, staring at each other. They looked stupidly, idiotically happy.

"So I guess we're doing this," Joshua said.

By way of response, Leo grinned and tugged him into a sweet, lazy kiss that wasn't intended to be shared with the world; a kiss that was just for them.

Just them.

AUTHOR'S NOTE

Hello, and thank you for staying with me! I so hope you enjoyed the ride.

If you're not yet ready to let go of Joshua and Leo, they show up again halfway through *Be My Endgame* to deliver a plot twist. Also, there's a little bonus interview with Leo that I shared with my Facebook readers group *Zarah's Zarlings*.

Before you go, I have a small favour to ask: **would you have a minute to leave a review?**

Writing is a lonely business—I spend hours stuck in my own head, rolling around sentences and scenes, thinking through plot twists even as I run through forests or wait for a train. As such, it's *wonderful* to read reactions. It makes it feel a little less lonely and signals that maybe, if there are people who care about these characters and their stories, it's all worth it.

Reviews also help in spreading the word. We're all overwhelmed with things we could be doing, so why would anyone pick up this book instead of another? A review can make all the difference, and I didn't know how much they matter until I started writing.

Let's stay in touch!

- Check out my website for more books. You can also join my newsletter for updates and bonus content, including a free 2-hour read: **www.zarahdetand.com**,
- My **Facebook readers group Zarah's Zarlings** features book chatter, things that make me laugh, sneak peeks, and bonus content, or
- Find me on Instagram @zarahdetand.

Again: thank you for joining me on this journey!
—*Zarah*

P.S. I should mention that this is a self-published work of writing without any financial resources behind it. While a lot of care went into catching mistakes, some may have slipped through the cracks. If you spot any, I'd love it if you let me know via my website.

MORE BOOKS BY ZARAH DETAND

This Shifting Ground: A law student and part-time waiter befriends a new-to-town customer seeking casual connections. This slow-burn MM romance novella combines fast-paced dialogue with a simmering attraction that blurs the lines of friendship until they cease to exist. **Free on my website!**

Be My Endgame: Liverpool midfielder Alex Beaufort and Manchester United striker Lee Taylor go from rivals to roommates during England's World Cup campaign in Spain. This MM sports romance tackles family legacies and personal struggles as unexpected feelings kick in. A love story as thrilling as a last-minute goal. (Prince Joshua and Leo appear for a couple of scenes!)

Amid Our Lines: In this small-town romance set in the Swiss Alps, London songwriter Eric recognises his new boss Adrian as the adult film star he fancied as a teenager. Their awkward encounter sparks a comedic, slow-burning friends-with-benefits arrangement, amidst a backdrop of snowy charm and heartwarming romance.

You're My Beat: In this slow-burn friends-to-lovers tale, a dancer and a rockstar rekindle an old connection during a world tour. Realistically messy feelings meet lighthearted banter for a hard-won happily ever after.

Change My Ticket: A Hollywood heartthrob seeks help from lab researcher to prepare for a movie role as a molecular biologist. Expect a sweet, slow-burning and mostly lighthearted read with just a dash of angst.

Pull Me Under: After accidentally outing himself, a soccer player enters a fake relationship with an openly gay music student. As they navigate public appearances and the media spotlight, their friendship deepens and romantic feelings emerge, leading to a heartwarming and cheerful tale of love in the limelight.

...and several more!

Printed in Great Britain
by Amazon

40955918R00219